Wizardream

BOOK ONE

The Return of Maradass

Wizardream

BOOK ONE

The Return of Maradass

Bruce Chatfield

Press

Published by 99% Press,

an imprint of Lasavia Publishing Ltd.

Auckland, New Zealand

www.lasaviapublishing.com

Copyright ©Bruce Chatfield, 2023

Illustrations by Bruce Chatfield

Marbling by Bruce Chatfield

Edited by Rowan Sylva

Designed by Daniela Gast

ISBN: 978-1-99-118980-6

To Joanne

Foreword

I first read the manuscript of *Wizardream* when I was twelve years old. At that age I loved the books: the chases, the savage evil dogs called marauders, the magic, the clambering over ravines in the Broken Lands, the map and the illustrations. Reading the manuscripts anew as an adult and editor, I was impressed, enjoying it possibly even more than I had as a child. I found myself wanting to flick ahead, to read on into the night to discover what would happen. There were things that appealed to my adult sensibilities that I had forgotten or not noticed as child: the way the narrative explores the landscapes and peoples of Australia and New Zealand; the depth of the lore and careful take on colonisation, war and destruction; and the play on Wizardream and dreamtime. I approached the manuscript with scepticism, worried that I would find a perhaps wooden or stuffy high fantasy. I am delighted to say that my scepticism was unfounded. *Wizardream* is innovative, imaginative and enchanting. It is true that it displays some of the foibles of its genre: plenty of lore and back-story that could, to readers of thrillers, seem tedious; a dichotomy between good and evil, heroes and villains; and a certain stiltedness in the dialogue. Yet it also displays the strengths of the best of high fantasy: A rich and self contained world you can get lost in; daring quests and epic battles; and a quality of timeless appeal. *The Return of Maradass* is the first book in the *Wizardream* Trilogy. It is followed by *Of Wizardry and War*, and *The Wizards Way*. There is also a fourth book, *The Last Wizard*, a stand alone novel set in the same world.

Rowan Sylva

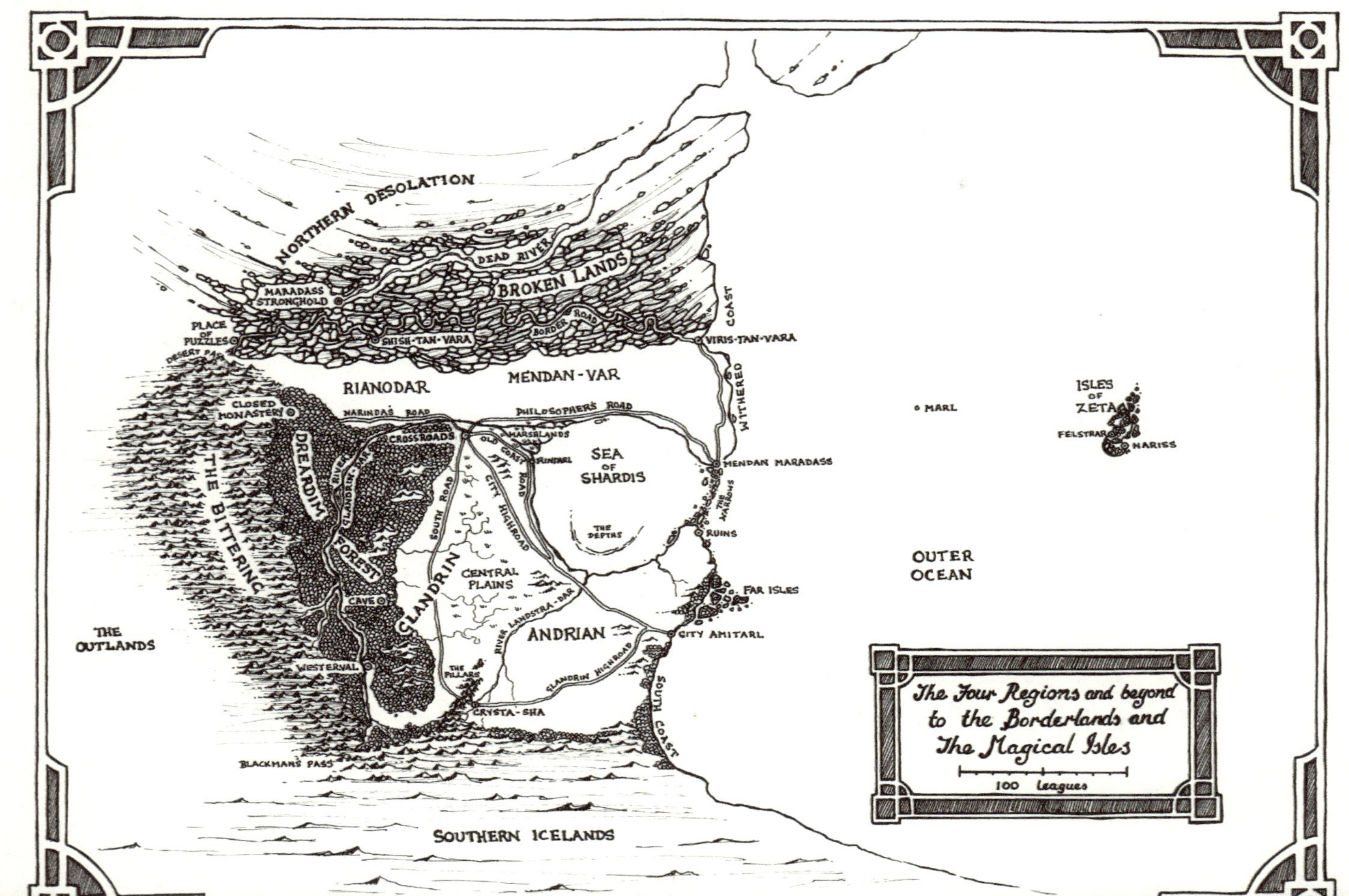

The Four Regions and beyond to the Borderlands and The Magical Isles
100 leagues
NORTHERN DESOLATION
DEAD RIVER
BROKEN LANDS
MARADASS STRONGHOLD
PLACE OF PUZZLES
DESERT PASS
SHISH-TAN-VARA
BORDER ROAD
VIRIS-TAN-VARA
WITHERED COAST
MENDAN-VAR
RIANODAR
CLOSED MONASTERY
NARINDAS ROAD
CROSSROADS
PHILOSOPHER'S ROAD
OLD MARSHLANDS
COAST ROAD
FUNFALL
SEA OF SHARDIS
THE DEPTHS
MENDAN MARADASS
THE NARROWS
RUINS
MARL
ISLES OF ZETA
FELSTRAR
NARISS
OUTER OCEAN
THE BITTERING
DREARDIM FOREST
RIVER GLANDRIN-VAR
SOUTH ROAD
CITY HIGHROAD
GLANDRIN
CENTRAL PLAINS
CAVE
THE PILLARS
RIVER LANDSTRA-DAR
ANDRIAN
FAR ISLES
CITY AMITARL
GLANDRIN HIGHROAD
WESTERVAL
CRYSTA-SHA
SOUTH COAST
THE OUTLANDS
BLACKMAN'S PASS
SOUTHERN ICELANDS

Contents

Swords in the Forest   11

The Old Coast Road   29

Flindas   50

The Sea of Shardis   63

Beyond the Horizon   82

The Magical Isles   95

Council of Zeta   113

The Games   129

Wizard Dreams   149

To Viris-Tan-Vara   165

Thief in the Night   191

The Border Road   222

Shish-Tan-Vara   245

The Parting of Companions   268

Crossing the Broken Lands   285

The Dying Mountains   310

The Evil One   332

Swords in the Forest

Kerran could see that Storm was disturbed by something deep within the old forest. The white hawk flew swiftly through the trees, leading Kerran further into the overhanging gloom that was Dreardim, the vast and most ancient of forests. Kerran had come to gather herbs and mushrooms for his mother, but his curiosity now drew him deeper beneath the lofty primordial trees than he had ever ventured before. Storm soared aloft, then again swooped in a hunting dive into a distant narrow valley overhung by a jagged outcrop of rock. Kerran urged the old family horse down the gentle slope, wondering what could be the cause of the hawk's excited behaviour. There was little undergrowth and he managed to get a fast walk from the old animal, and after a short time he could hear the distant sound of steel striking steel.

At first he thought it must be some blacksmith living deep in the forest who served a community other than Kerran's own village of Westerval. He had never heard of anyone living so deep in the forest and rode on until the sounds became unmistakable. Not far ahead, two adversaries fought in a battle of swords. Though never having heard the sound before he was sure that in this quiet corner of the land, sword now clashed on sword, the sound ringing clear through the forest. Kerran rode on slowly, unable to see the battleground through the trees. Suddenly an anguished cry came from the forest ahead of him, dismounting he crept forward through the thinning trees until he reached the edge of a small clearing.

The midday sun lit the open glade where two knights fought. One was armoured in white silver that gleamed in the sunlight, though the metal was battered and rent. This knight was on his knees, warding off a blow from the mighty blade which was wielded by a man of huge proportions. Fully head and shoulders above any man Kerran had ever seen. This knight's armour was the colour of the darkest night. It did not shine, but instead seemed to absorb the light around it so that the very air shimmered, grey and forbidding. A deep and wicked laughter came from the Black Knight and Kerran shuddered, knowing that only evil could come from this man's victory. Blood flowed from wounds that the White Knight had received, splattering the grass with red, and Kerran could see that he could not endure for much longer.

The White Knight struggled to his feet again but was crushed by yet another blow; on his knees he swung his sword in vain at the Black Knight's legs. His adversary stepped back to avoid the blow then kicked his enemy viciously. Stunned, the White Knight sprawled backward onto the grass as the sound of black laughter rang through the gloom of the forest.

"'Tis time for you to die," sneered the Black Knight, his voice filling the glade. "Then I will take the prize you carry."

His words became softer with wicked pleasure, knowing his foe to be defeated.

"Your father cannot protect you now! Did you think it would last forever? Fools! I am back, and my father's power protects me; soon the lands will belong to Maradass alone."

The White Knight tried to rise but was knocked to the ground, his sword spilling from his hand.

"Your mistake was to let us live," the Black Knight snarled. "The corruption of the Broken Lands has strengthened us."

There was a pause, as though the Black Knight was remembering some delight. The White Knight stirred.

"Do not try to rise," the Black Knight spat the words as another kick found its mark.

With a soft groan the White Knight slumped onto his side, one hand reaching out to the fallen sword. A heavy foot came down upon the clutching armoured fingers, grinding them into the earth. Lifting his visor now the Black Knight smiled down upon this vanquished foe and Kerran looked for the first time into the dark face.

"You thought us lost and never to return," said the Black Knight. "Rubon gave chase and paid dearly for it, though he lived longer than you may believe he had no reason to rejoice in that time."

The Black Knight was taking pleasure in his speech. "We were driven north but turned in the night," he rejoiced. "The numbers were against us but the victory was ours. I can still see the look of surprise on your ancestors' faces as their heads were lifted from their shoulders. How many of your family were lost that night I care not. I now only wish to slay those that remain. Maradass will return to rule the lands and soon your line will be dust. The people of the Southlands are weak and soft. War is something they no longer understand. Your life is now at an end, and soon the remnants of your family will die beneath my sword until no Amitarl remains to save the Regions."

At hearing the name Amitarl, Kerran gasped. Amitarl was a name from the deep ancient past, so old that it had become legend. Not in any living person's lifetime had there been in the land a bearer of the name Amitarl, though Kerran had heard of a city which still bore that family's name. Legend spoke of magical times and of ancient ones who had lived for many years longer than ordinary mortals. Kerran knew now that the White Knight must be descended from Darna Amitarl, who was said to have left the West to sail for Zeta, the Magical Isles, and was never heard of again. It was hard for Kerran to believe that the legends were coming to life near his own home, here on the edge of Dreardim Forest.

The Black Knight stepped back from his enemy. "Enough now," he said. "I would make your death slow, and with much pain, but I have more important game to ensnare, that cripple brother of yours is loose somewhere on the northern borders. I have many eyes and ears and he will be found soon. Your father too will not remain hidden for long; my own father's power will cross the oceans and strike him. All that he cares for will soon be overcome, but for you there is now no more protection."

He raised the great blade above his head and cried in a mighty voice, "Father! Maradass! This death I pledge to thee. It is a good day when an Amitarl dies!"

The sword began its swift and final descent, but quicker still had been the flight of Storm. From a high tree the hawk had watched the one-sided battle, and as the sword was raised for the deathblow the bird swooped downward, speeding toward the open visor of the Black Knight. The sound of feathered wings caused the sword to hesitate, and then into the dark face flew the white hawk, talons sinking into flesh, tearing, screaming. The sword fell from the powerful hand as the Black Knight clutched at his face. In that instant the White Knight lunged for his own fallen sword, and in one movement thrust upward with his last remaining strength. The blade came up beneath the black chain-mail skirt, slicing through the leather garments beneath and plunged deep into the Black Knight's body. An unearthly scream filled the clearing as Storm escaped and took to flight, away from the ravaged face. In horror the Black Knight looked down upon his slayer. The giant man's knees gave way beneath him, sinking downward, his own weight forcing the blade deeper into his body. His lips opened in a silent scream and blood gushed from his mouth as he fell in a clash and clatter of armour, to lie still and silent beside the White Knight.

Kerran could not move for some time. The battle had taken but a short time. The sun had barely moved in the sky. The forest lay in silence as he looked to the air but Storm was nowhere to be seen. Kerran did not know why the hawk had attacked. Never before had his friend done such a thing. Slowly Kerran walked out from beneath the shelter of the trees towards the place where both knights lay motionless upon the bloody grass. Kerran moved cautiously until he came to kneel beside the White Knight, not knowing what best to do he gently removed the elaborately figured helmet.

A cascade of golden, blood-soaked hair tumbled out onto the grass and Kerran, in great surprise, beheld the face of the most beautiful woman he had ever seen. How could one so fair be the slayer of the giant who lay nearby he wondered? Even to bear the armour she wore showed that her strength was far beyond that of any woman Kerran had ever known. Her eyes were closed but she breathed still. Blood continued to pulse from a wound at her neck, while more escaped from beneath her armour and mail. Kerran took his water bottle and gently cleaned the blood from her neck, searching for the wound. Her eyes fluttered and opened, looking up into his face. There was much pain and with difficulty she spoke.

"Who are you?" she asked the youth, her eyes searching his face.

"I am Kerran Shalastar," he replied. "I live to the west of the forest. I heard swords and saw the end of your struggle."

"Was it your hawk that attacked the Black One?" Turning her head a little she could see her fallen enemy.

"I cannot own him," replied Kerran. "We are friends. I have never seen him do such a thing before."

"I am glad," she said. "The emblem of my family is the white hawk. I am Leana Amitarl."

She coughed as blood came to her lips and a shudder of pain passed through her body. She took a long slow breath then paused, gathering her strength to speak further.

"Kerran, are you brave?" she asked painfully. "The one who lies beside me is Zard, son of Maradass. The armies of Maradass return and will have no pity on the Regions... I must ask you for your help Kerran, there is no one else... Take the talisman that is around my neck... Take it now. You are my only hope."

She lifted her head slightly and as though in a dream Kerran slipped the leather cord from around her neck and held it in his hand, taking little notice of the small piece of blue-grey metal which hung from it.

"There will be no safe place," Leana continued through her

pain. "There are marauders to the north. Beware these black dogs... If the prize you carry falls to them there will be no hope, and all choices will lead to death or worse... You must do this Kerran."

She gripped his arm. Kerran could see that more blood had seeped from beneath her battered armour, staining the earth and grass. He found that he could not speak.

"Travel to the ocean and beyond," she whispered. "Find my father Tolth on the Isles of Zeta... To the east... that is the way you must go."

She paused, her face ashen.

"The talisman has powers and it may protect," she said softly. "Take my horse... there is gold. Promise me Kerran that you will do this thing... I am dying... I can do no more."

Her voice was now a faint murmur and Kerran could barely understand her words. A flood of sadness for her filled his heart, while the urgency in her dying voice told him that in truth the fate of the lands hung here in the balance.

His words came as if they were not his own.

"Do not fear," he told her. "I will do this if I can. I will find Zeta and place this thing in your father's hands, and I will tell him of your bravery, this I promise."

Kerran held his ear close, catching Leana's dying words.

"Do not return to your home," she whispered. "The dogs are coming... Go deep into the forest... lose your trail... then eastward to the sea... Find Tolth... Go now... I will rest... all I want now is to rest."

"I cannot leave you here," said Kerran.

"You must," she gasped clutching his arm feebly.

Though she was near death she suddenly found the strength to speak further.

"Every moment is precious. Armies draw nigh to the northern borders. Tolth must have the talisman to protect the land; it is what the Black One fought for today. It is a piece of the wizards' tool called the Seacrest... Go... quickly... there are no longer any choices... Farewell and may all that is good go with you... Go!"

Far to the north Kerran heard the baying howl of some evil

dog. He stood quickly as Leana's eyes closed, a look of peace coming to her face as she lay still and silent.

Kerran turned and walked to the far side of the glade where a tall horse stood patiently, and then he looked back. Leana Amitarl lay in the sunlight, perhaps dead already; the white armour had begun to fade. From the shadows of the trees he saw it shimmer for a time and then slowly disappear. Where before had lain the White Knight, now only a blood splattered body could be seen.

"Farewell Leana Amitarl," he whispered.

He mounted then turned the powerful horse to the east and rode deeper into Dreardim Forest, knowing that his own family horse would easily find its way home. At a great distance he heard again the howl of a strange dog. It was answered from the south as Kerran urged the horse on as quickly as the old forest allowed. The shadow of Storm flickering now and then on the thick layers of leaves that carpeted the way ahead; Kerran was very pleased to have the white bird's company.

The afternoon began to pass and Kerran found that he was beginning to ride steadily downhill. He could see that this part of the forest lay within a vast depression in the land. The way forward was becoming steeper with occasional outcrops of old and weathered rock that forced Kerran to retrace his trail at times. He thought of turning to the north in an attempt to avoid the wide valley but somewhere behind him he knew there was danger.

"Beware the black dogs," Leana had said.

As he descended into the valley Kerran began to remember some of the old stories, those that his father had told him by the fireside on cold winter's nights. The names Maradass and Amitarl conjured up times long past, times of war and magic and the fall of great heroes. He remembered how Amitarl and Maradass had once ruled the lands in peace and friendship, and then had come Maradass the Mad. Kerran tried to remember again his dead father's words and stories, though he had been but seven years old when his mother had become a widow.

The Mad One had fought to overthrow Amitarl, and Zard his son had led the Black army. War ravaged the lands for centuries until Rubon Amitarl, aided by his valiant kinsmen, was finally victorious, though Rubon himself and much of his family had died in the final battle. Maradass was driven into the Broken Lands to the north, a vast place that ancient sorcery had cursed for all time. It was a land poisoned and torn by ancient wizardry; to some parts of it not even the diggers of gold and gems dared go. Many did not come back from the Broken Lands and for centuries there had never been a word of Maradass. The name had slipped from the memory of most, and into the depths of time.

Kerran rode on into the late afternoon. He knew now what his father had never known. The family Maradass had survived and once again desired the rich lands of the Four Regions. Kerran thought sadly of his dead father. He remembered the day that the men from the village had come to their house bearing his father's shattered body. An accident in the forest they said, a tree that turned and fallen the wrong way. Kerran had lived on in his family home with his mother, and though they had been poor there was always enough food on the table. Living on the edge of Dreardim Forest Kerran had learned many skills in hunting and foraging, and his accuracy with a sling could not be matched by any other from his village. He had lived happily there for seventeen years now, a quiet solitary boy, preferring the company of Storm and the wonder of the forest to the rowdy village life of Westerval. Now he thought that he may never see his mother or his home again, for he rode eastward on a tall war horse, in search of a mythical island called Zeta, a place about which he had heard only tales.

Kerran shook his head in disbelief, and then he remembered the amulet that hung around his neck. The day had passed so quickly with the fear of black dogs behind that he had all but forgotten the reason for his journey. Lifting the cord over his head he examined the piece of old magic in the late afternoon light. The horse was cleverer than he at finding the easier path and so he gave the creature its head. Leaning back in the saddle Kerran looked closely at the fragment of strange blue metal that he held in his hand. It seemed almost transparent, with radiating lines and runes unknown to him carved deeply into one face. His father had once mentioned its name, the Seacrest.

"You are still young and the story is best left for a later time," his father had told him, though of many other things he had spoken freely.

The amulet was the shape of a quarter circle, yet its two roughly straight edges were not cut cleanly. They were broken unevenly and showed incomplete designs; it was obvious to Kerran that it had once been a part of a full circle. Towards its centre there were lines that if continued on the other three quarters would form the shape of an eight pointed star. A small clasp at the point of the two broken edges took the stout thong and held fast the fragment of old magic. Kerran clasped the piece in his hand and wished for the appearance of a delicious meal. Nothing happened and he laughed at himself as he again passed the cord over his head.

The way continued to descend, and now only a few scattered trees broke the barrenness of the hillside. Below, the floor of the valley lay in silent darkness, while far away he could see the far wall of the valley ringed by the haze of distant trees.

"I will not push the horse too hard", he said to himself. "It may be many days to the ocean. It cannot be helped."

Kerran rode on until darkness began to overtake them, and then he built a small fire to be a cheerful companion in the night. He was thankful that in his pouch he carried flint and steel. As he ate the last of the bread and cheese he had carried into the forest with him that morning he wondered about the road ahead. Tomorrow he would not hunt. He had not forgotten the urgency in Leana's voice and must hasten to the coast as quickly as possible. After placing more wood on the fire he stretched out and was soon drifting into sleep. An owl hooted and a distant reply comforted Kerran as the sound always had, and then a dream came to him but like no other dream he had ever had before.

His mind was fully awake and he felt himself inside his body. He walked he knew not where while his eyes saw only a soft mist. It frightened Kerran; his wakeful mind knew that he lay by a small fire deep within Dreardim Forest. Without thought his hand reached to his throat and he clasped the fragment of the wizards' talisman. A strange voice came instantly into his waking sleep.

"Kerran!" it cried. "You are in great danger. Leave this place. Quickly! Go upward now! Awake! Go!"

Kerran sat up quickly and looked around and it seemed as if the dream continued for a mist had risen from the valley and was becoming thicker by the moment. He could see nothing to fear. It was cold and he shivered, his fire now a small flickering glow of embers. From far down the slope he heard a low moan that was almost human. It seemed to echo amongst the nearby rocks and boulders, and then one by one, other voices took up the dreadful lament. Kerran leapt to his feet and untying the reins of the horse he clambered into the saddle, then he urged the charger uphill, away from the cries. The horse stumbled, stones flying from steel shod hooves. The wailing cry grew louder as the mist began to gather and swirl about them. The horse screamed in fear as more rock was loosened beneath its hooves. Something from the rising mist brushed against Kerran's leg. He saw a soft grey hand reach from the night and caress his cheek. More hands stretched out towards him, soft grasping hands clutching at his clothing, entangling in his long fair hair. The horse cried out again as more of the disembodied hands came from the mist, trying to drag both horse and rider back down the slope. One of Kerran's own hands was torn loose from the reins. The horse swerved and stumbled. Kerran was thrown heavily to the ground. He was grasped from all sides and felt finger-nails sinking into his flesh.

"The amulet!" cried the dream voice in utter despair, "quickly!"

Reaching through his horror Kerran clasped the piece of ancient wizardry in his hand. A cold heat raced through his shuddering body, and then from the Seacrest fragment white light suddenly exploded outwards. Kerran could see the stars above; a wide opening had been torn in the mist. He leapt to his feet and began to run, as from the darkness came the screech of Storm, the white hawk swooping close above him and flying up the slope. Kerran followed as quickly as he could, running and stumbling in fear and not looking back for a long time. When his pumping legs could push him no further he stopped, sucking in huge gulps of the cool night air, he looked back down the hill to where the mist lay far below, still and yet forbidding.

Kerran leaned against a massive boulder and through his fear he realised he was safe, but that the horse and all that it had carried was gone. He knew he would not return down that slope again, not even in daylight. Climbing much higher Kerran finally sat down to rest. He lit no fire, and it was almost daylight before he closed his eyes and slept; untroubled by further dreams or voices. When he woke at noon Kerran felt bruised and hungry. Storm perched on a rock shelf nearby, watching him quizzically. Kerran had not even been able to save his water bottle. All he had was in the pouch at his waist: his knife, flint and steel, his sling, and the strange talisman which hung about his neck. Water was not a problem as there were many streams and pools in this part of the forest, and he could do without gold for now, but the horse was a terrible loss. He climbed further until he reached the tree line and turned to the north, keeping well beneath the shelter of the comforting trees. During the previous afternoon he had been able to study the wide valley of the forest, he had seen that the northern end was much closer than the south. Dark tales of this most ancient of forests returned to him as he walked. There was said to be many ferocious beasts living here that few had ever survived to tell of. The thought of perhaps hundreds of leagues on foot and fearful creatures behind and still further on crushed Kerran's hopes. He touched the amulet through his shirt and wondered at the strange voice; it had not seemed quite human, neither woman nor man, not old nor young. It had been able to save him once; he hoped that in need it would aid him again.

During the afternoon Kerran managed to kill a rabbit with a good throw that brought the animal down in a flurry of twitching legs. A lively fire and an appeased stomach helped to ease him into sleep. By sunrise he was again on his way, eating the last of the rabbit and a few wild vegetables as he walked. He wasted nothing, sucking the marrow from the bones and rolling up the skin, keeping it for later use. He walked softly, his sling and a stone held in his hand, always on the watch for rabbits or any of the larger forest birds. Lizards he caught by hand, while he usually gave way to any snakes in his path; most were poisonous and best left to their own ways.

Days passed in the forest and Kerran began to wonder if he was moving eastward at all. Keeping to the ridge lines for fear of being caught again in the mist shrouded valleys his journey seemed to be taking him ever northward. His father had taught him much about living from the land, while his mother's healing skills and medicinal needs from the edge of the forest had also prepared him well. By firelight he scraped and cleaned his rabbit skins, stretching them out by the flames to dry and harden. When he had collected enough of them, he fashioned a bag to carry his food and even more of the skins. Winter was not far off and rabbit hides, if only partly cured, could still mean the difference between being warm or freezing in the approaching cold from the south. Almost a half moon had passed and still the forest seemed to go on forever. Occasionally at night he heard the distant howling of dogs. Whether they were the marauders of which Leana had spoken or wild hounds that roamed in much of the lands he could not tell. Of any larger beasts he had seen and heard nothing.

One night Kerran camped by a clear pool that was fed by a small bubbling stream. He built a larger fire than usual, stripped, and then leapt into the chilling water, he felt strengthened and his meal of several small lizards roasted on the fire was most welcome. He ate two of the wild apples he had found earlier that day growing in a clearing by a stream, then after scraping at a rabbit skin for a time Kerran felt his eyelids drooping. He stretched out by the fire and turned his mind to sleep, his hand resting on his chest touching the fragment of the Seacrest.

He dreamed that he walked through a soft mist and after a time the strange voice came into his mind again, but this time it spoke softly and without haste.

"Kerran I am here. I have come to tell you things that you should know."

"Who are you?" asked Kerran in his wakeful mind, surprised that he could talk with his thoughts into this dream world.

"I have no name," the voice replied. "I am not anyone or anything. I am nothing but this voice and these words. I am part of the amulet that you bear. I am a teacher and a warning in your dreams. I am the past, but not the future. I cannot see the times to come but I have true knowledge of parts of that which you call history. I will try to answer the questions that you now wish to ask."

"Tell me what happened in the mist? What were the hands?" asked Kerran, shuddering as he remembered the fear and the soft grasping fingers.

"The valleys of mist here in Dreardim are places of death and madness," replied the voice. "In the time of the wars between the wizards, many were driven insane by the wild magic of the sorcerers. In love with power, some of the wizards cared not for mere humans who were used as players in their games. Huge armies were raised and annihilated in contests of magical strength, and into these valleys came many of the dead who could not rest and were lost in those violent times. Throughout the forest there are many of these places, to find safety from these undead you must sleep on high ground or beside flowing streams. Beware stagnant pools even in the day, for it is there that they rest and wait. Their madness formed the mists that surrounded you. They are undead, their bodies lost in time. They have only their hands so to be able to capture any who stray into their domain. Your fate would have been to become one of them. You came very close to being lost and this must not be." The voice became silent.

"Tell me of history," said Kerran, having always enjoyed tales and legends of the distant past. "Tell me of the House of Maradass and those ancient times," he said intrigued. "Tell me of the amulet."

"The power that you carry is but one quarter of what was once known as Ma-Zurin-Bidar," said the voice. "The Seacrest in the modern tongue. It has powers that vary with the one who bears it. There are unknown strengths within you Kerran. Your use of the Seacrest has already shown that. The history of Ma-

Zurin-Bidar goes back many thousands of years to the time of the wizards. There is much hidden to me of the ancient days, though some things I know. It was made by Rishtan-Sta the White Wizard and was used by him to end the Wizard Wars. Much later it was found in the Sea of Shardis, and magic was still in it. It would not be tamed and many were corrupted by its power.

"Finally the great houses of Maradass and Amitarl rose in the land. They made an alliance, and to weaken the harmful powers within the Seacrest they decided to divide it in two, but when the dividing was made Ma-Zurin-Bidar broke into four parts. Maradass the Philosopher who had brought about the alliance chose the piece which was concerned with Death. His eldest son Zard received another piece, that of Life. Another fragment of the Seacrest went to Barthol Amitarl and he studied the possibilities of the Future through the powers of his fragment. The last piece went to his eldest daughter, Narinda. Her fragment was of the Past and is the piece that you now carry."

"For a thousand years there was peace. By ancient oaths and the magical powers of the Seacrest the Philosopher and his family lived for a great many years. Amitarl lived shorter lives but often as long as two centuries. Zard was killed and by oaths sworn at the dividing of the talisman the father also died though not all of this is known to me. What I know is this, Darss, the second son of Maradass the Philosopher, and twin to Zard came to power. It is he who was called the Mad One. Zard returned to the world, tied in oaths which were forged by his father. He came again as one of twin sons to the Mad One, who then turned to war against Amitarl and the Southlands. Using the power within the Seacrest fragments he drew together great armies, with Zard the Black Knight at their head. Then, in a great battle on the Central Plains Zard lost his piece of the Seacrest, and the Black Armies were driven to the north and beyond the borders of the Regions. It is here that Maradass has again prepared an army with the aid of his lone but most powerful piece of the Seacrest."

"The other three parts were passed down through the eldest

of the Amitarl line. Tolth on the Isles of Zeta now holds one, the piece that is concerned with the future. Landin Elfhand, his eldest son, carries yet another piece on a mission to the northern borders, Zard's piece, the one concerned with life. The third piece which was carried by his sister Leana is now in your keeping. The Seacrest is ancient magic, so old that no made thing in these lands is older. It escaped the purges in the Dark Times when almost all of the wizards' talismans and wands were destroyed."

"The house of Maradass is stirring and may soon march on the Northern Regions with but one piece of the Seacrest at their command. They have sought to capture at least one more piece, for with the power of a full half the House of Maradass could not be destroyed except by wizardry. Their armies are vast and have been centuries in preparation. Now Zard has been vanquished once again, but not destroyed, for he will come again as before. The Mad One in near death if the oaths remain true, Darss, his second son will come to power now and his own twin sons will soon be conceived. The new head of the Maradass family is unknown to me, yet I fear him, and I believe that the lands are still in great peril. Soon the new Maradass will hold the Death piece. On the new moon which is this day, the Mad One will end his reign."

The voice had weakened slowly through this telling. "There is much that I could tell you Kerran but I must go now, my power is almost gone. If I can warn you of danger in you path I will. It is easier for me to come into your dreams than it is in your waking. Find Tolth, he will know what to do." The voice had become a whisper, and then it faded and was gone.

Kerran slipped into true but unusually vivid dreams where there were castles and far off lands, beautiful people and violent terrible deeds. A great plain spread out before him and a battle was being fought there, where towering war machines were drawn by fearful creatures of mighty strength. Armies of horsemen and foot soldiers slaughtered each other in great numbers. Kerran dreamed then of a land that burst asunder. Tall fires reached into the skies, and mountains melted and flowed across the land. Troubled dreams and dreams of terror which only dissolved as he woke shivering in the forest, touched by an early frost. The cycle was turning further towards winter, and the times of winds and snow were not far away.

Kerran spent much of that morning tying and stringing together his rabbit skins to form a sleeveless hooded jacket. The journey seemed so impossible that he wanted to turn and go home, but he knew he could not. There was no choice as Leana had said; around his neck he wore the fate of the land. If nothing else, the dream voice had convinced him of that. One day while climbing a difficult escarpment Kerran had the strangest feeling that he knew the place, but it was not like a memory. It was as if his whole body, sight, taste, smell, somehow knew that he was close to something important that he could not understand. He would have liked to ask the voice about this but it had not returned.

He walked on for several more days, struggling to overcome the terrain as well as his fears and eventually began to notice a change in the forest. There were no longer the pockets of hoary old trees that had towered above the dense lower canopy of the deeper forest. Groves of tall straight-trunk giants were now mixed with thickets of small wiry many limbed trees and pockets of overhanging ferns. Then Kerran finally began to come upon signs of other humans. He saw footprints in a wet hollow by a stream, and soon after a narrow path crossed his own. A dog barked somewhere far off to his left, and there was the faint smell of wood smoke on the wind. For two days Storm was not to be seen, and Kerran felt utterly alone and almost desperate, then to his great relief the white hawk returned, flying in long slow circles above the forest. Kerran had always thought that Storm was special in some way and he remembered back almost ten years to a cold and black winter's day not long after his father had died.

A fierce wind had blown, and rain had thrashed the country about Westerval; bolts of hard lightning splintering the dark sky. Kerran had been standing at the window looking out on the yard when there was a flash of lightning and a violent shattering burst of thunder. A young white hawk was suddenly blasted from the sky to fall dazed and injured a few steps from the front door of the house. Kerran had rushed out into the rain and scooped up the stricken bird, and then with his mother's knowledge and help they had been able to save the hawk which Kerran had named Storm. The white hawk had stayed with them until completely cured and then Kerran had set the bird free. Storm had flown westward, disappearing toward the distant mountains of The Bittering. Kerran had been saddened to lose his new and wonderful friend, but it was only a few days later that Storm had returned, flying into the yard much to Kerran's surprise. Storm would not often allow himself to be handled but remained in the area, and he was always above when Kerran went foraging in the forest. Kerran was pleased to have such a companion. He knew that he would feel much more alone without the presence of the majestic bird circling lazily in the skies above.

One cold windswept evening the forest finally came to an end. There were no signs of dwellings close to where Kerran emerged from the trees and something told him that he should avoid contact with the small villages and towns that were scattered along the edge of the forest. The fragment of magic which he carried near his breast was too important to be lost to some ruffian's hands. Spread out before him as far as his sight could reach lay a vast unsheltered plain, and a new stage of his journey was about to begin. He heard the dog pack hunting in the forest, howling as they ran, and wondered again that he had not met any of the beasts or any other dangerous creatures during his many days crossing Dreardim Forest. Kerran made camp in a sheltered hollow on the edge of the forest, and as he cooked the thin rabbit he had managed to kill that day he wondered as he wondered every night what the morrow would bring.

The tall powerful man became aware of the distant howling deep in the forest, as the huge dog that lay stretched beside him lifted his head, his sharp ears also taking in the sound of the pack as it hunted in the darkness. After a few moments the mountain dog dropped his head to rest it across his paws, and the man turned his gaze back to the glowing fire where he roasted two small rabbits. Winter was soon to come to the Southlands where his journey would take him, but the man was accustomed to the hardships of the road and living from the land. He was an outlaw and a much wanted by the Governor of the City Amitarl, but it was to this very place that he now travelled. With the toe of his boot he pushed a glowing branch further into the fire sending sparks swirling on the light evening breeze. He wondered again at the strange white bird he had seen earlier that day. At first he had thought it must be a gull, blown inland from the coast, but it had been too large for any seabird he knew and had soared like a bird of prey. It was said that white hawks still inhabited the mountains of the Bittering, but in all his years under the open skies he had never seen one.

Somewhere nearby three or four of the wild dogs began to howl menacingly, and the man reached across for his arrows and bow. His companion, the mountain dog, came to his feet with a wild threatening roar and continued until the lesser beasts slunk away into the darkness. The man smiled, knowing that they would not be disturbed again that night. After eating his fill he stretched out beside the low burning fire, wrapped in his heavy blanket. Yawning, he pulled his wide brimmed hat down over his eyes and was soon walking in the realm of dreams where a white hawk flew high on the wind.

The Old Coast Road

Kerran stood at the muddy roadside. The weather had turned to rain and puddles were collecting in the wheel ruts worn by the carts and wagons that had passed this way. The choice of which way he should go was not so clear to Kerran. If he was to follow the road he must choose north or south. The other possibility was to go directly east, out into the vast flat land that spread to the horizon. He saw wetlands there. Reeds grew in waving fields amongst wide stretches of water and he did not feel it to be a wise choice to go that way. Food was becoming a major concern, winter was not far off and there would be little game anywhere in the land. The road to the north made the most sense as winter deepened from the south, and he decided that by going that way he could avoid some of its bitterness.

Shouldering his bag Kerran took to the road again. He passed by a number of poor villages and larger towns. All were encircled by walls of logs and earth, and poor ragged travellers were not welcome there. He had travelled little more than a league and passed a larger settlement when he became aware that he was being overtaken by a slow moving horse and wagon. Few travellers had passed him going north, and they had been furtive and mistrusting, treating Kerran like an irksome beggar or worse. Kerran continued to walk and it was some time before the other traveller came up close behind. Kerran looked back as the wagon began to slow, and a great bearded mouth boomed at him.

"What of all devils are you doing boy? Where do you think you're going in you're hairy garb?"

Kerran found it strange to be hearing a human voice.

"I go east to the ocean," he blurted.

"That you do not," came the gruff reply. "You are heading north to the Crossroads is my best guess, and then you will probably have to go some place else. My guess would be Mendan-Maradass, unless of course you wish to continue walking in circles while going the wrong way. In any case you look like you could do with a ride at least as far as the Crossroads. Climb up boy. I will not bite you, not yet in any case. Come, I could do with some good company. You *are* good company I hope?"

Kerran climbed up beside the friendly jovial driver. He had taken an instant liking to the man who at that moment flicked the reins and got the wagon under way again, speaking as he did so.

"By appearances you are not some magic devil sent to waylay me, so I guess I can introduce myself in safety." His eyes twinkled and he winked knowingly. "My name is Redrah and I move things around." He poked his thumb at the load of boxes and packages on the tray behind.

"My name is Kerran' he replied. "And I thank you for this ride, Redrah."

"Tell me Kerran, why do you want to go to Mendan-Maradass?" asked Redrah.

"I am not going to Mendan-Maradass, at least I do not plan to," replied Kerran. "I am going to the ocean."

"Yes, as you said, you go to the ocean," grumbled Redrah in jest. "Then what? The ocean is a big place."

Kerran wanted to trust this good-humoured man; he wanted to ask questions without having to hold back anything.

"I go to find a boat that will take me to Zeta," he said quietly.

"Zeta!" bellowed Redrah looking at him in astonishment.

"What are you boy? Some sort of simpleton? Zeta? By the ten thousand devils, what world are you living in, boy?"

"I have to go, it is very important," said Kerran, almost overcome by the man's ridicule.

"Excuse me Kerran," Redrah said a little more kindly. "I did not mean to offend you. One does not hear of someone going to Zeta everyday. Tell me, what do you know of the Magic Isles?"

Kerran was pleased that Redrah no longer scoffed.

"My father told me stories of the old times," he replied. "Zeta was a land of islands, a magical hidden place, a place of sanctuary. I know little more except that I must find a man called Tolth."

"Well I have never heard of Tolth," said Redrah. "But as for Zeta you know about as much as anyone I have ever met. A place of sanctuary in the old days," Redrah nodded, remembering. "And you must go there, Kerran? Will you tell me why?"

"I must go to Tolth and tell him that his daughter did not die in vain," said Kerran. "I must give him something that she gave to me."

Redrah did not ask what this thing could be and both travellers became silent for a time. The wagon trundled on to the north and the plains went on forever in every direction, a few trees and the occasional distant spiral of someone's hearth fire somehow making it seem even emptier; the haze that had been Kerran's last sighting of the forest was several days behind. Redrah told Kerran of the Four Regions as the boy did not seem to know a lot about the lands he lived in. They travelled through Glandrin in the south and west, he told the unschooled boy. It was a land of farmers with no great city except for the ruins of Crysta-Sha. Kerran, who indeed knew little, discovered that he had been born in a narrow corner of Glandrin, between forest and mountain, where the beginnings of the great river Glandrin-dar flowed. It was such a secluded corner of the land that Redrah was not surprised at the young man's lack of knowledge of the outside world.

"Then there is the Region of Andrian in the south and east," he continued. "There by the sea is the crumbling but fair City of Amitarl. Much has now come to ruin and disrepair in these later days. Since the breaking of the Seacrest Alliance, and the later disappearance of the Amitarl family, the strong hand of decadence has crept into the courts of the city."

Kerran felt surprise at the mention of Amitarl and the Seacrest. He held the piece of the talisman through his shirtfront as Redrah continued his telling.

"The present governor is an unkind man and tempted by all things," Redrah told him. "The peace that was, is no more."

Redrah was silent for a time. "Ah, it must have been a wonderful land in the old times," he eventually continued. "Even Mendan-Maradass was said to be a city of wonder, though the old castle, long in ruins now, was said to have no beauty in it at all. It was destroyed in the Wars of the Broken Alliance and never rebuilt. Mendan-Maradass is a totally debauched city now. Trade still goes on, but it is a place of wickedness and treachery. There are few to trust. If you go there Kerran watch your back and keep away from the docks. Now if you want a fair and peaceful land you must come to Rianodar, the Region that is my home. Ever since Narinda was made the governess of that corner of the lands two thousand years ago war and decadence has left little trace there. Tis said that on our land a good spell is cast. I am not hard to find if you are ever in the west of Rianodar, at the foot of the mountains you will find me. You are welcome, even though I still think you rather odd; I will pry no further into your journey and I hope that you find Zeta."

Day moved towards evening, and at dusk they stopped to camp beside the road, where Redrah quickly built a fire from dry firewood he kept in the wagon and prepared a delightful meal. Kerran had never tasted anything so good. The pot of stew bubbled happily by the fire and Kerran ate three bowls. Huge chunks of bread dipped in the juices were sucked from his dripping fingers. After a hot mug of sweet fragrant tea Kerran felt warm and full for the first time in many days and he slept deeply under a warm blanket from the wagon, untroubled by dreams. Over the next few days Redrah and his wagon passed through a number of the small towns and villages, sometimes dropping off a package or two, and sometimes picking up freight to be delivered further to the north. Kerran helped when he could but kept away from any who showed any curiosity about Redrah's ragged passenger.

"Today we will come nigh the Crossroads and the parting of our ways," Redrah said one morning. "You may keep that blanket, winter comes and you will need it. Besides I would never be able to get the smell of rabbit out of it. I will dig out a small cooking pot that I think you could use, even roast rabbit must get tiresome after a time." Redrah was silent for a while then spoke again. "Have you decided which way you go after the Crossroads?" he asked.

Kerran had indeed thought a lot on this question.

"I do not like the sound of Mendan-Maradass," he replied. "I think I will take the Old Coast Road that you spoke of and hope to find an honest sailor to take me to Zeta."

Redrah looked with disquiet at the road ahead. "Do not go on with this fool's quest," he told his young companion. "Go home, or come and visit Rianodar, but do not go in search of Zeta. None have ever returned of those who went looking. Why is it so important? A woman's dying words, and something she gave you; it does not sound like enough for you to risk your life and die for as well. What is it that is hung from the thong around your neck? The thing that you clutch in the night?"

He paused, regretting his words. "It is none of my business, I know," he said quietly. His words trailed off and he became silent.

Slowly Kerran lifted the thong over his head and held in his open palm the quarter piece of the Seacrest. Redrah looked at it and his eyes grew wide in astonishment.

"It is," he said incredulously. "It really is. I have seen its likeness in a book somewhere."

He reached out and touched the piece of blue metal.

"So this is what you must take to Zeta," Redrah said amazed. "I understand now. I do! I do! Well, well, you are indeed a very odd one Master Kerran. For so long the Seacrest is lost, then here in the middle of nowhere, I meet this boy, who just happens to have a piece of it hung around his neck."

He mused, his mind absorbing this amazing revelation. "If you are sent to Zeta then it may well be that the Amitarl family survives there," he said. "I hope this is so. As for the Seacrest, if one piece survives then perhaps the others do too. There may be hope for the lands yet. Good news Kerran. Good news indeed."

Redrah chuckled away to himself for some time, and then Kerran noticed his friend peering up at the sky now and then, looking for something.

"His name is Storm," he told the astonished man. "He is my friend, and I hope above all things that he plans on coming to Zeta too."

"He *is* a white hawk?" Redrah said incredulously.

"Yes," replied Kerran. "He has been in my life now for ten years."

"You travel under mysterious and wondrous stars," Redrah said solemnly. "The white hawk is the emblem of the Family Amitarl, if anyone is destined to find Zeta it must be you my young friend."

Redrah did not question Kerran further. He began to tell tales of Amitarl and the old times for most of the morning, but eventually grew silent. Finally he spoke again.

"The Crossroads," he said pointing.

Ahead Kerran could make out an interruption in the road. The land rose slightly and was crowned by a tall dead tree and a tumble of huge cut stones. As they approached Kerran saw that a castle had once stood on this small hill overlooking the vast flat plains, though now it was but a circle of massive stones, fallen and broken. A feeling of dread came down upon him, as though the sky had grown heavy with a silent warning.

"It is an evil place, but all travellers must pass through it," said Redrah who kept a very careful watch, expecting danger. "Those who have tried to force new roads through this country have never succeeded. The plains are covered with swamps and treacherous marshlands, not to mention outlaws and dogs. Whatever the curse is on this place, it cannot be avoided. All roads pass this way."

They were beginning to climb the rise when Kerran saw

a human skull lying half hidden in the grass. Further up the slope he could see pieces of rusted armour and still more skulls and bones.

"They are the ones who were caught here at night," said Redrah, answering the unspoken question. "It is only during the day that any can pass through the Crossroads."

"But there are so many soldiers who have died here," exclaimed Kerran as he saw more remains of the fallen dead. "What could have destroyed them?"

"No one can say, but I have heard the story of these soldiers," said Redrah. "They were a troop from the City Amitarl in a time, not so long ago, when the Southlands still had a real army. Their captain was a bold and arrogant man and he camped here on purpose to test his men. They were indeed tested in the night it seems for none survived. A messenger who had been sent on to the next garrison returned in daylight to find them hacked to pieces. The messenger fled and the bodies were left to the dogs and crows. No one lingers here, even in the daylight."

They came to the top of the rise, entering through what had once been the castle walls and came upon a large open courtyard. Kerran saw that four other roads had converged on the old castle and each entered the courtyard through the broken walls.

"That is the Old Coast Road," said Redrah, pointing to the gap in the wall, second to their right. "It is not a road for horse and wagon, but you will fare well on foot."

He slowed the wagon to a halt in the centre of the Crossroads, then leaned across and grasped Kerran's hand.

"Farewell Kerran," he said with a look of wonder still in his eyes. "May you reach your journey's end in safety."

Kerran jumped down from the wagon and stood looking up at his large, bearded friend.

"Farewell Redrah," he replied. "Thank you for everything. I would like to visit Rianodar one day. I hope we meet again. Do not let the ten thousand devils tangle your beard."

Redrah chuckled, and then passed Kerran a small bundle wrapped in the warm, soft blanket. "A few things to help you on your way," he said. "A bit of food and that pot to cook your skinny rabbits in."

"I will always be grateful to you," said Kerran as he dashed away a tear.

"Go now, we must both leave this place," said Redrah, ever watchful. "Robbers haunt this place, but not the Old Coast Road. You will be safe there for no one else ever goes that way." He paused a moment, loath to leave this brave young man. "Beware of the dogs," he said quietly.

Redrah smiled one last time at Kerran, then flicking the reins he turned the wagon to the road into Rianodar and waved goodbye. Kerran stood watching as the wagon trundled down the gentle slope and into the gathering gloom..

The Old Coast Road was deeply cracked and broken in places. It had been built in an ancient time when great care had been put into the building of this first connecting road between the two great cities. Made of stone it stood a man's height above the surrounding wetlands and ran perfectly straight for many leagues at a time. Often there were living trees which had grown into ruined sections of the road, slowly tearing it apart, while in the marshlands, which had caused the near destruction of this marvellous feat of road building, there were many ghostly white skeletons of a long dead forest.

Kerran lay down to sleep that night wrapped in Redrah's gift. The warm woollen blanket still smelt of the various contents of the now distant wagon; Kerran did not sense the smell of rabbit at all. Storm uncharacteristically perched in a living tree, which grew close to the stonework of the roadway and overhung Kerran's campsite. Normally the bird did not come near the firelight, yet he remained in the tree all night, watching over Kerran as he slept. Kerran dreamed of the ocean, until on the edge of sound he heard a high wailing cry that trailed off as he tried to focus on it. All was silent and he lay down again, though he did not sleep again that night and dawn found him on the road early.

The day passed, cold and bleak. During the thunderous afternoon Storm flew above the road scanning the countryside, unperturbed by any problems other than food. Food was also on Kerran's mind. With the cooking pot, Redrah had given him a loaf of bread, a small round cheese and several apples. It would not last him forever and game was not plentiful. There were ducks and other water birds in the wet marshlands, but they were not easy to approach. From what he had learned of this country, unknown to him before leaving home, he knew that he had perhaps seven or eight days walking before he came to a fishing village on the coast of the Sea of Shardis. There he hoped he would find someone who would sail to Zeta.

"But why would anyone want to take me to Zeta?" he asked himself. "What have I got that I can offer?"

He saw little real hope unless he was to steal a boat, though he knew nothing of sailing. The thoughts and questions kept running in circles through his mind as the leagues slipped by beneath his feet. The country he was passing through was becoming more swampy and silent; the bleak dead forest had little to offer a hungry traveller.

Kerran halted suddenly when he saw the large black bird paddling quietly near the edge of the old highway, intently peering into the large pool where it swam. He had easily been able to come within range, and the bird was unaware of his soft approaching footfalls, intent on its own hunt. Kerran readied for his throw, but then found that he could not do it, the bird was so beautiful with its long elegant neck and its soft plumage. Kerran took a step forward, knowing that the creature would soon become aware of him and take to flight.

Without a sound Storm suddenly plummeted from the sky and fell upon the screaming bird. There was the sound of violent splashing as together they disappeared from view beside the edge of the roadway, with a single last sharp cry from the doomed bird. Kerran ran forward but before he had reached the spot, Storm flew up from beside the pool carrying the dead bird in his talons. With a disdainful cry, the hawk dropped the bird at Kerran's feet, and then flew off to disappear into the approaching night.

Kerran was astounded. He could not believe what he had just seen but he would have to believe it, for there at his feet lay the black swan, almost decapitated by the hawk's attack. Kerran puzzled over this new event, Storm had done some surprising things since they had begun their journey, and now here was the white hawk helping to supply food for his travelling companion. Kerran had never thought of Storm as belonging to him, there was a bond between them that Kerran had tried to explain to his mother, but he had not been able to put words to his feelings.

Kerran carried the carcase of the dead bird in his rabbit-skin bag, which had grown quite large. The evening turned to darkness with a thick mist rising from the wetlands and Kerran made camp, once he had found a dry place on the southern side of the road. He clambered down quickly and after starting a fire he attended to the bird. It was not long before he had pieces of white meat bubbling in the pot with assorted herbs and the few wild vegetables he had gathered. He ate well and finished with one of the apples that Redrah had given him. He thought of the great bearded man and tears of gratitude and loneliness came to his eyes.

Once again he began to have doubts about his ability to see the journey through. He thought of home and his mother. What would she think? The old horse would have found its way home and his mother would have searched for him. The neighbours and local farmers would have joined in eventually, but there would be no sign. He was sure that no one would search so far into the forest that they would find the small glade, where the two fallen knights must be lying still. He was so sorry that he could not explain to her, and he hoped that he could return quickly when his journey was done, if indeed it was ever done.

During the following afternoon Storm seemed unsettled, something that was beyond Kerran's vision, somewhere off in the trees and misty swamplands was disturbing the hawk. Storm, after being aloft for a time, would dive below the tree tops in a hunting swoop, then come flying upward again to circle low for a while, gaining height slowly and then repeat the dive. Kerran neither saw nor heard a thing, though Redrah had warned him of the dog packs which sometimes came this far east from their usual hunting grounds in the forest. The history of dogs in the land was more ancient than that of the wizards he had learned from stories his father had told him. In the village of Westerval almost every family had at least one dog, and Kerran knew much of their nature. He looked at his thick staff and knew that it would deter or damage any dog that he had ever met, though he wondered if in the wild, dogs could grow larger or stronger than their village counterparts.

The Old Coast Road was the only way through the marshlands and he would not leave it. Whatever was disturbing Storm, so long as it stayed out there in the misty gloom, he cared not to discover its identity. As the day passed Kerran's thoughts went often to his home, nestled in the quiet valley on the edge of Dreardim Forest. He missed the fireside talks with his mother. There were many chores that she would have to cope with now. His heart ached when he thought of her grieving over him, lost or dead in the forest.

The weather was turning to rain again and it was time to look out for a campsite, but the land beside the road had almost completely vanished under dead stinking pools and soft boggy ground. Kerran clambered across a broken section of the road hoping to find a little shelter. Rain was pouring down when he finally came upon a narrow space between slabs of fallen rock. Wedging himself through a tight gap, he found himself in a open space beyond where he could crouch and lie down, and it was dry, much to his delight. When night came he lit a small fire, having collected dry leaves and twigs along the way. Dead trees and broken limbs could always be found, as many dead trees had fallen against the roadway. It was as if the plants had given a final slap at the effort of the builders, who had not foreseen the advance of the wetlands that would destroy their work.

During the early hours of the morning Kerran was woken by a growl and a scuffling sound outside his shelter. He sat up quietly, reaching for his staff. Pale moonlight came slanting through the gaps in the tumbled stonework. There was a snarl and a yelp, then a crunching sound. The bones Kerran had thrown out earlier were being eaten and Kerran cursed himself for a fool. Far off in the swamp a single howl came floating on the air, and then from much closer another dog replied. There was a snuffling near the entrance in the space between the rocks, then a head with pointed ears appeared, blocking out the light. Kerran swung his staff, catching the dog squarely on the snout. The creature yelped in pain and surprise, howling as it retreated. A cry went up amongst several dogs close by.Kerran did not know how many dogs answered the call from afar but it seemed a great many.

He was well protected in his narrow shelter but did not like the prospect of being trapped for very long. He heard dogs scratching in the loose earth and rubble above him. Kerran sat alert and waiting as the night grew long, again a dog appeared in the entrance and received great pain for it. Kerran dozed between bouts of howling, and towards dawn all became quiet so he lay down and slept. The sun, shining into the small cave, woke him from a dream. Kerran drank a little of the water he had collected the evening before, the small pot was perhaps half full. Taking a piece of meat from his pouch Kerran pitched it through the gap. There was silence. He waited, listening, then a shadow passed across the entrance, a soft sound of the meat being taken and that was all. Kerran knew he could not stay in this tiny sanctuary, he would have to go and face whatever may be outside. He prepared his bag, and then clasping his staff he crawled to the entrance.

Kerran did not see any dogs as he emerged, he moved quickly, rolling out and coming to a crouched stance. All was still and Kerran breathed a sigh, he seemed to be out of trouble for a time. Turning, intent on putting some distance between himself and this place he saw the dog facing him. Large, and mostly black, the creature snarled at him, vicious teeth bared. Kerran attacked, he had met fierce dogs before and he knew it to be the only thing he could do that would make the dog go.

Leaping forward he landed a sharp blow on the creatures shoulders. It leapt sideways away from the staff but Kerran had expected this, swinging the wood above his head he brought it down full on the animal's brow and it fell, stunned. Kerran was almost congratulating himself on the ease of his triumph when a number of smaller dogs rushed at him from behind. He turned and caught one a heavy blow to the ribs. It howled and ran from the fight. Kerran landed another blow, and then he felt sharp fangs bite deep into the muscles of his lower leg. He cried out in pain as the teeth clung to him, then he fell to his knees. The dog let go his hold and screamed as Storm tore at its back with raking talons as Kerran crawled, in great pain towards the gap in the rocks. He swung his staff but the dogs did not come at him. Fear of the hawk had scattered them. Kerran scrambled through the narrow space again and dragged himself further into the stone sanctuary. A burning pain pulsed through his right leg, and blood seeped through his torn breeches.

His flesh was torn and there were deep blue puncture marks that oozed blood. All was quiet outside as Kerran tore strips from his blanket and wrapped them tightly about his damaged leg. Lights began to swirl before his eyes and he shook his head, fearful that he might lose consciousness and become easy prey for the dog pack, certain that they were not very far away. Kerran wished he could clean the wounds but he had no water left. All he could do now was lie still and hope the blood would soon stop flowing. He knew that he would not be able to travel for some days now, even if no infection came from the bites.

Holding his staff in his right hand Kerran leant his head back against the wall. Suddenly everything seemed so hopeless. He was trapped and unable to move, his pouch contained only a little food and he had no water. He could expect no help and could now hear the movements of dogs outside. Soft padded feet scuffed around the entrance of Kerran's refuge. Tears fell from his cheeks to his shirt front and pain kept shooting through his wounded limb. He could do nothing but lie on the dirt floor. Easing his leg, and thinking about the predicament he was now in. There seemed little hope, unless the dogs gave up on their trapped prey and went away. Kerran did not hold out much hope for this. Despair weighed heavily on him, overpowering him, until a low growl brought him back to his surroundings.

A large dog stood in the entrance. It had an ugly short nose, cunning yellow eyes and a mouth that snarled and salivated. Kerran knew that if this dog were to defeat him, all that would remain of Kerran Shalastar and his quest would be a few bones scattered through the ruins of the old highway. He let out a loud and enraged yell, swinging his staff at the face of the dog, but the blow went wide of its mark. The beast did not move, growling, it stood unblinking, well aware of the vulnerability of its prey. Kerran, his knife in his left hand, swung again with his staff catching the dog a glancing blow to its shoulder. With an angered roar the dog leapt forward barking savagely, fangs bared. Kerran brought his staff up and was able to force the dog backward, slashing with his knife hand, barely missing the underbelly of his adversary. Swaying from side to side the dog hunted for an opening, out of reach he eyed Kerran, growling low in his throat. Other dogs were pressing in from behind and the large dog turned and snarled viciously until the pack withdrew to await the outcome of the confrontation.

The shrewd calculating eyes once again rested on Kerran, smouldering, unmoving, willing its prey to drop his guard for just a moment. Kerran gave another enraged cry trying to drive the creature from the entrance but the dog stood still, tormenting him, just out of reach of the swinging staff. Kerran lowered his weapon slowly. He was tired. The bleeding from his leg appeared to have ceased but a large amount of blood had soaked into the dirt floor. Breathing heavily, he sat looking at the dog as the creature slowly lowered itself to the floor of the shelter, as if taunting Kerran into an attack. The dog's eyes never left his own and a great fear crept into the deepest recesses of Kerran's mind. If he slept the dog would leap upon him, followed shortly by the rest of the pack.

Just out of reach Kerran could see a good hand-sized stone. Stretching slowly to his left his fingertip brushed against it, and taking his eyes from the dog for just a moment. The stone slipped into his left hand. The beast growled raising its head. In a quick movement the rock was transferred to Kerran's right hand, and in the same motion his arm flicked out, sending the stone quickly across the short space between himself and the dog. The animal could not retreat in time and the heavy stone crashed into its head. Blood spurted from a jagged wound above the beast's eyes. A howl of anguish filled the small cave and the dog retreated quickly, drops of blood splattering on the surrounding rock.

Kerran lay back again. If the dogs rushed in he did not know if he had enough strength to fight them off. His throat was dry and he ate one of his last apples. It helped the dryness, but Kerran was very aware that with only one apple left. He could be trapped for days without water, with a wound that he could not tend. The dog pack would not give up easily; even now he could hear the scratching of paws digging again at the earth above him. No dog dared enter by the narrow passage for now and Kerran spent some time sharpening his staff to a fine point. He ate some bread and cheese then rested against the cold rock.

Kerran dozed through the afternoon, waking abruptly at the slightest change in the sounds around him. Once during the afternoon two young dogs rushed in, tearing at his legs. With a powerful thrust of his sharpened staff Kerran stabbed one of the dogs in the throat. There was a gurgled bloody cry and the beast lurched back through the entrance followed rapidly by its mate. Outside there was turmoil. Dogs yelped and barked and a great howl went up, then a terrifying scream from just one dog. Kerran realised that the pack had turned on their wounded companion. The dogs were growing hungry as winter began to descend on the land and the struggle did not last long.

Evening came. Kerran had enough wood to build a small fire that would last well into the night and he set it just inside the entrance, hoping that it would keep the pack at bay. He could see that, dig as they may, no dog could come at him from any direction other than the narrow gap between the two rocks. Rain began to fall again and the pack was quiet. Kerran, not knowing if they had gone or were silently waiting for him to emerge had no intention of going anywhere. The pain in his leg became agonising at times and he cried out as shafts of hot fire rushed through his torn flesh. At other times the leg felt almost numb and Kerran was able to sleep for a time.

The night wore on and the rain fell heavily. His fire spat and hissed as a few drops found their way into his shelter. He could almost taste the rain on his tongue and his thirst grew, even though he kept a small pebble in his mouth which helped to keep his throat moist, something he had learned from his father.

Early morning light crept softly across the floor of his refuge. Kerran lay propped against the wall and for a time he could not remember if he was alive or dead, or how much time had passed; his mind swam in a delirium of fever. Hot and cold waves passed through his body and all memory would pass for a time. He could not remember what it was he feared that was just beyond the old stonework, and then he would smell the dogs.

During the day his mind was at times clear and the pain not so acute, though he was weak and parched. Unless he had water soon he knew that he must surely die. It had been quiet outside for a time when Kerran crawled across the dirt floor and carefully peered through the narrow gap. A soft drizzle fell and there was no sign of the dogs. Puddles had formed, and with little thought other than the desire to slake his thirst. Kerran dragged his body through the confined space and drank a long marvellous draught.

Using the fallen stonework Kerran struggled upright, his left leg taking all of his weight. There was still no sign of the dogs but for how long he knew not. Though his mind had begun to find confusion in simple things, he knew that he must work if he was to heal himself and not die in this miserable place. He spent some time scooping up water into his cooking pot and after passing it through to his refuge he began to scrape a channel from the closest puddle to the entrance. It took all of his remaining strength but finally he had a small stream that allowed rainwater to trickle into his sanctuary. Crawling back inside he scooped out a hollow in the floor and placing a rabbit skin in the hole he watched the first few drops collect. Thankful, he took another drink from his cooking pot and ate a little bread and cold meat. The water had done much to revive him and Kerran cleaned his wounds as best he could. Quite a puddle had formed in the rabbit skin and he took another long drink before he lay down to rest. His leg was swollen and the bites were inflamed and blue. Kerran had seen blood poisoning before, and his heart sank as he realised that there was very little chance that he would ever leave this place. He fell into a disturbed and tormented sleep.

Night had almost come when the howling began. First there was a single startling cry from near the entrance, and then others nearby took up the call. They had returned, hopeful of taking an easier prey. Kerran woke from his evil dreams to find the reality of his situation to be far worse. He barely had the energy to lift his sharpened staff before dogs began to rush in. Either they expected to find him past resistance, or there was something outside which had driven them from behind he could not say. The first dog lunged at Kerran but was met by the pointed end of his staff and with a scream the beast was impaled on the spike. A second dog caught hold of Kerran's boot, teeth sinking through the heavy leather. With a wide swinging blow Kerran plunged his hunting knife into the animal's neck. Blood sprayed around the enclosure as dogs howled in pain and fought to escape, while others struggled to enter, hampered by the two stricken creatures that thrashed about in the approaching darkness.

Kerran felt a terrible nausea coming on him. His vision swam and he thought that it was surely over, that the dogs would soon have him. Then with a dark inhuman cry, that seemed to come from much deeper than his weakened being, Kerran lunged out in raw fury with his knife. Once, twice, and then again he struck flesh and bone. Crawling over a dying dog, his own cry was more animal than human. In the gathering darkness he lunged again with his blade, finally the dogs could take no more and all retreated quickly from the narrow passage. Kerran collapsed over the still quivering body of a dying foe, the last of his strength torn from him as he slipped into darkness.

"Kerran, I am here," said the strange voice into his nightmare world. The voice was urgent and it seemed in pain. "I cannot stay long," it continued. "I will not let you die here. The Seacrest must reach Tolth, and it is you who have been chosen to carry it. I will find a way. Wait for me. Take water, much of it. Dream now, for it will sustain you... I am gone."

Kerran slept and continued to dream. The visions were vivid, wide lands with tall cities of glass and stone. Strange people clothed in finery that could never have imagined. He saw the ocean and it was beautiful in its blue vastness. He flew above a green forested land and then descended into a gardened clearing where he slowly entered an old ornate home. He passed through solid walls and eventually came to a large room which held him; there was warmth and gentle pleasure here. He was not surprised when an old woman with long greying hair spoke to him from her seat by a large warm fire.

"Hail young Shalastar," she said as though to an old friend. "You are most welcome here. I have a story to tell you that one day may help you to see more of who you might become."

Kerran found he could not speak but it mattered little. He did not understand the meaning behind her words but was not troubled by them either. This was more than a dream he knew and he listened closely.

"This is the history of how the ancient wizard's magic that you carry returned to the lands, and eventually corrupted all who tried to wield it. Listen well Shalastar, for this touches on your history and your future."

In his sleeping world Kerran thought that he had never been as awake as he was now.

"Back in a distant time," she began. "But long after the wizards had gone, there lived a poor fisherman named Trarl. One day, far out on the deep waters of the Sea of Shardis, he pulled in his line to find a strange object entwined with it. It was made of blue metal and had markings that he could not understand. His son Larnus was enchanted by the object before he could even walk. Larnus became a man and his fortunes began to change. He had wealth, and business was good. He was an orphan now and had been an only child. He liked to travel, and walking one day in the old forest he came upon a cave. There he met an old black man who told him that if he took the charm to a place that would be shown to him, great rewards would be his. The black man told him that he could even be king. Larnus believed him implicitly. The charm brought him to a place on the open plains where a walking track crossed a well rutted wagon trail beside a low hill. Larnus was told to bury the charm there and to leave for his home of Viris-Tan-Vara.

"The knowledge that he could have anything, made him want to be a king. He gambled and won every time until he owned half of the richest city in the land. He told the city council and the citizenry that he wished to be king. The inhabitants of the city all laughed at him. He kept a small army and became more ruthless. Eventually he owned Viris-Tan-Vara, the entire city, then again he said he wanted to be king and the people called him ridiculous. He stopped supplying the city with food. People began to starve, until finally the city voted in favour of his kingship. For ten years Larnus was king, and then into his court came the wizened, old, black man. He stood before the throne, bare foot, a skin of some animal covering his body, a twisted staff in his hand.

"'It is time to go and get your charm back,' he said to the king.

"Larnus was puzzled. 'Why must I retrieve it?' he asked. "What good is it to me?"

"'You will see,' said the black man.

"So the king, again hearing truth in the old man's words, travelled to the place where two wide roads now intersected on the small hill. An inn had been built over the site and Kind Larnus had it knocked down. When the family complained Larnus had them killed, except for the youngest son who escaped.

"The talisman was found and king Larnus decided to build a mighty castle at these crossroads that would be his new home. More years passed and a city grew around the castle. Then reports came of a great horde of wild horsemen that had ridden unannounced into his kingdom from the south. The king's army was sent out but very few returned, battered and wounded, the enemy not far behind.

"The king stood on the high turret of his castle, the talisman in his hand. "Why?" he asked himself, for his kingdom was about to fall.

"Suddenly the old black man was at his elbow.

"'Why indeed?' he asked in return.

"'You said I could be king!' cried Larnus. 'Now you destroy me.'

"'You have destroyed yourself,' replied the black man. 'They want what you have these invaders from the south. Your greed has been your downfall.'

"'But you made me king,' cried Larnus.

"'I said that you could be king,' the black man said. 'I did not say that you should be king. There are few who sit on thrones that are indeed worthy of being there. The talisman had to be buried in that place for a time to work a future magic. The reason for this is not important to you.'

"'But what will happen now?' asked the king.

"'You have the amulet,' said the black man. 'One wish is all that can be granted to you now. You cannot ask for mercy from him who come for you. So what is it that you would have?'

"'I would like to die in peace,' said Larnus. 'I was far happier as a fisherman's son than I have ever been as a king.'

"If that is your wish then yes, you may die in peace," said the black man. 'But you must first pass the talisman to the one who now comes; you will know him.'

The castle was taken and the king faced his enemy.

"'King!' called the man. 'I am Drangmar. You killed my family at the Crossroads. Now you will die.'

"King Larnus remembered the small boy who had run from his soldier's blades. "Before I die there is something magical that I was told to give you," said the king and handed the amulet to Drangmar. 'I was also told that I could then die in peace.'

"Drangmar stood holding Ma-Zurin-Bidar, feeling its power, as King Larnus lay upon a divan and closed his eyes. After a short time he gave a peaceful sigh and died."

The old woman grew silent and smiled at Kerran. "That

is how Drangmar became the first of his ruinous lineage to rule from the castle in the Crossroads of the lands. You carry a fragment of that which corrupts all who hold it. The Seacrest may bring you what you wish, but you must be sure that it is what you really want." The old woman smiled again then nodded. "Remember these words well,' she said softly."

Kerran woke. It was dark and there was no sound of dogs from beyond the entrance. The voice of the old woman had somehow comforted him and he drifted back into an easier slumber. During the following day the pack did not come for him.

For two long days Kerran fought the poison which ran in his blood. Nightmares came again and pain tore at him. The dogs had not returned and in moments of clarity Kerran knew that when next they did come, he would be lost. He drank when he remembered but could eat nothing. Storm had gone, Kerran had not seen his friend since the white hawk had attacked the dogs, and had probably saved his life for a time. He hoped that Storm had not been caught himself and killed by the beasts.

There was a morning when Kerran woke with the knowledge that he would die soon. He clasped the Seacrest fragment in his hand but no power came. The last thing he saw before unconsciousness took him again was the appearance of Storm at the entrance of the enclosure, squawking and beating his wings. Then Kerran's mind fell into a world of fever and nightmare from which he did not expect to return.

Flindas

Kerran opened his eyes and looked up. Above him was an interwoven roof of branches and leaves sheltering him from the weather. Beside him was his cooking pot partly filled with water, and a small fire burned close by on which another pot bubbled, sending out delicious food smells. Kerran realised he was alive and famished. He tried to lift himself onto his elbows, but the effort was too much and he slumped back again. His head came to rest on an unfamiliar jacket that had been rolled up to cushion his head from the cold hard stone. He managed a sip of water. Lying on his side he let it dribble into his mouth, then he lay back again, amazed at his good fortune. Though he was weak he knew that he would live, someone had found him and tears of relief ran down his cheeks. A sudden thought came and he reached for the Seacrest fragment at his chest. His fingers clasped the talisman through his shirt and he sighed. The touch comforted him and he closed his eyes, sliding into a half conscious rest.

Later he woke to see a man crouching over the fire stirring the delicious smelling stew. Kerran could see that his rescuer was like no farmer or villager that he had ever met. The man was tall, his skin darkened by much exposure to the elements, and a long braided tail of hair hung far down his back from beneath a wide brimmed hat. His clothes were sturdy and made for travelling, as were his boots that looked as though they had walked far. Kerran remained as if asleep and continued to study the man. The traveller was beardless and Kerran guessed that he was close to forty years of age. When the man moved from his squatting position to gather more firewood Kerran could see that his long-limbed body held much agility and strength. His travelling pack also told much of the man when Kerran finally espied it beyond the fire. It was leaning against a fallen slab of stone and Kerran could see that attached to it was a sword in its scabbard and a longbow with a pouch of many arrows. The man also carried a heavy knife that he now thrust into the stew, drawing forth a piece of meat which he blew on and began to chew. After he had swallowed the mouthful he spoke, still looking into the fire.

"You must be hungry?" he said, his voice soft and careful.

He turned towards Kerran who looked into the man's dark, sombre eyes. A smile came to the stranger's face.

"Well my young friend, back from the dead I see. I am glad I did not waste my time on someone who had no will left to live." He paused a moment, looking at the young man who had almost died despite his care. "My name is Flindas," he continued, beginning to fill a bowl with the delicious smelling broth.

"I am Kerran Shalastar," was the weak reply.

"Do not speak now," said Flindas coming to him with the bowl. "Eat, rest, and get well. There will be time enough to tell me your tale later."

When Kerran could not feed himself Flindas took the spoon and carefully fed him until the bowl was empty, then exclaimed.

"For someone who was barely alive two days ago you have quite an appetite," he said. "Would you like more?"

Kerran shook his head and sighed with a smile. Inside he felt a wonderful warm glow, then at a great distance he heard the plaintive cry of a lone dog.

"Lay still and rest," said Flindas, seeing the startled look in the young man's eyes.

"There is no need to fear the dogs. I think they have enough to worry about without coming back to trouble you. I have treated your wounds with a poultice and already it begins to work. Do not worry yourself. All is well."

Kerran realised that his leg was bound in bandages which he had not applied, he smiled in disbelief and then a heavy drowsiness came over his mind and he again travelled into the world of unremembered dreams. He woke late in the night and saw Flindas sitting silently by the fire gazing into the embers. Kerran felt reassured and did not wake again until well into the following morning.

"Have some more soup," said Flindas coming to him with a bowl. "It will make you well. There are healing herbs in it."

Kerran was able to sit up and eat, and with the soup he took a little bread. "How did you find me?" he asked. "It is not likely that many people would take this road out of choice."

"Tis a strange thing," said Flindas returning to the fire and squatting beside it. "I was coming from the north on my way to the City Amitarl. I arrived at the Crossroads and was met by a very persistent bird, a white hawk no less that kept flying into my face as I tried to go on my way. Then it would fly to the beginning of this, the Old Coast Road and land on the roadway squawking and making a terrible noise. The Crossroads are not a place to linger but I was very curious about this hawk. I have never seen before such a creature. It seemed to want me to follow the old way which I have only once before travelled. It was at that time a mistake and I have not chosen it again. Now here I am, led here by a wild bird which seemed to know that you needed help. I have never seen a hawk behave this way and in truth I thought the white hawk only appeared in fables."

"His name is Storm," said Kerran leaning now upon his elbow. "He is my friend."

Flindas raised an eyebrow. "Well Kerran Shalastar," he said. "I must say you have rather unusual friends. A most unlikely companion, but there is no doubt that he saved your life."

As if he had been listening Storm swept across the campsite and Kerran was very happy to see the bird alive and well. Their eyes followed the hawk as it flew higher on the wind.

"Storm," Flindas mused. "A good name for such a bird. Tell me, Kerran, what are you doing out here on a deserted road with winter coming on? You seem ill equipped for a journey of any sort. Your clothes are just a little unusual."

"I go to the coast," replied Kerran, his voice falling almost to a whisper. "I am bound for Zeta. I must reach the Magical Isles."

Kerran was still exhausted, his words coming in short tired bursts. Flindas looked at him with intense curiosity.

"You go to Zeta you say," he said. "That is a fanciful destination for a boy to dream of. The Magic Isles have not been heard of for a very long time. Those who go looking for Zeta do not return they say. Why should you want to go there Kerran?"

Once again Kerran was in a predicament; it was hard to explain his journey without speaking of the Seacrest. He looked at Flindas, knowing that this man had saved his life. He owed Flindas his trust.

"I have a piece of the Seacrest," he said "I must take it to Zeta and give it to one called Tolth. It was his dying daughter's wish."

"The Seacrest," murmured Flindas. "You talk of old fables again. How could a boy like you fit into those stories? And the Seacrest! I cannot believe it. You have dreamt all this in your illness."

"No," said Kerran, and he lifted the talisman from beneath his shirt as Flindas leaned forward over the fire.

"I saw that earlier but took it for a trinket," he said.

The tall man came from the other side of the fire and knelt beside Kerran, looking closely at the piece of strange metal held in the young man's hand.

"Well I do not know what the Seacrest could possibly look like," said Flindas. "But that certainly seems to be something from the old times. What does it do? The Seacrest was said to be most powerful. Could you not have used it to defend yourself against the dogs?" The tone in the man's voice held much scepticism.

"It has power," replied Kerran replacing the Seacrest beneath his shirt. "It has saved me once, and in my dreams it talks to me."

"Talks to you!" said Flindas in surprise. "What does it say?"

"It tells me of the past," explained Kerran. "It does not know all of history but I think it knows much. Leana entrusted me with it and I must get to Zeta."

"You talk in riddles that I do not know the answers to." Flindas said as he sat beside the youth. "If you are strong enough, I would like to hear your tale from the beginning."

Kerran began to tell Flindas of that day in the forest and the clash of swords in the sunlit glade, of two fallen knights and a promise. He told of Redrah and the coming of the dog pack, and then there was not much more to tell."The last thing I remember was Storm arriving at the entrance of my cave," said Kerran. "You could not have been far behind, and here I am alive when I thought I would be dead. Thank you Flindas."

"Thank your hawk," was the reply. "I think he would fit very well into the old tales. The white hawk was once the emblem of the Family Amitarl before they disappeared from the land. It can still be seen fashioned on the walls of Celisor castle. I spent much of my youth in the shadows of those walls."

"Are you from the City Amitarl?" asked Kerran. He was curious about this lone traveller and wanted to know more.

"I was born there," said Flindas. "But it is fifteen years or more since I lived in the city."

"Will you tell me of it?" Kerran asked. "Is it as beautiful and sad as Redrah told me?"

"You are full of questions today," said Flindas.

The tall man paused, looking at the grey moisture laden sky, then he seemed to make up his mind to speak further. "It was once the most elegant of cities, the greatest city of the Regions," he began, almost as if reciting the words. "The house of Amitarl lived on the South Coast until the sixth century of the Alliance, and then Erindas founded and built the city. It flourished and grew until the time of Maradass the Mad. There is much blurring of history and few scholars in the lands now, so the old stories change much with the telling. Celisor

Amitarl built the walls around the city and then the castle, which overlooks the lands about. Built on a high crag, it is impregnable if defended even by a few.

"Celisor had died and so too had his son Rubon and much of the Amitarl family. The golden age of the city was over. Tis said that Celisor the Second was a greedy man and the line of Amitarl declined by his hand. It is not known what happened to the Seacrest since that time. The last Amitarl were Darna and his sister Anrin, who left in search of Zeta and were not seen again in the lands, perhaps the talisman went with them. The city sank further into degradation as did Mendan Maradass. Trade ceased between the Regions and outlaws ruled the Highroads as the family of governors in the city became the greatest criminals of all."

The words of Flindas became scathing as though he had a personal grievance against the family who had ruled since the departure of Amitarl. "The city became a dangerous place and still is today," he continued. "Few will go walking at night. It is graceful and beautiful, but it crumbles and falls. The city and courts are corrupt. They grow rich while many of their people go hungry."

Flindas stopped speaking. There was something in his voice that told Kerran there was more behind this man's solitary life than he was telling. Kerran did not pursue the matter but would have liked to have heard more. Even his home Region of Glandrin was little known to him. He thirsted for the stories that his father had never had time to tell, and his mother had not known. Kerran closed his eyes, resting with a sense of safety which he had not felt for many days.

He woke late in the night and could just make out Flindas sitting on the far side of the fire, his dark eyes looking into the low flames. Kerran could also see a large shape beyond Flindas that had not been there before. He could not see what it was and returned to sleep, marvelling as he did so that neither dogs or rain had come to disrupt the peaceful night. Dawn came slowly, the sun striving to penetrate the grey mist that lay on the land. Flindas was nowhere to be seen but his pack remained where it had been the night before, though there was no sign of his bow, or of the thing that had lain near him in the night. Kerran sat up; he was weak but knew he was mending. Whatever the healing was that Flindas had applied it seemed to be working fast.

The morning passed and Kerran found that he was able to stand with the help of his staff. He limped about amongst the tumbled stones testing his leg and Flindas found him thus

"You should not be walking on that leg yet," he said leading Kerran back to his resting place. "Lie there while I prepare us some food."

Kerran could see three rabbits and a duck lying by the smouldering ashes. Flindas began to breathe life into the fire, adding twigs and dry leaves, and then from behind the man a huge brown head appeared from amongst the rubble. The most enormous dog that Kerran could ever have imagined leapt to a vantage point atop the broken Highroad. Kerran cried out in fright and grabbed for his staff. Flindas sprang to his feet and as he whirled to face the danger his sword sang from its scabbard then seeing the huge animal above him Flindas laughed and lowered his sword, turning to Kerran with a smile.

"Do not be afraid of Rark," he said. "I should have told you of my travelling companion. He is the reason that no wild dogs have come to attack us. He would not avoid taking on the whole pack."

"I think he already has," said Kerran amazed at the creature.

The large beast stood watchful above them, traces of matted blood amongst his shaggy fur. Kerran still felt uneasy and hoped the dog would be friendly towards him. As if in answer Rark moved down to the side of Flindas, sniffed at the rabbits, accepted a scratch behind his ears, and then ambled leisurely towards Kerran. Kerran stroked the beast's neck and shoulders and Rark, with a great sigh, sank down beside Kerran, enjoying the attention he was receiving.

"I have never seen such an animal," said Kerran. "He is not of any breed that I know of."

"No, and you may never see his like again," said Flindas. "He came from the west beyond the Regions. I was travelling in the high country near the western borders and one day came upon him. He was near death, an arrow deep in his side. I often find lost and damaged animals on my travels."

He looked up and smiled at his jest.

"I have learned many things travelling the lands," he said. 'But the most valuable is perhaps what I have learned of the healing arts. Rark mended well and when I was able to release him back to the wild he would not go. Such a dog does not have a master. Just as you and Storm, we travel together and have done so for almost three years. In these dangerous times that we live he is a fine companion and friend."

"I would much rather be his friend than his enemy," said Kerran.

"Yes," agreed Flindas. "I know of no animal in the land that could overpower him except an armed warrior, and then only one who is highly trained."

Flindas paused, cutting a piece from the rabbit that he had been skinning and tossed it towards the dog. In a lazy movement Rark stretched his neck and deftly caught the morsel in his mouth, one swallow and it was gone.

"You will not be able to travel for some days," said Flindas. "Your leg needs rest. I will stay with you here, and then if you care for the company I will go to the coast with you. That is if you still wish to go."

"I am in your debt and most grateful for your company," said Kerran. "Do you know the coast? I am going to have to find a boat and someone to take me to Zeta."

"You talk as if finding the Isles of Zeta is easily accomplished," said Flindas with a hint of annoyance in his voice. "Even if it does exist I suspect that you will never get there. You will drown, or be killed by pirates, or be eaten by some sea monster. It is a fool's journey Kerran. Take your talisman and go home. The Alliance is no more and the other pieces of the Seacrest are surely lost. This Leana, even if she was of the family Amitarl is dead now as you say and no one knows the course to Zeta."

"I will go," said Kerran with conviction. "There is no choice. Maradass returns and the family Amitarl will need this piece of the Seacrest; this I know to be true."

Flindas looked intently into Kerran's eyes, trying to discern a shadow of doubt in the youth's conviction, but he saw none. Kerran's intent would not be denied. It was a foolhardy journey but Flindas could only admire the youth's bravery. To have travelled this far Flindas knew that Kerran was no ordinary young man.

"I was in the north no more than six moons passed," said Flindas. "I have seen the corruption and depraved lives that people must accept when they live there. but I saw no armies."

For three more days Kerran remained unable to travel. He exercised his leg and Flindas replaced his dressings each day, closely examining the torn flesh.

"It heals well," he said one evening. "You were lucky I think. Your youth and strength are on your side. Tomorrow we should be able to walk for a time."

Flindas spent the evening telling Kerran tales of the Four Regions. He knew a great deal of history and Kerran went to sleep to wander in ancient times of knights and castles and old battles, lost and won. Then a most vivid dream invaded his sleeping mind. It was as though he had woken but knew that it was not so. He saw the Seacrest in the hand of an aged bearded man who stood alone on a hill top. The old, white robed figure stood holding the talisman aloft as storm clouds raged about him. Light and power emanated from the Seacrest, spreading out across the lands that lay below. Armies fought on the plains. Great beasts of war drew huge battle towers, crushing friend and foe beneath their wheels. Mighty birds of war flew above the battleground, swooping down to snatch up soldiers of the opposing army, carrying them to dizzying heights, only to drop them screaming to the earth far below. Wizards walked unscathed amongst the warring armies, and from their fingertips coloured light flashed, slicing through armour and chain mail as easily as a hand passes through water. Kerran watched it all from above, aware that it was a dream, and yet at the same time knowing that all he saw had certainly happened deep in the past.

The great and terrible wars between the wizards were alive behind his sleeping eyelids. Packs of huge dogs, not unlike

Rark, tore their way through the armies, their massive jaws ripping the throats and limbs from the lightly armoured foot soldiers. Mounted horsemen charged, spears lowered, breaking the ranks of enemy troops, impaling or crushing them beneath the steel shod hooves of their mighty war horses. Kerran could hear the slow incantation of the wizard who stood above them on the hilltop, the Seacrest held aloft. Strange words rose and fell from the ancient bearded lips with one phrase repeated over and over many times.

"MA-ZURIN-BIDAR ARN ZARID MINDARL
    AR MURA DA-FARA DARBIN VIRAR."

To Kerran it meant nothing except that he recognised the first words, MA-ZURIN-BIDAR, as the ancient name of the Seacrest. The wizard, robes flowing about him, brought his chant to an end. There was a pause in the battle as all looked to the old bearded man atop the hill around which they fought. Many cowered under his words. Dogs howled, and the huge beasts shuffled about, trampling many beneath their feet, then the earth erupted in fire, shaking, cracking. Kerran saw the high towers of an old and beautiful city fall into rubble and mountains of shattered glass. The armies screamed as one and were swallowed by the earth. Fire blazed around the other wizards who fought against the light and were finally consumed, and then the fire turned on the one who wielded the Seacrest, then he too burned and was gone.

Kerran woke in darkness shaking with fright. Sitting up abruptly he reached about himself, clutching for something real that would bring him back to the present time. His hands came to rest on the fur of the great beast Rark, and Kerran, still trembling, crawled in closer to the dog, feeling his warmth and taking comfort from the beast's heavy breathing. Rark roused a little and brought his head to nuzzle into Kerran's neck, accepting a scratch. Eventually Kerran slept again and no further dreams disturbed him that night. It was not until much later that he recalled the chant of the wizard, and would remember the sound of the words.

"If your leg gives you much trouble we can rest," Flindas told Kerran the next morning. "Do not overwork it, for it will take some days before it is fully recovered."

Flindas was right, and for five days they slowly travelled the Old Coast Road, which became more broken as they went further to the east. At times Kerran's leg became too painful to take his weight and they would rest, finding shelter where they could from the rain that had dogged their way to the coast. Winter closed in upon the Regions and bitter winds swept across the swamplands, the cold biting deep into Kerran's body. At night he slept close to Rark, sharing body warmth, and the dog seemed to understand Kerran's need.

One day Kerran began to notice that the surrounding landscape was changing. The swamp was slowly giving way to low rolling hills, interspersed with pockets of sand and low scrub. The road had begun to sweep further to the south while far ahead Kerran could just see a long, blue-green line on the horizon.

"What is that?" he asked Flindas, breaking the silence of their journey.

"It is the ocean," replied Flindas surprised, and then added, "I had forgotten that you have never seen it before."

"Only in my dreams," said Kerran and gazed at the distant wonder.

"We will reach the coast sometime tomorrow," said Flindas. "Do you have any plans on how you will find a boat? You have no gold to buy one and you have never even sailed! Do you not see it is impossible! You will never reach Zeta."

"I will get there somehow," Kerran muttered, almost unheard.

Flindas was troubled by his companion's stubbornness, but he had not been in the forest and heard Leana Amitarl's words, and for some time there was a gloomy silence between the two travellers. The journey did indeed seem impossible Kerran thought; he would have to steal a boat and would probably drown during the first day, or be shipwrecked on one of the many isles that guarded the Narrows. Flindas had told him of this place and how many sailors and fishermen had been lost travelling through those treacherous waters.

"Do not go that way," Flindas had told him. "Travel with me to the City Amitarl and find a boat there."

But Kerran knew that he could not walk that far without many days of rest, and he remembered again the urgency in Leana's voice: 'The Seacrest must reach Tolth'.

That night Kerran went to sleep holding the Seacrest through his shirt. He walked in the soft mist, familiar now and welcoming.

"Kerran I must speak with you," said the voice. "Do not go to the City Amitarl. I cannot see the future but it is not yet your time to go there. Tomorrow you must take to the sea. My strength is not great, but I may be able to protect you once you are upon the ocean. I am part of the Seacrest and the name is no accident. Ma-Zurin-Bidar was formed from the ocean itself. This is most ancient knowledge that comes from an age of which I know little. I understand that it was Rishtan-Sta who made the Seacrest, Rishtan-Sta was the White Wizard, the Master, the most powerful of High Wizards. In the final battle of the Wizard Wars, Rishtan-Sta took the Seacrest to a hilltop above the battle. There he ended the lives of all those about him, wizards and warriors alike. He destroyed all in the hope that peace would come to the lands, but final peace has never been possible."

"I saw him," Kerran said in his mind. "I saw him in a dream. He held the Seacrest. There was a great light, then darkness. All were swallowed by the earth or burned."

"Yes," said the voice. "You saw the end of the world as it was and is no more. The time of the wizards will never come again. Only in the Seacrest does a little of their power live on. Together the four parts are most potent."

The voice paused as if remembering, and then continued. "Kerran, know that there are no accidents. All things have a design and a cause. It was not by chance that Flindas came to your aid. You must try to convince him to sail with you to Zeta; your success may depend on him. Hold to your path Kerran. You have much courage and strength. Trust in yourself and have faith in your own powers and that of the Seacrest. I must go now."

The voice had become a whisper.

"Trust in yourself," were the last words, and the voice was gone.

The Sea of Shardis

"There is the town called Rhindarl," said Flindas pointing towards a distant gathering of grey buildings sprawled along the edge of the sea. "If you are to find a boat it is there you must look."

The morning had passed in silence and Kerran had been unable to ask Flindas to come with him to Zeta, but now he took a deep breath. "It is much to ask I know, but I must," he said. "Will you not come with me Flindas, and seek out the Magic Isles?"

"Come with you!" cried Flindas. "On a fool's errand that would get us all drowned or worse! No Kerran, my life will be short enough without going to my death willingly."

Kerran could do no more and they walked on in silence. Before long they came to the top of a small rise and below them lay the town and the wide open Sea of Shardis. Kerran looked in awe on the vast expanse of water. The ocean seemed to go to the end of forever and beyond, with a sweep of land disappearing into an emptiness north and south.

"Kerran, I cannot go with you," spoke Flindas softly. "But I wish for your success, and there is something else." He took from his pouch a small bag which he bounced in his hand, it rattled a little. "There are eighteen pieces of silver and eleven of gold," he said. "It will help you to get your boat, and before we part company I will give you a lesson or two in sailing and how not to drown."

Kerran could not speak. He knew it was much money for a person like Flindas, and indeed for most people in the land.

"Let us go now," said his benefactor. "Let us at least get you sailing in the right direction."

They walked down the slope and came to the outskirts of the shabby town.

"I have been this way before some years ago," said Flindas, as they began to pass the first dilapidated buildings.

An old woman peered through a dirty window. Children left the street and stood behind walls and fences, their mouths gaping when they saw Rark; while small filthy dogs bolted from the street howling.

"There used to be a boat builder near the other end of the town," Flindas continued. "I think it would be a good place to start."

They walked on and passed through what must have been the town centre. There were shops selling ocean supplies and food stuffs, but the streets were muddy and almost deserted. Music and a raucous song came from an inn called the Seafarer as the three travellers passed by unnoticed.

Eventually they came to a yard with two large wooden gates, Flindas hammered on them with his hand. A dog inside began to bark furiously and it could be heard running backwards and forwards behind the gates, then a man's surly voice called to them.

"What do you want?"

Then an eye peered at them through a hole in the fence.

"We would like to speak to you about buying a boat," Flindas replied, the howling dog almost drowning out his words.

"Quiet, curse you!" the man's cried, there was a thump and the dog yelped. "A boat you say," said the ugly voice again. "Well perhaps I can help you and perhaps not. Go down the side of the building and I will meet you there."

So saying he shuffled off and the travellers, taking his

instruction, proceeded down the filthy alley. On emerging they found themselves beside a small river where floated many of the local fishing boats. There was a jetty built out into the evil looking brown water. A bolt protested as it was forced to slide, and then the man stepped through a small doorway, kicking his dog back inside and closing the door behind him. His clothes were filthy and his hair a tangled mess. He shuffled up to them, taking much of his weight on a gnarled walking stick; he eyed Rark with suspicion.

"A boat hey?" he grumbled. "A boat, a boat. You appear not to me as ones who would need a boat! You be not going fishing I guess?"

He swivelled, blinking at them with suspicious eyes, unable to keep them at rest. He kept well away from the huge mountain dog who seemed not at all interested in approaching the evil smelling man.

"We wish to sail a boat along the coast of Shardis," said Flindas, unable to stop his feelings of disgust. "Do you have something for sale?"

"Yes I have a boat," said the man. "It will not be cheap."

"Let us see it and we can discuss the price after that," said Flindas.

The man grumbled something and led them to the jetty, where he pointed at a small craft that floated beside it. Flindas stepped down and into the boat. He spent some time studying the craft, hauling up the single sail and peering closely at the steering gear. He tested all the pulleys and ropes and finally seemed satisfied.

"It is a sturdy craft," he said, coming back onto the jetty. "Now you must name a price."

The man muttered to himself, flashing a look at Flindas, and then shuffled along the jetty to stand looking down at the boat. "A fine craft," he said. "Indeed a fine craft. It is the last boat my brother built before his sudden demise." His voice turned to a sly whisper. "You are lucky to find such a one," he said. "You know the tree from which it is made. It is Rinswood and you will find none better. Yes, yes, it is worth much. You must give me sixteen gold pieces, and not a coin less will I take."

Flindas smiled, knowing the boat to be worth perhaps half of what had been asked. "You are mistaken if you think we are so rich and foolish," said Flindas. "I would not give more than six gold pieces for such a craft."

"Six!" squealed the man, becoming agitated and shuffling back and forth. "No, no, that is impossible. Fourteen gold pieces and you steal the bread from my children's mouths."

"Eight," said Flindas with no further comment.

"Twelve!" cried the man "I cannot go lower. You would starve my family."

"I will give you ten," said Flindas. "No more. Your family will not starve with such a profit."

The man stood muttering, rolling his hands one through the other as if trying to wash them clean of a foulness, or perhaps blood.

"Give me the ten," he sneered at last. A thought flashed in his eyes and was gone.

"Not yet," replied Flindas, not trusting the man. "We need supplies. We will be back later and pay you then. Do not try to change any parts while we are gone. I will check everything when we return."

With that the travellers went to the main street and walked the short distance to the centre of town. During the remainder of the afternoon there was much more bargaining to be done. Kerran was surprised at the experienced way in which Flindas was able to reduce the price of the various things he found necessary for the voyage. There were two small barrels of sea biscuits and two more empty ones for water. There were packages of salted meat, dried nuts and fruits, and fishing lines with all the necessary extras. Flindas also bought a large sheet of waterproofed sail cloth for covering the supplies against the sea, and to collect rain water. They needed to borrow a small hand cart to transport everything to the boat.

They had finished loading and filling the water barrels when the back door of the boat yard was pushed open and the old man shuffled out demanding his money. He left the door ajar. Flindas had just counted out the last coin when nine or ten large men with wooden clubs suddenly rushed at them from the boat yard.

Before he could defend himself Kerran was dealt a sharp blow to the side of his head. He fell to the ground as he heard Flindas draw his sword and a great howl go up from Rark. Kerran was dazed but still conscious. Through shrouded pain he saw Rark dive at one of their attackers, bearing the man to the ground, his great fangs tearing at the upraised arms. Another fell with a sword thrust to his chest, a deathly cry coming from his lips. Kerran held his head and began to rise, then another blow took him on the shoulder and sent him staggering sideways. He stumbled to his knees as another club fell hard on his back. Rolling away from the blows he felt a body crash down and cover him, the smell of blood and the limpness of the body telling him that this was a dead man who had him pinned to the ground.

"To the boat!" cried Flindas. "Quickly Kerran!"

Heaving the body aside Kerran crawled along the jetty to the boat. He could do little more than roll into the bottom. His head swam and his eyes fought back tears. Another man cried out and there was a splash as he fell into the water. Kerran struggled upright and saw that Flindas was hard pressed. Though three men had fallen to his sword, more came at him. Rark crashed into their flank knocking two down and scattering the others. The blows that rained down on the dog only seemed to inflame him. The great jaws tore at the men, holding them at bay for a few precious moments.

Flindas rushed to the boat slicing the ropes that tied it to the jetty. He leapt aboard and thrust the craft with all his strength out into the channel. In an instant they were caught by the current and began to move down stream. With a last howl of anger at their attackers Rark turned and leapt into the water in pursuit of his friends. He soon caught up with the boat, swimming strongly, and with much difficulty Flindas managed to drag him aboard. There was not a great amount of room in the boat, and Flindas had to climb over the dog to get to Kerran's side.

"How badly are you hurt?" he asked, taking a piece of cloth

from his pack and beginning to clean the blood away from Kerran's matted scalp.

"I think I may live," said Kerran painfully, easing his back against the ribs of the boat. His head had cleared somewhat, which just seemed to make the pain worse."My arm hurts badly," he said.

"Not broken I think," said Flindas lifting and turning the limb gently. "That was a very near thing," he continued. "It could have been the end of us. There are men who will do anything for a gold piece. Times are evil and there are few to be trusted."

"Once again I am indebted to you Flindas," said Kerran. "There is nothing that I could ever offer that could repay you."

The boat continued to drift along with the current as the stream widened, soon they were at the mouth of the river, with the Sea of Shardis stretching out before them.

"You may be even further in my debt by the time we get to Zeta," said Flindas smiling down at Kerran.

"Then you will come?" cried Kerran in happy surprise, the relief on his face made Flindas laugh.

"Yes I will come on your impossible journey," he said. "I have travelled to many places in the Four Regions and the Borderlands. I have even been to the red Outlands, but I have never been to Zeta. I think it may be worth a visit."

His understated words made Kerran laugh, though it hurt him in numerous places to do so.

"Yes," he agreed, "I think it may be worth a visit too."

Kerran was heavily bruised and his head sang for some time, but he felt strong enough to sit up in the bottom of the boat leaning on Rark, who did not seem to mind. They were under sail and a south-westerly wind was pushing them from the coast. From above there was a loud cry; Storm suddenly arrived, alighting carefully on the upper spar. In the urgency of the moment Kerran had forgotten the bird, which for the last few days he had seen only from afar.

"We are an odd crew," said Flindas. "I hope we can all learn to eat fish. The dry food we must ration. It will not last forever."

Fish they soon had. Kerran looked at the strips that Flindas was cutting to dry, and pulling off a small corner. He chewed it slowly. When the unusual taste and texture became too much he swallowed it quickly.

"It will take some time to get used to," he admitted and took the apple that Flindas offered.

"The fruit will not last long," said his friend. "We must be very careful with the water. The barrels are lashed but we must always close the lids tightly. Tomorrow we will fish again, for soon we will be over the northern reaches of the Depths."

"What are they?" asked Kerran.

"The Sea of Shardis is only shallow enough for fishing near to the coast," replied Flindas. "Some thirty or forty leagues from the shore the sea floor drops away to much greater depths. In the south of Shardis it is more so. No one has ever bothered to measure how deep it is as far as I know. Rest now, you sound tired. Tomorrow you will learn to sail for I cannot stay awake forever."

Kerran drifted into sleep, thinking that if the men had not attacked he may have been here sailing alone. That night, through the pleasant befriending mist the voice came to him once again.

"Kerran I am here. All is well and you sail to Zeta. My strength is returning. When the Seacrest, or any part of it is near the ocean, it is at its strongest. I will come to your aid if you call, and give you protection if I can."

"What should I call?" Kerran asked within his mind.

"You have heard it before," replied the voice.

"'MA-ZURIN-BIDAR ARN ZARID MINDARL
AR MURA DA-FARA DARBIN VIRAR.'

They are the words of Rishtan-Sta: 'Ma-Zurin-Bidar, unite the lands. Let peace prevail and may all be one.' Call me in need, and if it is in my power I will come to your aid," said the voice.

"May I ask something?" said Kerran though he had yet to think of a question.

"Yes, I have time now," replied the voice. "My strength was much diminished but now it returns."

"I do not know where to begin," thought Kerran. "What of Leana and her father? Yes, tell me of Tolth and the family Amitarl."

"Tolth is Amitarl but he is also something else," said the voice. "His mother was an Elveren. Tolth is one of the few half children born to the woman of the deep ocean world, who at rare times come to the land to seduce men. The Elveren, for they are all born female, then take the beginnings of life back to the depths. One called Ni came to Darna Amitarl on his voyage to Zeta, and yet did not return to the oceans; Tolth was their only born. He has powers of memory and learning that other humans have lost. He holds the one quarter part of the Seacrest that is concerned with the Future. He sees much and understands much, though the piece he holds is the most difficult to master. He has lived a long life and his children have inherited some of the Elveren magic of their grandmother."

"Tell me of Leana," asked Kerran. There were many questions he wished answered, but he did not expect the voice to remain with him for long.

"I felt her thoughts clearly, though we were never able to speak together as you and I do," said the voice. "I was able to give her much protection, but finally it was not enough. Her armour was of my making and would come to her in need. She drew physical strength from the Seacrest and through the ancient powers of Narinda, her ancestral sister. Her life's blood flowed from her wounds as you took the piece from about her neck, for she had no magic over final death. Maradass alone holds that power."

"Tell me of this," asked Kerran intrigued, and the voice answered.

"In the two thousand years that have passed since the Alliance was made there have now been only three men known as Maradass, men who have led the household and carried the fragment that governs Death. Into the Seacrest Rishtan-Sta wove the four elements of: Life, Death, Past and Future. The Seacrest was divided at the Crossroads, and though it was meant that the amulet should split in half. It fell into four quarters. At the Crossroads I too was made. How I cannot say.

Oaths were sworn, and though not all is remembered, I know that Rishtan-Sta came to those gathered there. To Zard fell the piece of Life. Already he was the most powerful of men in the lands, though he was also the most gentle of men. Maradass the Philosopher swore such oaths that his family may live forever, though no one can escape death for ever. The Philosopher could not bear to leave behind his beloved family and so he contrived to make it most difficult for death to find any of them. Only should Zard die would his father die. Zard was all powerful and the oaths and spells that were contrived made it that only in single combat could he be killed.

"Twice now in the last two thousand years Zard has been slain, and yet he will always return as a new born. Darss, the younger brother o Zard becomes Maradass at the death of his father, who dies at sundown of the first new moon day following the death of his son Zard. Soon after this, to Darss there are born twin boys. The first born is Zard returned, and he grows to his full strength in the space of just one moon, while the new Darss, his younger brother, ages as a normal child. This new Darss is the incarnation of his grandfather, and so in this way the Maradass family has perpetuated itself, with so few deaths, throughout these last twenty centuries. The vulnerable time for the Maradass family is now. Until this new Darss reaches manhood and can father children, the family faces annihilation should Zard be killed. Darss would be unprotected, and as a child he would have not the strength to wield the Seacrest fragment commanding death. Then and only then can the family of Maradass die.

"The man who is now Maradass I have no understanding of, except that he is ancient in years, and is now the elder of the House of Maradass. He will be wed soon and father two sons. Zard and his twin brother will soon be amongst the living again."

After some time trying to understand this most complex of families Kerran asked about the fourth piece of the Seacrest, the one concerned with Life.

"It is with the one known as Elfhand who is Tolth's eldest son, Landin Amitarl. He is beyond the northern borders and I know not how he fares."

"Elfhand," said Kerran in his mind. "It is a strange name."

"Elf is an old wizard word," replied the voice. "It is said that in the ancient Northern Lands from whence the wizards came there were people other than those that we know of in these lands. An elf was a magical smaller person, and it is for this reason that Landin gained his affectionate name of Elfhand from the people of Zeta. He was born with a left arm which is very small and has no movement. He was recently sent by Tolth to the Broken Lands in search of Maradass, while Leana went to the Southlands in search of allies. Landin Elfhand is a clever spy, and with the power of the Seacrest piece which he bears, he is the mightiest warrior of Zeta. Even Zard had fear of Elfhand.

"There are two other sons of Tolth who remain on Zeta," said the voice to Kerran's further questioning. "Leana was the older twin of Verardian, and his strength is in the power of healing. He is a gentle man and a cleansing comes from his touch. Then there is Mindis, the youngest son of Tolth. He is many years younger than the others, being born of another mother, and in him there is a great difference. He is silent, almost mute, and no one sees into his mind. Even with the three fragments of the Seacrest in his hands I have sensed nothing of him.

"His mother was not the mother of Landin, Leana and Verardian. Ellenen, Tolth's first wife lived long but died a mortal death. Tolth lived on for many years and did not look for another woman to share his life; he buried his grief in study and learning. Then Luista was found washed up on the shores of Zeta. She had no recollection of her past, and none could find a way to unlock her memory. No one who comes to the shores of Zeta can leave again, except that it be willed by Tolth and the Greater Council. Those who somehow penetrate the magic veils that protect Zeta and do come are welcomed and soon find a home. A few men have reached the magical isles over the centuries, but in all the years that Amitarl have been on Zeta no other woman has ever arrived there. Drawn to her beauty and charm Tolth among others soon became her admirer. Luista lived on Zeta for three years before she became Tolth's wife. She bore him a son, Mindis, and then she disappeared one night while walking alone by the sea. She vanished as incredibly as she had appeared and no more is known of her.

"I tire," said the voice after a pause. "There is more I could tell but this dream time fatigues us both. Sleep now and may a fair wind speed you to the east and to Zeta."

Kerran slept deeply, warmed by Rark. Once he opened his eyes to see Flindas silhouetted against a vast starlit sky. A light breeze still blew from the south and by morning it had freshened. Small waves crested and the air was tangy with the taste of salt spray.

"The elements are on our side," said Flindas as Kerran woke. "We will be across the inner sea and amongst the Narrows within a few days if this wind holds. We will need all our strength and fortune to pass there unscathed. There are no safe passages through the walls that we will sail against. Some say that all this inner sea was once a land above the ocean. In an upheaval the land split and fell in upon itself, and then the sea entered. Tis also said that a great city, a whole civilisation, was lost here in the time of the wizards, though tales from those ancient times can never be truly known or believed."

Flindas stretched and then stood up still holding onto the helm. "Come Kerran," he said. "It is time for you to learn some basics of sailing before I fall asleep."

Kerran went aft where Flindas instructed him in the art of steering the small craft, with the wind from the westerly quarter the instructions were reasonably simple and soon Kerran was alone in the stern of the boat steering with the wind. He watched the vast ocean slip by, having left the land far behind and lost beyond the horizon. Flindas woke in the late morning having only slept a short time, and as Kerran felt comfortable sailing the boat Flindas lay back and told tales of his and other's adventures. Eventually Kerran asked him of the sword play that had taken place back at the boatyard.

"I think you killed three men back there on the jetty," said Kerran. "For a person who appears to wish for a peaceful life you fight like a man trained in the arts."

"Yes I am trained," replied Flindas thoughtfully. "It was part of my upbringing. My family is not a poor one in the City Amitarl; they have much. When I was younger I broke away. I visit at times and enjoy some of my family's company. My father is different. He hates me for a reason I will not speak of just now, perhaps another time. Suffice it to say that we do not enjoy each others company, my father and I. To him I am the errant son and I was never going to come to any good. While my two brothers were themselves part of the Governor's Court, and highly esteemed, I would never have traded places with them. The corruption is finely tuned at the top, and for twenty years I watched the deals and deceits, with my father as a major player. So yes, I am trained in the fighting arts. It was compulsory, and my two brothers saw to it that I complied with my father's wishes, though they did not really take to it themselves. Much of it I learned gladly. At archery I won my colours at seventeen years. When I am hungry I can easily bring down game if it is about, so I am thankful for some things from my days as a somewhat wayward member of the court. Now that reminds me of something about you that I find curious, Kerran. You are covered over in rabbit skins and yet you carry no bow. Do you throw rocks at them, or does Storm bring them to you?"

Kerran slipped his sling from his pouch. "I throw rocks with this," he said, holding it up.

"Ah!" exclaimed Flindas. "An ancient and noble weapon. I did not think of it. A sling was not customary training in my schooling." He paused a moment looking up at the rigging. "Sailing was not on the list of required lessons either," he said. "It was not thought dignified for those with money and power; it was something only fishermen and the foolish did. Sometimes I would be gone for days, sailing along the coast, even as far as the Far Isles. Occasionally my sister Darbra would come too. The family was furious of course, but since beating was not considered fashionable either, they could do very little. It was easy to quietly slip away."

Flindas became thoughtfully quiet, and for a time they

sailed on in silence. Kerran found that chewing on the raw fish was becoming a habit. In small pieces and dipped in the sea water he was finding it quite palatable. Rark did not enjoy the fish very much at all. First he turned up his nose at it, but when he discovered there was nothing else except the occasional sea biscuit, he gave in and ate the boneless chunks that Flindas and Kerran served up for him.

The fortunate breeze kept up for several days, pushing them quickly across the Sea of Shardis. Gulls followed them, diving for the scraps of fish that were discarded from each catch. A good rain had fallen the night before and again the water barrels were full. Flindas had rigged the sail cloth to funnel water into them. as well as keeping some of the rain off themselves. It was winter and the sky dropped ice cold pellets. They had seen several dark storms on the far horizons but the turbulent winds and high seas passed them by as though a protection hung over their small craft. When the breeze turned again to the south and became slight, they had reached a point where Kerran could see far ahead of them to a long dark line on the horizon.

"It is the Narrows," said Flindas to his inquiry. "I have never sailed here, though I have heard many stories of shipwrecks and drowned sailors. There are passages that lead to dead ends and ferocious undercurrents. Most of the islands fall sheer into the sea. If we are shipwrecked there is little we could do to save ourselves. Let us hope for a fair day and only a little wind. The boat is small and this I think is an advantage; also it is made of Rinswood. We could not have hoped to find better, even if swamped it will remain floating for some days."

As they continued to the east Kerran could make out more details of the islands. Many of them protruded as tall solitary giants from the depths beneath the sea, while others clustered in groups, as though in deep silent communication. For another full day they sailed amongst them and on into the tightening grip of the Narrows. The islands drew closer together, at times forcing them to change their course, until far ahead the isles became a continuous line of sheer cliffs with many narrow defiles. It was mid afternoon when they found themselves sailing offshore from the dark menacing walls of rock. Some were as huge as mountains while others appeared like castles rising up out of the shadowed depths. Currents swirled; at one moment it would be calm, and then at the next a great suction would pull at the water, drawing the sea downward and exposing the jagged rocks below.

"We will keep well away and sail north," said Flindas. "It is said that the best passages are there, though I have never met any sailor who has passed through. There is no real need as the fishing in Shardis is good and the old trade routes between the City Amitarl and Mendan-Maradass are all but unused these days. The moon will be close to full tonight. With enough light I think we will be able to keep sailing. If we see a likely passage, we can hold off until morning to get a better look."

None of the narrow chasms that they had seen so far had looked possible at all. There were close gaps that wound deep into the sides of the islands only to meet a sheer wall of impassable rock. Others were so narrow that a person could barely swim through, even if they were foolish enough to try. By nightfall they had found no way through, and by moonlight they sailed northward under a starry sky. They ate biscuits, dried fish, and the last of the apples.

That night Kerran's dreams were disturbed. There were men trying to kill him with clubs, and suddenly he was drowning, going deep into the waters, the ocean closing over his head. He woke in fright, startling all on board.

"What is it?" asked Flindas concerned.

"A dream," Kerran replied, "I was drowning."

"Then it is but a dream," said Flindas. "Rest easy. It is almost dawn. I think I have found a possible passage through. I can see much light at the end of this opening."

He pointed to his left which surprised Kerran until he realised that in the night Flindas had turned the boat to the south and into the light wind.

"We will stay here till dawn and see what we have," said Flindas.

The pale light of morning grew slowly from beyond the dark walls of the islands where gulls nested closely on the lofty crags above. After some time Flindas turned to Kerran and pointed to the wall of rock. Where one particular island fell sheer into the sea the next one had crumbled. Huge pieces of rock had fallen away and Kerran could see a small gap. It was roofed over with a slab of fallen rock and the sunrise was shining through from the other side.

"It is very small," he commented to Flindas dubiously.

"Yes," replied his friend. "But it looks clear to the other side, and the currents are not so strong. We will watch for a time and see if it changes. When we go we will have to lower the mast and pull ourselves through with our hands."

For some time they watched as the sunlight crept further into the sky. Suddenly, around the narrow way, the almost calm waters became a boiling mass as undercurrents forced the ocean upward in a great crashing surge. Any boat attempting to pass under the fallen rock when this happened would be crushed against the roof of the tunnel and sunk. Kerran's heart sank when, after just a short time of quiet, the sea boiled up again, great spouts of compressed water spurting violently from the enclosed space.

It was not in any way predictable. There was one long period when all was calm and Flindas was tempted to go. On the point of lowering the sail and making a dash for it with the oars the water rose again, more violently this time. The boat lifted a little and was pushed further away from the cliffs.

"After the next time it surges I think we should try to pass through," said Flindas. "It does not seem to have any pattern."

He took down the sail and mast. Rark woke up and stretched. It was hard on him being cramped like this and he let out a deep discontented sigh. When the ocean erupted again they were ready. The eventual subsidence had been unpredictable also, at times the calm would return quickly and at others rage on for some time. Flindas decided to go. He cut deep with the oars and the boat surged forward. Kerran marvelled as his friend showed a great deal of strength, and rowed from long experience. They were not far from the opening when the sea began to rise. Water compressed somewhere far below, now pushed upwards in a moving wall of energy. Kerran clung to the boat in fear as it hung precariously on the swell. Flindas tried desperately to turn the small craft, and then they began to be pushed backwards. Water cascaded over them; a large wave formed by the crashing of the sea against the wall of rock fell upon the boat, swamping it immediately.

Kerran was thrown from the craft and found himself thrashing wildly for the surface. He gulped air and saw that Flindas had managed to keep a hold on the boat and was looking about for him. Kerran was about to call out when into his mind he remembered his dream of drowning. Without a sound his head sank below the surface and he began to go under. Soft compelling whisperings told him to sleep. It would be so easy just to go to sleep. He felt as though he could even breathe the water. The faint whispers beckoned to him and he could not resist.

A sudden dragging at his sleeve stopped his death dream. Kerran felt panic then and fought his way to the surface, helped by the strength of Rark who had come to his rescue. Kerran gasped at the delicious air and knew that something frightening had just happened. In fear he paddled clumsily to the boat but said nothing of it to Flindas as they clung there together, the current slowly taking them away from the rocks. Bailing out the boat was impossible; the sea was too broken and choppy. Storm flew down and considered them for a while, before returning to his hunting on the cliffs above.

"There is no way we can empty the boat without solid ground underfoot," said Flindas anxiously.

He looked towards the high cliffs but saw nowhere they could possibly land. It was quieter now that they were further from the rocks and the more broken water, though emptying the water from their boat was still impossible. They wallowed in a lull of uncertainty for a time, and then Kerran remembered the words of the dream voice.

"There is something I may be able to do," he said as he began to recall the chant.

Flindas did not query him as he began to hear the strange unknown words come from his young friend's lips.

"MA-ZURIN-BIDAR ARN ZARID MINDARL
AR MURA DA-FARA DARBIN VIRAR."

Kerran chanted the words three times and then grew silent, waiting for what may come, if indeed anything was to come. He had almost given up hope when something smooth slid against his leg. Kerran felt a long sleek body glide by him through the water and in fright he called out.

"Ahh! There is something in the water!"

Flindas felt it too and exclaimed loudly as an unseen sea creature pushed by him to a position beneath the boat. Kerran and Rark slipped back into the wallowing craft as it began to lift a little from the sea. The small boat was just above the water line and they began to bail frantically. Whatever it was below the surface was trying to help them, and they took advantage of it.

Kerran could see long blue-grey bodies swimming beneath the boat as they baled quickly, the boat finally becoming buoyant without the help from below. Some of the creatures suddenly broke the surface. They made the strangest chatter that Kerran had ever heard, and seemed to smile continuously beneath their long smooth noses.

"What are they?" he called to Flindas as they worked.

"They are dolphins," Flindas replied, a look of great relief on his face. "Some say they are the early ancestors of humans."

Flindas was slowing in his work as the boat now floated well clear of the lapping waves. "Whatever it was you chanted, it could not have brought a friendlier creature to our aid," he said with a smile.

The last of the dolphins swam from beneath the boat and came to smile and chuckle at them, flapping about in great humour.

"What marvellous creatures," said Kerran laughing with them. "I did not know that such animals existed."

"There are few who have come so close to them," said Flindas, still marvelling at the miracle of their rescue.

"It is said that there was a time when the seas abounded with them," he continued. "I have only ever seen a few before from a distance, when I sailed amongst the Far Isles."

The dolphins called to them one last time and then were gone, playfully diving and splashing away. They seemed to Kerran the most happy of all creatures he had ever met.

"We will rest then try again," said Flindas with a grim smile, as he looked towards the narrow passage. "We were unlucky that time, with only a very short pause between swells. I hope it will not be so again. If we do not succeed I hope your friends can return to help us again."

Kerran heard the doubt in his friend's words. Flindas began to adjust the ropes that held their supplies against the mast, fortunately nothing had been lost. Then he sat at the oars as again the powerful swell of water thrust upward from the depths, crashing against the rocks, subsiding slowly.

"We go," he called, and began to row hard.

They covered the intervening stretch of water quickly, Kerran and Rark in the stern. Waves sprayed about them but the gap remained clear. As they reached the opening Flindas quickly brought in the oars. They passed under the shelf of rock, the water echoing eerily with drips and soft splashing. Indeed the space was smaller than it had seemed from the outside where the light and reflection had played tricks on their eyes. It was also much longer than it had appeared. The roof of rock went on for a great many boat lengths.

They were almost through, dragging the boat along by their fingertips, when what they feared most began to happen. The boat started to slowly rise, though the main force of the upward thrust of water seemed to be far behind them. The craft began to scrape against the sides of the watery cave as a wave rushed at them from behind, thrusting the boat forward, gouging the stout craft's timber work. They were catapulted forward, water splashing and tumbling all around them, and then they were hurled violently from the narrow opening. Water cascaded down on them. The boat was awash as it plunged down the side of the bulging wave into the bright sunlight. Kerran felt that the craft must surely turn and roll but it held true as Flindas fought the helm, and in moments they were clear of the tall looming islands. The boat was carrying much water and they had to bail again; Kerran's hands shook as he worked.

The sun was a memory of warmth but they took off their clothes to dry them in the fresh breeze. Huddled in blankets that had been kept almost dry by the sailcloth, they watched the cliffs recede behind them. The current was taking them away from danger, and as the sail was undamaged they raised it, then turned to the east and entered the vastness of the unknown ocean.

Beyond the Horizon

It was late evening, the moon hanging like some magical ball in the dark sky. Only a few stars fought to combat its brightness and barely a cloud floated on the light breeze. They talked into the night, once again dressed in their dry clothes that were becoming thick with salt. Kerran had a question that he wanted to ask though he wondered if he should.

"I saw the scars on your back," he said carefully. "They look like they came from a whip."

"You are too observant," Flindas replied. "It is said, 'Take some caution at what you ask, for you will know a man by his questions, not by his answers.'"

Kerran felt rebuffed and they were silent for some time.

"My father gave them to me," Flindas said finally. "Beating was not fashionable in the City Amitarl but one time I provoked him so much that he had me tied to my bed and he whipped me. I was just eighteen. My pride was as much hurt as my back, which was bloody and raw. He is a sordid man, dishonest and cruel, and I wish I could disown him as my father. It is a hateful thing to say perhaps, but the beating was one of the lesser tortures he put me through; with my brothers his ever willing supporters. I was hounded by them and their allies, who were the rich untouchables. I went to many distasteful lessons just to avoid them."

There was a pause. "I talk too much," said Flindas and grew silent.

The sail gave a sudden snap and the steel housings protested at a change.

"I think the wind is going to get up by the morning," said Flindas. "We could be in for an interesting time. If it keeps coming from the south and west we will travel at some speed. I hope that going directly to the east will get us to Zeta. I also hope it is big enough that we do not miss it."

Kerran looked up to where the constellation of the Six Sorcerers hung high in the clear sky to the south. He too hoped that Zeta lay in their path.

As he slept Kerran again was dreaming of drowning, sinking beneath the surface of the ocean in total surrender, then the voice came and the soft mist enveloped him.

"Kerran I am here. Listen to me. Today you were in great danger, the Seacrest also. Not from the ocean, nor the rock, but from another source. When you were drowning what do you remember?"

"I remember feeling peaceful, and that nothing really mattered any more," Kerran replied.

"Do you remember a voice?"

"Yes," said Kerran. "There was a whispering voice. It told me to sleep. It was you."

"No," said the voice. "It was not me and it was not from the Seacrest. Something came and blocked my way to you. I think it was Maradass, the new Maradass, the unknown one. If it is so, his power is even greater than that of his father. He holds but one fragment, and yet he had the power to reach you. He wanted you to sleep, to drown. With this piece of the Seacrest lost forever, his power would grow. Kerran, you must stay out of the water, for this dark magic came from there. The dolphins were friends that I called on for help, but I felt him and felt that his power is far greater than mine. Maradass is searching for you, and in less than one year, when his two sons are born and age but one moon, the Black Army will again march from the north under the command of Zard. I cannot see the future but I know the House of Maradass. It is not from greed that they will march, it is from revenge and the pleasure of destruction. The strength of this new Maradass increases, this is certain. Less than one year, that is all the time that the Regions now have to prepare for war. Without Leana's stand and final victory in the forest the armies would be advancing now. Good speed Kerran. Do not enter the ocean again. Take heart, for Zeta is in your path."Then the voice faded, drifting into the mist and was gone.

For several days they continued to be driven along by the favourable wind. Very few had ever sailed these waters, for what trading ships there were hugged the coastline, while the Sea of Shardis provided most of the fishermen with their needs. The Outer Ocean was unknown to all but those who had ventured beyond the lands and had never returned. Legends told of many things about the sea but no one in living memory had ever found land out beyond the horizon and returned to tell of it. Flindas seemed pleased with their progress; he told Kerran that he was surprised at the placid nature of the sea and wind. He pointed to the south where a dark squall was spread across the horizon.

"They pass us by," he told his young friend. "So many winter storms I have seen and yet none have come to test us. Perhaps it is the magic you carry that protects us."

He smiled at Kerran with a curious look in his eyes. Flindas became silent and Kerran watched as his friend's dark eyes scanned the seas ahead, searching for any sign of land. Kerran knew now that he would never have been able to make this journey on his own. It was impossible to think that he would have gotten this far alone. The following morning Storm was not to be seen aboard or in the skies above. During the day Kerran grew concerned for his friend, not knowing if the bird could land upon the ocean to rest and it was well after midday when Storm finally returned to the boat. Kerran was glad to see him but there was something else which Flindas was even more pleased to see.

"Look!" he exclaimed, pointing at Storm.

Kerran was wondering what had excited his friend when he noticed the particles of sand clinging to the white hawk's feet.

Late in the afternoon Flindas gave a cry and stood up in the stern of the boat. "Land, Kerran!" he cried. "There is land ahead."

Kerran strained his eyes but could see nothing. They had sailed on for some time before he saw a darker patch on the horizon directly in their path.

"It will be dark before we reach it," said Flindas. "We can take in the sail and drift on the wind. Tomorrow morning we will be on dry land for a change. It may even be Zeta."

They drifted through the night and sometime during the early morning began to hear the sound of distant breakers on a shoreline. The wind had died away completely and they found themselves on the western side of a low forested island. Flindas rowed them in closer. He could see an easy landing and pulled for the shore, bringing the boat to rest on a sandy bottom. They hauled their craft further up the beach and looked about.

Rark would not be controlled and leapt from the boat. He walked around with stiff movements for a time, sniffing about him and eventually bounding ahead of them up the beach. Flindas and Kerran also found walking quite difficult; joints unused for days were stiff and loosened up slowly. Storm flew across the beach and above the trees as Rark came running back shaking and spraying water on them. Then with a loud joyous bark he leapt away again, leading them into the edge of the tree line. There was a stream with a clear pool and both travellers leapt in as they were. The water felt marvellously cool and refreshing after the days of sea air. They drank deeply and cleaned the salt from their clothes and bodies. There were fruits growing in the forest and Flindas selected what he thought would be edible, tasting them carefully. He eventually passed several to Kerran who delighted as the wonderful sweet juices flowed down his throat. They collected more fruit and returned with them to the boat.

"Let us fill the water barrels before anything else," said Flindas. "We do not know if we are alone on this island."

They filled the barrels and stowed a great number of fruit

in the boat.

"Now to explore a bit further," said Flindas taking up his bow. "It would be good to find some game."

They had been having problems with drying out the fish they caught as the sun had not yet shone strongly during any part of their sea voyage. A hot fish stew would be most welcome.

The companions went back into the trees. The undergrowth was thick in places, abundant in tangled vines, broad leafed ferns, and a tall grass that was sharper than swords. Unknown plants stood tall in what was becoming a dense forest. Some of the trees were huge; Kerran had never seen such giants. Flindas estimated that one they found was at least six of his arm spans across.

"One could carve a home out of the middle of this," said Kerran as they left it behind.

The island was not high and they had no problems getting to a vantage point to view the far side, and what they saw astounded them. There in a clearing, not far below, lay an immense ruin. It had not been a castle as it did not appear defendable: Flindas thought that it was probably an old temple of some long forgotten people. They moved down the hillside towards the tumble of giant stones. Some high columns remained standing, stone upon stone, rivalling the mighty trees. One long graceful arch curved across a great distance, seeming to hold up the sky.

"They were masters whoever built this," said Flindas, looking with wonder at the lasting workmanship. "It is an odd place to find such a structure. The stone did not come from this island I think."

He studied a tall central stone beneath the arch. It stood above the ground which was laid in slabs, many pushed upward and cracked by the advancing forest.

"A mystery it must remain I think," said Kerran.

Standing on top of the central stone he looked about as Storm came to land on the sweeping arch and seemed to scold Kerran.

"Yes," agreed Flindas. "There is no one left to tell us their tale. Let us go now. I see no sign of game, but at least we can cook fish on a fire tonight. I do not think one night's delay will sorely harm the outcome of this journey."

Kerran was pleased.

"It will be good to stretch out by a fire, and on a bed that is not moving all the time," he said.

They returned to the beach and Kerran collected firewood while Flindas prepared the previous night's catch. The meal was a feast, baked fish and crab, numerous sweet fruits, the last of their nuts, and a sea biscuit each. The clear spring water was a pleasure after the frugal sips they had been allowing themselves from their water barrels. Kerran lay by the fire and looked up at the wide starlit sky.

"My father called those the Six Wizards," said Kerran pointing to the well known grouping of stars which formed a cross, high to the south and west.

"The Six Sorcerers," said Flindas. "That is what they are usually called."

The four stars in the cross, and the two other bright ones which followed them across the darkness dominated the southern sky at night.

"Though they have always had that name there are so many stories about those stars that none can say which might be the original," said Flindas. "I could tell you any number of them but not now. Tis time to rest and sleep I think."

Flindas became silent, lying on his back and gazing for a time at the passing constellations.

Kerran's eyes eventually closed in sleep, the fire burnt low and Flindas was about to turn to sleep when from the corner of his eye he saw a flicker of light, but when he looked towards the forest the light was gone. He thought it may be the last of their firelight reflecting on a shiny leaf, and then the light came again near the top of a small hill. Flindas saw the small flame before it faded into the trees. He stood up and Rark lifted his head, watching his friend intently.

"Guard," said Flindas quietly and walked towards the tree line, sword in hand.

Kerran woke much later to find Flindas gone. Rark gave a

deep growl and stood up.

"What is it?" said Kerran.

In reply Rark moved towards the trees and then returned. It was obvious to Kerran that the dog wanted to go into the forest and wished him to follow. All was dark and silent as Kerran picked up his staff and followed Rark to the edge of the trees. Beneath the canopy there was only blackness.

"Rark come here," he called softly.

Rark returned and Kerran held him by his coat.

"Let us find Flindas," he said to the dog. "Flindas."

Rark started out, following a trail that only he could find. Kerran stumbled and fell, often scraping his knees and hands on fallen branches and rocks. All else was quiet and Kerran found that they were ascending the hill that they had gone up earlier in the day. He began to see light shining from beyond the brow. It was coming from the old temple. He began to hear the muffled sound of drums as if it came from the very ground beneath his feet, and as they crept to the top of the hill it was certain. The earth itself throbbed with the beat.

Crouching behind the buttress of a large tree Kerran looked down upon the ruins. Torches burnt in a great circle around the edge of the clearing while in the centre he could see people gathering. They were all dressed in blue robes and appeared to be coming from beneath the ground. After a while he was sure that there must be large underground caverns below the ancient temple. The throng was beginning to spill out beyond the ruined walls as the many people in long, pale blue gowns continued to gather and with many hand gestures talked in groups. Some pointed to the centre to where torches were being set beside the central stone. From below the drums beat out with a greater intensity, the rhythm taking a pace forward, quickening. A slow jarring chant started softly in the circle of people. Others caught it up until all chanted discordantly but with the same rhythm, their feet drumming on the ground which throbbed beneath them, echoing the loud pounding rhythm from beneath the ground.

Kerran covered his ears. The sound was deafening, and the great tree beside him pulsed and seemed to sway with the beat.

In the final pulsating cry, Kerran was physically shaken to the earth. He could do nothing but lie there, hands tightly thrust against his ears. Rark too was down on his belly, his paws trying to deaden the sound. The last beat echoed through the forest and a violent strange cry went up from the assembled people. Kerran lifted his head and looked down into the light. The number of people had grown, and now filled all the space inside the circle of torches. At the centre, stretched and bound upon the high alter, lay a figure wrapped in a white robe of soft flowing material which hung draped all about the stone. Kerran could not make out the features of the prone figure but feared it may be Flindas. He had to get closer.

Stepping slowly down the slope, Kerran and Rark made their way, tree by tree, shadow by shadow, until they stood in the darkness thrown by one of the last broken stone columns near the outer circle. They were only a few paces from the backs of the robed throng and a little higher so Kerran was able to see above the many heads. He looked across the intervening space to the high central stone. The figure lay there and he could still not see if it might be Flindas, or some other. Two figures in darker blue robes ascended from beneath the floor of the temple. One was tall, a great beaked nose protruding from the darkness of his hood, while the other was shorter and bore before him a carved wooden box. They moved slowly and in silence up the steps to the prone figure, who lay there, unmoving.

All was absolutely silent now and yet Kerran felt a tension and expectancy in the air. The intent of the hooded ones was revealed when the taller man bowed low to the other, who then opened the lid of the box. The tall one reached in and took up a broad bladed knife. He held it aloft as unheard words came to his lips. The silence was complete; the only sound was the occasional spark from the burning torches. Kerran reached into his pocket and took out his sling and a handful of stones. With good aim and the help of Rark, he hoped to knock down the man with the knife and charge the crowd. He did not expect success but there was nothing else he could see that was possible. He loaded his sling and prepared to throw, then a voice called out from the forest not far to his right.

"Kerran do not throw. Wait!"

It was the voice of Flindas. Not one of those gathered seemed to notice, and Flindas called again. "They are all deaf," he told Kerran. "The drumming has destroyed their hearing. Wait until you see me shoot then take the short one if you can. Send in Rark. He will keep them busy and I will try to reach the stone. I see no weapons except one; I do not wish to have a sacrifice done here. There has been too much death in the name of gods and wizards. Wait until I shoot."

The tall priest spoke silently over the knife. There was a sudden loud moan from the figure that lay on the stone alter as the man raised the knife above his head. The sound of an arrow sped across the open space and the tall priest screamed as the shaft passed through the hand that held the knife. The next sound was a thud as Kerran's stone hit the side of the hood worn by the other man. He went down like a falling tree. In the next instant Rark charged, crashing into the backs of those who craned forward to try and see what had happened at the sacrificial stone. They fell inwards. There were cries of pain and confusion as Kerran came through behind the mountain dog. Though he was unused to combat Kerran swung wildly with his staff and the people began to scatter, running blindly into the darkness. Others fell back giving no resistance as Flindas fought and battered his way through from a different direction.

Rark reached the sacrificial stone first, turning to face any who might challenge him, but none did. The tall priest knelt, weeping in an unearthly voice as blood flowed from his wounded hand, the arrow protruding from both sides. Kerran and Flindas reached the stone together. The woman was tied and Flindas quickly sliced through the ropes. Several robed figures had gathered under the ring of trees now, and armed with sticks and rocks they charged, a scream of wild madness in their throats. Rark took them front on, his strong body crashing into their midst and they flew like sack dolls in all directions. Flindas lifted the now unconscious woman, and was about to retreat to the forest when the tall priest came to his feet, holding the sacrificial knife in his undamaged hand. Flindas had not seen him and the knife began to descend, aimed at the warrior's back. Time seemed to slow; Kerran could count the moments between heartbeats as the knife descended. His throat had tightened. He could not call out a warning; it was too late. Flindas was moving away but the knife would reach its mark first.

A blur of white wings smashed into the face of the priest and Storm's talons tore at the soft flesh. The knife missed its mark and the priest screamed in pain, still swinging the blade wildly towards Flindas. Some deep instinct took over Kerran and in a sudden instinctive movement he thrust his own knife deep into the dark robes, where it sank into the bony chest. With a gurgle and a look of surprise in his deep sunken eyes, the priest crumpled to the ground and lay still.

"Quickly, Kerran, to the boat!"

Kerran heard the words through his sudden horror, Flindas turned in the direction that he had attacked from.

"I must get my bow!" he called.

Rark and Kerran ran beside him and at the edge of the forest Kerran stooped and retrieved Flindas's weapon. They began to climb the hill, struggling through the undergrowth and the increasing darkness. Vines tripped them and branches slapped their faces, while from elsewhere there were distant screams in the forest. There was no sound of pursuit. All was chaos in the forest behind them.

"I hope they did not find the boat," said Flindas. "Let us go quickly."

He thrust his way through the trees towards the beach. All seemed quiet now, the hill and forest blocking off all sound from behind. They reached the beach where their small fire still glowed in the sand. Flindas lay the woman down on his blanket and stood looking back at the forest.

"Guard," he called to Rark, who walked up the beach and stood there listening for any sound from the trees.

"I doubt that they will come after us," said Flindas. "They were not fighters, though I dare say they have much blood on their hands. It was a close thing though. I can still feel that knife between my shoulder blades. Kerran, Storm flew at night and must have been watching the battle. I have never heard of such a thing. He saved my life."

"I saw him fly at night once before," replied Kerran. "He has done some strange things since we began this journey."

Kerran had been standing near the boat looking up at the tree line when his knees went weak and he sank to the sand, a cold shiver running up and down his body. He wanted to be sick and he retched, holding onto the side of the boat. Flindas came to his young friend, holding him around the shoulders.

"It will pass," he said. "The man deserved to die. It was a good thing you did. Perhaps now there will be no more sacrifices in this place."

Kerran recovered slowly. He still felt the knife in his hand and the feeling as it had passed through the robes and into flesh. He shuddered and took a deep breath. "I am better now Flindas. I think you have a more urgent patient there." He indicated the unconscious woman, who had not moved since Flindas had laid her down.

Turning to the boat, Flindas reached in for a ladle of water and a cloth which he wet and then used to moisten the face of the young woman. She moaned softly and curled into a ball, holding her knees close to her chest. Strange words came from her lips, she seemed to be chanting.

"Her body is not harmed except for rope burns, but I do not know in what realm her mind is roaming," said Flindas. "Kerran I think we should go now. Let us stow our things and depart."

"Something seems strange to me Flindas," said Kerran as they prepared to leave the dark island. "It was certainly a sacrifice that we prevented tonight, and yet earlier, when we came upon the alter, there were no signs of blood to be seen."

Flindas paused a moment.

"They may have cleaned it well, but blood is difficult to remove completely from old stone," replied Flindas. "Perhaps they are not as bloody as we thought, though we at least saved one life this day. Perhaps it was not chance that brought us to this place on this very day. Perhaps the magic that you carry has an answer to this that we cannot understand."

Kerran saw from the look that his friend gave him that Flindas was not joking. They were laying the silent woman in the bottom of the boat when lights appeared along the edge of the forest, and they could see torches being passed from hand to hand. Rark howled, then from the darkness along the shore came the splashing of many feet running at the water's edge.

"Quickly Kerran, the boat!" called Flindas.

Heaving on either side they dragged the small craft to the water's edge and launched it. A cry came from the forest and then those amongst the trees charged onto the open beach. Rark stood his ground as a shower of stones rained down on the boat; several struck the woodwork. Flindas gave a loud grunt as one took him on the shoulder. Now they could see those who were coming from the darkness along the beach. Rark was being pelted with stones and then he charged his attackers. They had not expected it and he broke their line, scattering them, torches spluttering in the sand. Again Rark charged and the attackers turned and ran.

Flindas and Kerran had the boat deep enough in the water to board when the wave of men and women who came along the beach threw a bombardment. Kerran was hit but his heavy clothing managed to deflect most of the stone's power. Flindas loosened three arrows into the midst of their assailants then he and Kerran leapt aboard. Flindas took up the oars and the boat was perhaps waist deep in the water when a stone caught him on the side of the head. Without a sound Flindas fell backwards into the boat, and then Kerran was under attack from several men who had finally reached the boat. One slumped back into the water as Kerran's staff smashed into his head. Another gave an anguished cry as his knuckles were broken with another blow. Rark was swimming toward the fight, howling as he came. A man, still in his blue robes, scrambled aboard. With an upward thrust Kerran caught him a blow to his out thrust chin and he fell back into the water. Rark was almost to the boat and his jaws closed briefly on the leg of another attacker, then he swam back and forth, clearing the immediate area around the boat, the southerly wind eventually pushing them beyond danger.

Rark could not get into the boat and swam alongside, seeming to understand, as Kerran went to Flindas who still lay in the bottom of the boat. Kerran took the ladle and splashed seawater into his friend's face. Flindas spluttered and reached for his painful head. With a moan he opened his eyes.

"What happened?" he asked, his voice coming through clenched teeth.

"It is safe," said Kerran. "They have gone. Do you have the strength to help Rark aboard?"

Flindas came to his knees and with much struggling they got the mountain dog into the boat. It was now a very crowded ship as the wind freshened and they drifted further from the darkening shore.

The Magical Isles

During the night they hoisted the sail and left the island far behind, a light southerly wind pushing them to the east. Flindas was at the helm, a small wound just above his left eye the only visible scar from the struggles of the night before. Morning came quickly, the events of the night running through Kerran's mind like a dream. Much had changed in him since the darkness of the previous evening. He thought of the man he had killed at the altar and of the men who had probably drowned from his desperate blows that had saved their quest from sure destruction. He did not feel like a child any more. Battles and danger were the things of stories and legend, and he had never expected to have to kill. The woman who had been destined for sacrifice remained still and silent in the bottom of the boat, breathing softly.

"She has had a great shock," said Flindas. "I hope there is no further damage. She has a fever and may be in the grip of something I cannot see and cannot heal."

He took herbs and powders from his pack, mixing them with a little water, then he took the concoction and began to feed it slowly to his patient. Her protests were weak, with Flindas eventually managing to get her to take nearly half of the mixture. At times during the following night she would wake with a scream, her wailing voice penetrating far into the darkness. By dawn she was extremely weak and could only manage a sip or two of water. The sun was warm and they rigged the sail cloth to give her shelter.

"I do not believe that there is very much hope for her," said Flindas with a sigh. "She does not appear poisoned. I think it is a drug she craves and the need for it is killing her."

The woman's fits became weaker and less frequent during the afternoon and as the sun lowered to the horizon she quietly died. On the instant of her death many voices called to them from the sea.

"Give her to us!" was the cry.

Flindas jumped in astonishment, Kerran dropped the helm and Storm gave a squawk and flew aloft. Rark seemed unperturbed by the ruckus.

"Give her to us!" said the voices again. They were women's voices coming from below the surface of the waves, and then one voice alone spoke to them. "We will take her body and give her life again; we will make her one of us."

The voice was soft and compelling. "It must be done quickly. She will be safe here with her sisters."

Kerran and Flindas looked at each other and in silent agreement they lifted the woman's body and lowered it towards the water. There was a stirring on the surface as many slender hands came up from the water to hold her, then very gently she was lowered to the water. For a moment she appeared to be floating on the surface and then she was gone.

"There are many of the old stories that are becoming real," said Flindas as he sat back in wonderment. "They were Elveren, nothing surer. Soon I may even begin to believe in Zeta."

He smiled at Kerran through the softening light as they settled back into the boat. The light southerly had died and they drifted on a calm, empty sea. The wind did not rise again during the night and the dawn broke clear and warm.

"I hope this does not keep up," said Flindas. "To be becalmed is not to a sailor's liking."

Days passed without a breath of wind. They were hot and

cramped; Rark was the most uncomfortable. Flindas looked to the stars at night, their drift, he said, was still east and perhaps a little north. Though they had fish enough, the remainder of their stores were very low. The fruit from the strange island they had eaten already for it had begun to spoil quickly. Only a few biscuits and fruit remained of their dry foods, and though they drank their water sparingly, one barrel was empty, without a sign of a rain cloud in the sky.

It was in the early dawn of another clear morning when Flindas shook Kerran awake and pointed to the east where a tall white cloud seemed to hang in the gathering light. Kerran strained his eyes and after a time he could see tall pinnacles of white thrusting up through the distant haze. As the light grew they watched in awe as a range of lofty, snow covered mountains came slowly from beyond the horizon. It took the rest of the day before they could see the foothills of the towering crags.

That night a fortunate light breeze came out of the west and Flindas steered with it, intending to sail to the south and east of the land that grew before them. They sailed yet another day along what seemed to be an uninhabited coastline, then during the following night they began to see lights twinkling on the shore. A small town appeared to be nestled into the tree covered foothills of the southernmost mountains.

"We will wait until dawn," said Flindas. "We do not know what this place is. It may be Zeta or it may not. We can judge better by morning."

They lowered the sail and during the rest of the night Flindas kept them just offshore by rowing in close and holding against the gentle wind and currents. When light came he rowed them in, eventually beaching the small boat in a secluded bay a league or more from the town.

"Rark! Guard!" said Flindas and touched the boat.

The mountain dog moved about stiffly for some time. He drank from a small stream then came to stand beside the small boat. A path led from the beach up a steep rise. Kerran and Flindas began to climb, their legs ached with the sudden exercise. On reaching the brow of the hill they came upon a cleared place on a high point above the sea, a circular fireplace of large rocks stood there. A tall pile of firewood and kindling was set, with black oil coating many of the logs. All that was needed was a flame to ignite it.

"It is a signal fire," said Flindas. "By day it would send up smoke, and by night, from this point, it could be seen for some leagues up the coast. A lookout for enemies coming by sea I think, but if that is so, I wonder where the ones are who should be here keeping watch?"

There was a rustling in the bushes as two small figures leapt up and dashed away along the path. Flindas and Kerran gave chase. The two children pursued. They were perhaps ten years old and no match for the long strides of Flindas, who caught them both by the back of their shirts and almost lifted them off the ground. They struggled and cried until Flindas put their feet back on the earth.

"Keep still!" he told them loudly.

They stopped their squirming, one still whimpering softly.

"Do not fear," said Flindas. "I am not going to hurt you."

First one then the other turned to look at him. Kerran had to look twice. They were almost identical though one was a boy and the other a girl.

"If I release you are you going to run away?"

They shook their heads.

"Now, let me ask you some questions," said Flindas. "You can speak? Yes?" They both nodded their heads in silence.

"What are your names?" he asked them in a friendly voice.

The girl, who was slightly bolder, replied. "He be Naral and I be Lor," she said.

"What is this place?" asked Flindas gently.

"Tis the village Inverill," she said, her voice had a strange almost musical sound to it.

Flindas smiled at the girl. "And where is Inverill?" he asked.

"Why, 'tis here," she said, looking at Flindas as though he were a fool.

Kerran smiled.

Flindas knelt down to come eye to eye with the children.

"It is Inverill and Inverill is here, so tell me what land this is?"

The girl looked at him quizzically. "Why 'tis Southlin, that be where Inverill is," she smiled at her brother.

Flindas almost laughed at the frustrating answer. "And tell me," he said with great patience in his voice. "What land does this Southlin belong to?"

The children looked at him in astonishment, their mouths open.

"On Zeta of course," the quiet boy said finally. "Where else do you think you would be?"

Kerran spoke the word in a whisper. "Zeta." They had arrived. "Tell me," he asked them. "Do you know a man called Tolth?"

Again the children gaped in amazement. "Of course we know Tolth," said Lor, assured now that the man was mad. "Who would not know Tolth? Have you been sick or something? Are you one of the ones who do not remember?"

"No," replied Kerran. "We come from another place far away and I am here looking for Tolth."

The children were silent for a time. They looked into each other's eyes and made signals with their hands. "We will take you to our grandfather," they said together.

"Come," said Lor and they began to walk up the path.

Kerran and Flindas came close behind, ever wary of the children taking flight. They soon came from the forest onto a well-worn road.

"Our grandfather lives not very far from here on the edge of the village," said the girl and led the way to the south.

They walked on in silence, until on rounding a turn in the road the small village came into view. Looking down on it Kerran could see well-constructed wood and earth buildings. Vegetable gardens covered one hillside, while a large herd of goats could be seen higher up. Smoke drifted from a number of chimneys, and people were gathering in the town centre where a market seemed to be in progress.

"This be the home of grandfather," the children said as they came to a small tidy house on the hill, just before the road ran down into the village. "He will be home, he never goes out."

The children were becoming a lot friendlier and talkative, no longer fearing their strange captors.

"Grandfather! Grandfather!" they called into the open doorway. "There be someone here to see you."

A noise came from the back of the house, a chair scraped and something clattered.

"Well come in then," called an old man's voice along the passage. "No point staying out there. Come in."

Flindas and Kerran followed the children along the hallway to where sunlight flooded into the kitchen from a northerly window, bathing the room in light. At a table sat an old man. His grey hair fell to his shoulders and his beard reaching to his belt. He had been cutting vegetables when the party arrived in his kitchen but, with a startled look at the two travellers, he leapt to his feet holding the knife before him.

"What is this?" he called. "What do you want?"

"Do not fear," said Flindas. "We are weary travellers and mean no harm. We have come to Zeta to find Tolth. Your grandchildren here said that you may help us."

"You are not from Zeta?" the old man marvelled. "Though from your appearance I should have guessed as much; weapons are not worn openly here."

He eyed the sword which hung from the tall warrior's belt and the bow across his shoulders.

"Your clothes are a little more than peculiar also."

He was looking at Kerran's coat of rabbit skins, now much patched and repaired. Kerran's shirt had become rags and eventually fallen apart. His breeches were torn at the knees, and his boots, after all the walking, were almost worn through.

"Can you tell us of Tolth?" asked Kerran. "It is important that we go to him."

"Yes, yes," said the old man who returned to the table and put the knife down. "Tolth is in Nariss, the Green City. It is a day's journey by wagon. If your urgency can be delayed until tomorrow I will take you then. I daresay you would like some hot food and perhaps a bath. Out of politeness I will not mention how bad you smell."

He chuckled at his joke, completely at ease now with his

very unusual uninvited guests.

"You will take food then?" the old man inquired again.

"Your offer is most kind," said Flindas. "Tomorrow will do very well, but first I must return to our vessel. We have left one of our companions on guard there and he too would appreciate your hospitality."

"Yes of course," said the old man. "Go and get him."

"You lad," he turned to Kerran. "You could help an old man by setting a fire under that water pot outside. Tis sure a good bath is what you most need."

Flindas left Kerran and returned to the boat, he secured it firmly to a tree that clung to the water's edge and then he and Rark returned to the old man's house. He met no one on the road and when he came to the door, Rark followed him inside. The exclamation from the old man seemed to rattle the crockery on the shelves.

"What is that?" he called as the two children rushed to his side, clinging onto his legs in fright.

"This is Rark, a mountain dog," said Flindas. "He is our companion and is of no danger to you."

As if to confirm this, Rark went up to the old man and stood there as though asking to be accepted a curious look on his face. The old man laughed.

"You are an interesting lot, that to be sure," he scratched Rark behind the ears. "Are there any more of you in this travelling circus? If so I had better know how many I am cooking for."

"Yes," said Kerran "There is one more but I have not seen him for some days. He is a white hawk and travels as he will. I think perhaps that he came ahead and is now on Zeta too."

"A white hawk!" exclaimed the old grandfather. "Now that is the strangest of all. A white hawk has not been seen in this land for many centuries. Tolth will be very interested to hear it I think. Come! Into the bath with you, and I will see if I can replace that smelly hide of yours."

After they had bathed in the small tub open to the sky they spent the remainder of the day sitting in the backyard, for Shindara did not want his neighbours knowing that he had `foreigners' staying with him.

"They would just come around and stick their noses in," he said with disdain. "Tomorrow night you will be in the Green City, but for tonight you are mine. I want to know everything about the Regions, news does not come often. Tolth has ears there but we have heard little of importance for years. For instance, how is it that scoundrel who now holds the governorship of the City Amitarl?"

There would be many more questions as the day wore on. Shindara gave Kerran an old work shirt to replace his rags and smelly jacket. It was patched at the elbows but still had much wear left in it.

"This should keep you covered and decent," he said. "It belongs to my grandson Eron, and that reminds me." He turned to the twins. "Where is that brother of yours? He should have been on watch, not you."

"He told us to stay there," said Lor with a defiant look, which turned to a radiant smile as her grandfather shook his head.

"That boy!" exclaimed Shindara turning to Flindas "He will not take his duties seriously. We have been asked to keep vigilant watch on the coast these days. There may be war in the Regions they say, even with the old magic to guard us Tolth and the Council wish to take no chances."

Shindara laid a friendly hand on Kerran's shoulder. "Take a bowl and help yourselves from the pot. It is fish and vegetables. You are probably tired of fish but it is the only meat that we on Zeta will eat. Please have what you will. I made the bread this morning and the cheese is good."

The afternoon passed with Flindas telling much of the goings on in the four corners of the lands. At the evening meal Eron, the older brother of the twins sat with them, surprised and delighted at the strangers in their midst. He was scolded by the old man for leaving his younger brother and sister to remain at the signal fire alone.

"I came back and they were gone," he said in excuse.

His grandfather grumbled and gave him a friendly cuff about the ears. Eron, who was fourteen or fifteen, listened in awe to the stories that Flindas, and sometimes Kerran, told of their journey. When Kerran mentioned Storm, Eron blurted out that there was word in the village that a white hawk had been seen flying high up amongst the southern mountains.

"Good," said Kerran "I am glad to hear that he is safe."

"You do not know the significance of the hawk," said Shindara to Kerran. "It is said that when the white hawks return to Zeta the lands will be healed. One bird does not mean a return but it is a hopeful sign."

Kerran felt a comfortable exhaustion begin to creep upon him and he yawned.

"To bed young man," said Shindara, and led him to a cot in a bedroom that he was to share with Eron.

"Sleep well," said the old man. "The last leg of your journey begins tomorrow and by evening you will be with Tolth."

Kerran slept heavily and awoke to the smell of breakfast coming from the kitchen. Eron's bed was empty. Kerran dressed slowly, his joints still stiff from the many days on the boat. When he reached the kitchen, Flindas and Shindara were at the table eating bowls of steaming oatmeal and fruit.

"So, the lazy one has decided to join us," said the old man. "Have some breakfast. We will soon be on our way to the city. Eron is out harnessing the horse now."

Kerran ate the delicious gruel and was on his second bowl when Eron came in to say that all was prepared. Kerran gulped the last of his hot sweet tea and joined the others in the yard, where a sturdy farm horse stood harnessed to an old four wheel working cart.

"It is not a princely coach but it will get us there," Shindara said.

Eron and the twins wanted to go too but Shindara told them there would not be room, and besides they had chores to do.

"You will have to stay," said their grandfather. " You all have lessons today too, so mind you attend. I will return tomorrow. Eron, you make dinner for the others, vegetables mind, and not just bread and honey."

Eron smiled. He knew what they would be having for dinner.

They climbed aboard, Shindara took the reins and Flindas sat up beside him. Kerran and Rark were in the back, and they were soon under way, returning along the road that they had walked the day before. The forest was thick and Kerran could see only a short way into its depths. Huge trees stood like guardians, their great limbs sheltering the smaller trees beneath. Many different ferns grew on the forest floor and a great variety of song birds called to each other from the sunlit treetops. Shindara talked much during the trip, mostly about the land they passed through and how it was managed.

"We do not cut down trees unless it is necessary, and then we plant and replace," he told them. "The forest helps us keep a balance here on Zeta. The people live mostly in communal villages, and the work is shared and made much lighter because of it. Everyone learns what there is to know about many occupations. It makes for a strong bond between people knowing that everything is shared."

"What of your grandchildren's parents?" asked Flindas. "You obviously have charge of them. Are their parents dead?"

"Oh no," said Shindara. "Their mother has work of importance in the city and their father has been called to the Army. We have never had war on Zeta as no enemy has come here in the time of Amitarl, but Tolth is still the Guardian of the Four Regions. Even though few have ever seen it, we keep our army prepared to protect the great western land against the return of Maradass and his black son."

"We have been prepared for many years. Only volunteers train for the army but it is a peculiar thing. Ever since the army formed there has not been a man or woman who did not volunteer to train. It is a tradition I suppose. This year Eron will go to the city and study the fighting arts. He looks forward to it. When the training is done, in his own eyes he will be a man. There is great pride for the young people when they gain their colours. Eron wishes to join the elite who are taught by Elfhand and his training masters. One must be very skilled to enter the ranks of the Elbrand. It is said that Maradass prepares for war, well we will be ready."

The old man went silent for some time. The trees had thinned and they found themselves bumping down the road through fields of vegetables and fruit trees. As they entered a small village the people stood staring, their mouths gaping at the huge hairy beast that had risen from the floor of the cart. Some called out and Shindara called back importantly. "They are from the Regions! We go to see Tolth!"

Then they were gone, rattling down the road and back into the forest before any could waylay them in talk.

The sun dipped behind the western mountains. The afternoon had passed and evening came softly. Far ahead the lights of a large city could be seen. The twinkling began in the hills above it, and ended in two sweeping arms of light that partly encircled a large bay. The lights of much water traffic could be seen further out, plying between islands and tall ships.

Kerran became apprehensive; once again he was just a boy from a far off corner of the land. He had never been in a city, nor had he ever met anyone as important or powerful as Tolth Amitarl. He looked at his clothes. The shirt that Shindara had given him was patched and frayed, though compared with the rest of his clothing it was in good condition, and he still carried his staff and a battered rabbit skin bag.

Shindara broke the silence. "We will be going down to the port for that is where the Council Buildings are," he said. "Tolth will be there, or at his home which is close by. I know that he will want to see you as soon as we arrive, and I doubt if you will be having an early night. News direct from the Regions does not come to us every day."

Though the old man knew that his guests had important news from the Regions, he had not asked what it might be. They drove on in silence and the first houses of the city began to pass. They were built of wood, stone and earth, and most had their own gardens and fruit trees. The darkness began to close in, making the lights shine brighter. The road they had been following began to broaden out into a wide avenue lined with trees. The fragrance of many flowers filled the air, while shrubs and ferns filled every bit of open ground, houses nestling into the surrounding greenery. People sat in roof gardens and cheerful lamplight shone from many windows. As they got closer to the port there were many businesses and stalls. On some street corners stood large fireplaces where crackling fires burned. Many people stood near them, warming their hands and discussing the events of the day. Some carried lamps on poles, while others cooked a meal in the open air. The whole feeling of the city was one of light and greenery. Plants of many sorts unknown to Kerran grew from balconies and rooftops, and long tendrils hung down covering the walls of the buildings. Every spare space seemed to be taken up with the growing of some sort of vegetation.

"It is why we call this place the Green City," said Shindara. "Nariss in the old tongue. Everyone is encouraged to grow things. Even children have their own little plots. It helps to keep the air clean and many of the city's vegetables are grown above us on the roofs of the houses."

Kerran in his imaginings had always seen cities as tall buildings, spires and castles. Here it was not so. He had not seen a building that had more than two floors. The roofs were almost always flat, giving an outside living and gardening space for the occupants. Large parks and groves of old trees broke the city into many parts, and a river had been diverted and channelled into many ponds and lakes. They began to drive through a large park that stretched down to the docks where tall sailing ships floated on the tide. Far to the right Shindara pointed out a long two story building. It was the largest structure that Kerran had seen so far.

"That is where the Council meet," he told them. "Tolth is more likely to be there than at his home. He has workshops and special rooms for teaching; it is said that he does not sleep. That may be an exaggeration but in his waking time he does a great deal of work and study. He teaches, he instructs, he listens, he counsels. Though he does not claim leadership, everyone looks to him for guidance, and of course people talk of him. There are many stories, and I wonder often which ones may be true. He has lived long and done many things."

Often during the journey Kerran had imagined the time when his quest would end and he would pass the Seacrest fragment on to Tolth. The simple stone building seemed too common a place to be the seat of power on the Magical Isles. They climbed down from the wagon: there was no one to greet them, no guard, only a single flame that burned in a metal bracket above the door.

"I will leave you now," said Shindara. "Tolth is here. The torch shows that. I do not come to the city very often, but there are people I like to visit when I do. Perhaps we will meet again, Zeta is not so big. Farewell and may Tolth be as gracious as he is wise."

He held out his hand to them and they thanked him, and then with a flick of the reins he was gone back up the road and into the city. They stood looking after him and then turned to the entrance of the Council Building.

"Well, here we are," said Flindas. "I never thought that I would ever be knocking at an Amitarl door."

So saying he rapped on the large wooden slabs which formed the high door. The companions stood for a time in silence, then Flindas knocked again. The door eventually swung back and a young boy stood there. He gaped at the group standing before him.

"We have come to see Tolth," said Flindas. "We come from the Four Regions."

"Yes, yes," gulped the boy, who was perhaps nine or ten years old.

"Please come in. I will tell Tolth that you are here," and he scuttled away. They stood in a large hallway which contained a number of comfortable chairs and other pieces of furniture. On the walls were hung several well-executed paintings. Most were portraits, while others showed tall cities or sweeping landscapes. Kerran thought he recognised the forest and far distant mountains depicted in one.

"It is not far from my home," he said to Flindas in surprise. "It is the Bittering Mountains. The river is the Glandrin-dar."

. Then he thought of his home and his mother. A tightness came to his throat and his eyes glistened, Flindas laid a comforting hand on his shoulder.

"You will be able to go home soon Kerran," he said. "Your work is almost done."

A door opened and closed somewhere in the back of the building and brisk footsteps came their way. From around a far corner Kerran saw the young boy coming towards them quickly, he beckoned to them and they followed him down the hall, Rark's claws clicking on the stone flagging. Kerran ruffled the great dog's coat, stroking his neck and shoulders as they walked, the great head moving back and forth studying the nature of his surroundings. They turned the corner and found themselves in a hall similar to the one they had just left. At the far end a door stood ajar and bright light streamed from it into the more dimly lit passageway. The boy led them to the door and entered the room which was large, and would have been spacious if it had not been for its contents.

Two large tables stood against opposite walls, both covered with books and many papers and scrolls. On a third table, and on numerous shelves, stood a great number of curious things. There were old weapons and pieces of armour, sea shells encrusted a number of old jars, glass globes and metal contraptions strove to find space on the tall sets of shelves. There were pots and jars marked with strange runes, things made of glass and light, a great many Kerran wanted to reach out and touch, beautiful things, dark indescribable unknown things. He stood in the doorway and his eyes travelled around the marvellous room, and then they came to rest when Kerran realised that amongst the small mountains of books and treasures, he himself was being observed. An elderly bearded man sat at yet another table which stood in a far corner. He was eyeing them with great curiosity.

Having been noticed the man stood and walked towards them, his hair was long and almost snow white. He was tall and walked with strength and purpose, a smile spread across his remarkable face. He did not appear to be exceedingly old though Kerran knew he had lived for almost two centuries, that this was Tolth he had no doubt. In a few strides the head of the Amitarl household was across the room, his hand outstretched.

"Welcome, welcome," he beamed. "Visitors from the Regions! Amazing! Wonderful! We have had no unexpected guests for many years. Welcome again. I am Tolth Amitarl and I believe you have come all this way to see me. What could possibly make someone face all that danger and the wide unknown ocean to get to Zeta? Please sit and tell me your tale."

In some way Tolth seemed to know that it was Kerran who brought him news.

"My name is Kerran Shalastar" said Kerran. "I come from the west of Glandrin, and this is Flindas and Rark my travelling companions."

"A most marvellous animal," commented Tolth. "Please go on."

They sat, after Tolth had cleared away some of the books and other things that lay scattered on a low wooden bench. Kerran found it hard to begin.

"I have a message from your daughter Leana," he said finally.

The old man appeared to stop breathing. He seemed to know, thought Kerran. "I am very sorry to tell you that she died in a battle with the one called Zard Maradass," he continued. "He died there also. She entrusted me with this to give to you."

He slowly lifted the cord from around his neck and passed the Seacrest fragment to the old man, who sat before him in silence.

Tolth remained still and did not take what was offered as tears suddenly came to his soft blue eyes. The tears streamed down his cheeks and fell, to be absorbed by his simple deep green robe; his face did not change expression.

"You bring me sorrowful news young man," he said with a deep shuddering sigh. "Leana is gone. I knew that some calamity had come about, but her death I did not even imagine. I cannot believe it and yet I must." He took the Seacrest fragment and touched it gently. "Yes," he sighed again. "I knew that something of great importance had happened in the land. I sensed that Zard had come to yet another end, but I did not guess that it was by my daughter's hand. You bring me much sadness Kerran, and yet you bring me hope also." He wiped away the tears. "Maradass the Mad is dead and the family is vulnerable for a time," he said quietly. "Please Kerran, tell me all."

Kerran began to tell his story from the beginning and as he did so he relived many of the dangers that he had passed through. Tolth was very interested in Kerran's experiences with the Seacrest.

"Each person who has carried a fragment finds that it works in different ways, if at all," said the old Amitarl. "It is interesting that it gave you such assistance, particularly in Dreardim Forest when you had only carried it for less than a day."

Tolth delved into Kerran's dreams and when he was told of the part that Storm had played throughout their adventures he gave Kerran a penetrating look. "A white hawk you say?" said Tolth in wonder. "There have been stories reaching Nariss that such a hawk has been seen on high up in the mountains. If it is true then it may mean the fulfilment of an old prophecy."

"It is true," said Kerran. "Storm has been with me from the beginning of my journey. We have been together for some years. He will go off on his own at times but always seems to find me again."

"You are fortunate to have such a friend," said Tolth, who rose and took down a scroll from a shelf.

Unrolling it Kerran saw a family crest at the centre of which flew a white hawk.

"This is the Amitarl family crest," said Tolth. "The white hawk lived on Zeta for many centuries until the Mad One sent his armies here, long before the return of my family. All animals including the hawk were slaughtered during those dark times, the forests were burnt and the rivers poisoned. It was thought that the white hawk had been totally exterminated. Then stories came from Glandrin and the Bittering that the white hawk had been seen again. Now I am very pleased to know that it is true. It is said that peace will come to the lands when the white hawks return to breed on Zeta."

Though his eyes showed great sadness Tolth encouraged Kerran to continue. Many times he interrupted, wanting Kerran to elaborate on some minor part of his tale. Flindas joined in occasionally, remembering things that Kerran had forgotten, or not known of.

"Dolphins..." Tolth said in quiet surprise.

During the evening he sent Nup, his young assistant, to find them some food. The boy returned with large bowls of soup, bread and cheese, a simple salad and goat's milk. They ate and

Kerran continued with his tale, though there was more to be told that would have to wait for another time. Kerran was tired and Flindas had been quiet and had spoken little.

"There is much to be done," said Tolth eventually. "We need news of Maradass and his armies. Landin, my first son, is at this moment somewhere in the Broken Lands to the north of the Regions. I have had no news of him for some moons."

Tolth stood and paced the room as best he could amongst the ordered clutter that surrounded them. "We live in troubled times," he said. "Tomorrow I will call the Council together. They will wish to hear your tale, Kerran, and there will be much to discuss." Kerran felt his eyelids begin to droop and he stifled a yawn.

"Forgive me," said Tolth reaching out and touching his arm. "You must be weary for you have travelled far. I sleep seldom and forget at times the needs of others. Come, there are beds in the rooms above. The rest of your story can wait until morning; it will be a busy day."

Tolth led the way along the hallway and up a flight of stone steps. He showed them to a large room where a number of beds stood along one wall. Opposite was a long window and balcony which looked out upon the parklands and the lights of the city.

"It is no palace," said Tolth. "We on Zeta have done away with much of the trivial and unnecessary things of the past. Simplicity has its own rewards. Nup is next door, so if you should need anything please ask."

"Thank you," said Flindas. "After so many days in a small boat any place that I can stretch my legs out seems luxurious."

Rark seemed to agree with Flindas for he spread out on the carpeted floor with a long contented sigh. Tolth looked at the great dog.

"You must tell me sometime how you came by such an animal," he said. "His kind is rare in the lands nowadays and none have been seen on Zeta since the purges of Maradass. Goodnight my friends and may your sleep be untroubled."

He bowed slightly and closed the door behind him. The sound of his sandalled feet disappeared down the steps to the floor below.

Kerran was very tired and in a short time was deep in sleep. He dreamed that he was in a dense forest where strange twisted trees, unknown to him, grew close together, impeding his way. There was something important that he was looking for and could not find. Suddenly he was falling, the earth rushed up to meet him and with a jolt he woke in a cold sweat. Sitting upright he clutched at his breast for the talisman that was no longer there. He sat still, his mind beginning to calm. The sound of Flindas breathing softly in the next bed reassuring him. Rark lifted his head and looked at him through the near darkness, and then Kerran lay back down, trying to understand the dream, and eventually he fell into a troubled sleep.

Council of Zeta

Kerran woke late when Nup roused him gently to the smell of breakfast that was laid out on a table near the open window. Flindas sat there looking out upon the bright sunlit day.

"Good morning Kerran" said his friend. "I thought that you would sleep through the day by the nhsound of your snoring. Come, have some breakfast. We are requested to attend the Council shortly."

Kerran rose and dressed. With a cup of sweet tea in hand he walked onto the wide balcony and looked out on the park and the bay with its many and varied ships. A tall single masted vessel was just leaving the port. Seagulls swooped down upon the beach where fishermen cleaned the catch from their nights work, and carts carried the cleaned fish towards the markets in the city. Small boats sailed across the bay to the distant headlands and islands. Families were arriving at the sea shore, the children rushing to the water's edge, splashing and diving. Gardeners worked in the parklands, pruning and preparing beds for winter flowers. Everyone seemed busy and cheerful in the activities of the day.

Kerran returned to the table, taking another piece of bread and honey and pouring a third cup of tea. He had almost finished it when Nup entered with a summons to the Council. Kerran and Flindas followed him down to the lower floor and along several hallways until they came to a large room. It was simple in design, with many windows and a large round table at the centre. Tolth was there alone and turned to greet them as they entered.

"Good morning my friends," he said cheerfully. "I have called you a little early so that I could explain what will happen here today. Most of the men and women of the Council are elected by the people. Today's meeting will be concerned principally with your news, and there will be many questions. Though Zeta has remained at peace for years, there is much apprehension at the events in the Regions and to the threat from the north. Some fear for the future and wish to act swiftly. Others would like us to stay on Zeta and not be involved with the struggles of the land at all. All roads seem fraught with danger and I cannot see the outcome. Last night I studied the two parts of the Seacrest together, little was revealed and much is obscured. The people call me wise. I think wisdom comes from knowing that I do not know what I do not know. There are many answers; it just seems that the right questions are unknown. Yours is the first news that we have had for a long time. Landin and his company are delayed, and I believe a decision will be made by the Council to send another band of the Elbrand to the Borderlands to find him."

Tolth stopped speaking and turned thoughtfully to look from a window into the parklands beyond.

"The Council come now," he said. "Please be seated. The meeting will begin soon."

Kerran and Flindas sat in the seats that he indicated and then Tolth made himself comfortable in a chair further around the table. The doors opened and people began to enter. All looked toward the two travellers in curiosity and many smiled and bowed slightly, then they took their seats, some of which remained empty. Kerran was surprised when the meeting was begun, not by Tolth, but by a tall dark haired woman three seats to his left. She stood and asked for quiet.

"Firstly I would like to welcome our visitors from the

Regions," she said. "My name is Orlar and I lead the Council during this moon. The Council is called to hear and consider the news that you bring. Greetings Kerran and Flindas, we hope that you have found our hospitality to your liking. Now I would ask you Kerran to tell us your tale. Take what time you need and tell us all that you remember."

She sat again and all eyes in the room turned on Kerran who felt his face redden. His life had been a quiet one and he had never had to address a group of any sort. Tolth saw his discomfort and spoke to him.

"There is nothing to fear Kerran, we are all friends here."

This just seemed to make things worse for Kerran but he found the courage to stand and begin. He spoke of that day, which seemed so long ago, when he rode upon the old family horse into the forest and Storm had led him to a sunlit glade. Kerran talked on into the morning, interrupted many times to be asked question after question. The Council were fascinated by many of his revelations. The presence of a white hawk in his story startled many of them. As different members of the Council asked their questions they introduced themselves. There was one man who sat opposite them whose eyes never left Kerran as if by his intent gaze he could read the thoughts behind Kerran's words. There was something very familiar about the man's slim face and features. Golden locks adorned his head and hung to his shoulders, and his eyes were a colour Kerran had never seen before; they almost matched his hair colour. The man wore a loose white shirt with a small circle of embroidered gold around his neck. Finally he stood to ask a question.

"Greetings Kerran and Flindas welcome to our home," he said. His voice was soft, and yet it seemed to fill the chamber with kindness. "My name is Verardian Amitarl and Leana was my twin," he continued. "You speak of the white hawk Storm, but how is it that he is not with you now? And when you tell of the things that Storm has done, do you not feel there is an understanding between you and this white hawk, something that is more than a coincidence?"

Kerran thought for a few moments before he answered.

"Yes," he finally said. "There have been times when I have felt that Storm knew my mind. Once on the Old Coast Road, before I met Flindas, there was a beautiful bird that I was loath to kill, even though I needed the food. In that instant Storm fell on the bird and killed it himself, leaving the dead creature for me to eat. I could not understand how he had known to do that."

Verardian nodded. "It is as I thought," he said. "There is a bond between you that goes beyond mere friendship I think. I wonder if you would try an experiment for me. Your companion has been seen circling high above the city this morning, and I believe he may be looking for you. What I would like you to do is to will Storm to fly here and come to the window."

Verardian stood, then walked to a tall window and opened it wide. He came back to his place and spoke again to Kerran. "What I would ask is that in simple words you attempt to will the hawk to come to you," said Verardian. "Try, we can but see what happens."

Kerran closed his eyes and his mind formed the words. "Storm, come to me."

Over and over he spoke the words in his mind while all was silent in the room. Finally Kerran ceased and opened his eyes. There was many an expectant gaze fixed on the window but nothing happened.

"I am sorry," said Kerran. "He has a strong will of his own."

"No need for apology," said Verardian. "It was but a thought."

Kerran looked closely as the man sat down. The strange voice of the Seacrest fragment had told him briefly of this second son of Tolth. Finally Verardian spoke again, his voice a tone deeper, he held back tears.

"I always thought that if Leana was to die, no matter how far away she might be, I would know," he said sadly. "It is only since you arrived and brought us this news that I feel this sorrow. You carried her piece of the Seacrest safely to our shores and we are so very grateful to you. She would not have passed it on if she had felt that there was any hope for her, and yet we were closer than two pages of a book as they say, and I thought I would have known."

The members of the Council sat a long time in silence, their thoughts travelling back to their own experiences of the one they had lost. Even though Kerran had known Leana for the briefest of times he too felt a great sadness.

The sombre mood was suddenly ended by a sudden fluttering of wings at the open window. All looked up and there was Storm, walking backward and forward on the sill. He gave a low squawk and peered about at the assembled people. For a moment his eyes came to rest briefly on Kerran, and then he flew off again and was gone. Laughter broke out amongst the Council and the spell of sadness was broken. Tolth stood and went to the window, a whimsical smile on his face as he stood looking out at the sky.

When Kerran began to tell the Council of their experience on the small island west of Zeta several people in the room exclaimed loudly.

"You have been to Marl?" asked Tolth.

There was a look of dismay on his face; this was part of Kerran's tale that had not been told the previous evening.

"I do not know if it was Marl," replied Kerran. "Are there more than this one island to the west of Zeta?"

"There are no islands out there," said Verardian quietly from across the table. "Marl is a place that is known of but seen by few," he continued. "It does not exist for most that have sailed that way. You must have a strong protection to come away unscathed, ancient and corrupted wizard's magic lies there."

Verardian leaned back in his seat, looking at Kerran thoughtfully. Time passed and finally the story was told, and all questions had been answered, at least for now.

"It is time now to decide what must be done," said Orlar. "If any wish to speak to this they will do so now."

She sat as the room became very quiet. Everyone seemed to be deep in thought, and it was Verardian who spoke first. "I think as many do that we must send a group of Elbrand in search of Landin," he said. "My brother travelled with others and would have sent news by now if he could. We need to know of the preparations of Maradass. I do not believe that the new head of the Maradass household will be any more agreeable than the one who has now passed, but of this we cannot truly know for certain. All we have ever learned of the second son of the Mad One has never been good. He is said to be unlike his insane father, rather he is more cunning and evil they say. We must use this coming year wisely. I would not recklessly send men and women to their deaths, but the people of the Regions are of our own blood, though they know it not. Landin has not been captured, that is almost certain. If Maradass the Mad had held a full half of the Seacrest these past moons I believe that he would have attacked the Regions by now. I feel that Landin is still somewhere in the Broken Lands. We must find him and the piece of the Seacrest that he carries."

A tall man, a few seats to Kerran's right stood up and spoke for the first time. He introduced himself to the two travellers as Davin and then turned to Verardian. "You know my thoughts on further involvement in the Regions," he said, his voice seemed troubled to Flindas. "Our independence here is complete. For hundreds of years we have left the Regions to their own devices and it has become a place of mistrust and fear. It does not appear to me that it deserves rescue. With the three parts of the Seacrest on Zeta, Maradass, with all his armies, could not gain mastery over us. Yes, we should find Elfhand and bring him home, and all others of Zeta who are in the land should also return. Withdraw totally from the Regions and leave it to its own ends. These are my thoughts."

Davin then sat and turned his head to observe Kerran closely. Now Tolth stood and spoke "I am sworn to protect the Regions," said the old Amitarl. "And even if it were not so I would still do it. To withdraw all help from there would mean an end to the heritage of the people of Zeta. It would mean slavery and an awful death for those in the lands, and I could not let this be. I agree that Landin must be found and that he return to Zeta. We need his strength to lead our army for the war that is certain to befall the Regions soon."

For some time no one spoke, and it was Orlar who eventually broke the silence. "We have one year, perhaps a little less," she said. "Elfhand may still be searching for the secrets of the Maradass Army, or it may be that he will be back on Zeta soon.

He expected to be gone six moons and five have now passed. Though we have had no word from him I do not doubt that he is alive and still in the Broken Lands. So I suggest that we wait one moon. Wait until after the Games have ended. If he does not arrive by then we should send Elbrand to find him. Those are my thoughts."

Others spoke now though to Kerran much of it seemed to repeat the thoughts of others. Finally it was decided by all that after the Games, which would begin in twelve days, a small band of the elite Elbrand would be sent in search of Landin Elfhand. Only when he returned to Zeta and the three parts of the Seacrest were safe, could further decisions be made. At the last moment Flindas stood and all looked to him.

"When the Elbrand go in search of Landin I would like to go with them," he said. "I have spent much time on the Border Road and I may be useful. Few who have gone to the Broken Lands can truthfully say that they know the country well, and I think my knowledge may help this expedition."

He sat and Kerran noticed that several of the Council members attempted to hide their smiles. Tolth now spoke. "I applaud your bravery, Flindas," he said gently. "But we will be sending our very best in search of Landin. They have trained for many years. I do not wish to cast doubt on your abilities, but it is very important that only the most skilled are sent on this journey. There will be no more than four or five in this group. It is difficult to say this without giving offence, but it may be that you are not good enough and would slow the group. Also your wonderful beast, Rark, could not go. There would be much need for stealth and concealment. I am afraid your friend would be like a cut diamond amongst river stones. My apologies but we could not allow it."

Flindas spoke, his voice calm and untroubled. "I do not take offence at your words Tolth," he said. "I would not volunteer to go unless I felt that I was equal to the task. A thought occurs to me. I understand a little of the games you speak of from your kind and talkative assistant Nup. He spoke of competitions in the arts of battle and endurance. My teacher was a master and taught me with care, and since I left his teaching I have learned much more. Life in the Regions and particularly on the Border Road is a hard one, and I do not ask to go without you knowing my abilities. As for Rark, I believe he would be quite happy to remain on Zeta with Kerran. So will you allow me to use the Games as a test?"

The Council members looked about the table and several nodded. Finally Orlar spoke. "Yes Flindas," she said with a smile. "If you can match our best then you may go. Your knowledge of the Broken Lands would be an advantage. It is only in recent times, since we heard that Maradass was stirring in the north that we have had our people go there, but you must pass the tests and I warn you it will not be easy."

Flindas thanked the Council and sat. There was little more to discuss and the meeting concluded as the sun vanished behind the western mountains. Flindas and Kerran remained seated as the Council members began to leave, and soon the only others left in the room were Tolth and Verardian. Tolth came to Flindas and placed a fatherly hand on his shoulder.

"It is a brave man who will volunteer to go to the Broken Lands and seek out Maradass," he said. "You must tell me what you know of this place. Perhaps you would care to dine with us tonight. My house is not far. I could send Nup to get you."

Both Kerran and Flindas agreed.

"Good, good," said Tolth. "When you return to your room you will find a bath has been drawn in the room at the end of the hall, and I do believe that you will find fresh garments there. Excuse my frankness but I believe that what you are wearing now are only of use as cleaning rags or worse."

He smiled and bowed slightly, his hands together at his chest. "I thank you for your patient answering of our questions today," he continued. "It has helped us on the Council to have a clearer picture of what transpires in the land. Now I will leave you and Nup will bring you to dinner, until then."

He turned and with Verardian left the room. Kerran looked at Flindas.

"I thought you wished to stay and explore Zeta just as I do," he said to his friend. "And now you want to go off on another journey far more dangerous by the sounds of it than the one we have just completed. You are a puzzle to me at times Flindas."

Flindas smiled at his young friend. "When I left my father's home I vowed that I would not be like him," he said. "I would try to heal in my own way some of the damage that people like him have brought to the Regions. I could remain on Zeta and no doubt have a pleasant time, but this journey to the Broken Lands is something I can do that may help. Perhaps I am trying to prove my worth, to compensate for my worthless father, or perhaps tis just the adventure of it. You will take care of Rark for me Kerran? He would be well loved and cared for amongst these generous people, but he needs to know who it is that acts in my stead while I am gone."

"I will look after him as long as I remain on Zeta," Kerran told his friend, and then he paused and looked at Flindas.

"You are very confident of being chosen," he said. "Are you that good?"

Flindas smiled broadly and clapped Kerran on the shoulder. "I have no idea," he laughed. "One thing that my master taught me was that confidence in oneself is at least half the battle won. If I am beaten it will not be because I am not as good as I think I am; it will be because the others are better. We shall see. I look forward to the competition. I think it will be very interesting, but come now; let us see to this bath and new clothes."

They walked back up to their room, and while Flindas soaked himself Kerran studied his new garments. They appeared quite grand for a country youth of his simple upbringing. The jacket was a marvellous deep red while the shirt and breeches were a soft brown cloth, plain but well tailored. The boots were of a material Kerran had not seen before except on Zeta, they were not made of leather but were surprisingly pliant and strong. He had seen no leather clothing since coming to Zeta, not even a belt. The boots fitted as if they had been made for him, someone had measured him by sight and had a keen eye. After his bath he donned the comfortable clothes. All he kept from his original possessions was his knife and sling and the cooking pot that Redrah had given him at the Crossroads.

Flindas had similar clothing except that his jacket was a

deep forest green. There was some time remaining before they were expected for dinner and he spent it sorting through his pack, his weapons he put on a spare bed by his side. Kerran had not seen this full array of arms before, for besides his sword and bow Flindas also carried a variety of knives. There was several of a design Kerran had never seen before. They had four blades in the shape of a cross and no handle. He asked about them.

"They are for throwing," replied Flindas. "If your aim is true then at least one blade will find its mark. Finesse with a single blade is admirable, but when outnumbered and speed is of the essence then I would prefer these to the single blade."

A rather small and insignificant carved stick caught Kerran's eye. It was less than a hand span in length and he thought it may be a small flute, but could see no holes, except that it was hollow through its length.

"You are very curious today Kerran," said Flindas picking up the carved stick and a small pouch that lay beside it. "I will demonstrate," he continued.

There was a blur of hand movement from pouch, to stick, to mouth and with a sudden blow from his lips Flindas sent a small dart hurtling across the room to embed itself in the wooden door. Kerran stepped back in astonishment.

"It is what the black men of the desert call a Dujarn. Sometimes the dart is poisoned, though in that case the victim usually has time to raise an alarm. I prefer another less potent mixture that does not kill, but will halt an enemy in the space of a heartbeat. It is almost silent and has its uses when stealth is required. Dantas my teacher taught me the use of many weapons; he was most thorough."

Flindas retrieved the dart carefully and replaced it in the pouch, and at that moment Nup arrived. He carried a large bowl with food for Rark, while another of water had been placed by the door already.

"Tolth requests your company for dinner," said Nup with extreme politeness. Kerran was not used to such courteous behaviour. The people of his village were mostly abrupt without please or thank you. The house where Tolth and his family lived was no different than hundreds that Kerran had passed by on their journey through the city. It had two floors with the living space below and sleeping quarters above. In the long room that was both for dining and comfortable sitting, Tolth greeted them warmly.

"Welcome to my humble dwelling," he said bowing deeply. "Come sit by the fire for a while. Dinner is not quite ready."

A thick carpet was underfoot and many paintings hung upon the walls. In a far corner, appearing deep in thought, Kerran noticed a boy, perhaps a year or two younger than himself. He sat quietly, acknowledging no one, his long, slim hands clasped lightly in front of him. His hair was as black as hair can be and matched his clothes from shirt down to his boots. He did not move but continued to look into the air before him, seeing nothing. His face was pale and gaunt, his expression exhibiting no emotion at all. Kerran remembered what the voice of the Seacrest had told him of Tolth's youngest son and he tried to remember the dark one's name. Tolth followed Kerran's gaze.

"His name is Mindis," Tolth said. "He is my youngest son. Though I am almost two hundred years old he has but fifteen years. An old man's infatuation with a beautiful young woman, won and then lost." Tolth grew silent, thoughts flickering across his saddened brow.

"I know of Mindis," said Kerran. "The Seacrest told me of him and his mother Luista."

"Did it now?" said Tolth, his penetrating gaze holding Kerran's eyes. "And what did the Seacrest tell you of an old man's vanity?"

"It told me that Luista came to Zeta and that you fell in love with her," replied Kerran. "Mindis was born and then she disappeared. The Seacrest also said that Mindis was closed to it, that it could not read him."

"Yes," said Tolth sadly. "That is so. With my own powers and the aid of the Seacrest I cannot penetrate his mind or his heart. He is closed, as you say. He does not sleep and barely eats. He will sit like that for days, then he will rise and walk about the island as if in a dream. To my knowledge he has not spoken more than eight or ten times in his entire life, though he somehow knows the language. He appears to listen and understand at times, but there is something terrible that ails his mind and holds him apart."

At that moment Verardian entered the room by a side door carrying a tray laden with platters and glasses.

"Dinner will be here shortly," he said. "The cook has had a long day in Council and will not be rushed."

He smiled and returned through the door and Tolth looked after him tenderly.

"I have been blessed with a fine son in Verardian," he said smiling. "He is a true healer. His strength is in his pure heart and the love he holds for all living things. To be simply touched by him is to experience that purity. My children have all been of a special kind."

His eyes once again flickered down the room to Mindis, and then returned to Kerran.

"With your news of my only daughter's death you bought me great sadness Kerran," said Tolth. "Landin is far away and I feel that trouble dogs his path."

He paused.

"Forgive me my friends," he said softly. "So much has been said in the last brief day that I am in a somewhat melancholy mood and I did not ask you here to listen to my lamentations. Come, tell me more of the lands, Flindas. How is the City Amitarl faring without my family's guiding hands?"

"It does not fare well," replied Flindas. "Corruption is everywhere and there are few to be trusted. I have lived there in the past but no longer. It is not a place with a good heart."

"The Regions are in dire need," agreed Tolth. "The Amitarl family will return, but not yet. A time will come when we must face Maradass. Only when that family is vanquished completely will lasting peace return to the Regions."

Verardian and Nup served dinner. There was of course fish, but there were many varied vegetable dishes with a delicious combination of tastes and flavours. The table was circular and they sat around it. All except Mindis who remained in the far corner of the room with a bowl at his elbow.

"He will eat perhaps, and then he may not," said Verardian

as he held his hand for a time at the top of his dark brother's back.

For a brief moment the face of Mindis came to life, and then returned to stare into empty space. Talk at the table came around to the Seacrest and Kerran asked about the fragment that Tolth carried, the piece concerned with the future.

"There are things there that I am not able to see," said Tolth. "Like a dark shroud hanging in the deepest of the caves. There is a power in the future that even when the three pieces are in my hands I cannot penetrate. It is understood that there are no accidents, no coincidences, and yet it is also known that the future can only be a variety of possibilities."

Putting his hand to a pouch that he wore at his waist Tolth took the two pieces of the Seacrest from it and placed them on the table. The fragment that Kerran had carried was now free of its cord and clasp. The simple metal objects lay beside Tolth's platter of food.

"Kerran," said Tolth thoughtfully. 'Since you have carried the piece that Leana held, and I believe it gave you great protection. I wonder what affect the piece of the future may have in store for you. It will not harm you."

So saying Tolth passed his piece across to Kerran who gently held it and felt its warmth. He sensed that a colour emanated from it, and the room took on a soft orange-red glow.

"If you close your eyes and relax your mind you may see something useful," said Tolth. "Perhaps you could tell us what you see."

Kerran closed his eyes and began to speak. "It is dark," he said and relaxed further "I see a moving shadow. It comes slowly towards me." He did not speak for some time, and then his face grew pale and fearful. "No!" cried Kerran suddenly, as he opened his eyes and looked around the room in search of unseen enemies.

"What is it?" said Tolth with an anxious frown.

"Large black dogs," said Kerran, and shuddered again. "Vicious creatures with huge jaws and blue fire in their eyes; they were hunting for me I believe. I care not to see more of the future I think."

"Marauders," said Tolth knowingly as he took the fragment of talisman from Kerran's outstretched hand. "I wonder why you saw such beasts. It was Maradass the Mad who created this barbaric animal. Tis said that they are cunning beyond any other creature except man. What of your travels Flindas? Have you any knowledge of these foul creatures?"

"Only what I have heard, and that is little," replied Flindas. "They are ferocious in a fight and they are silent when they wish to be. I have never seen one. I have heard of them but I did not know they were part of the Maradass armies."

The conversation continued by the fire as Nup cleaned up the table. It was some time later, when Flindas was speaking of the Border Road that there came a sound at the window, a tapping and scratching could be heard through the shutters. Verardian eased them open and to his surprise and delight Storm appeared on the windowsill. With a cry, the bird flew across the room and alighted on the low table, which stood before the fire. Nup gave a cry and fell from his seat. Storm ignored all others and went directly to Tolth, and then began to peck at the pouch which hung at the old man's waist. Tolth looked at the bird in surprise but allowed Storm to do as he wished. Storm pulled at the contents of the bag with his beak until he was able to take out a piece of the Seacrest. It was the one that Kerran had carried. Then the hawk walked across the table and dropped it in Kerran's lap, who hesitated until Tolth said quietly.

"Pick it up please, Kerran," said Tolth, still amazed. "This must be important."

Kerran took the piece and immediately the voice of his travels came into his woken mind.

"Kerran I am here," the voice sounded subdued and exhausted. "You must not return home to Glandrin, not yet. There are evil people and dark creatures searching for you in the Four Regions; beware the black dogs."

Kerran remembered Leana saying these exact words just before she died.

"Something happens to the oceans and it saps my strength," the voice continued. "Stay on Zeta, learn, and understand. I know that your part in this is not yet ended… "

The voice became a distant whisper and then trailed away.

Kerran came back to the room and its occupants, only moments had passed. He repeated for those by the fire what the voice had said. Tolth was concerned at the words about the oceans. He too feared that the powers of Maradass grew in some way within the waters. Storm meanwhile returned the way he had come, once again flying by night, a soft white ghost against the starlit sky.

Kerran handed the piece back to Tolth who replaced it in his pouch as he spoke.

"We are approaching a great and terrible age," he said. "It will all come to an end and perhaps a new beginning within the next few years."

The following day Verardian showed them the sights of Nariss and he proved to be an excellent guide. There were the trade markets where the complex barter system allowed those with much of one thing, produce or services, to trade with someone who wanted some of what others offered. Individual names and village names were written down or remembered. Verardian told them that money was not used on Zeta, and that gold and jewels were of little value as the southern mountains were filled with both. At the end of the day much of what was left of the food was divided freely until little remained. Verardian showed them the Old City. It lay to the north of Nariss, a tumble of ancient ruins that had been found on Zeta even before the Alliance. It had been a vast warren of a city with a high castle built on a low hill where it commanded an expansive view of the harbour.

"It is said that Rishtan-Sta, who forged the Seacrest, did so on Zeta," Verardian told them. "It is believed that he was attacked and defeated here but managed to escape with the incomplete Seacrest. These ruins are believed to be the result of that war, and though the protective spell that keeps Zeta safe had been broken it was not completely destroyed. When the Mad One came to power he took Zeta before any could guess at his plan, and by treachery the spell was broken and Zeta was burned and destroyed. Few creatures and no humans were left when my grandfather came to these shores, but in time Zeta regained the protection of Rishtan-Sta's spell. If any come here with evil intent all they will find is ocean. It is a very powerful spell to last these many centuries."

They explored the tumbled walls and palisades, and then delved into the upper tunnels of a complex system of underground caves and waterways. Verardian told them that they reached to the ocean. The view from the highest point was sweeping and gave the travellers an excellent view of the Green City. There were several more solitary hills that the new city had spread around. These conical mounds were green clad and Kerran could see monuments and sometimes ruins at their summits.

"They were once volcanoes," Verardian told them. "There are fourteen of them."

The day was drawing on and they walked back towards the city. The people they had met during their walk were all excited to be meeting or seeing the two travellers, and their great beast. They were respectful of their privacy, though the children could not be kept from stroking and patting Rark who accepted it all in his placid undisturbed way. The streets began to be lit and families stood or sat around the communal fires. Some cooked as children danced playfully and sang old songs from the Regions, while many men and women stood close in earnest conversation, discussing the happenings of the day. Verardian and his companions eventually made their way back to the Amitarl household where Nup had prepared a delicious soup for their supper.

The Games

Tolth welcomed Kerran and Flindas to the fireside and was pleased that they had enjoyed their day exploring the city. During the evening meal Flindas asked of the Games and what would be expected of him.

"The Games are in several parts," Tolth began to explain. "There are tests with various weapons, mainly sword, knife and bow. There is unarmed combat and also specialties where each finalist must compete against others with their own favourite weapon. The final armed contest of all has the last two opponents choose a specialty of their own without the other knowing. This is where a contestant may outwit his opponent.

"On the last day there is the test of endurance. This is a contest which will sap every last fragment of your energy. First you must swim one league, and then run one league, then again another swim and a run. You will keep going until you cannot continue, there is no time limit but you must not stop. There are judges, and the crowd is everywhere. In all events there is great pride in winning the green belts that are the mark of the champions, though to win the test of endurance is the most favoured by the crowd."

The next day Flindas began to train, realising that he

did not have long to prepare. Kerran watched him in some of his exercises and was amazed at the strength and skill of his travelling companion. Though slim in appearance his build was deceptive, every muscle working with strength and purpose. Flindas swam for much of each day and ran all over the surrounding countryside and along the coastline. Sometimes Kerran watched from afar and could see that Storm was accompanying the lone runner. Kerran still felt that something drove Flindas. He was not a contented man, though he seemed well suited to the life he had chosen to live, he was a loner, an outsider, and seemed to want it so. His hate for his father seemed to have influenced his choice of the dangerous life on the road, and it was just this that Flindas did not appear to have come to terms with.

One day while Flindas was resting, Kerran asked about his reasons for his solitary nomadic life, and for the first time Kerran heard anger in the voice of his friend. "Why do you ask so many questions?" Flindas snarled. "Is it not enough that I wish to?"

He walked off, leaving Kerran stunned. He had not realised that he was on such sensitive ground with his questions. Much later Flindas returned. He apologised for his manner earlier, but then became quiet and lay on his bed as if dead. When it was dark Kerran went with Verardian to eat in the town, yet Flindas had remained on his bed and not responded when they left.

"There is something wrong with Flindas," Kerran said to the gentle man who walked beside him. "He is very unhappy about something."

"I think I understand him a little," said Verardian in reply. "He is in a dilemma and that dilemma is partly because of the times we live in. He is a fighter who does not want to fight. He was taught for years how to use his body to kill others, but I think he does not wish to do so. He is also pursued by a bitter memory of which I know not the nature. There is something in his past that does not sit well with him. Perhaps I will talk with him and try to help. Sometimes the pain of the mind is the hardest hurt to cure."

The first day of the Games arrived. Kerran and the Amitarl family were amongst many other early arrivals at the gates of the large circular pavilion where the Games were to be held. Thousands of gaily dressed people poured through the four entrances, carrying their food parcels, laughing happily, while holding their small children on their shoulders so as to see them come to no harm in the crush. Tolth, Kerran and Verardian made their way to a vantage point high in the open stands. The large excited crowd was eventually accommodated, and the beginning of the Games was announced.

The first event was archery, and for much of the morning men and women shot their arrows in continuous rounds of elimination. The people in the audience would hush, and then roar in approval at a particularly good shot. Apart from the contestants there were others on the field, dressed in a deep forest green they stood at the edge of the sandy arena and continually announced the scores and the names of those who had managed to pass through to yet another round of elimination. Flindas shot high scores consistently and saw many others leave the competition.

"Flindas does well," said Tolth. "He has surprised not a few people already."

Flindas drew with an easy motion and there was little time between his aim and release. His score remained high and the crowd roared as they had taken to this stranger as though he was a favourite lost son. The man from the Regions was now assured of a place in the finals. A third man did not shoot so well and it came down to the last two. Flindas and his opponent, whose name had been announced as Brook, stood together and spoke. Brook was a big man, taller than Flindas, and to Kerran and many in the crowd it appeared that Brook was trying to intimidate his opponent. Flindas, who did not appear to care for his adversary turned his back and walked away.

"Brook is the winner of many green belts," said Verardian. "Archery has always been the one he was most certain of."

The final part of this first contest was now to come. Tolth had earlier explained it to Flindas who said that it was well known in the Broken Lands, where gold often changed hands in deeds of such rash daring. It was an unusual finale and was a test of skill as well as bravery. The two archers were to shoot six arrows each, they would send them up into the air and have the arrow fall as close to their standing position as possible, or as their courage allowed. Tolth told Kerran that the closest any had come to serious injury was many years ago when a contestant had received an arrow in his foot, he was hailed as a hero and his green belt was marked with his own blood.

"I believe he lives in a village nearer the mountains to the west," said Tolth. "He still wears the belt and hops about with a stick. He is an old man now."

A hush came over the crowd as the two archers made ready. Brook was to shoot first. He aimed directly above him and sent his shaft aloft. It sang away into the sky but its fall was almost silent and it thudded into the dirt five paces to Brook's left. The shot that Flindas made was closer by perhaps a pace. Both men now understood something of the upper air currents. The following arrows continued to get closer to the two contestants, and as the last arrow fell to earth it struck the ground no more than a hand span from the heel of Flindas's right boot. He said later that he had felt the wind ruffle the back of his shirt. The crowd began to applaud and the sound grew deafening. The stranger from the Regions had won the green belt for archery; his skill and bravery were the only topic of conversation as the people adjourned for the midday meal.

In the first event of the afternoon the men, and not a few women, fought with hardwood swords, wearing stout body protection of very fine chain mail, and layers of woven goat's hair. Though the wooden swords caused no blood to flow there were many cries of pain from those competing. Flindas fought three matches and won them with ease, though the last warrior had scored several points against him. Kerran watched many more battles until Flindas returned to one of the distant fighting circles. As well as a test of skill it was also a trial of the combatant's stamina. By the late afternoon the final was decided, and in this Brook had won his green belt. Flindas had not made it to the last four, but had great credit put on his swordsmanship. He had lost just the one bout and that had been to Brook. During the evening meal Flindas was quiet and thoughtful, and his dark eyes turned inward.

During the following day's competition, which included the throwing of light knives, Kerran had a sudden vision, as if he was flying above the arena in the body of Storm. In the same instant that a competitor named Simo was bringing his arm forward for his final throw, across the arena flew a white grey streak. A shrill cry came from the hawk's throat and Simo missed his throw completely as Storm swooped and soared aloft into the gathering darkness. It had happened so quickly and a great roar of astonishment went up from the crowd. The judges and attendants rushed to the centre, and it took some time for the announcement to be made. Because Simo had specified one throw only, without exception, the judges had to give the round to Flindas. From his seat Kerran could see that Simo argued the point and finally left the centre in anger.

"Simo will surely argue the outcome for the rest of his life," said Verardian. "Storm may well have cost him a green belt and the chance to travel to the Regions. It is something that he has wished for a long time, though he is still quite young It seems that your feathered friend wants Flindas to win at all costs, and the crowd are beginning to show who their favourite is. It will be an interesting final I think."

"I wonder," said Tolth. "Perhaps Storm had another reason for his actions. Perhaps he did it not so Flindas might win but so that Simo might lose."

"I do not understand," said Kerran.

"Nor do I," replied Tolth smiling.

"Flindas is indeed skilled in many weapons," said Verardian. "I do not know who his teacher was but he was surely a master."

Kerran turned to Verardian. "Flindas told me of his teacher," said Kerran trying to remember. "His name was Dantas if I remember well."

Both Tolth and Verardian exclaimed loudly and turned to Kerran.

"Dantas! Are you certain?" said Tolth, holding Kerran in a powerful gaze.

"Yes, I am sure that was his name," replied Kerran. "You

know of him?"

"Yes," said Verardian softly.

"Yes, we know him," agreed Tolth, but the two men did not elaborate.

"Who is he?" asked Kerran, it was an intrigue that he did not want to let go of, and Tolth finally answered.

"If it is the same man, and observing the skill of Flindas today I have no doubt that it is, he was once an Elbrand," he said. "Dantas was a commander and a champion. It is at least fourty years ago that he did not return from a special mission, one that took him and his command into the city of Mendan Maradass. Of the thirty soldiers under his command there were but two who managed to return here to Zeta. They told that they had stumbled upon Zard and marauders within the old castle ruins. In the fight that followed Dantas ran in fear from the Black One. No one ever speaks of him without scorn, and it is only as a curse if that name is used these days."

"Dantas," Tolth mused. "He was my friend, and he could have come back. He was too proud I expect. There would have been shame for him, but he had proven himself in many dangerous situations before. So he lived to teach his arts, I am pleased, to have run and not survived would have been a great waste. He was a skilled warrior in many ways, and now, here in the arena, we have his student."

Flindas was in the centre preparing to meet Brook and a small man named Teaker for the final green belt of the day, the throwing of various knives. The competition continued until with his last throws, Flindas found that with a perfect score in this final round he could win his second green belt of the day. In such rapid movement that was faster than the eye, Flindas threw his six blades. His timing was exceptional but he had just missed the central dark circle of one small target. His score had come between that of Brook and the man called Teaker who, with many smiles and amusing almost comical bows accepted his green belt. The cheering hurt Kerran's ears. Teaker was a most popular man on Zeta and his wide smile could be seen from high in the stands.

The crowd did not disperse for some time and there would

be many beakers of ale and red wine drunk that night in the communal taverns, and around the open street fires. Flindas rejoined Kerran and their hosts. There would be no celebrating for the contestants if they were wise, for the following day was to be a long and exhausting one. Flindas ate little during the meal in the Amitarl home; he spoke of it as being part of his training. When Tolth told him that Dantas had been an Elbrand from Zeta, he was much surprised.

"He told me little of his past," Flindas said of his old teacher. "He never said where he had come from, but I see now that in truth he could only have come from Zeta. Nowhere in the Regions or beyond have I met one with such skill and command of weapons, and many other talents, though it is hard to believe he once ran from a battle, even against Zard."

Later that evening Flindas swam for a time in the bay and slept soundly until dawn. The first event of the day was an unusual mixture of wrestling, with sometimes one and often two opponents and there were also a series of tests for agility and balance. By the late morning there were twelve finalists with Simo, Flindas and Brook amongst that group. There was a further series of bouts and then Flindas met Brook in a one on one wrestling match. It would possibly be a fine bout but with only one outcome expected by the crowd. The gathering cheered as each man managed to throw his opponent, but it was Flindas who was hurled to the ground a third and final time and so retired. Brook laid a friendly hand on the shoulder of this deceptively powerful man from the Regions, before going on to win his second green belt of the Games.

There were few who left the arena at the noon meal. It was such a struggle to get out and return that most had brought with them a larger meal than necessary so as to share with any who cared to join them. The afternoon contests began within an extensive maze where various battles were fought. Many were slowly eliminated including Brook which surprised many. The last contestants trickled out of the labyrinth until it was Simo who arrived into an open square to find empty ground, with Flindas high on a wooden structure observing his arrival. Quietly Flindas slipped from his perch and disappeared from

Kerran's sight. Simo had at the last moment sighted Flindas and he slunk along a wall toward the spot where the tall warrior had disappeared. He was guessing the direction that the man from the Regions would go when Flindas suddenly arrived from a totally unexpected quarter. Kerran did not know how he could have gotten there so quickly and in a sudden battering conflict, Simo was down and succumbed to a painful hold. The crowd erupted and only then did the two contestants realise that they had been the last two finalists. Simo's look was of hate when he found who had beaten him to the green belt, and he stormed from the field. To the crowds continuous cheers Flindas received his second belt of the Games.

"Even if he does not do more I believe he has won a place on the coming mission," Tolth said, and Kerran heard a deep satisfaction in the old Amitarl's voice.

For one who had achieved a position of honour and esteem amongst so many people, Flindas seemed sombre and spoke little as they all ate together by the fireside that evening. Nup bubbled in and out of the kitchen; he was serving the stranger who had won two green belts. He would have a tale to tell his friends now, and for a long time to come. Verardian glanced at Flindas with a look of worry on his brow.

"Are you ailing Flindas?" he asked with deep concern in his voice. "I can see that all is not well with you."

Flindas looked up at the healer, his dark eyes held those of Verardian. "I am ailing, yes Verardian," he said slowly. "I have been like this now for many years, but there is no cure. There is no herb, or touch, or spell that can rid me of this."

"To tell of it may ease your troubles should you wish it so," said Tolth, bringing the eyes of Flindas to his own. "Speak of it. We are friends here."

There was a long silence, and then Flindas finally spoke. "Seventeen years ago," he began. "When I was but twenty, and living in my father's house, I one day found my elder brother attacking a young woman who worked in our kitchens. I only hit him once, but it was a trained blow and I did it without thinking. Kaylan, my older brother, died by my own hand. I did not love him, but would not have wished him dead. I ran, for

I could do nothing else. Kaylan was the oldest, heir and most favourite son of my dangerous father. I took my father's purse, and after a last word to my sister I fled. I return in disguise now to my own birthplace. Since that time I have lived in fear that again I would kill someone who meant me no physical harm, that my training would take over without thought. There have been times on the road that have tested my restraint. It is a past that I am not proud of, and is a thing I would undo if I could. It is murder to any court in the land, and the price on my head is now five thousand gold pieces, alive. My father wants me that much but I have made myself hard to find. Dantas taught me that."

There was silence around the small table until Tolth broke the stillness. "It is seventeen years and I think you have paid much for this deed my friend," said Tolth. "You have a cruel family I believe, and that is a hard thing for the younger ones of such kin. Dantas may have trained you over well. Let it go Flindas. You are admired here on Zeta for who you are now, and not you're past. You came on an impossible journey to help Kerran bring to us the Seacrest, and to the people you have proved yourself a quiet, unassuming champion. The people love you Flindas. Enjoy this time. You are a good man. This is something that all can see. One rash act, no matter how damaging, is still just a moment in an entire lifetime."

Flindas smiled slowly looking into the fire, and then he turned to Tolth. "You could tell that to my father if you ever meet him." Flindas laughed softly.

Kerran only then realised that he had not heard Flindas laugh for a long time. "I will try to take your advice Tolth," said the sombre warrior and for the remainder of the meal Flindas became more animated.

He began to tell of his life in his father's house and of the many struggles of his youth, yet it still seemed to the others that he held back something important that he could not yet say.

The evening's competition was hard and ferocious, more injuries occurring in this test of various weapons than in all others combined. When it finally came down to the last physical encounter the crowd roared with approval as Flindas and Brook again faced each other across the central ring; each contestant was to declare his as yet unnamed weapon. Brook had secretly chosen the hardwood spear used earlier in competition and this was announced, then the judges announced that Flindas would fight without weapons. The crowd were stunned, unarmed against an exponent of the fighting spear; it had not been done before. Brook seemed sincerely concerned. He did not want to fight an unarmed man.

"You must," Flindas said quietly to him. "Otherwise I will have the green belt. If you fight me you may still have a chance."

He smiled at the big man and Brook also smiled. "I will try not to hurt you too much," he said as he picked up the spear.

"Do not hold back," said Flindas quietly, and Brook frowned a little in doubt.

The two men came together in the middle of the circle and for many beats they circled each other, then Brook lunged with the spear, a blur in his hands striking at the body of his opponent. To all who watched Flindas seemed to quickly turn away from the fight, in the next moment Brook was careering backwards to fall beyond the boundaries of the fighting circle. It was over so fast that most of those in the audience had not even seen the strike. There lay Brook holding both hands at a point just below his breastbone. He was in pain and was obviously having trouble breathing. Flindas went to him quickly. Word went around the arena from those who had actually seen the blow. It had been a kick that had won Flindas his third Green Belt.

"It was a method of attack that Dantas often used," said Tolth as the people continued to cheer. "Landin also, but one does not expect it these days. Three green belts, it is not at every games that one will win three. I believe our friend Flindas will do great things in the times to come."

Kerran now saw that Tolth was holding both future and past fragments of the Seacrest in his hands.

"There is much danger for him that is hidden from me," said Tolth finally. "Also, if he so chooses, there is much reward to be had in his future, again that is if he so chooses."

Tolth quietly replaced the two pieces into his pouch, his lips touched by a curious smile. They congratulated Flindas as he rejoined them, the crowd clapping him on the back as they made way for their new hero. Tolth beamed.

"I only wish that Landin were here," he said. "He would have enjoyed the competition very much."

Now that the events of physical contact were completed Flindas relaxed a little as the last competition was the run and swim. Over dinner he spoke with a contented look on his face.

"I will go to the Broken Lands with the Elbrand," he said confidently. "And there we will find Landin."

The following morning dawned clear and still. The day's event began in the arena with a dash to the ocean for the first swim; there were always a great many entries in this event. Any of the populace could enter and there were many lesser prizes and other minor competitions built into the event, many children of all ages were at the starting line. The main prize of the green belt was for the person who went the greatest distance without stopping, slowing to a walk, or treading water. The people of Zeta were the judges with a great many boats spread along the watercourse.

The race began and the crowd cheered happily. All of those competing were barefoot and the ocean suddenly foamed with lines of lunging bodies. The first swim would spread the field. Kerran and Tolth remained expectantly in the stand while Verardian had joined the swim. Then as unexpectedly as ever Storm dropped from the sky and landed in a clear space next to Tolth. The people around were surprised and amused. Storm took little notice as he pecked at Tolth's pouch until the pieces of the Seacrest were produced. Taking Leana's piece in his beak Storm crossed to Kerran and offered it to him. Tolth smiled incredulously and then nodded as Kerran took it into his hand.

Kerran closed his eyes and as the soft mist dispersed he saw a far sweeping landscape. He did not recognise the land but was somehow aware that it was deep in the past. He thought it could be an area of Zeta that he had not yet seen but he was not sure. The sky was dark and threatening, storm clouds climbing to dim, unseen heights above. Kerran was aware of his own body. He touched his hands together. He stood on firm ground and felt stones beneath his bare feet. A gust of wind pushed him from behind and he began to walk down the path which lay before him, descending slowly into a deep wooded valley surrounded by mountains. A dark forbidding forest lay before him and high to his left he saw a promontory which looked like a face carved into the rock. As if propelled, Kerran plunged into the shadows beneath the trees.

Kerran pushed onward and eventually thrust his way into a dark clearing, one side of which was hard up against a sheer wall of rock. He stood and waited for what he knew not; the air was heavy with expectation. Kerran was gazing at the solid rock face when an opening began to appear in the hard surface, as if a curtain were being drawn back. There was a shimmering light and a stairway slowly appeared. Kerran stepped forward. The stairs were lit with a blue mist that seemed to contain its own illumination. Kerran began the ascent. The stairway climbed upward in a spiral, with the only light coming from the mist enshrouded stonework. Kerran did not know how far he climbed, though he felt no fatigue and took each step looking to the next. From far above a soft breeze touched his face, and then he could see another light reflected on the walls above but it was not blue light. Not far above him the sun was shining.

With a final turn of the stairs Kerran found himself on a high stone shelf above the forest. Where before had been gloom. Now all was sunlit and vibrant green. A carpet of tree tops swept away to a far distant ocean sparkling in the sunlight. The shelf was smooth, almost polished, and near the edge of the precipitous drop stood a large rock. The top was flat and Kerran saw that an object lay on the smooth surface. He moved forward, and then he could see that it was a plain circle composed of the same translucent metal from which the Seacrest was made. He stood looking at the piece of metal the size of his palm. It could have been the Seacrest but it showed no runes or markings. Kerran could not go further forward. A force held him and he continued to stand still as time flowed by. The sun sank behind him and the moon began to rise full from across the ocean, then an unfamiliar pattern appeared on the lower half of the moon. A blood red stain spread across the face of the silver orb, and then appeared to fall into the ocean. The moon was held in the sky for a long time. It felt as if it did battle against the red stain but it could not rise, and then it began to sink again into the sea. The redness spread until it enveloped the whole of the moon's face as it disappeared into the depths. All was dark then except that the stars still shone, dominated by the constellation of the six sorcerers.

Time passed and eventually the sun rose on a changed land, before Kerran now lay total desolation. The forest was in ashes and all the land was grey and scorched, while far off near the ocean a castle stood in ruins, smoke rising from its shattered stones. The circle of metal was no longer on the flat surface of the rock. Suddenly a feeling of immense horror touched Kerran, and terrified he turned and fled down the stairs, a great fear and dread rushing at him from behind. He fell through the closing vale of rock and landed heavily amongst boulders and tall green grasses. In the briefest of moments he saw a pale skinned woman sitting near the rock face. She was smiling as tears streamed from her sightless eyes. Suddenly a terrible pain shot through Kerran's body as though he was consumed by fire. He cried out and then he felt a gentle hand touch his shoulder. In moments the pain had faded into memory. His vision was blurred, and then slowly he began to take in his surroundings. Tolth sat beside him, holding Kerran's shoulders, a very troubled look on his face. The people about him were offering their aid.

"I am all right now," Kerran announced, and slowly returned the Seacrest to Tolth, his hands were shaking.

"Tell me," said Tolth. "I believe it is important. What did you see? What was it that made you cry out?"

Kerran began to relate his dream vision to Tolth who interrupted at times to clarify and ask questions. The sound of the crowd near the ocean announced that the first swimmers were returning.

"Soon we will not be able to hear each other," said Tolth. "Remember as much as you can. I do not know what it means, yet it may be the answer to an old question that goes back to the times of Rishtan-Sta and the forging."

The crowd began to roar, and the sound soon became deafening as the first runners entered the stadium. Though Kerran had suddenly grown tired, he strained to see the faces of the four who had begun the gruelling fifteen laps, but Flindas was not amongst them. Brook was there and three faces that Kerran did not know, one was a young woman. Flindas was eventually welcomed by the crowd, where he ran in the middle of the field that still remained. The first runners had completed most of their laps and would soon return to the ocean for their second demanding swim. Kerran realised that his friend did not swim as well as many others on Zeta. Most of the hopefuls of village and city had not made the first complete swim. Still the running track soon became crowded and Kerran could not see how the judges or the crowd could tell who was running in what order. Brook and others were now returning for their second swim while some of the runners were retiring. None now were entering the stadium. There were now quieter times when Tolth questioned him on his vision. He was very interested in the piece of metal that Kerran had seen on the mountain.

"There is a story," said Tolth. "So old that only Rishtan-Sta, were he alive, could know the truth of it. The Seacrest was created and came from the ocean with him, and there was one who saw him who should not have seen. A woman of the Elveren was on the land of Zeta. It is said that she was struck blind by the vision of Rishtan-Sta emerging from the ocean, a dazzling fire coming from his hand. The story has been told and retold, yet there is no evidence of the Seacrest ever having been on Zeta, and now there is your dream. The place that you describe is a valley in the mountains near the bay of Shoalwater. The castle and the rock face that is like a face tells me this is so. I have been there but did not see the stairs and rock shelf you describe, perhaps they are no longer there or remain hidden. I have often wished to know of the creation of

Ma-Zurin-Bidar but without success. I have never had much fortune in searching the past through the talisman. There is an affinity that you have with it that I have not seen before in anyone, including Leana. It held a protection over her but little more. Would you hold the piece again? Do not do so if you fear it, but I am close and if the experience is too terrible I can bring you back."

Kerran reached out and took the fragment of the Seacrest; it felt warm from the hands of Tolth. Kerran closed his eyes and immediately felt again the searing pain of fire through his body. He was prepared this time and he found that he could remain with the vision as it began to appear through the mist. He saw across a vast distance, and he was flying. Again he was a hawk in the skies and far below lay the ocean. For a long time there was only the passing water, until on the distant horizon he saw a dark scattered shape, and as he flew on it became a fleet of many ships. He saw a crest at the masthead of the leading ship. It was on a black field and depicted a red circle enclosing the white skull of a dog. He knew it was a fleet of Maradass and he turned, following it into the gloom of evening.

In the darkness fires broke out. A great splashing of men as they leapt into the water. Battle was joined on a beach. Fires tore through the ships rigging as sword clashed on sword. The invaders were all powerful. They thrust their enemy backward and burned everything in their wake. No one was left alive. The darkness grew to dawn and Kerran flew above a high mountain range. He looked upon a scorched land where all was silent and still except for the drifting smoke. He knew that it was the land of Zeta that had been plundered and left in ruins. He flew quickly to many parts of the islands but nowhere was there any sign of life. The destruction had been complete. Slowly he returned to the arena where Tolth heard his story.

"Yes," said the old Amitarl. "The skull of the dog, old Maradass the Philosopher took his emblem to be a living dog. When the Mad One came, he changed it to a dog's skull. The living dog was too tame for him. I think you saw the invasion that almost destroyed Zeta nearly a thousand years ago. It still does not answer the questions that I would ask; so much is still unknown."

"I have a question that you may be able to answer," said Kerran. "What of Zard, the son of Maradass the Philosopher? How did he die?"

"The strange pact that gave the Maradass family a long life was designed by the Philosopher," replied Tolth. "He wished to live forever, his family also, and so he made the agreement and sealed it with the Seacrest. His son Zard was a mighty but peaceful warrior, and he had never been bested, so in this the idea was born. Only should Zard die in single combat would the family ever change, and so for a thousand years they ruled two of the Regions, undying, ageless. They ruled wisely and peace lay on the lands for all of that time. Only invaders from the north disrupted the Four Regions, and they were easily repelled each time by Zard and his army."

"It is believed that his brother Darss, who was to become Maradass the Mad, killed Zard after provoking him into a fight. Darss wished to rule and forced an argument with his brother. As soon as Zard made to repel Darss his fate was sealed, for this was single combat and Darss carried a hidden blade. He killed his brother, and by doing so his father the Philosopher also died on the following new moon. Zard was reborn with a new twin named Darss, the one who now rules the household of Maradass. The Mad One warped his son Zard into the horror that he became. In a way I pity Zard. He did not begin the evil. In his previous life he had been a peaceful and kind ruler. Now, he will soon be reborn yet again and I do not know what new evil his father will instil in him, though I believe the new Maradass may be even more of a demon than his mad father."

Tolth grew silent and gazed across the arena, his hand reached into his pouch and he touched the Seacrest fragments.

"Please tell me more," asked Kerran. "What do the other pieces of the Seacrest do?"

"The piece of the Seacrest that is of the Future is the most difficult to interpret," said Tolth. "It holds the answers to all questions, though it is difficult to know the correct questions and how to ask them; the other pieces are much simpler to understand. The one that you carried holds much of the past within it, since the time of the Alliance and the dividing. I think that your upbringing, isolated as you were from much of the troubles of the lands, left you open to delve into its power, though I find it strange that in danger it also seems to have held a protection over you. The tale of your sea voyage is most strange to me. We here on Zeta have experienced the customary storms of this season, yet you tell of little but favourable winds on your journey, and to be becalmed is a most unusual event in these wild waters. A small boat such as yours could never have been expected to cross the leagues between the Regions and Zeta."

Tolth paused as though he had pondered on this before. He shook his head. "Then there is the piece that Landin inherited and carries," he continued. "Life is in it. It gives long life, but more than that it gives strength and a power in action. Landin is not just a formidable opponent; he is a force that is guided by a power far greater than that of any mortal man. He is attuned to the finest point, and it would be a most ferocious battle if Landin and Zard were to ever face one another. No one can say who might win that struggle."

"Then there is the piece that the Philosopher was given, and is now in the hands of the one who is the unknown Maradass. Death is its guide and force. Maradass cannot die tis said, for he will always be reborn in the body of his brother's youngest son, and so the Mad One will come again as the new Darss. It is not known what would come about if one were to attempt to kill Maradass while Zard still lived, but it is believed that he would not die. Perhaps the only way to truly end the line of Maradass is to end the life of Darss who is yet to be born. This is not known. So much is uncertain."

Tolth frowned deeply and grasped the Seacrest. "Landin where are you? Return quickly!" Tolth exhaled his breath in a rush. He looked at Kerran who could see the pain in the old man's eyes.

"Excuse me Kerran, there is so much danger, and my family is at its centre. I fear for us all." He looked away, his eyes travelling across the arena.

Kerran reached out a hand and rested it on the old man's

forearm. "Do not fear," he said. "Flindas will go to the Broken Lands and he will find Landin."

Tolth smiled slowly and turned again to look at his young friend. "Your faith in Flindas gives me hope," he said. "He is indeed a gifted one, not only in combat but also in his ability to survive. Few come back from the borders unscathed."

"As I have said I have never had much success in searching the past through the Seacrest," he continued. "Would you hold the piece again? You seem to be appointed to this task and I would not ask you otherwise."

Kerran reached out and again took the fragment of the Seacrest. He closed his eyes and immediately felt again the searing pain of fire. It was too strong this time and he let the talisman fall to his lap, and just as quickly the pain was gone.

"I cannot," he told Tolth. "There is much pain now that I cannot bare."

Tolth retrieved the fragment thoughtfully and returned it to his pouch. The morning passed and it was almost noon when the gathering began to show more interest in the day's event. Some stragglers were still struggling to complete their run but it was not them who stirred the crowd now. Cheering could be heard outside the stadium and it was moments later that Kerran saw three men enter the far gate at a run. They appeared strong and ready for the next stage of the gruelling race. Brook was there as was Simo and another man who Tolth named as Rian; he had featured well throughout the Games but had not yet reached a final. Others began to enter, some in pairs and others alone. Among those still running near the front was the young woman Kerran had noticed earlier and he guessed her to be about his own age. She was slim and strong, her hair dark and cropped short. Her face, though somewhat strained with the run was captivating and he asked Tolth who she was.

"There are many people on Zeta," he replied "I regret that there are some whom I have not yet met. Her name has been announced as Piata from the village of Felstrar. It is on Shoalwater, the large shallow harbour to the north west of Zeta at the foot of the mountains. She is very young to be running with such elite company." Tolth's eyes smiled at Kerran from beneath his thick brows. Kerran blushed and pretended to look away as yet another runner entered the arena, then his eyes returned to Piata who ran on strongly around the track.

There were now perhaps twenty runners on the course and Flindas was not amongst them. Brook was alone at the front of the field and he had almost completed the run and was about to return to the water when Flindas entered to the cheers of the crowd. He ran hard but it was obvious that the swim was not to his liking for he now trailed the field. None came behind. He ran several laps with the others. Finally the contest became too much for the young woman, and she came to a slow frustrated standstill, watching in pain as the others ran on. Flindas was the last to leave the arena and ahead lay yet another exhausting league in the water. The crowd knew that whoever finished the swim and returned would need to complete nine laps of the track to break the long standing record. The year before Brook had taken the green belt in this arduous event but not the coveted record. This year he wanted both dearly and when he returned later in the afternoon the people stood to cheer him on.

Brook stumbled several times but always managed to regain his feet before the judges ruled against him. He was on his fifth lap and no one was expecting any others to remain in the race when a delighted cheer was heard from outside the stadium. Flindas arrived running slowly to the admiring cries of the people. He too showed great exhaustion but did not stop as the laps slowly slipped by. Brook got through his sixth lap and then his seventh, then the prize was in sight. The big man finished his eighth lap and the crowd were all on their feet, cheering him on. Brook stumbled and almost fell and a huge gasp came from the gathered citizens of Zeta. Another stride and another, a green ribbon tied to a post marked his goal. Flindas was far behind and did not appear to have the strength to go much further. Brook fought on and the green ribbon was not beyond his reach. He cried out in pain and pleasure as he stumbled past the post and kept on for another few paces, then his legs gave out and he fell to the ground, attendants rushed to him but he waved them away.

Brook dragged himself to the side of the track to watch his last adversary, the only person who could take the prize from him. Flindas ran another painful lap and then another, and each time Brook saw the grim determination on the warrior's face as he passed. The crowd became unusually quiet and eventually total silence took over from the cheering, perhaps this stranger and champion could also take the record and rob Brook of victory. Flindas finally completed his eighth lap, he forced his stumbling legs to keep moving, slowly closing the distance, then Flindas rounded the last curve and the green belt and the record were in his grasp.

What happened next was for a time totally inexplicable to those who watched. Brook lay still and knew that he was beaten, but when Flindas came to the spot where Brook had finished his race the stranger slowed and then stopped opposite his rival. Flindas looked at the big man and then his knees gave way, he collapsed into a sitting position by Brook and then lay on his back, sucking air into his lungs. The crowd erupted, but they did not know whether to applaud or be disappointed. Eventually the applause won out and all cheered the two record breakers. Finally the two men helped each other to their feet and were assisted to the rooms of healing beneath the stadium.

"Not only a champion and warrior but also an honourable man," said Orlar, who had watched the race avidly. "He will win more friends and goodwill from that gesture than from any number of green belts. He would make a leader among the Elbrand."

Wizard Dreams

The Games were at an end and there would be much celebrating in the city that night. No one was expected to rise very early in the morning. The day after the Games being an unofficial but traditional holiday. Tolth led Kerran to the underground levels and eventually found Brook and Flindas together in a room where their feet were being dressed and bandaged.

"I shall not walk for a full moon," growled Brook in a deep rasping voice. He smiled through the pain. "Welcome to Zeta, Kerran Shalastar," he said. "For a young man you have a brave heart I hear, but are there not enough champions on Zeta that you have to bring someone from the Regions to best us all?"

He gave Flindas a hearty clap on the back which drew a gasp.

"Careful Brook," said Flindas with a wincing smile. "Or I may be a far worse casualty for the healers to repair."

"You are both the high champions of these Games," said Tolth. "I congratulate you and invite you to dine with me tonight."

"I would do so with pleasure," said Brook. "But Flindas and I have already made other arrangements. We intend to enjoy our fame while we can. Tonight the city is ours and we intend to have it all."

He again laid a heavy, friendly hand on the shoulder of his fellow champion. "Flindas and I will not rise early tomorrow. In fact we may not sleep tonight at all. I have a great thirst and it will take many an ale to slake it."

"The Council will meet the day after tomorrow," said Tolth. "There is no need for either of you to attend, though your names will surely go forward as two who go in search of Landin. It will be but a few days before your journey begins. Do not tax your bodies too much. You must be fit to travel."

"A blister or two and a sore head will not stop me from going," said Brook. "I have always wanted to return to the Regions." He turned to Flindas. "I was there as a young Elbrand with Dantas on an early expedition," he said. "It does not have the peace and beauty of Zeta but I am trained for battle and I seek adventure in my life before I must return, and age sends me to the fields or the nets. One great undertaking would settle me into my dotage with a satisfied mind. I would even take on Zard, were he in my way."

"Do not wish that fate on yourself," said Tolth hastily. "Even you, with all of your strength and skill would lose such a fight, and that would be a great loss to Zeta. It would be no shame to run from the Black One. Dantas ran once and survived. I do not know if he was right to do so, or if he should have died with his men."

"I would not run," said Brook. "Dantas was a coward and brought dishonour on the Elbrand. If I met him I would not hesitate in killing him."

"If you got the chance," said Flindas. "He may surprise you and win out."

"You know him!" exclaimed Brook. "How is this? It is thought that he died in the Regions. His name has not come to us for many years."

"I know him as Dantas," said Flindas. "Though to all others that is not his known name. He was my teacher and friend and I would defend his honour. Any man can be overcome by fear. More than once I have run when I could see that no other option lay open to me."

Brook became silent and thoughtful.

"Well Kerran," Tolth said. "It seems our champions here have other plans for the evening and Verardian also I believe. I hope I do not dine alone tonight."

"No Tolth, it would be my pleasure," replied Kerran.

They left the two victors to their treatment and rode back to the parklands where Kerran found Rark being made a fuss of by a parade of colourfully dressed children. A large fire burned and it was obvious that a party was being organised for the evening. Rark wore garlands of flowers and allowed the small children to ride him around the park. Nup was there and assured Kerran that Rark was in good hands.

"Come to my workrooms," said Tolth to Kerran, leading him to the Council Building. "There are things there that may interest you. I have not shown you before as I have been busy with other work. Let us see what we can find, for I saw your interest the first night you arrived."

As they entered the doorway of the building Storm suddenly flew down from above and landed on the step. It was obvious that he too wanted to enter the old man's study and workshop.

"Well, well," said Tolth with a laugh. "This bird certainly does have its own mind. Come, let us go in."

They walked down the hallway, Storm's talons scratching on the stonework. With a sudden beating of wings the hawk landed on the shoulder of Tolth, who took it as no surprise.

"He has never done that to me," said Kerran in wonder. "I have often wished that he would allow me to carry him, but he has always remains aloof."

"I think Storm and I understand much about each other," said Tolth as he opened the door to his rooms. "He is a wise bird and I believe that one day his offspring will hatch here on Zeta and fulfil the prophecy."

They entered the rooms and Storm left Tolth to alight on a table covered with papers and thick parchments. Once again Kerran marvelled at the display of wonderful and mysterious objects that cluttered the many shelves. Tolth went to the end of the room and took down a flat piece of stone about one hand span in diameter and showed it to Kerran. Carved into the surface was the likeness of a hawk, wings spread, about to take flight.

"It comes from the original house that was built by Barthol Amitarl to the south of the City Amitarl," said Tolth. "The exact site is not known but this piece has come down through the centuries. When Barthol and Maradass the Philosopher made their pact at the Crossroads it was decided by them who should govern which parts of the land. Barthol chose Andrian for his home and built his house by the ocean on the South Coast. You can see in this stone the remains of small shells, it is the face of the key stone above his doorway."

Tolth took the stone and returned it to the shelf.

"Here is something interesting," he said, taking down a strange contraption of metal and wood that moved and swayed in his hands. Putting it on a table he asked Kerran to place his hand onto a metal plate that faced one side of the apparatus.

"Hold your hand there for a while," said Tolth. "It will take a short time to work."

Kerran watched the instrument closely. Nothing happened for some time and he began to wonder what Tolth was expecting, when all of a sudden it began to glow softly and some of its parts began to move. Kerran pulled his hand away in surprise and for several moments the machine continued to glow and move, then it became still once again.

"One day we will use the heat and light from the sun to bring power to Zeta," said Tolth. "The heat from your hand was enough to begin this toy's machinery. It will take some time to perfect but it will come. With the power of the Seacrest I can do the same thing, but it would be no fun for me to spend my life standing in one place, giving power to all of Zeta." He chuckled at the imagery. "No, no fun at all."

Kerran was curious. "I do not understand," he said. "Do you mean that you can draw light and power from the Seacrest?"

In answer Tolth took the two pieces of the talisman from his pouch and held one in each hand. A light began to glow from his hands and soon the two lights became so bright that they outshone the smokeless torches that had been burning when they had arrived. Kerran shielded his eyes from the yellow brightness as every detail of once dim corners could be seen clearly. The light slowly faded and for a while Kerran had trouble adjusting his eyes to what now appeared to be a very gloomy room.

"It was so bright!" he exclaimed. "I did not know it could do that."

Tolth laid a hand on Kerran's shoulder. "It takes much time and practice to draw forth the true powers in the Seacrest," he said. "I have lived now for many years and still I am not even close to understanding its full potential. The little I do know did not happen in a few days, and of course I have never held all four pieces. The original Seacrest had much power that is for now unknown, though it must be immense."

"What is this?" said Kerran pointing to what appeared to be a ball made of blue glass. Inside he could see an intricately fashioned castle, minute and perfect in every detail. Tolth took it from its place on a wooden cradle and handed it to Kerran.

"There is no magic power in this piece," he said. "Except that the one who fashioned it must have had amazing powers of workmanship. It was found in the ruins of Maradass Castle after the Mad One was vanquished and disappeared into the Broken Lands. It is indeed a model of that castle itself, as it was before its destruction. A child's toy I believe, but a very carefully made one. Perhaps it belonged to Darss as he grew from child to manhood. I do not know. It was discovered and given as a gift to our family."

While they were examining the various objects Storm had been fluttering from table to bench to shelf. He had poked his beak into many corners and turned over a number of scrolls as if looking for something. Tolth had watched him at times and then turned his attention back to Kerran's questions. With his beak and talons Storm was now pulling at an old and tattered scroll that had lain hidden beneath a small mountain of others. He got it free and Tolth went over to the now quiet bird and took up the parchment. Unrolling it he held it under a lamp and Kerran saw that a large section appeared to have been burnt and was missing.

"Ah, so this is what you were searching for," Tolth said, and looked up with curiosity as Storm came and stood at the corner of the scroll.

Kerran looked closely at the old parchment. There were many lines on it as if it were a map of some kind. Words were scrawled across it, and though Kerran had never learned to read he could see that the writing had not been executed by a tidy hand. The scrawled lines ran in many directions and even overlapped in places.

"What is it?" he asked Tolth who stood pondering the scroll, but the old Amitarl did not reply for some time.

"You ask what is it Kerran," Tolth finally said. "Do you know that I have been asking that same question myself for many years. I have never been able to decode its message. It came to me from Landin who took it from the dead hands of one who was a messenger for Maradass. I am sure it is a map but what of I do not know."

Again he looked at Storm. "It is no accident that he should select this," said Tolth. "I believe that it is important and yet I cannot say why."

Tolth drew up a chair and sat bent over the map for some time. Finally he drew a deep breath and leaned back in his chair.

"I do not know," he sighed. "Much detail was lost with the burning. My belief has always been that it is a map of the area surrounding the stronghold of Maradass, somewhere in the Broken Lands. Though where, and to what scale I could not even guess. It is even something of a guess that it has anything to do with where Maradass might be found, though the man who tried to destroy it appeared to be desperate to avoid having it fall into the hands of the Elbrand. There are parts that I think I understand but the whole is a mystery. If Storm believes it important then I must spend more time studying it to try to find the answer, for it may help us in the war that is surely to come."

Storm suddenly pecked at the scroll. He continued to strike at one particular spot, a dark circle that showed near the top of the scroll.

"Yes, the answer is there," said Tolth. "I know it is. If only I could read what Storm can see. Kerran, perhaps you can help.

I have looked into the past for an answer but none has ever come. Would you try? It may work and I believe it could be of great importance."

"Yes I will try," replied Kerran, and then repeated quietly as if to himself. "I will try."

Tolth took Leana's piece of the Seacrest from his pouch and handed it to Kerran. Through the mist the voice came to him. "You must sleep Kerran. It taxes me greatly unless you sleep."

Then the voice was gone and Kerran turned to Tolth. "The voice came," he said. "It has told me that I must sleep, though I doubt if I can just yet. It has been an exciting day and I am not at all sleepy, perhaps later."

"If you wish, I can make you sleep now," said Tolth.

"Yes, if you think you can," smiled Kerran. "Now that would be magic."

"It is no magic," replied Tolth. "It is an ancient art taught to the people by the black men of the desert a long time ago. Here Kerran, lie down on this couch and we will begin."

Kerran lay down and Tolth sat beside him. His voice became soft and slow.

"Look at the light above you Kerran. It is bright, see the brightness and watch it closely.

Tolth's voice grew quieter. "It is becoming dimmer. You can see it losing its strength. It is losing its power. Your eyelids are getting heavy. The light is fading. Your eyes are closing. Let it happen. Do not fight it. Sleep now, gently sleep."

Kerran's eyelids became so heavy that he could not keep them open. They closed and slowly he drifted into an easy sleep.

Kerran walked in the safe comforting mist and the voice came again.

"I am here Kerran. What is it that you wish to know?"

"Tolth has a map," said Kerran in his mind. "It is a scroll taken from a messenger of Maradass. We need to know what it means."

"Yes," said the voice again. "I can see it in your mind, and yet I cannot tell you what it may be for I have no memory of it. The only way that you may find the key is for me to leave you, then your unguided dreams may reveal the answer."

There was silence in Kerran's mind. He was aware that his body slept, but his mind wandered in thoughts of the past days, and a soft mist continued to surround him. Kerran then heard many running feet. There were others in the haze, all hastening in the same direction, and then Kerran was moving with them.

Ahead there was a sudden clash of swords and a scream of pain pierced the fog as the runners joined in the battle. All was confusion. Men in heavy black armour fought against the lightly clad Elbrand. There was one of the Elbrand who fought so swiftly and with such mastery that none could stand against him. Kerran saw three powerful men fall quickly to his short sword. The warrior held no other weapon or shield. Indeed he had but one arm to fight with and Kerran could see that the other must be strapped inside his breastplate. Kerran knew then that this was Landin Elfhand who fought against the soldiers of Maradass sometime in the recent past. With a final cry the last of the enemy died and Landin leaned on his sword. He stooped and took a scroll from the dead hand of one black swordsman who had been attempting to burn it. Landin looked at the map briefly and then placed it in his travelling pouch, then he turned away and the Elbrand disappeared into the thickening fog.

Kerran dreamed on, flying high above a forbidding land which he knew must be the Broken Lands. Below him lay a barren realm where huge fissures cut the threatening terrain into many bleak mountains and ravines. Scattered dark plants grew there, and only an occasional stream of brackish water was to be seen. Red brown earth glared up at him from below and in all directions nothing moved. The sun was lowering to the horizon as he flew northward into the coming darkness. All night he flew, a pale thin moon lighting his way. It was just as the sun was rising on the following day that he saw far ahead a bleak and desolate mountain range surrounded by a flat open plain. Occasionally he saw the thin band of a road which twisted its way through the shattered land. He flew over many crumbling peaks until ahead he could see one mountain loftier than all the others. Clinging to its side stood a dark and forbidding castle; Kerran saw no gate. A vile and putrid river, as red as the surrounding deserts, ran sluggishly from a gap at the base of its walls. It oozed down the rock face and collected in a stagnant lake in the valley below. The river did not appear to have an outlet and yet it must, for it did not fill beyond a certain height. A road skirted the lake shore while hills of broken stone filled a large part of the valley.

Kerran flew above the castle. There was a corruption there that was beyond anything he had ever felt. It was as if totally evil hands reached up to clutch him and draw him downward in its grasp; suddenly he began to fall. Kerran cried out. Fear grasped him and he cried out again. A hand came from nowhere and held his. He clutched the hand and the great fear and darkness slowly lifted from him. A voice called his name over and over, and his mind began to return to the real world. His eyes fluttered and opened. Tolth sat beside him holding his hand and calling his name.

"Kerran, come back," he said one last time.

Kerran blinked and was once again in the cluttered room, Storm stood on a table nearby, watching closely. There was concern in Tolth's voice.

"I am sorry Kerran," he said. "It was too much to ask. I should not expect so much of you."

"No," replied Kerran as he wearily sat up. "If it will help to defeat Maradass then it is little to pay."

His head swam and his throat was parched. It took some time before he was able to describe his dream to Tolth. "It is an evil place of power and dread," he said. "If you go in search of Maradass I believe that you will find him there. It is far to the north and the land is burnt and hostile."

Tolth passed the map to Kerran. "Do you recognise anything here?" he asked. "Can you say if this is a map of those lands?"

Kerran studied the parchment. "Yes," he said finally. "If the centre of this top pattern is the mountain and castle then some of it appears to make sense. I saw a road that passed through tunnels and many deep gullies." He pointed to a line that wriggled like a snake through the central part of the parchment. "If this line is the road," he said. "Then the places that it does not appear could be where it passes beneath the rock."

Tolth was encouraged and pawed over the map. "We have no idea of the scale," he said. "Can you say how far you travelled above the actual mountain range before you saw the castle?"

Kerran thought for a time. "I would guess perhaps three or four leagues," he said. "It is hard to judge when you are flying like a bird."

Tolth chuckled then spoke slowly, calculating. "So if this area is the mountain range, and we assume that the map is oriented to the North then..." He puzzled over it for a few moments. "We are fortunate that the burning did not destroy the bottom corner," he said thoughtfully. "It is only a rough calculation but I would say that it is approximately thirty leagues to the bottom of the parchment. I hazard that the bottom of the map, though it is burnt, could prove to be near the Border Road. Somewhere thirty leagues north from that road may lie the stronghold of Maradass, how far east or west I could not even guess."

Tolth wanted to make an exact copy of the map and as Kerran wanted air he decided to go outside and watch the festivities in the parklands. Rark joined him as he left the building and he soon found himself drawn to the largest fire, where people sang and danced. A keg of ale had been broached and food lay spread on long wooden tables. Tolth had forgotten completely about dinner but at the fire Kerran's presence was welcomed by all.

"Our young hero has come to join us," one called to the others.

He was clapped on the back and a tankard forced into his hand. It was a dark brew and Kerran sipped slowly, unaccustomed to the bitter taste. He stood by the fire, a flush in his cheeks, and told his story to those many who wished to hear it first hand. There were countless questions, and as new people joined the circle he found himself returning several times to the beginning of his tale. There were many children and young people at the fire and some listened, while others imitated their heroes from the Games and fought out mock battles upon the grass. Wooden swords and spears were wielded by the young ferocious warriors. There were faces that Kerran knew from the Games, either in the field or in the crowd. He sipped at his tankard which never seemed to be quite empty, and retold so many parts of his story that soon he was confusing himself.

For a time he joined some of the older boys in a wrestling match and though he was strong, he was thrown by all of them. The art of wrestling came to them almost as soon as they were able to walk. Some of the young women also joined in the matches and Kerran was amazed by their skill. Piata, who had run in the Games, was also there, and he watched in admiration as she threw one of her larger male opponents. Kerran applauded and she caught his eye. It was a look of curiosity and after her bout she came across to where he was standing.

"You look a little drunk, young hero," she said to him with a smile.

Kerran felt his face flush even more and could not seem to speak.

"You need not be bothered by it," she continued. "'Tis a good night to celebrate. I would like to hear your story sometime but not now, I have quite a few young men to annoy. Enjoy yourself tonight."

Then she was gone, back to join the wrestling.

That night Kerran dreamed, his mind wide awake while his body slept on his bed in a dark room on Zeta. He walked in a wood of tall and slender trees with white and grey trunks; they shed long strips of bark to the forest floor. They did not grow closely together and it was easy for Kerran to walk through the low undergrowth. A flock of large black birds flew over him, Kerran counted more than forty of them. Yellow feathers decorated their tails and as they passed there was a single raucous call. He disturbed the strangest of animals. It stood on its hind legs with the help of a large tail, and its forepaws were like small hands able to hold its food. It had a long grey face with deep watchful eyes that looked at Kerran without fear.

Its ears were large and stood up from the sides of its head, listening, then in a bound it turned and disappeared into the underbrush.

Kerran had never seen or heard of such an animal. He then looked above to where a large white bird with the most raucous cry startled him, and then he almost fell over a cliff, it had been screened by the bush and he felt his body jerk sharply as it lay in bed. He stepped back from the edge and looked beyond to where a deep green valley spread before him to the far blue horizon. Looking down onto the tops of the forest his eyes were drawn to far off cliffs.

To his right, in a curve of the nearer cliff he saw a waterfall that cascaded in long drops to the valley floor. Near the waterfall, and perhaps halfway down the cliff, he could see a thin stream of smoke emerging from what appeared to be an overhanging cave. Kerran saw where a path led down to this precarious abode and he made his way along the edge until he came to the stream, beyond it he could see a cleared area. Assorted wooden implements lay about near a cold fire, and a path led to the edge of the sharp drop. It was not an easy descent and both hands were needed at times to negotiate the narrow way, sometimes the path led behind the falls. The sunlight turned the drops to glittering strings of gems and sparkling bands of colour.

He came to the wide rock shelf before the cave. It was a deep overhang open to the magnificent view to the south and west. Kerran stopped at the entrance to the cave. A black man sat by a small fire at the back of the cave and turned some meat that cooked in the embers. The man was old, long grey hair flowed over his shoulders, and thin whiskers covered his lower face.

"Come in Kerran Shalastar," he said in a strongly accented voice without turning from his fire.

Kerran thought that he pronounced his second name quite differently, but did not know where the difference lay. Soon he had forgotten it as the ancient black man continued to speak, as if he knew his young visitor.

"You have come this far so you may as well sit by my fire

like real people do," he said.

Kerran approached and sat on the earth floor near the low flames. He opened his mouth but found he could not make a sound.

"No," said the black man with a strange glint in his dark eyes. "There is no need for you to speak just now; all you need do is to listen. My name is Manzanee and I am able to enter your dream world if I choose, and today this is what I choose. I am older than all peoples, and I have lived far into your future."

The black man paused, turning the dark meat again. "You will need great courage young Kerran," he said quietly. "When the time comes you will know. Be strong, and think then of what you are about to learn now." Manzanee leaned forward, his dark searching eyes peering into Kerran's own.

"The key lies in the mind of Zard," he said. "A time will come when you must place your life into his hands, though I will not tell you why. Do not be afraid of it. Remember this when the time comes."

The meat seemed over cooked and charred but Manzanee gave it another turn.

"Give me your hand," he said, and Kerran held out his left hand.

Manzanee took it, and then with a deft movement of his knife he made a small cut at the base of the thumb. Blood flowed from the wound and Manzanee scooped a little into a small bowl with the blade of his knife. Kerran put the cut hand to his mouth and tasted the blood, there was no fear in him, only wonder.

"Go now," said Manzanee with a leering almost comical grin. "Tell Tolth. He will not know the meaning any more than you do, but he too will understand it in the end, as indeed you all must. Remember to answer Zard with your will, for all of the lands, as far as the Western Sea will be affected by this. All who live in these troubled times will be touched by your choices young Shalastar. Go now and dream your dreams in peace."

Kerran woke late and felt almost light hearted. Dreams after all were usually just dreams, and then he saw the small cut near the thumb of his left hand. He was wondering about the small sharp knife from his strange dream when Nup looked in to announce breakfast; Kerran dressed quickly and ate hungrily. After breakfast he called on Tolth to tell him of the strange dream. Tolth was in his rooms below and was working over several ancient scrolls, the map being one of them.

"Come in Kerran," he smiled. "I am attempting to decipher some of that which is written on the map."

"I had a most unusual dream," said Kerran and Tolth looked at him quizzically. "There was a black man in it called Manzanee."

Tolth let out a sharp strangled cry. "Manzanee! Did you talk with him? Tell me."

Kerran told of his dream, with Tolth making sure he left nothing out. Even the terrain down to the smallest detail interested him.

"Who is this Manzanee?" asked Kerran finally. "You know him, though somehow I think not in this world."

"He comes into many of my attempts to decipher the future," replied Tolth. "I have talked with him at times over my lifetime but not often. He tells of things that may happen centuries into the future or in the ancient past. He describes it all as 'the larger circle', and he says that the future can determine the past. He treats it as something of a game I believe and has set me many riddles. His intent seems neither for good nor evil. There are times when a simple word has had me puzzled for days, often without answer. He is older than all, and if he is to believed he lives on into the future. I puzzle now at his words on Zard. You still seem bound in the happenings of these times Kerran. You carried the Seacrest to us and perhaps thought that your task was done, as did I. I do hope that it never comes to you placing your life in the hands of the Black Knight. I will think on this for a time, the words of Manzanee can mean many things, even things that will never be, or ever were. Manzanee is a paradox in himself, a puzzle that I have never been able to solve."

"I have another piece of a puzzle that may not even concern this Manzanee," said Kerran. "But it sounds like the same strange man."

"Tell me," said Tolth, his eyes searching Kerran's face.

"On my journey here I had many dreams," replied Kerran. "I have told you of these but some that seemed to be less important or even forgotten for a time have yet to be told to you. I had almost forgotten this one as I dreamed it when I was near death from dog bite on the Old Coast Road. There was an old woman who told me a story. It concerned one called Larnus who was the son of the fisherman who found the Seacrest in the Sea of Shardis. The Seacrest came to this Larnus and with its power he became rich. He met a Blackman who said that he could be king. He was told to bury the Seacrest for a time at the place that would later become the Crossroads. This was part of some magic need that I was not told of. Larnus became ruthless and greedy and finally became king.

"His kingdom was destroyed by one who's family Larnus had killed at the Crossroads years before. The Blackman came to Larnus as he stood near defeat. Larnus complained, saying the Blackman had said he could be king. The Blackman replied that he could be king, but not that he should be king. The Seacrest was passed on to his conqueror, one called Drangmar, who in turn became a tyrant along with his heirs. It is the ruins of Drangmar castle that remain at the crossroads of the Regions. The old woman told me that the Seacrest would eventually corrupt any who held it. I believe she meant the complete talisman and not the fragments. She said to mark these words well as they are in some way connected to my own family history."

"Drangmar," said Tolth darkly. "That family were the scourge of the lands for centuries, long before the time of Maradass and Amitarl. Yes, that sounds like the Manzanee that I know, yes, a play on words that destroyed a kingdom. How your own family history can possibly be connected with Drangmar I could not even guess at. You are a strange young man Master Kerran Shalastar. I think it was not by mere chance that you were there in the forest on that sad yet surprising day."

The Council met the following day, the meeting was held in a much larger chamber of the building and many people came to listen. It would be a decision open to a vote. Tolth spoke and told of the discovery of the night before and a copy of the map was passed through many hands. Discussion moved from the map to the sending of Elbrand to the Broken Lands. It was not until the afternoon that the members of the company were decided upon. There would be five in the party and Brook would lead. Of the other three Kerran knew them all from the Games: Teaker, Simo and Rian were chosen, while Flindas would be the other member of the company. Time was felt to be of great importance and a sailboat stood stocked and ready at the quay. They would sail with the early tide on the following day.

That last evening Flindas ate his meal on Zeta in the home of Tolth Amitarl. He would board in the early morning and the conversation at dinner was mostly of the coming journey and search. Flindas talked about the prospects of discovering the whereabouts of Landin. If he was in hiding he could be impossible to find; if he travelled then he would be noticed.

"There are many eyes in the Broken Lands," said Flindas, "I do not wish to venture into the Northern Desolation unless we must. We take a copy of the map but I hope we do not need it. We will be looking for Elfhand not Maradass."

It was a sombre evening, even Rark felt the occasion. He kept coming to Flindas and resting his great head on his friend's shoulder. It was late in the night when Flindas was called to the ship and his last farewell was brief.

"Look after Rark for me Kerran," he said scratching the mountain dog behind his ears. "I will miss his great presence, and you Kerran, I will miss you also. We may be gone a long time. Enjoy Zeta for me while I am away."

He turned and walked down the path and was gone into the night, a shadow flew low across the sky as Storm followed the figure towards the docks. It was remarked in the early dawn that Storm was seen flying above the small ship as it sailed south around the coast and into the open sea.

To Viris-Tan-Vara

On the first day of their voyage Brook called a meeting on deck after the noon meal. There was not much discussion as the plan was simple; they were to land south of Viris-Tan-Vara at a place that was known to be a safe harbour. They would then travel north until they came to the old city, and there they would begin their search. When Flindas spoke of his knowledge of the Broken Lands Simo scoffed.

"You expect us to believe that you have spent years on the Borders and yet not lost your mind. Tis said all go crazy who stay there long."

Simo had been noticeably unfriendly to Flindas since they had arrived on board and Brook spoke strongly to him.

"I trust this man and his word," he said. "He has spent much time in the Broken Lands. Few of the Elbrand have travelled that way. Forget your differences, Simo. Call a truce."

There was silence for a time and then Flindas continued.

"It is possible to survive in the Broken Lands without being caught by their diseases," he told them. "Or by the pollution that brings the sickness of the wandering mind. Much is corrupted there but not all go insane. We were not born in the Broken Lands. We are strong and healthy and can survive there."

Simo turned away and looked to the sea as Brook spoke.

"With a fair wind the captain has told me that we should make our crossing in ten days," he said.

Then Teaker spoke up for the first time, the small man had a voice that always seemed about to turn into laughter, and often did. "Can you say how long we may be away from Zeta?" he asked. "If Landin is not to be found we must return sometime."

In reply Brook turned to Flindas. "How long do you think Flindas?" asked the big man. "How long to find out what we need to know?"

Flindas thought for some time. "If we have no word of him in Viris-Tan-Vara then we could search for years," he said with a wry smile. "I know people in the old city and it may be the information they hold that will determine how long we stay on the Northern Borders. I cannot say until we reach Viris."

Rian now spoke, he was a strong quiet man, tall and broad in the shoulders. A thick beard and long hair obscured much of his appearance. "Has anyone else noticed that we have company?" he said and pointed to the sky where Storm flew above the main mast.

"Cursed bird," said Simo scowling at the sky. "If it were not for that creature I could have won a green belt. If it comes near me I will wring its neck."

"No you will not," said Brook. "And I cannot believe you would either. It is the sign of Amitarl and if it were not for that family Zeta would still be a dead and terrible place, and our lives, if we lived at all, would not be as they are. Leave the bird, Simo. I do not know why it spoilt your aim at the Games."

"It wanted our outsider here to win," was the bitter reply. "If I had not scored high in the other events I would not be here. It almost cost me my one chance to go to the Regions. Just keep it away from me."

Simo left the group and went below.

"He will come around," said Brook. "He is a good man, though a little hot headed."

"Tolth had a thought on why the bird spoiled Simo's aim," Flindas said quietly as if Simo might hear his words.

Brook looked at his friend with the question unspoken.

"Tolth thought that Simo should not be on this quest," Flindas continued. "He said that he feared that Simo would not return to Zeta."

"If any other had said such a thing I would laugh at his words," said Teaker. "But the words of Tolth are not to be taken lightly in such things."

"We will watch and wait," said Brook. "There is little else that we can do in this matter without annoying Simo further."

The meeting was over and the men went about their various callings. Teaker and Rian played a throwing game using three pieces of wood carved into pyramid shapes and covered with runes. They played it at great speed, having learned it as children. The small man's laughter would burst forth at each throw, and at times he would leap to his feet in glee and dance about the deck. Teaker had been to the Regions before and had fought marauders; scars from the dog's fangs showed on both of his arms. Flindas stood by the railing, watching the ocean go by and felt the pleasant pulsing of the ship as it chopped through the small waves.

"And why are you here?" he said, turning to Storm, who had found a good berth amongst a coil of rope near the tall single mast.

Storm ignored him and continued to sit quietly, unmoving, as Flindas turned back to his contemplation of the sea.

Their ocean voyage for the first seven days was uneventful. An almost constant wind from the south had pushed them further to the north than the captain had wished. He did not seem overly concerned with their situation until the morning of the eighth day, when in the early dawn he called for all to come on deck. The five fighting men joined the crew at the rail, without a word the captain pointed to the ocean. Flindas could see nothing unusual until he looked into the depths. There he saw fish, schools of many kinds, and all swam the same way in great haste. They fled from the north, with none caring to eat or interfere with their usual prey that swam beside them. There were dolphins too. Leaping from the sea but not in play, they swam as fast as they could southward. A school of whales, creatures that Flindas had rarely seen before, came to the surface, their great tails arching gracefully above the tide, they too were turned to the south in haste.

"I do not understand it," said the captain. "I have sailed many parts of the great ocean but I have never seen this."

Members of the crew shook their heads and talked among themselves, and there was fear to be heard in not a few voices. Brook spoke to the captain.

"What do you suggest?" he asked. "They flee from something; perhaps we too should alter our course."

The captain stood stroking his beard. "Today I was to make the decision of when to change our tack and sail south and west," he said. "It appears that the time has come, for there seems much amiss to the north."

He called instructions to his crew and in a short time the ship was heading south and west, the small ship complaining as it lurched into position.

"The going will be harder now," said the captain to Brook. "The wind is no longer with us. Whatever lies to the north may well be upon us before we make landfall. I do not know what it is, but I fear it all the same."

For the remainder of the day and part of the next the fish continued to travel south. They took no heed of the ship and swam by in great, fast moving schools. Their numbers diminished during the late afternoon, and then just at sunset, all on board the ship noticed a dark red line on the horizon far to the north. It was not the setting sun but none could say what it was, and it was soon lost in the gathering darkness. Flindas spent the night on deck, the moon watched over the sea for a time and Brook joined him in the early dawn.

"I do not like this business," he said confiding with Flindas. "I will fight any enemy that I can stand against, but who can stand firm on a ship that may sink at any time. I cannot stand firm on water."

"I like it not myself," said Flindas. "I have sailed much, but my heart and strength are on dry land."

He was about to continue when Storm gave a cry and flew aloft, the bird climbed high into the dawn until the sun caught his white wings far above.

"The dawn comes," said Teaker as he joined them at the rail. "I am not a superstitious man but I feel a great weight on me that I cannot laugh away." He chuckled all the same. "Perhaps if I go back to bed it will disappear," he said and then became silent.

Together they watched the sun rise behind the ship, and then they all saw that the ocean had turned an ugly muddy red colour, stretching to the distant northern horizon. It spread from east to west in an unbroken line as far as they could see.

"What in the name of all devils?" exclaimed Rian as he and Simo joined them, but none could answer him.

"Maradass," someone said.

Captain and crew were now all gathered at the rail.

"We will not outrun it," said the captain. "It has gained much on us during the night. There is nothing we can do but sail on."

He ordered his disturbed crew to work, and the smell of breakfast was soon wafting up through the main hatch. As they ate their meal the redness overtook them. It lapped against the side of the ship and they watched it with anticipation but nothing happened. The ocean turned red all about the ship but did no harm. One of the crew threw a metal bottle overboard attached to a string.

"Do not touch it," called the captain but it was too late, the crewman had poured a little into the palm of his hand.

"It seems to be just red water," he said as the captain approached.

"I care not," was his reply. "Get it back over the side. I feel evil in it."

The seaman obeyed the order, throwing the bottle and string to the sea.

"No one else is to touch it," called the captain to his crew and passengers.

During the afternoon the sailor who had touched the water became violently ill, a savage fever raging through his body. His hand, where he had touched the water, became swollen, with streaks of red running up his arm beneath the skin. At times he screamed in pain. Flindas offered his healing knowledge but found he could do nothing for the stricken man. No herb or potion that Flindas tried would do any good.

"It is something stronger than any medicine I have," he said. "We can do little but give him water and wait."

They did not have to wait long, before the sun rose the following day the man gave a last cry of pain and died.

"I will not put him over the side," said the captain looking at the red sea about them. "He was a good man and deserves better than to be put into that."

They wrapped his body in sail cloth and stowed it below.

"I will give him a decent burial when we reach land," said the captain. "If this red horror has reached Zeta then I fear for our people."

During the day the wind, which had remained constant from the south for several days slowly died, and the sails hung loose from the mast. The crew who had been showing the strain caused by the strange sea now became vocal in their dread, and there was little that the captain could do to allay their fears.

"We are not far from land," he told them. "Few of us have been becalmed before but it is part of a sailor's lot. Do not touch the water and we will get through this. We would be in much more danger if a storm blew up."

Flindas and the Elbrand sat about the deck. They talked little, turning often to look at the redness that surrounded them. The day wore on and the wind did not return as they drifted at the whim of the currents. They were not alone on the ocean. Many dead fish and occasional seabirds floated on the surface. Nothing seemed able to live in the poison that had once been their natural home.

Many of the men aboard slept restlessly that night. Flindas, who slept on deck, found himself joined by most of the crew and passengers at different times during the night. Conversation was held in hushed voices as if the ocean may hear them and bring forth some greater horror. Brook and Teaker sat with Flindas, talking of their lives on Zeta, of their families and the tranquil life they had left behind. Flindas was a little envious as they spoke of loved ones and the joy of their children. Both Brook and Teaker had found it hard to leave Zeta but the adventure was the culmination of all the training they had been through. This is what they were best at. The constant threat of Maradass had kept the Isles of Zeta in readiness, and when a person found they were suited to the ways of the warrior, they would risk everything to test themselves against the real enemy.

The dawn came bleak and cold, but to their relief, far ahead, they could see the mainland. During the afternoon a slight breeze came from the north and stirred the sails and the captain ordered his crew to their stations. The breeze grew into a considerable wind by the late afternoon and the captain spoke earnestly at the evening meal.

"There is a storm coming," he said, and pointed to the north where dark clouds had been climbing behind them. "We will not reach our hoped for landing to the south. To get out of this red horror we may have to take the ship through the narrow headlands and into the harbour of Viris-Tan-Vara. We would probably lose the ship to the town's council but we would get away with out lives. I do not wish to die from this evil. I know where we are on the coast now and if this wind keeps up we will be at the harbour mouth by early morning. The wind is increasing a little all the time, so because of the danger I feel that all who are not needed should remain below. On deck we will wear our oiled clothing and cover our faces. I do not know what a single drop of this red ocean could do and I care not to find out."

After the meal all went below where Flindas found the confined quarters not to his liking. He attempted to sleep, and during the night was awakened a number of times as the ships timbers creaked in complaint at the increase of movement in the ocean. He looked from the hatchway and saw that the captain was at the helm. All the crew were below with only two men on watch from another hatch. Every so often a wave, a little bigger than the rest, would send fine spray through the air and Flindas watched as the captain ducked away from it. Flindas slept again until he was shaken awake by Brook.

"The captain is sick," he said.

Flindas went to the man and found him in deep fever and

pain. One side of his face was covered in red blotches with dark bruising spreading from his neck to his shoulder. A sort of insanity had crept into the captain's eyes, his second in command now stood at the helm, covered totally except for a narrow slit from which his eyes gazed in fear. If he were to fall ill there was little hope that others of the crew would take his place. One of the crew told them that he thought their chances without sail would be small. The wind was now coming from a more easterly quarter of north and being shipwrecked on the inhospitable Withered Coast, that stretched a great many leagues either side of the safe harbour, would be most likely. Viris-Tan-Vara was a safe harbour but its narrow heads could be easily missed in darkness.

About this time the captain breathed his last and for much of the night they sailed on until far ahead they could see the lights of the old city.

"The harbour entrance is close," said one of the sailors hopefully. "We will attempt it, but you must all stay below."

The wind pushed them hard as they neared the coast and the lights had gone now. All that could be seen in the gloom was the darkness of the cliffs as they loomed above the small ship. The crew returned to the deck as they would soon be attempting the heads. In anticipation Flindas and the Elbrand waited. In days gone by it was said that a prudent captain would wait for dawn rather than attempt the narrow passage by night. In a high wind and near darkness none but desperate men would even consider it.

There was a call from above as the ship gave a shudder and turned towards the wall of cliffs. Ahead of them could be glimpsed the flicker of the city lights. They were into the narrow space, waves beating against jagged rock and high windswept cliffs. For a time it seemed as if they would pass unscathed, then a strong gust pushed the ship sharply until it scraped against rock. Timbers cried out and splintered and water began to enter the ship and the men below rushed up on deck. There was little wind now and they were almost through the heads, but the damage had been done. The ship was doomed.

"We do not sink fast!" called the first mate. "We have a chance of reaching a beach to the south of the harbour"

They were through the heads when the gale that had been increasing came on in a fury, waves crashing onto the deck. The ship floundered, a splintering of wood told that more of its hull was giving way under the pressure of the ocean. There was now no possibility of avoiding the deadly water, and soon all on board were drenched. The doomed ship crashed against the rocks and began to break up, while the lights of the old city beckoned to them enticingly from across the wide bay. Another violent gust tore at the ship. Flindas heard a scream and was thrown against the railing. He clung to his pack. There was little else he could do but wrap his arms around the wooden rail and hope that they stayed afloat. His hope was in vain.

The ship was again forced onto the rocks, and then heeled over and began to go down. Flindas found himself in thrashing water, and then a crashing wave flung him against the rocks. Battered into submission he let go of his pack. The weight of his weapons and other gear sending it to the bottom. He swam away from the cliffs then removed his heavy jacket; his boots had to go too. Voices called to his left nearer the cliffs, and then he struck out for the lights of Viris-Tan-Vara. The storm drove him southward and the crashing of waves on rock warned him away from danger. He swam with all his strength. In the Games he had shown that though he swam slowly he could swim for a great period of time. Someone was swimming not far away from him. It was Brook who called out to him.

"Make for the beach on the south side," called the big man. "It will not be far."

His voice died away as the wind howled at them from the narrow passage of the heads. Flindas struck out again, the distant lights his only guide. Waves thundered onto rocks nearby.

"Is it all in vain?" he asked himself. "I am swimming in a poisoned sea. Tomorrow I will die in a raving fever."

It seemed hopeless, but he kept swimming and the sea became quieter as he reached more open water. Flindas kept to the south side, avoiding any sound of waves breaking on rock, he was alone and when he called to Brook he received no answer. Rain began to fall and obscured the lights ahead. All grew dark and he could see nothing about him, the sound of waves thundering onto rocks seemed to come from a number of directions. Suddenly, just above his head, there was a flash of white, then it was gone. A few moments later it came again, much closer this time, almost touching the surface of the water directly in front of him. The beat of white wings flashed by and disappeared into the gloom.

"Storm," Flindas thought to himself.

The bird was there and trying to help. Again the white hawk flew by and again in the same direction from what Flindas could judge in the near darkness. He struck out, following the course that Storm had shown him, and twice more the bird flew close by, guiding him. Flindas changed his direction slightly each time to follow the hawk, until finally he could hear waves thudding onto a beach not far ahead. He let his feet float down and they eventually touched sand. Flindas stumbled through the breakers and collapsed on the beach. He lay there for some time, the waves reaching him as they broke on the sands. Struggling to his feet as rain lashed at him Flindas was driven to seek shelter in the darkness, moving up the beach until he felt vegetation underfoot. Tall reeds of some sort grew thickly amongst the sand and boulders. Flindas was cold and bruised and the wind cut through his shirt like iced daggers. Crouching, and finally crawling, he made his way amongst the reeds and finally found a sheltered place behind a large rock. Still the darkness enveloped him. With his training he began a practice which he had learned from Dantas many years before. He quietened his mind slowly, taking his thoughts through his body, imagining fire and warmth in each limb, each joint, and each tired muscle. He concentrated in this way for a very long time. Any thought that came to his mind he let go of it and returned to the fire. The chill in his body began to disperse. A warm glow took over Flindas as he continued to fight the cold. He did not know how long he spent in this way. The night was old now, the storm abating, passing south down the coast. Flindas pictured a roaring fire and kept it before his concentrated mind. The rain ceased and he lay, crouched behind his boulder, and not long before dawn he fell into a weary but warm sleep.

Flindas woke with a start. The sun glaring sharply into his eyes. He could hear voices not far away and he rose cautiously from his position to find himself near to the foot of a cliff that towered above him. He looked from behind the boulder. The voices came from beyond the reeds and he made his way towards them with quiet stealth. Eventually he came to the last of the vegetation and looked through it to where he could see Brook and Simo, who sat talking with one of the sailors from their ill-fated craft. He was the first mate who had braved the ocean after the fall of the captain. Flindas stepped from his cover and the men turned with surprise.

"Flindas!" called Brook with a broad smile. "We thought you were gone. I am glad to see you made it here alive."

Simo barely acknowledged his presence.

"What of the poison?" said Flindas. "Are none of you ill yet?"

"Look," said Brook in reply and pointed to the ocean.

To his surprise Flindas saw that it was the colour that the ocean should be.

"Either we sailed beyond it in the night," said Brook. "Or for some reason it did not enter the harbour, whichever way we are safe and alive it seems."

"What of the others?" said Flindas, his eyes searched up and down the beach.

"No sign of them," replied Brook. "Teaker and Rian are both good swimmers. Perhaps they and the rest of the crew managed to land elsewhere. We can only hope."

Flindas sat with them now. The sun was warm and the stiffness of the night began to leave his limbs.

"We have been talking," said Brook. "Now that you are here it will be easier for us. We have lost almost everything, but before we left Zeta Tolth gave me these for an emergency."

From a small pouch he shook loose a number of gems and glittering stones. "Though these stones are common and of little value on Zeta, Tolth said that much store is put on them in the Regions," he said. "We can make our way with these for a time if we can get a good price in this place Viris-Tan-Vara. You know its ways, so what do you think? Can we find weapons and all of the other things that we might need?"

"To find a good price will be impossible," said Flindas. "We will get a price, perhaps half what they would be worth in the City Amitarl. We should be able to re-equip and have enough to spare for a while. Horses we will not get for any price. They are treasured, and well guarded by those few who own them. There is little game in the Broken Lands and horse meat is a great prize here. Some will eat anything, including other humans if they can get a chance. Guard against even the feeblest looking hand. It may carry a knife that seeks to carve your flesh."

Brook shuddered and said nothing.

"And you tell us that this is not a place of madness," said Simo with scorn. "How soon before a hoard of mad ones descend on us and begin to gnaw our bones?"

"I did not say there was no madness here," said Flindas, a flicker of anger in his voice. "The madness is everywhere and is always more intense in those who are born here, but there are sane people too. There are business men who deal with those from the north. There are weapon makers, and there are those who make a living from supplying or growing food. Even the mad are not without some understanding. The totally insane do not survive for long on the borders. Many are killed when young, their parents knowing what they are, cannot let them live."

"It sounds like a wonderful place," said Simo contemptuously.

Brook turned again to Flindas.

"Is there some way to reach the city from here?" he asked. "All I see is sheer cliffs. Do we swim again?"

"No," replied Flindas. "I have not been this side of the harbour before but I have been told that there is a path that reaches from Viris to the heads."

"We will probably have to climb these cliffs," he said glancing upwards. "They do not look easy."

All looked up and surveyed the possibilities.

"Let us walk further along the beach," said Brook. "Perhaps

we can find an easier way."

They stood and began to trudge through the deep sand. Each at times would turn to the sea, hoping to find their missing companions coming ashore, but there was no sign of them. Apart from the beach where they walked, there seemed to be nowhere else that a man may have landed in safety. Ahead of them the beach came to an abrupt end, overhanging cliffs undercut by the ocean looked impossible to pass. They had almost come to this point when Simo pointed upward.

"There," he said. "Can you see the path against the cliff face?"

"It looks more like a goat trail," said Blass the ship's mate. "And you would have to be a fly to get up to it."

Blass had not been trained as the others, his expertise was with the sea and he looked in dismay as Simo began the steep ascent.

"I will not make it," Blass said to Brook. "You will have to leave me here."

"We will not leave you," replied Brook and he carefully studied Simo as the young man continued to climb. Brook then turned to Blass, who was a small and wiry man.

"If you can cling to my back I think that I can climb this," he said.

"It will be hard," said Flindas. "Why not wait until we can find a rope? Simo and I can go ahead and search."

"No," said Brook. "We go together. Who knows what dangers you may come upon?"

Saying this he flung the surprised Blass across his shoulders and began the climb. Blass clung to Brook, fear showing clearly in his weather-beaten face.

Flindas watched them until Brook was well above. Simo seemed almost to reach the top and soon disappeared from view, then Flindas began to follow. His weariness from the battering of the ocean had not yet left him. He climbed carefully, not wishing to make a mistake. The top seemed a long way off and he heard the words of Dantas in his memory.

"Do not look down when you climb," his old teacher had told him. "Only a fool reflects on what is gone. Stay totally in the present. Move one limb at a time, hand or foot, never more. Test each hold before putting your weight on it."

He remembered the terrible test of height and strength that Dantas had once asked of him, a climb that had taken him up the sheer stone walls of Celisor Castle. It was an extremely dangerous undertaking that struck fear into any who had attempted it. Flindas kept this in mind as he continued up the cliff face. He was weary and bruised and there seemed to be no feeling in his fingertips. He hung on for some time unable to continue, breathing deeply, his face pressed hard against the rock.

"No time for resting," came a booming voice, and the large hand of Brook was hauling him upward.

Flindas forced his limbs to move and within moments he was lying on flat ground staring up into the blue sky. The others sat looking down upon the ocean and towards the city, against the cliff far below and to their right Brook pointed out some of the wreckage of their ship. Wooden spars and planking floated near the narrow heads. For a time they rested, then an exclamation brought Flindas upright. Simo was pointing towards the heads, and then they could all see it, the muddy red colour was beginning to make its way through the narrow passage. It came against the tide; inexorably it began to invade the large enclosed harbour. They watched for a time until Brook stood.

"Let us go to Viris-Tan-Vara," he said. "We all need clothing and food. We will not find them here."

They began to walk along the cliff top and it was not long before they came upon an ancient path, partly paved but fallen into disrepair.

"This is the work of an ancient time," said Flindas. "The city of Viris-Tan-Vara is far older than Mendan Maradass and the city Amitarl. Tis said it was a city even in the time of the wizards. There are ruins here that date back to those distant times."

The city was perhaps a league away and the four travellers, ragged and barefoot, made their way towards it.

"Why did you first come here?" asked Blass as they walked.

"I am an outlaw," replied Flindas with a wry grin. "I came to escape and to hide. My father himself has put a very large price on my head. He wishes to take me alive and have the pleasure of seeing me hang, I care not to be found and Viris was a good place to hide for a time."

"What did you do?" asked Brook. "It must have been something terrible for your own father to hate you so."

"I killed his favourite son," said Flindas quietly. "My elder brother. He did not deserve to die perhaps but it is done and cannot be undone."

Flindas became silent and there were no more questions from Blass. It was mid morning and they were nearing the city's outskirts. Dirty shacks, smelling of every kind of waste, were spread along the side of the paved way. A long straight avenue led them into the city. Its well executed design stood in stark contrast to its dilapidated surroundings. There were many people about. Some sat and stared at the strangers as they passed, while other inhabitants sat huddled over fires and cooked in large metal pots. Many just lay on the ground; there seemed little else for them to do. An old woman rushed at them screaming, and it took some time before they could leave her behind, wailing and cursing at their backs.

"This is worse than I thought it would be," said Brook to Flindas. "How do they survive? What do they eat?"

He did not care for the smells coming from the cooking pots that they passed.

"Most are able to survive on oats and grains that are one of the few crops that grow well in these parts," replied Flindas. "Anything else that is edible goes in the pot. Rabbits, cats, snakes, lizards, rats and mice. There is much food poisoning here. Notice that there are no dogs or any other animals amongst these desperate people."

He left the rest unsaid. They continued down the roadway into the heart of the city and were accosted several times but were never in danger. A weakness and feebleness clung to most of the people they saw. Each of the travellers carried a knife somewhere beneath his clothing; it was a customary part of their training. Even Blass would not have felt properly dressed if he did not wear his long dagger beneath his shirt, but the blades were not needed here.

"What is your plan Flindas?" asked Brook of his companion. "I know I am supposed to be in charge of this ill-fated expedition but it is you who must lead the way for now."

"There is a man we must find," replied Flindas turning to his friend. "His name is Hogarn. He does much business in Viris-Tan-Vara and on the Border Road. I have dealt with him before, while at other times I have irritated him with my own dealings. We are not complete enemies and neither are we friends, but he will deal with us for he loves the shining stones that you carry. I only hope he is in the city. He travels much, and though he has many in his employ, he will not allow any of them to have dealings in his name. He is a very careful thief and extremely successful. Of course he is never to be fully trusted."

"Wonderful," said Simo. "Now we must deal with a thief, and I know not what else. How do we know that you will not strike a deal of your own with this Hogarn and disappear with our gems?"

Simo did not see the blow that caught him on the bridge of his nose and sent him reeling to the roadway. He sat there looking foolish, holding his face as blood splattered his shirtfront. Thin dirty hands applauded from the surrounding street. Voices called and cheered as if this was the finest entertainment they had ever seen. Simo was now coming to his feet, a flicker of steel in his hand as Brook blocked his way and held him by the wrists.

"Enough," he said harshly into Simo's face. "You have been calling for that blow since we began this journey. I would trust Flindas with my life, even though I have known him but a short time. You have no reason to call him a thief."

Simo snorted. "A man who would kill his own brother would not turn from a bit of thievery, if I do not miss my guess," he said. He called to Flindas as the crowd grew more vocal. "Tell me killer of kinsmen, did you strike him a fair blow, or did you do it without warning as you have just done to me?" Simo spat blood into the street. "I do not trust you, outsider."

Flindas had stood quietly while Simo let his feelings flow, he now turned, and pushing his way through the crowd he continued down the road. Simo stood, knife in one hand, the other attempting to stem the flow of blood from his nose.

"Leave it," said Brook and turned to follow Flindas.

The crowd began to hiss and cry out disparaging words at Simo, until in a rage he lashed out with his knife, driving the people away from him. None in the crowd stood in his way now. He remained several paces behind the others and did not speak for a long time as they continued into the heart of Viris-Tan-Vara.

"We are not far from the place where Hogarn does his business," Flindas told Brook. "If he is in the city he will be there. I will do the talking; there are methods for dealing with such as him. Give me three of the gems and keep the pouch with you. We do not want to show all of our hand immediately. Also, Hogarn does not know my real name. To him I am Mardin Treska of Rianodar. There are not many on the Borders that know who I really am. The price on my head is large and there are few who would not turn me in if they knew.

Brook withdrew the small pouch and passed three glittering jewels to Flindas. Even though they were watched by a number of curious people the exchange was not noted by any. Flindas indicated a narrower side street and they entered the darkened way where tall ancient buildings blocked out the late morning sun. A man raved at them from an upper window; his words made no sense and were soon left behind. They moved along the haphazard streets off the main avenue, and in places the houses seemed to reflect the madness that touched so many of the people. Buildings leaned against each other. Some were so dangerously poised that they were abandoned and appeared about to fall. There were piles of rubble where buildings had indeed collapsed in on themselves or into the street. Little effort had been made to clear the way and no vehicles could pass. It was difficult enough for those on foot.

Flindas turned to his right down an extremely narrow alley and they emerged into an open space, a courtyard between tall decaying buildings. A roadway entered from the far side and

Flindas pointed at a building to the left of this road.

"That is the house of Hogarn," he said quietly. "Let us see if he is home."

They walked across the paved square to a large wooden door in the side of the four story building. Flindas took hold of the iron door knocker and struck it three times. For a while there was silence from within. Again Flindas used the knocker and immediately a thin voice called to them from behind the door.

"What do you want?" squeaked the man.

"I want Hogarn," called Flindas gruffly. "I have business."

"Hogarn is not here," was the reply. "Who wants him?"

"This is Mardin Treska, and I have good business for Hogarn, very good business indeed."

There was silence for a time, and then footsteps receded from beyond the door.

"Hogarn is here," said Flindas turning to the others.

"How do you know?" said Blass. "The man said he was not."

"I know the owner of that voice," said Flindas. "His standard reply is that Hogarn is not here. Until he knows who is calling that is all that can be gotten from him. Now he has gone to the rooms above to let Hogarn know who calls. When we enter I do not think that we will all be able to go above. Hogarn is a rich man and fears being robbed. There will be a guard inside. The house is like a fortress, and easily defended. Brook, I believe that the two of us should go above. The others must wait here." He turned to look at Blass and Simo. "Guard yourselves and trust no one," he told them.

As he said these words there was the sound of steel bolts being drawn on the far side of the door. With a groan it swung back to reveal a wizened old creature, and beside him a huge and powerful man carrying a short stabbing spear, his belt hung with a sword and numerous shorter blades.

"There are too many," squealed the old man. "Hogarn will not see you."

He began to close the door. Flindas put his left hand against the wood and in his other he flashed a large red gem.

"He will see us," he said simply.

The old man eyed the stone and licked his lips.

"Perhaps so, perhaps so," he muttered. "But not all of you, there are too many."

"Just two," said Flindas indicating Brook.

The old man thought for a moment then nodded. The door swung open again and the two men entered, the door shut behind them and the bolts slipped back into their housings, after the light of the street the gloom took some time to adjust to.

"Hurry up, hurry up," said the old man. "Hogarn does not have all day."

He shuffled ahead of them up a narrow flight of steps. At the top they entered a large well furnished room, a great contrast to the derelict city outside.

At a table sat a man who Brook was later to liken to a great fat frog or toad. He seemed to overflow from the large chair where he sat, and his completely bald head shone in the sunlight that entered through narrow slit windows on the north wall. His gowns were rich with gold thread, and his fingers glistened with numerous stones. His pale complexion stood witness to the fact that he rarely if ever went abroad in the sunlight without covering himself well against the harsh climate. As they entered he was stuffing a sweet cake into his thick-lipped mouth. Crumbs spilt down his front and he wiped them to the floor with great care.

"So Mardins, I hears you wish to do business wiss me."

His voice slipped over his words like soft butter, it made Brook shudder and think of yet another animal. This time a large fat snake came to mind.

"We wish to do business, yes," replied Flindas, his voice calm and soft.

"Well, wass is it you haves? I has not all day to wastes."

Flindas placed the red stone on the table before Hogarn who looked at it contemptuously.

"Iss that it?" he hissed. "You troubles my eating with thats. Ha! Iss but a baubles, a trinkets for a child's games. Nothing else?"

His eyes widened a little as Flindas placed before him a

larger green gem that caught the light and shot blue flame to the table's surface.

"Better," said Hogarn. "A little better." He deigned to pick this one up and looked into its heart. "Yess, perhaps more?" he queried slyly.

Flindas now placed before him a clear sparkling stone, and Hogarn's intake of breath was unmistakable. This stone was very fine and a rarity not often seen. The fat man picked it up and held it to the light.

"Not so bad," he said finally. "I haves a number of these but I suppose I could takes them off your hands. I is short of gold just now. Business is so poor these days... so poor." Brook swore that a real tear came to the fat man's eye."So poor, so poor," continued Hogarn as he reached to pick up another sweet cake. "Wass is your price?" he asked, his voice now full of cunning.

A look of greed flickered across his face as he held the stones in the palm of his hand. The other forced the cake into his mouth.

"We do not want gold," said Flindas. "There are four of us and we need clothes, food, weapons, horses and information."

Hogarn almost choked on his cake. He spluttered and was finally able to speak. "My dear Mardins, you asks for the impossibles," he muttered. "Foods yes, clothes yess, information perhaps, but weapons and horses. Ridiculouss. You asks the impossibles." He repeated these words slowly and then grew silent.

"Weapons," said Flindas sharply and then he too was silent.

"You haves perhaps more offs these trinkets?" said Hogarn quietly, not looking up from the hand where the stones lay.

"Perhaps," said Flindas. "Perhaps not. Show us your stores. You may not have what we want and we will have to seek elsewhere.

"I haves it, yess I haves everything, but nots horses," drooled Hogarn. "I ams the biggest dealer in this most awfuls of places. One days I will be a nobleman of Amitarl City. I wills be so famous and fabulously riches." His face went off into a dream.

"Show us," said Flindas.

He certainly hoped that one day Hogarn would join the

wealthy of his home city. The man would soon find that he was but an amateur when it came to deceit and trickery. Slowly the large man rose to his feet and as he did so he rang a small bell that lay at hand. The old man entered, the large armed guard never having left the room. Hogarn spoke briefly with the old man but Flindas could not catch what had been said, then he turned to Flindas.

"We goes to the basements," he said. "The other twos companions will join us. You sees I trusts you Mardins. We wills do good business yess?"

It took quite some time for Hogarn to negotiate the stairs to the ground floor, and then into the deep basement. The guard lit lamps as the old one went to get Simo and Blass who soon joined their companions.

The basement was large and stacked high to the ceiling with a huge assortment of merchandise. The travellers first went to the stores of clothing. There they found what they needed, each selecting a stout pair of walking boots and a traveller's pack as part of their attire. There was much dried food, smoked meats, fruit and grains, cooking vessels and implements. Next came the weapons in the next room and each man soon found all that he required. Flindas took an old but very well made sword, numerous knives, and a stout bow with long shafted arrows. Deep in a secret pocket of his breeches he still carried the small blowgun with its darts and potions. It took a long time before each was satisfied with his arms, and Hogarn watched them like a hawk, noting each item as it was finally selected.

"You must gives me more stones," he protested. "This iss much too much." Flindas looked at Brook and nodded. The pouch was produced and two more gems were finally agreed upon.

"Information," said Flindas to Hogarn. "We want to know about one who has been in this city and travelled the Border Road in the last six moons. He is a warrior and has but one good arm. They call him Elfhand."

"No, no, I knows of no ones like thats," said Hogarn. "He has not beens here in Viris-Tan-Varas. No, no, nots here."

Hogarn was lying. Flindas could see it in his eyes. With a

flick of his hand Flindas sent a small knife flying across the basement. It embedded itself in a large timber beam less than a hand span from Hogarn's cheek. In the same instant both Simo and Brook had arrows trained on the guard, who froze in the process of drawing his sword.

"Treachery! Treachery!" screamed Hogarn. "I trusts you Mardins. Why does you do this?"

"Information," said Flindas again, and placed the tip of his sword neatly between two of Hogarn's great chins.

The fat man collapsed to the floor, blubbering and crying for mercy.

"Mercy you will get when we have our information," said Flindas. "Elfhand the warrior was here, where is he now?"

"I do not know," cried Hogarn. "He was here and is gone. I do not know." The fat man's voice had changed from a snake's to a whining puppy. He cowered on the floor, unable to rise.

"Where did he go?" said Flindas. He nudged the great man's belly with the toe of his new boot.

"West, west, I do not know," gurgled Hogarn. "He was looking for the Black One and the Black One was looking for him. Tis all I know. Have mercy now on poors Hogarns. Do not kill me. I know not more." He grovelled on the basement floor.

"I have no intention of killing you," said Flindas. "The Black One, you mean Zard of the House of Maradass?"

"Yes, yes," whined Hogarn.

"What do you know of Maradass?" said Brook, towering over the terrified creature.

"Nothing, nothings!" cried the fat man. "The Blacks One came looking for Elfhand, but I did not know of him then. Elfhand came later and turned west. They seeks each other and perhaps they are both deads now. I do not know, not care." Flindas stepped back from the prone figure.

"Get up Hogarn," he said. "You are in no danger, we have what we need and will leave you now. You have a very fair price for what we have chosen. Show us the door and we will be gone."

With a great effort and help from his guard Hogarn rose to his feet and shuffled towards the stairs. The guard they left locked in the basement, while the old man was nowhere to be seen. They reached the door and Blass quickly had it unbolted. The sunlight streaming in.

"Good day to you Hogarn," said Flindas smiling. "As always it has been a great pleasure to do business with you, though I think it will be for the last time."

He bowed slightly as all four men crossed the threshold and emerged into the street. The door closed behind them and as the bolts slid to they heard Hogarn call out.

"Now! Gets them now!" he screamed.

The travellers turned and found that the square was filling with armed men, all carrying swords or clubs. There were at least twenty of them and they blocked every exit.

"Curse that man," said Brook. "We are trapped. What now?"

In answer Flindas launched an arrow at the mass of men, there was a cry and one of them fell, an arrow quivering from his chest.

"We fight," said Flindas as the men charged them.

Three arrows were loosed simultaneously and three of the attackers staggered and fell to the ground. Before the battle was joined the bowstrings sang once more and again three men fell then the swordplay began in earnest. The attackers were no match for the craft of their opponents, but sheer numbers forced the travellers backward until they were wedged into a corner of the square opposite Hogarn's doorway. The paving became slippery with blood, none of the four had received a wound, but at least ten of their attackers lay dead or wounded in the square.

The men continued to charge and eventually one landed a crashing blow with his club to the head of Brook, the greatest warrior of Zeta fell like a cut tree and did not move, while Flindas stood over him, fighting for their lives. With a cry Blass received a blow to his arm; he swung around to protect his left side but did not see the sword that thrust at him from another of the attackers. The blade passed through his body and came out his back. Blass was dead before he reached the paving.

Simo and Flindas fought desperately side by side and soon the two men were in complete defence, large clubs raining down on them from many hands. With a clean thrust Flindas brought down another of their attackers, then Simo was beaten to his knees. He fought on but could not rise against the blows. Suddenly from above there was a cry, and someone crashed down upon the remaining attackers. In a fury, first one and then another man succumbed to this new attack. There was laughter and through the sounds of battle Flindas recognised it. The last time he had heard it was just the day before aboard the hapless ship of Zeta. In a frenzy Teaker scooped up a sword and struck again, then Simo was on his feet and slew one of the remaining attackers. This was enough for the others who turned and ran from the square. They had not expected to meet such opposition.

"Kills them, not runs, kills them!" came the crying voice of Hogarn from a slit window on the second floor.

Flindas could see the outline of the fat man's head as it looked out upon the battlefield. Within a fraction of a moment Flindas sent a knife flying toward the narrow window slit and Hogarn did not move fast enough. The knife caught him across the cheek and neatly sliced off most of his left ear. He stood for a moment, a look of utter surprise on his fat face, and then with a scream he reeled from view.

"Let us go!" called Flindas urgently.

He and Teaker took Brook under the arms and half dragged, half carried him from the square. Blass was dead and they could do nothing but leave him where he lay; Simo stumbled after them, blood streaming from a wound to his thigh. They found themselves in a jumbled street like so many others in the city, jeered and laughed at by many, they ran on until they could go no further. A ruined building lay at the next street corner and they stumbled over the rubble and into the lee of the one remaining wall. Piles of broken stone and mortar gave them concealment from the street and here they collapsed, breathing deeply.

Teaker kept watch for a short time, and then disappeared with one of their water bottles. He was not gone very long and returned, the bottle filled with brown but untainted water. Flindas tended to Brook who was slowly regaining consciousness, while Teaker bandaged Simo's thigh, it was a long wound but not deep. Brook sat holding his head in his hands and groaned as Teaker returned to watch for the enemy. No one came looking for them and soon they were able to rest more easily. Brook recovered enough to realise that Teaker had rejoined them

"Where did you come from?" he asked in astonishment. "We thought you were dead."

"So did I," smiled Teaker. "When we hit the rocks I was thrown overboard. I guessed that the ship was not going to survive so I swam for the city. I kept swimming and landed sometime this morning. I slept, and tis by chance that I later heard of powerfully built bare foot strangers who had passed into the city just ahead of me. I asked after you on my way, and though a lot of these people are crazy, there are many who are sane enough to give you a straight answer if you threaten them."

He chuckled, and Flindas realised how much he liked this small indomitable man.

"After I knew where you had left the main avenue, all I had to do was follow the sound of the sword play," chuckled Teaker. "The rest was easy."

He laughed again and even managed to bring a smile to the usually dour expression of Simo.

"Do you know anything of Rian or others of the crew?" asked Brook.

"No," said Teaker, a seriousness coming into his voice. "When we were hit, I heard Rian call out. I think he was hurt in the collision. He was a good friend. I do not think he survived. Of the rest of the crew I know nothing. Gone I think. We are warriors and trained to swim far. I think the ocean got them all."

He grew silent and looked up as the sun descended behind the buildings opposite. They ate their dry fare, none of them having lost their packs in the fight, though Teaker remained ill equipped. He held a bare sword taken in the fight and had no boots on his feet. His clothes were torn, and none of his companions were small enough for their spare clothes to be of any use.

"I will get by," he told them. "I will go in search tonight. This city must hold some things that I can find useful."

He smiled and began to build a small fire from scraps of wood he found amongst the rubble. They ate some hot food and felt much better for it. No one disturbed them and they were able to rest easily. During the night Teaker slipped away and returned much later wearing a solid pair of boots and a thick home spun jacket. He carried a pack much like their own, containing a little food and various useful items for travel. A bow was slung across his shoulder and assorted blades hung from his belt.

"Where did you get all this?" said Brook. "And who did you have to kill to get it?"

"I killed no one," said Teaker. "I got it all at the same place as you. I climbed to the roof of the building. It was difficult, made that way on purpose, but I got there and found a way in. It looks as though the whole building has been ransacked. There was little of value in the upper floors; a very fat naked body was the only thing of mild interest. Your knife did not kill him," continued Teaker turning to Flindas. "I think he died of fright and then his men took what they wanted. When I found the basement it had been looted. There was little food but a great many other useful things. I took what I needed and left."

He slapped the side of a boot and laughed again.

By morning they were recovered enough to leave the city. Landin was not there it seemed, and their way led west. Brook's head continued to ache and Simo's leg was stiff and caused him to limp, though he said that he could travel. The day was warm for mid winter and there were many people about in the early dawn. The Elbrand and Flindas now caught many a watchful eye, their weapons and garb made them stand out from all others. There were some that marked their passing with curiosity and suspicion. It was impossible not to be noticed and so the companions walked boldly through the city centre with its ancient buildings. As they finally left the last shacks of the city behind they did not see the small dark figure that slipped along after them, following them on their journey.

Thief in the Night

Flindas and his companions walked throughout the hot morning. The country about them was like nothing that the Elbrand had ever seen before. Though Brook and Teaker had both been to Mendan-Var, neither had been this far to the north. To the south of the road they walked. The land was flat and somewhat dry, though trees and low bushes managed to grow there in the poor grey soil. Flindas knew that there were villages further to the south that managed to survive, though there were no signs of animals except rabbits and the occasional bird. To the north of the road the land was more broken and on the horizon it appeared as if the child of some mighty giant had played with the earth, heaping up mounds in an unnatural fashion, while scooping out great hollows to do so. The far hills were a deep red-brown, jagged at times as if cut and hacked with a blunt sword. Sheer cliffs fell into deep ravines, and a pall of red dust hung on the breeze. A more inhospitable place they could not have imagined.

The road was broad and well paved. Though cracked and broken in places, it remained a legacy of the ancient times of wizardry. They met only a few ragged and destitute people during the day's march, and at dusk they stopped to make camp out of sight from the road. Teaker went in search of firewood while Brook began to prepare a simple meal. The big man was fully recovered now but Simo had been troubled during the day by his leg wound. He had said nothing but Flindas could see that the man was in pain.

"Let me see your wound," he said as they made camp.

"It is no problem," said Simo. "It heals well."

"Let him look," ordered Brook. "Flindas is as near to being a healer as we have on this journey. I do not want a sick man to slow our march."

Reluctantly Simo allowed Flindas to remove the bandages. The wound was inflamed and did not look to be healing. Flindas cleaned it with water from his bottle then made a poultice of various herbs and ointments that had been part of his requirements of the stores of Hogarn. It was a hot poultice and Simo flinched as Flindas applied it, and then bandaged it to his companion's leg.

"We will see what it looks like in the morning," he said. "I think there is dirt deep inside. Hopefully it will be drawn out overnight."

Simo said nothing in gratitude and the camp settled down to eat their meal and then to sleep.

"We should guard our stores," said Flindas. "Keep them close, and one of us should remain awake at all times. There are many in this country that will slit a throat in the night for as little as a piece of bread."

Brook agreed to this and took the first turn at guard. For the last watch before dawn Flindas was awakened by Teaker, and in the moonless dark Flindas sat in silence, his back to a tree, his ears trained for any sound. He had been on watch for some time when he thought he detected a slight movement far to his right. He did not move. He strained his ears, and without moving his head he looked from the corner of his eye into the gloom. There was the very slightest sound again. A soft footfall and then a darker shadow than the night crept out of his vision. Flindas sat on, knowing that whoever it was had now moved behind him and was advancing slowly toward him from the cover of the tree.

The person had much patience and stealth it seemed, and

Flindas remained in his seated position and waited, then he leant his head against the tree trunk as though he slept. It was a long time before he heard again the smallest of sounds, the rustle of dry blades of grass. He remained still, waiting. If someone was going to steal from them he did not want that person to dog their steps for the days to come. To let the thief know that he was aware of him would just frighten him off for a time.

There was the smallest of movements close by the bag of stores that Flindas had placed against the tree beside him. He came to his feet quickly as one of his heavy knives sang from its scabbard. There was a short cry of fright from the thief who leapt towards the safety of the darkness. Flindas sheathed his blade as he pursued the small dark clothed figure. There were calls from the others as they awoke. Flindas landed hard against the masked thief's back and together they crashed to the ground. There was a short struggle before Flindas tore back the black mask. In the soft light he looked down into the face of a young angry woman.

Though dirty, and with short matted hair, she must at one time have been fair to look upon, but great harm had been done to her beauty. Her face had been disfigured by some awful accident, or perhaps it had been done purposefully, for Flindas had seen many such knife wounds before. Two long scars crossed each other at her left cheekbone. One began high at her right temple, coursed down across the bridge of her nose, changing the shape of her right eyebrow and ended below her left ear. The other began just above that ear and cut a hideous groove across her cheek into the left corner of her mouth. She struggled wildly but could do nothing to dislodge her much stronger opponent.

"Caught ourselves a thief I think," said Teaker with a chuckle.

The others came and knelt beside Flindas, and eventually had her wild thrashing hands tied behind her. Apart from her initial cry she had not uttered a sound and sat glaring at them from her most unusual face. They dragged her to the fire and sat her down.

"What do we do with her?" said Simo, eyeing the woman as

though she were some deadly animal. "Is she one of the crazy ones. She looks as mad as any I have seen these last days."

"Not crazy!" she cried out, and then bit her lip as if to speak had worsened her position.

"What were you doing here?" said Brook, his voice threatening and cajoling at the same time.

She did not answer.

"If it was thievery then you should have picked easier game," he continued. "We are not robbed easily."

Still she remained silent, a look of hateful defiance on her scarred face. The men sat down at the fire. It was not long before dawn and Teaker began to prepare some food and hot tea. The young woman's eyes would not leave his hands; she watched every movement as he mixed oats and dried fruit in a small pot over the fire. Though the men occasionally spoke to her, there were no answers to their questions. It was not until the food was being passed to the others that she quietly said;

"Want some too."

The men looked at her and it was Brook who spoke.

"If we untie you, and give you food, will you try to run away?"

"No," was her simple reply.

Brook untied her and when she received a bowl of the gruel she ate quickly and licked the bowl clean.

"More," she said and held out the bowl.

Teaker looked at Brook who nodded. The second bowl disappeared almost as quickly as the first, then she lay back on the scant grass, luxuriating in the feel of a full stomach.

"What is your name?" asked Flindas, curious about this peculiar woman.

She was not one of the mad ones and she did not seem to have companions. A lone woman on the road was not a common thing in these wild northern lands. She did not reply and for a short time she lay on her back, then with a sudden flip she was up and running; Flindas and Teaker had been expecting this and leapt after her. She was fast and light on her feet as she turned towards the road, and then fled westward. Flindas followed while Teaker made to cut her off by running

TRiS

an angle. The smaller man caught her first, diving at her legs and bringing her down in a cloud of dust.

"She has a knife!" called Flindas as he saw the flash of steel, though he thought he had searched her well.

Teaker continued the momentum of his dive, rolling clear and coming to a standing position with his own knife in hand, facing the girl. The small dark figure came to her feet and saw that Flindas was now close; she did not continue her flight and stood panting like a hunted animal.

"Put down the knife," said Flindas having drawn one of his own.

She looked at him and then at Teaker, then with a frustrated gesture she threw the knife to the ground. Teaker bent and picked it up.

"Come back to the fire," said Flindas. "We mean you no harm."

They walked back to join the others.

"So you do not like our company," said Brook to the girl. "You could at least tell us your name before you run off again."

He sat easily by the fire looking up into the young woman's face.

"I am not going to run," she said defiantly, and then after a pause. "My name is Tris."

"Well Tris," said Brook. "Let me tell you that we are here on a search, and since you appear to live on the road you may have seen the one we seek. He is a warrior but may be in disguise. He has only one good hand and arm; the other is small and has no movement."

Tris did not reply for a time and when she did her voice was guarded.

"Why do you look for this man?" she asked.

"He is our friend," replied Brook.

"Where are you from?" she asked, continuing to do the questioning.

"You ask many questions for a thief," said Simo and he received a hostile glare from her.

"We come from Zeta," said Brook. "Now, have you seen him?"

"No, I have seen no man like this," she replied. Flindas was sure that she lied.

The sun was rising on the sparse lands about them and Teaker began to pack the cooking gear and the others their bedding.

"What do I do now?" asked Tris.

"You go," said Brook. "We travel west to find Elfhand. You can remain here and continue your thievery for all I care. Just do not try to rob us again."

"I want to go with you," she said.

"What?" exclaimed Brook. "Go! Get away! Vanish from us!"

He gave an old curse but she only laughed.

"You cannot stop me from following," she said, smiling now.

"Why would you want to do that?" asked Flindas.

"I can be your guide," she replied. "I can show you things. You can give me food."

Brook stood and shouldered his pack, the others stood ready.

"Go, be gone," he said, muted anger in his voice.

She stood defiantly. "I go where I please, and give me my knife back," she said turning to Teaker.

"We will leave it on the road ahead," Brook told her. "Meanwhile you stay here. Do not follow us. We move fast."

He turned away and they left her there, standing beneath the tree by their dead campfire. Teaker dropped her knife on the road and the four men fell into a long striding walk, which would take them perhaps ten leagues or more by sundown. Simo showed no sign of being affected by his leg wound and when Flindas had removed the poultice earlier, it had seemed clean and free of any more infection. Tris went to the road and looked after them as they began to recede into the distance. She spat on her knife and wiped it on her breeches, watching them for a long time, and then with a light footed run she also took the road to the west.

Ensuring that she was not seen Tris spent the day just out of sight of her quarry. Often she left the road when cover permitted and in this way she was able at times to stay abreast of the travellers. The land became more broken. Small ravines gashed the landscape to the north and the road deviated often from its straight course to avoid a deeper chasm. Tris understood the ways of this road and knew where foot tracks had been made to shorten the distance. Eventually she got far ahead of the four men and by late afternoon was in a position where she estimated they would stop to camp. A small clear stream cut across the roadway where a shallow ford allowed wagons to cross. Many had camped here and there was enough wood to make a good fire.

During the day she had hoped for at least one rabbit, but had managed to kill three, they were her favourite game food. There were few she had ever met who had the skill with a sling to match her. She had practiced for many years and was an expert. Tris began to cook the three skinned animals and hoped that she had judged well the marching time of the travellers. Perhaps they would make camp before reaching this place. She was afraid that her game may not work after all.

The rabbits were almost cooked by the time she saw the four men coming towards her along the road. The sun was close to the horizon and she lay back against the sheltering rock and waited, a smile creasing her scarred face. They were close now and had seen the rising smoke from her campsite; Tris saw the one named Teaker pointing in her direction, and then looking back down the road.

"He has good eyes" she smiled to herself.

The men approached her fire but none spoke until they were standing above her, staring at the cooked rabbits.

"Are we invited to dinner?" joked Teaker.

Brook looked embarrassed, and Flindas stared at the meal with amused wonder.

"Yes, you may eat," she replied, and waved them graciously to sit at her fireside.

They had flour with them and soon Teaker had made a number of thin pieces of bread in a small pan, dried fruit and nuts made it a feast. The men of Zeta were not used to the rich meat and Simo ate little.

"How did you get so far ahead of us?" asked Flindas through a mouthful of meat and bread.

"You have to know the Ways," she replied mysteriously.

"And what are the Ways?" asked Flindas.

"My father called them the Shortways," she replied. "They are the paths that make the road shorter. There are signs that show you, if you know where to look. In the Broken Lands there are many Shortways. There are some dangerous ones that I have never gone by, long jumps in places. The road between here and anywhere can be shortened if you know the Ways."

"You have travelled many of these Shortways?" Flindas asked Tris. "I have been on this road before but have only been shown a few of them."

"Many, yes, and I know of many more," she replied. "My father used all of them at times."

"What was your father?" Brook asked, instinctively knowing that her father was no longer living.

"A thief, like me," she said with obvious pride in her voice.

"You are proud to be a thief?" exclaimed Simo in astonishment.

"Of course," she replied. "It is an honest trade in these lands. It is not as if we are robbers. We steal but do not hurt people. thievery is an honourable trade."

She paused and chewed on a bone.

"I can show you the Ways," she said shrewdly, looking from Flindas to Brook.

"Why do you want to travel with us?" asked Brook suddenly concerned that she may be a spy as well as being an honourable thief.

"I want to go to Shish-Tan-Vara and the road is not safe," she replied. "Oats too."

Again Flindas felt that this was a deliberate lie.

"We need to talk," said Brook looking at the others and they left the fire to sit on a tumble of rocks by the stream.

"What do you think?" Brook asked them. "She seems to know the road well. Does she come along with us?"

Teaker spoke first.

"How do we know if one of her Shortways will not cause us to miss Landin somewhere on the road?" he said.

"A good point," conceded Brook.

"There are numerous towns and villages before we reach Shish-Tan-Vara," said Flindas. "It will be at these places that we will find news if any. It would be more than luck if we heard of his whereabouts while on the open road. Travellers go speedily between the inhabited parts of this desperate place. There are few but mad ones and robbers on this road. The girl knows the lands but I believe she lies. She goes not to Shish-Tan-Vara in particular and she knows of Landin. I am sure of it."

"Let us find out," said Simo beginning to rise.

"No," said Brook. "It is not our way. Simo, you know that. I think that she should travel with us. She will not stand guard and we must watch her for any trickery."

They spoke further for a time and then rejoined Tris by the fire.

"You may travel with us," said Brook. "We will take your Shortways except where it may bypass an inhabited place. We wish to visit all of these. You say you know nothing of Landin, the one we seek; are you sure?"

He watched her closely.

"Yes, I am sure," she replied bluntly. Her lie was covered well this time thought Flindas.

The others prepared for the night while Flindas stood the first watch. He let them sleep long and called Teaker well into the early morning, then he slept until dawn and they were on the road once again.

During the day's march they found the way more and more broken. The road was passable by wagon or horse, but had been rebuilt in many places to accommodate the shattered ravines and tall cliffs that began to bar their way.

"Here is the beginning," said Tris and pointed.

Just ahead the road suddenly plunged into a deep defile and they were soon truly within the Broken Lands. Flindas had travelled this way before but the three Elbrand were shocked by the devastated lands that they had just entered.

"The first Shortway is not far," said Tris. "We can gain a league or more on this climb. It is a well known one, many people have walked there."

Tris eventually called to them from ahead where she liked

to walk, and at times even run; showing the others how she had managed to pass them the day before. She carried a pouch, a small blanket, her sling and knife; that was all.

"Here we begin the Shortway," she said. "It is steep but not dangerous."

They began ascending a rock wall that at first appeared unclimbable. The path was narrow and hugged the cliff face. Tris took the stairs lightly and rested on her way. The others climbed with full packs and it was a heavy trudge before they reached the top. There was a final steep section where they needed both hands to complete the climb, and then the travellers came out on a narrow plateau where a path led them back to the paved road.

"A league or more," called Tris. "Am I not worth a mountain of gold?"

She laughed and danced ahead of them. Flindas heard Simo speak under his breath to Teaker.

"If she is not mad then I am the crazy one," he said.

Teaker chuckled.

During the day they took two more of the Shortways. One did not last long but the other gained a distance of some leagues. Little grew in this barren land, a few bushes and dry blades of grass did nothing to break the impact of the sheer red escarpments and deep valleys. They passed by two small villages on their way but even with the offer of a gold coin, they learned nothing of Landin's whereabouts. Finally they made camp and ate their evening meal, they had seen no one travelling on the road all day and Tris told them that in recent times this was common. Few ventured far from the inhabited parts of the Broken Lands; the black dogs had grown in number and roamed the Broken Lands at will.

"Marauders?" asked Teaker.

"That is the name I have heard," replied Tris. "Though there are other names I would not repeat. They are killers and merciless."

"I have met them," the small man said, with barely a smile.

During the night two riders galloped by without noticing their camp, they were in a hurry it seemed. It was almost noon the next day when the travellers came to a small town built above a vast chasm. The people were suspicious of strangers and most would not speak with them; those that did knew nothing of a one armed warrior. The travellers moved on and by nightfall found themselves at a high point in the road, which overlooked much of the surrounding land.

"It is not called the Broken Lands without reason," said Brook to Flindas as they stood by the road looking at the surrounding tormented country. "The wizards must have hated the earth to have caused such devastation."

"Yes," agreed Flindas. "No one knows how much they destroyed. How far these tortured lands stretch to the north no one can say except perhaps the black people."

"Do you know much of those people?" asked Brook surprised. "I have heard it said that they eat the white people they capture in the deserts."

"I would not believe all you hear," replied Flindas. "There was a time when I was forced into the Outlands. It is harsh out there and water is difficult to find. I met a family of black people and they gave me water and food. We did not speak the same language and because I was running for my life from my father's men I left them, so as not to bring danger to their peaceful lives. All I know is that they helped me and meant me no harm."

During the evening Tris told something of her life in the Broken Lands.

"My father could lift the food from the plate of a starving man," she told them. "Or so the saying goes for he would never have done such a thing. He knew these hills and the city of Shish-Tan-Vara like no one else. He was never shown anything but honour by the thieves that he mixed with."

Her voice grew sad and she became silent.

"How did he die?" asked Brook.

"He fell, a little more than a year ago, while taking one of the Shortways," she said. "I was not with him. It was a Way that he had gone many times before. The others that were there say that the path gave way beneath his feet and he fell a great distance. They returned to camp for a rope and we managed to bring his body back up from the valley. He should never have fallen; sometimes I do not think that the whole truth has been told."

Tris grew silent again, her thoughts wandering along Shortways with her father beside her. Suddenly she became fully alert, fear widened her eyes; her nostrils flared, sniffing at the air. The others sensed nothing and did not know what to make of it.

"Marauders," she said in a fearful whisper. "They are close."

The men leapt to their feet, scooping up their weapons.

"How do you know?" whispered Flindas.

"I smell them; they come on the road from the West," she said.

Simo began to scoff until Brook told him to stop.

"I am willing to believe her until she is proved wrong," he said. "Quickly now, get amongst the rocks. If they attack we will have a better defence there."

All picked up their packs and ran for cover. Soon the others could smell it too, a musty canine smell; then they heard the sound of padded feet, coming at a fast run. The moon was high and bright and the road stood out against the darkness. A black mass of moving bodies appeared upon it where the road began its ascent. The large dogs, perhaps ten or twelve of them became distinguishable from each other, their blue flamed eyes flickering as they ran. Behind them rode two men on horseback. They were armoured and cloaked in black, the white skull of a dog showing as the emblem on their tunics.

The marauders were almost passed when all at once the leaders slowed, until the whole pack was milling around sniffing at the road. The two riders also stopped and looked into the darkness, their eyes finally coming to rest on the last glowing embers of the fire. The beasts found it too and were soon following the trail to the pile of jumbled rocks where the five travellers were hiding. There was now no choice and Brook stood out from a gap in the rocks.

"Be gone," he cried. "There is nothing for you here. Take your hounds and go."

The dogs howled and stood their ground as a vicious laugh

came from one of the horsemen.

"Our beasts are hungry, and since you are here there certainly *is* something for them," one dark voice replied.

He laughed again and Flindas felt a shiver climb up his spine, then with a single howling cry the marauders launched themselves at the party. Three bowstrings sang and three of the dogs crashed into the dust, legs thrashing. The others stopped their charge and looked to the horsemen for guidance.

"Get them!" one called. "Take them! Kill them!"

The marauders turned and charged again. Arrows sang through the air and two more of their number fell, while another was hit sharply in the face by a hard flung stone. In a rush the remaining dogs reached the rocks, leaping through the gaps or clambering up onto the boulders. The fight was ferocious and brief, swords flashed and thrown knives found their marks.

Teaker gave a cry as sharp fangs tore at his arm where once before he had received similar wounds. The animal died with a knife in his throat. With a roar Brook swung his sword, cutting deep into the flesh of another marauder. From the corner of his eye Flindas saw Tris wedged into a space between rocks, attempting to fight off two of the beasts with her small knife; he sent three of his throwing knives at her attackers. With a howl one fell while the other tried to pull the knife from its shoulder, until Simo's sword ended its life.

The marauders were all dead or dying. Flindas scooped up his bow and strung an arrow as he leapt to a vantage point overlooking the road. The two horsemen were still there, surprised that their beasts were not to be seen, though their death cries echoed through the night. Flindas sent arrows across the space between him and the riders and with a cry one of them fell to the road, while the other dug in his spurs and before Flindas could shoot again the rider and mount were galloping into the darkness.

"We must leave this place," said Brook. "He may return with others."

Flindas fanned the fire back into life and attended to Teaker's wounds. There were a number of small gashes and punctures which would heal quickly if they did not become infected. Flindas was concerned about one cut on Teaker's right forearm. It was deep and the muscles were damaged. The little man sat without sign of pain as Flindas applied two large stiches, then an ointment and a stout bandage.

"Can you travel?" Flindas asked.

"Yes, tis but a scratch," smiled Teaker.

They divided part of his load between them and left the hilltop. The moonlit road plunged into a gorge where a small stream followed their path. They talked as they moved.

"I have not met with marauders in the Broken Lands before," said Flindas to Tris. "You seem to know them well."

"In the last three or four moons they have begun to be seen often," she said. "They come and take who or what they will. We were lucky they were a small pack and your fighting skills I have not met with before. Few can stand against marauders. They will return and hunt us I think. The black horsemen are not used to being thwarted. They have camps in the Broken Lands now, though I have not seen them so far to the east before. Soon they will push into the Regions and none will then be safe."

"How do you know all this?" asked Brook. "You seem well informed for a thief. What can you tell us of the dogs' masters?"

Tris did not reply immediately, their footsteps on the roadway were the only sound. High above, the moon slipped from behind a cloud and bathed the roadway in soft light.

"Do you know anything of the movements and intentions of Maradass?" Brook asked bluntly.

"Ssh!" she said quickly. "Do not mention that name again unless you wish to call down the black hordes upon us."

"But what of his intentions?" said Brook. "You have still to answer me."

"He will invade the Regions. This is the belief of all who live here on the Borders," she said. "No one can say when. That is all I know."

Again Flindas detected an untruth in her voice.

They travelled now in silence, marching quickly, watchful of the road ahead and behind. Flindas examined Teaker's arm again and found that the stitches and bandage were not stemming the flow of blood as he had hoped.

"We must find a place to stop and rest his wound," he said and Brook turned to Tris. "Is there somewhere near that is safe?" he asked.

"Ahead, not far, is a Shortway," she told him. "It is not one I have taken before. It goes up sharply and there is a leap that is most difficult I am told. If we can cover our tracks we may be able to lie there undetected for a time, without having to jump. I fear the marauders will not leave us to travel unmolested. We have killed their kind and now they want our blood."

They had travelled less than a league when Tris pointed to a large overhanging rock.

"We must climb around that rock," she said. "Then we go uphill until we come to the chasm that we must cross or turn back. There are many leagues to be saved by going this way but few ever have. Coming from the top it is not so hard they say. The jump is higher from that side. I have looked at it from above. I will not be able to jump from this direction. This I know."

"We have ropes," said Brook. "We will go this way and hopefully lose the dogs."

First they walked on for some distance to lay a trail that may fool the black horsemen and marauders. Then they backtracked, and leaving the road, they began the climb. Having wiped out any signs of their departure from the road, they knew that if marauders came the dogs might still find their scent. It was a difficult climb, hand over hand at times. Teaker had problems and blood continued to seep from his wound. They eventually came to the chasm. The moon was lowering and the leap looked impossible in the gloom.

"We will stay here until dawn," said Brook. "If marauders or soldiers have not come by then we will make our decision. I do not like the look of this jump. We may have to return to the road, black horsemen or no."

They rested, and there was little that Flindas could do for Teaker. The blood had ceased to flow now that they were not walking and the little man seemed at ease with his wound.

They lit no fire and there was little sleep in their camp for the remainder of the night. Dawn's first light was just beginning to touch a high cliff face when Simo called softly from his vantage point amongst the rocks above them.

"Marauders, many of them," he said.

The travellers peered down onto the darkened road; a troop of horsemen could be seen, while ahead of them went a large pack of the black dogs, perhaps a hundred of them. They came from the east and had not yet reached the point where the Shortway left the main road.

The advancing troops did not appear to be in a hurry, the leading dogs sniffing the road as they went, but then it was seen that even ahead of the dogs went two men on foot. They were black men, bare foot and almost naked. These two carried no weapons and Flindas finally realised that one of their legs was joined to that of the other by a fine metal chain. They stayed well ahead of the troops, scanning the road at their feet; eventually they came opposite the hidden path that was the Shortway. Here they stopped and then went to the side of the road. One held up a hand and the troops and marauders halted. For a time the two black men studied the roadside, then walked a little further on. It took some time for them to return but when they did, they spoke to the black horsemen who led the troops. After a few moments they pointed up the cliff face towards the place where the travellers lay in hiding far above.

"They have us," cursed Brook. "We must cross this chasm or die here. We cannot fight all of them."

He ran to the edge of the jump and looked down as a great howl went up from the beasts below when he was seen. Orders were called out and marauders sprang up the path, followed by many of the riders, now on foot. More dogs and several of the horsemen galloped ahead of the others and down the dusty road. They hoped to cut off the traveller's escape route far above on the road.

Brook realised that the leap to the far side would have been impossible except he could see that handholds and a narrow ledge had been carved from the cliff face opposite. If one could reach that point without falling then it was an easy climb to the top. Brook began to prepare for the jump, taking a coil of rope from his pack and hanging it around his shoulders.

"I go first," he said in a voice that broached no argument. "We will get Teaker across and the girl first. You must hold them off."

He had turned to Flindas and Simo. Brook then stood well away from the edge to gain as much momentum for the jump as he could. For a moment Flindas saw fear pass across the big man's face, then Brook took a deep breath and ran to the brink, his final footfall landing on the very edge. With a great roar he propelled himself outwards into the air. He seemed to fly slowly across the gap. An eternity passed before he landed heavily against the rock face opposite. His hands clutched at and then held the small holds, just as his feet came to rest on the narrow ledge. He roared with laughter, the relief in his voice was plain for all to hear. With ease he found his way to the top of the opposite ledge. For a time he disappeared from view then returned with one end of the rope.

"It is secure," he called as he threw it to them.

Flindas kept an eye on Brook and the other on the advancing enemy. Quickly they tied their packs to the rope and Brook hauled them across. The marauders were coming on fast, howling as they climbed, though it was difficult for them in places to find a foothold. Teaker would take the leap next, with the rope tied under his arms he was in no great danger of falling, but had to take care of how he landed against the cliff face opposite; with only one useful hand it would be difficult not to hurt himself further.

The time came and he leapt, his short legs racing. Brook took up the slack as he jumped and judged it perfectly. Teaker landed lightly, his good hand finding a hold; at the same time Brook hauled on the rope and was soon joined above by his small friend. The marauders were close now, but Flindas and Simo did not use their bows; their arrows were best saved, there were too many of the black dogs for them to make much of a difference. With the rope around her Tris made the leap safely.

"Simo you next," called Flindas, drawing his sword as the

marauders came closer.

Simo quickly tied the rope and leapt but misjudged the jump; he slid down the rock face, only saved by the strength of Brook. Flindas could now see that there would be no time for him to have the advantage of the rope, and the marauders were almost upon him. Quickly he sheathed his sword and ran for the chasm; the dogs were almost at his heels when he leapt into space, the rock face coming at him fast.

In his hurry he had jumped too far to the right and hit the rock hard, his clutching left hand just managing to find a hold. For a few moments he hung there, unable to find a place for his feet, his toes could not find the narrow ledge. From above he heard Brook call out, and then he found the rope slithering down around his back. As his grip weakened on the rock he clutched the rope with his other hand and was hauled aloft by the strong arms of his companions. The marauders howled in frustration, milling around the edge of the chasm, causing the dust to rise.

"We must go quickly," said Brook coiling up the rope. "It will not be long before they are on the road above and on our trail again."

He turned to Tris.

"Can you tell us of any escape from here?" he asked. "The road will be most dangerous now."

"There is another Shortway not far ahead," she told him. "We did not fool them this time. I doubt if we can lose them by taking this other way, but we can try. There is a river that may help us."

They gathered their packs and began down the road at a fast run. Teaker managed to keep up for a time, blood streaming from his arm, and then he fell with exhaustion into the road. Simo gathered up his pack while Brook lifted Teaker to his shoulders and they continued to run. They kept it up for a league or more until Tris showed them the beginning of the other Shortway. It cut sharply down to the right where far below a river ran strongly.

"This way!" she called and leapt down the path.

Flindas was the last to leave the road. For a time he stood

silently, listening to any sounds from behind. On the very edge of hearing he thought he could make out the distant howling of marauders. He left the road quickly and rejoined the others.

"They are not far behind and will not miss our trail," he called, as they ran hard down the path, they were almost to the river when Flindas looked back again. On the edge of the slopes above them he could see perhaps ten horsemen, but there was as yet no sign of the marauders. Tris who was ahead called back to him.

"They will send the dogs ahead to cut us off," she cried. "They will reach the end of this trail before we can. I am sure."

The five travellers came to the swift flowing river and halted where a bridge of logs spanned the gap. Brook eased Teaker to the ground.

"We cannot outrun them and we cannot outfight them. What of this river?" he said turning to Tris. "Can we swim with the current and get beyond them?"

He looked back at the horsemen who were beginning to descend the slope.

"There are parts I do not know of," said Tris. "There are rapids and then a waterfall I was told. With Teaker the way he is he may not survive. I do not know the full nature of this river; there are places that cannot be seen from the road. The falls are high and go into a large pool. If we get that far then we are beyond the road and will be safe perhaps. We may not be able to get out, but they will not be able to get in I think."

"Quickly!" called Simo urgently. "There is not much time and the river is our only hope. Cut a log from the bridge. We may save our packs by tying them to it."

Brook, without another word, ran to the bridge and began to hack a log loose from the rest. The others joined him and they soon had a short length cut away and ready to launch, which they tied their packs to.

"We will hold on to it as long as we can and steer it through the rapids," said Brook. "I will care for Teaker. Good fortune to you all!"

The black horsemen were descending the last steep section of the path when the five companions took to the river. With a heave they pushed the log and themselves into the rushing tide and were quickly swept away, out of sight of the black horsemen. For a time the river was swift but not dangerous, then they came to the first rapids. The log, a little more than a man's length, floated well and they managed to steer it between the rocks that at times almost barred their way. Brook held Teaker against the log, the small man's head just above the water.

With a sudden jarring crash the log hit a rock hidden beneath the surface. Flindas and Tris were shaken loose and swept ahead of the others. The log stuck for a moment then swung around and into the stream again. In the swirling foam ahead Flindas had managed to find a hold and was able to rejoin the log as it passed. Tris was far ahead and could not be seen. They passed through several smaller rapids and then came to a thrashing wall of water and rock that seemed to last forever.

The men were battered and forced under the surface continually. Flindas felt his leg scrape along a rough surface and then he was held, his foot caught between two rocks. His hands slipped from the log and it floated rapidly away from him. His foot wedged tighter, and water rushed by and at times covered his head. If he could not free his foot soon he would surely drown, for it was taking much of his strength just to keep his head above the foaming current. He felt his ankle twist between the rocks. Pain shot up his leg. Reaching into his belt he drew one of his heavy knives. Taking a lung full of air, he plunged below the surface cutting at his boot with the knife.

He felt the blade cut into his flesh but there was no time to be delicate. After another lung full of air he was finally able to cut himself loose and began to be pushed along by the river. There was much pain in his ankle, yet at the last moment he had managed to save his boot. Though it was cut in a several places, with binding it would still be useful. The redness of blood began to mingle with the water about him. He could not see the others and continued to be swept along, taking every chance to look to the river banks. He did not want to miss his companions if they had been able to halt their progress and get to shore. There was no sign of them, except on one jagged rock he saw the remains of a bow, the cord stopping it from being swept further downstream.

Alone in the water he avoided rocks as best he could until he finally entered a wider and less furious part of the river. Ahead he could make out the log, heads bobbing beside it. He struck out for them; his ankle was becoming numb with cold, the pain almost gone. The log lay close to the western shore of the river. Brook and Simo were steering it into the shallows while Teaker lay sprawled across it. Of Tris there was no sign.

When Flindas joined them Brook was carrying Teaker to a small sandy beach carved out of the overhanging cliffs, while Simo pushed the log to a position where he could untie their packs. Most of their gear seemed to have been saved. Only one pack was torn and spilling its contents. Flindas struggled up the beach and collapsed as the feeling returned to his ankle. He examined it gently. Blood flowed from two knife wounds. It was not broken but he suspected that he would not walk on it for some days. He retrieved his pack from Simo and dressed the wounds.

Teaker remained unconscious for the rest of the day. A fever had caught hold and Flindas did all he could to ease the small man's pain. After many attempts they managed to get a fire going with driftwood that lay about the beach and wedged amongst the rocks. It was not until late afternoon that they heard a call from downstream. It was Tris, clambering over rocks, and then swimming to their small beach.

"All safe and in good health I see," she said with an amused look at the bandages and bruises that seemed to cover at least half of each of the men's bodies. She seemed almost unscathed, though she winced when she had to use her left hand. After a time of warming herself by the fire she told of the river ahead.

"There are more rapids and then the river becomes very wide and peaceful, almost like a lake. That part cannot be seen from the road. I would have known. After that there is the high waterfall, and I could not see a way down from there and also it would not lead us on the right way to Shish. On the east bank of the river there seems to be a likely way to climb out, but not an easy one. The problem is that the road is on the west. The west side is steep and overhanging as far as the falls, I could not see a way up."

Though they had managed to save their packs, some of the food was now spoiled, and a number of things had been washed away including two of their bows. For three days they camped beside the river and heard no more from marauders. Teaker recovered and was soon able to move about. Flindas no longer felt pain in his ankle and after walking and exploring for a day he declared himself fit to travel. It was decided that they would go downstream as far as the falls, unless another route showed itself to the west. They set out early, sometimes walking and at times having to swim. There were more rapids but the companions were not much troubled by them. At midday they rested and ate. Cliffs, impossible to climb, many overhanging sharply, lined the sides of the narrow river valley. They moved on further and it was not until late afternoon that they began to hear ahead of them the unmistakable roar of a large waterfall.

Flindas marvelled that Tris had been able to reach the falls and return to their previous camp in one day. She moved ahead of them now as always, and though she did not appear to be moving fast she always seemed to have time to sit and wait until they reached her, then she would be up again, moving ahead as usual. They walked beside the river and all had noticed that it flowed more swiftly here. It rushed and foamed, crashing on the rocks, spraying them until they were as wet as when in the river itself. After widening to become a small lake the torrent narrowed and flowed between two cliff faces, disappearing to a canyon far below; a fine, misty spray hung on the air.

They passed through and finally came to the edge of the drop; the water was propelled outward in a great rush. There were many huge boulders and rocks at the bottom of the sheer cliff, a jump was hopeless and to climb down also seemed impossible.

"Well, here we are," said Teaker. "Perhaps we can sprout wings and fly."

His humour was not welcomed by Brook who stood at the

edge, studying the possibilities.

"A plague on these lands," he finally said and sat down on a rock ledge. Nowhere had they seen even the slightest possibility of an escape route to the west during their journey down river. They sat and talked about their situation for a time but no one had any suggestions that might help. It did indeed appear that they were trapped; the cliffs above them seemed to be leaning down and laughing at their predicament.

"We will have to go back," said Brook. "Perhaps we missed something, or we may be able to force a way upstream and back to the road that way."

His voice contained the doubt that they all felt, on their watery journey after they left the bridge no one remembered seeing an easy way out of the deep ravine. They were just beginning to shoulder their packs again when Simo called out in surprise and pointed. On the far side of the river there stood a small scruffy dog, which, on being noticed, gave a yelp and bolted off amongst the rocks. Tris was up and running before the others could react, she kept the dog in view, but after a short time she returned to the others.

"It disappeared," she said incredulously. "He was there and then he was gone. Unless it stopped to hide behind a rock I do not know where he might be; but if it got down here then we may be able to get out."

"Yes," said Brook. "We will look. I think we can cross over not so far upstream."

After a short time of clambering and a leap from rock to rock across a narrow point in the river, they found themselves approaching the falls from the other side, but there was still no sign of the dog. They spread out as much as possible and searched amongst the rocks.

"Here is where I saw him last," said Tris pointing to a tumble of boulders against the cliff face.

They began to poke and peer amongst them until they heard a low growl from somewhere deep within.

"I can see him," said Teaker, though having just recovered from a marauder's bite he was not willing to venture any further.

Flindas got down on his knees and peered into the darkness between two boulders, he could just make out the crouched form of the dog. There was something else too. It appeared to be a bundle of rags until a child's voice called out.

"Go away, leave us alone!"

In surprise Flindas looked at the others.

"I do not think we are welcome here," he said.

Again he peered into the dark place.

"We mean you no harm," he said gently. "Why do you and your friend not come out from there?"

There was silence within. Flindas spoke again.

"We have good food if you are hungry," he said. "We are friends and we do not hurt children. Come out and talk to us."

Still there was no sound, except a growl from the small dog.

"Let me try," said Tris, and she knelt beside Flindas. "Hey little one,' she said in a sweet friendly voice that none of her companions had heard before. "There is no need for fear. My name is Tris, and my friends are not bad people. Come and eat with us."

A growl met her plea. She turned to Brook.

"It is time for us to eat," she said loudly with a wink. "Let us make fire and perhaps we can entice them out with the smell of food," she said quietly.

"Yes," agreed Brook smiling. "It is indeed time to eat."

Simo collected wood and soon had a small fire started. They had managed to keep their food above water this time and the smell of camp bread wafted about in the late afternoon air, a simple fish soup bubbling in their cooking pot. A low whine came from the dog and there was movement from within the small cave. First the head of the dog peered out, followed by the dirty face of a small girl. Her hair was long and matted, her clothes torn and almost falling from her thin body. She knelt in the entrance to her shelter and gazed out at the travellers from smoky brown eyes. The companions remained by the fire, aware that the slightest movement could send the girl scuttling back to her burrow.

"Food," said Tris and scooped at the pot of soup with a lump of warm bread. Slowly the girl emerged and stood up. She was no more than eight or nine years old and held a short piece of branch before her in defence. Her feet were hard and bare. The dog stayed close to her and looked at the strangers with suspicion. Tris juggled a piece of bread in her hand and then tossed it across the space between her and the girl, who caught it easily and bit off a large mouthful. The rest she gave to the dog who gulped it down quickly.

"There is more if you want it," said Tris. "Good hot soup, come, we will not harm you."

Slowly the small girl and dog crossed the space and came close to the fire. Brook held out another piece of bread. The girl stood still and would not take it. Tris took the bread from Brook and held it out. It was snatched from her hand and consumed as before, the dog getting his share.

"It tastes much better with soup," said Tris and coaxed the girl nearer the fire, where she handed her a spoon and made room for her near the pot.

"He cannot use spoon," said the girl indicating the dog.

"No of course not," chuckled Tris.

She dug into the pot and scooped out a few pieces of fish which she placed on a rock near the dog. He sniffed at it and when it had cooled a little, gulped it down. The girl too ate a piece, accepted more bread and then a full bowl of the soup. Everything she had she divided in two and gave the dog a share. As they ate, their fears visibly subsided along with their hunger. The dog was soon being scratched behind the ears by Flindas and the girl had finally had her fill and returned the bowl to Tris, who spoke to the child.

"What is your name?" she asked.

"I am Gram and he is Wuff," came the reply as she indicated the dog.

"What are you doing here?" asked Brook but received no answer.

"I think a woman's touch is needed," said Tris smiling.

Brook gave a grunt deep in his throat and was silent while Tris continued. "Tell me Gram, why are you here?" she asked.

"I ran," said Gram. "I ran," she repeated, and tears began to flow down her cheeks. She cried silently.

Tris put an arm around her shoulders and the girl clung to her, Gram's crying became more vocal until she was sobbing loudly, her face buried deep into the sympathetic shoulder. Tris soothed the child, slowly stroking her hair and whispering soft words into her ear until Gram eventually ceased her weeping. Wuff came to her side and nuzzled into his young mistress, wiping a dirty sleeve across her eyes she calmed enough for Tris to ask.

"Why did you run Gram? What did you run from?"

For a time she was silent, her eyes darting up and down the river. Finally she whispered. "Black dogs."

The men looked at each other in disbelief, a man could not outrun a marauder, and yet here was a live girl with a story of running from the beasts. They wished to ask questions but it seemed the girl's trust was in Tris alone.

"We too ran from marauders," said Tris. "How did you get here?"

"I came that way," she said and pointed to the cliff face opposite.

"We have looked there," said Tris. "We found no way up or down. Can you show us where?"

"Yes, but we cannot go," Gram replied. "Black dogs there and they will get us." Tears welled in her eyes again. "They got mother and father and all my friends," she gulped hard, choking back her pain.

She looked up the cliff and shuddered violently. Tris held her and looked at the silent men around the fire.

"If she got down here, then we may be able to get out," said Brook quietly. "Yet I still cannot see any way up."

Tris rocked Gram in her arms until the child's tears again subsided.

"There is a way," Gram finally said, this time looking at Brook. "It is a small way and I do not think you will fit."

The others smiled, Brook carried no extra weight, but his body was much larger than that of most men.

"Can you show us?" he asked his voice soft and friendly.

Gram nodded. "But dogs," she said. "You not afraid of marauders?"

"Yes we are afraid," said Brook. "We have fought them already. If there are many then we will not go that way. Tell me Gram, how long have you been down here?"

Gram thought for a while. "Three nighttimes," she said finally then turned to Tris. "I saw you come this way. I was hiding. I thought you were hunting for me so I hid."

"You do not seem so very hungry for someone who has not eaten for three days," said Brook.

"Wuff caught a fish," said Gram proudly. "It was a big one, it tasted not very good but we ate it. He is a good dog is Wuff."

She hugged the dog who turned and licked her face.

All of them had now eaten and Brook stood and looked at the young girl.

"Can you show us now?" he asked.

Gram nodded and began to lead them back upstream to where it narrowed and they had crossed earlier. Before anyone could say a thing Gram and then Wuff took the short leap across the torrent. It was not a great distance but for the small girl it must have taken a great deal of courage. They continued to follow her, and soon she was clambering amongst a pile of rock that appeared to have recently fallen from above. They had seen it before but there did not appear to be any way from there to the heights and the distant road above.

"Here!" called Gram and stood smiling, pointing at a small dark cavity amongst the rocks. It did not look as if any but a child could pass through. "It comes out up there," she pointed up the sheer face of rock to a small overhang high above. "Wuff found the way," she said, again pride coming into her voice.

"I will try," said Tris, who was the smallest of the group. "Give me a rope that will reach. The gap is very small so I will tie it around my waist and you can feed it in behind me."

She discarded her pouch and blanket and then removed her heavier outer clothes. The others saw for the first time that the scars on her face were not the only ones she bore. Her left forearm had at some time been gashed horribly, and another vicious-looking scar ran up her right arm and disappeared beneath her sleeveless shirt.

Tris got down on all fours and crawled into the hole. Flindas fed the rope in behind her and it continued to disappear into the darkness until there was only a little remaining. He tugged on the rope and it stopped its slither into the hole. Quickly he tied another length to the first and pulled on it again. The rope again began to disappear, and for a time it continued, then stopped. From above they suddenly heard Tris call to them.

"I am up here!" and they saw her waving.

She went from view again and then the rope began to disappear quickly into the hole. After a time they saw it being lowered to them from the ledge. Brook took it in both hands and tugged hard, Tris had secured it above.

"I will go first, I wish to see what is up there,'" said Brook. "I will call if the way is clear."

He grasped the rope and in easy practiced movements began to scale the cliff, in places there were no footholds and the big man climbed using only the rope. Brook reached the top and disappeared amongst the rocks above, he soon returned and called down to them.

"It looks good from here," he cried. "Come ahead, Simo you next."

Simo skimmed up the rope, and then Flindas secured Gram, the rope under her arms.

"Quicker than your tunnel I think," he smiled in reassurance. "Do not worry about your hairy friend, Teaker will carry him safely."

As Gram was hauled above Wuff grew agitated and barked wildly, suddenly he dived into the small tunnel and disappeared. As it was, he beat Gram to the top and was there to meet her, tail wagging happily. Flindas tied Teaker onto the rope. The little man's arm was healed but still weak and he too was hauled aloft, while Flindas remained to send their packs up the cliff. Lastly he took hold of the rope and climbed steadily, to eventually find himself on a wide rock ledge where the others were gathered. Tris pointed to a crack in the rock behind them, it was the narrow way down. The ledge seemed to continue upward for a way and was not difficult.

"Thank you," said Tris to Gram. "Without your help we might still be trapped down there."

"It is not so hard from here," replied the girl. "It is a long way to the road though. I ran a long, long way."

"Were you on the road when the marauders came?" asked Flindas.

"Yes," she said quietly. "We were travelling, taking some food and other things to Viris. We had three wagons; I think dogs got everything. I ran and ran and ran. They did not see me I think. They were too busy."

She screwed her face up in pain and knelt to hug her dog.

They began the upward climb and Gram found the going much harder than coming down, eventually Brook put the girl high on his shoulders and continued, unaffected by the extra weight. Flindas was surprised at the ease in which they climbed what from below had appeared to be an impossible cliff face; a narrow defile in the rock, unseen from below, cut back deep into the cliff. A small watercourse, dry now, showed them the way, mosses and lichen grew amongst the stones. Eventually they came out onto a flat plateau. In all directions the country was the same broken dry landscape as before.

The companions walked a league or more before they rejoined the Border Road, where they found the remains of the wagons. They were burnt and broken and there was little else to show of the travellers who had been murdered there. They walked on into the evening, the road continuing flat and straight for a long way ahead. They did not camp near the road that night. After covering their tracks, they lay in a shallow depression amongst distant rocks from where they watched, but saw no movement, on the road that night.

For three more days they travelled, moving parallel with the road much of the time, and taking Shortways that Tris recommended. They met few other travellers and those that they did were in fear of them and ran as soon as they spied their weapons. The companions passed through a number of abandoned villages and towns, many of the houses had been recently burnt, the people dead or gone.

"He begins to play his hand openly," said Tris, not daring to name Maradass. When she learned that it was no longer the Mad One but his younger son who now commanded the black forces she nodded.

"I knew that a change had come but did not know what," she said quietly. "The troubles become harder now. I fear the death of the Black Knight has only let loose a greater curse on the lands."

Tris looked to the road ahead, undisguised concern in her dark and thoughtful eyes; she spoke little that day, and indeed they all walked in silence, deep in their own thoughts and fears.

The Border Road

They were on the Border Road, walking a particularly narrow section when Tris, who was far out in front, signalled for them to leave the road quickly. Deep canyons fell away on each side of the narrow plateau; it was a very dangerous place to have trouble find them. Tris leapt to a rocky outcrop and disappeared from sight; the others could see nothing, but they ran until they reached a vantage point amongst a tumble of boulders not far from the broken stonework of the road.

At first there seemed nothing to fear. The sky was still and warm, flies buzzing in clouds on the heavy air. Then they felt, rather than heard, a distant rumbling in the earth. Far ahead on the road they could see a cloud of dust rising from the dry lands to the west. Black specks eventually appeared from the cloud, which continued to approach ominously. Soon they were able to make out the nature of the dark figures. They were marauders, running far out in front of an approaching mass that moved along the road towards them. After a short time they could all make out the leading horsemen who rode at the head of a vast, moving army.

The travellers lay on the earth amongst the rocks watching as the faster moving marauders came closer. When the creatures reached the point where Tris had left the road one of them found her scent. Immediately his fellows joined him and all stood circling the spoor, but they did not leave the road. From behind them a group of horsemen spurred on ahead of the army and soon six of their number and six of the dogs stood on the road, conferring. Then the group split up; three dogs and three horsemen began to track Tris into the rocky land, while the other three began to backtrack on her spoor. It was not long before the dogs found the spot where Flindas and the others had also left the road.

It was obvious to the travellers that the dogs and men communicated much more readily than normal for man and beast. One of the riders removed a small bird from a pouch, and after attaching something to its leg he sent it aloft. The bird flew directly back to the approaching army. This time several horsemen and six more dogs rode out to join the others. One horseman stood out amongst the dark riders, he was a commander in the army and wore heavy armour. On his chest was the Maradass emblem, the white skull of a dog.

"We must go!" said Simo urgently.

"And where shall we go?" asked Brook of his fellow Elbrand. "We cannot outrun marauders here. There is nowhere to run to, just from one pile of boulders to another. No, we will save our energy for the coming fight and we will die, and that will be that."

His fatalistic words shook his younger companion. Gram held on to Wuff and said not a word. The men had two long bows left between them, Flindas held one and Brook the other; there were no more than ten or twelve arrows left. Each man began to go through the motions of checking his weapons, though they all knew exactly what they carried, while below on the road a decision did not seem easy for the riders.

"They may not want to stop the army for a few people hiding in the rocks," said Teaker, his face still carrying a grin.

"Let us hope so," said Simo.

The head of the army was approaching. Lines of marching men appeared in the clouded distance. The commander stood high in his stirrups and looked into the rocks where they lay in hiding, then he waved his hand and the riders and marauders began to follow the trail of the Elbrand.

"My mouth will turn and bite me," said Teaker with a chuckle.

They remained where they were, watching the approaching dogs as the army of foot soldiers and horsemen began to march by, the greater part of the army would not stop it seemed.

"Nine is not so bad," said Teaker.

"What do you mean nine?" said Simo. "I count twice that number."

"Tis only the dogs I am worried about," replied the little man.

Gram began to weep silently but the warriors who were now her protectors did not notice. Brook and Flindas strung their bows and waited. The horsemen came on until they were forced by the terrain to dismount, the marauders did not run ahead now, they came on as a group.

"They are within bowshot," said Flindas.

"Yes," replied Brook simply, and both men drew their bows.

The arrows sang together across the distance and buried themselves deep into two hairy bodies; two marauders fell thrashing in their death throws. The others howled in surprise and turned to flee but were kicked and goaded forward, only to have two more of their number fall. The animals would not advance now. They hung back from the horsemen who moved amongst the rocks, concealing themselves as best they could. Flindas felt surprise that the dogs showed such terror of their enemies. He had thought the marauders to be guided entirely by the dark magic of Maradass and would be utterly fearless. Two more arrows flew across the distance and this time two men fell. Flindas looked at their few remaining arrows.

One of the horsemen returned to his mount and galloped rapidly to the head of the passing army. Line after line, troop after troop marched by, six abreast. There was something very strange about this army Flindas thought. Though there were several large troops of well armed horsemen, almost all of the foot soldiers carried long spears, without a sword or bow to be seen. These peculiar troops marched stiffly and in perfect unison, they held themselves upright without showing any signs of weariness. Flindas also noticed something else; these men, if indeed men they were, took no notice of the skirmish that was taking place not far from where they marched; their grim stony faces stared straight in front, ignoring everything but the road ahead. Wagons rumbled along drawn by large horses with ordinary men at the reins, while packs of marauders moved by, most of them well aware of the happenings to the side of the road. At the head of the army a group now broke away, there were perhaps fifty horse soldiers returning to join the others.

"Now we really do have problems," said Teaker, and there was now no smile on his face, he turned to look at Gram but the girl was too frightened now to cry.

The horsemen dismounted and spread out below, then came on steadily. Four of their number fell and then no more, for Flindas had strung their last arrow. Brook looked out at the approaching enemy and then smiled at his friend.

"It is a very long shot for that bow," he said, and Flindas looked out beyond the soldiers to where the commander still sat astride his mount.

Flindas smiled grimly. "But worth the try I think," he said.

He drew the bow and aimed high into the air. There was little wind and though it was not a bow such as those to be found on Zeta, it had proved itself well. Flindas made a slight adjustment to his stance and then the arrow leapt soaring into the air. The commander's armour was sturdier than that of his men but when the arrow descended it caught him high in the shoulder, deflected a little and then tore into the shoulder joint. With a cry the commander fell backward. His horse reared in fright and the man was thrown to the ground, where he writhed in agony clutching at his shoulder. Some of his men returned to assist him while the others continued their hunt. There was a sudden tumbling of small stones behind the companions and they turned quickly, expecting marauders; Tris clambered breathlessly up the slope behind them.

"Quickly!" she called to them. "There is a way out, come, now!"

"Do not be afraid," she said to Gram. "We will be safe soon."

Flindas heard the fear and doubt in her voice.

Brook scooped up the girl, they picked up their belongings and ran without looking back with Wuff bounding along beside Brook; there was fear in the little dog for he had smelled the black dogs of Maradass. They were seen and the black horse soldiers quickly returned to their mounts, while the marauders milled around them and did not yet follow their prey. Tris was far ahead of the others, she seemed to fly across the tumbled rock. They were close to the cliff's edge running parallel with the road, while the massive army continued to pass unheeding; the ground was almost flat here and would not hinder the pursuing horsemen. Tris stopped and waited for them to join her behind a large boulder.

"I must explain quickly," she gasped. "There is a jump."

"Not another one," joked Teaker.

"This is urgent!" she scolded him. "It is a long downward jump over a chasm. First we run hard down hill, there is a corner, and then we jump. If you were not to know of this you would probably not reach the other side. I will go first and call out when we are about to get there."

She looked at Brook and he nodded, Gram was as safe as she could be in his powerful arms.

"Come here," said Flindas and picked up the unprotesting Wuff.

"We must run fast and keep apart," said Tris urgently. "Expect the leap or you will not survive it, come!"

She turned and ran on along the cliff top. There was a call from behind as they were seen again. A number of harsh blasts from a horn were heard, then from the dark ranks, marauders and a full troop of horsemen turned and joined the pursuit. The travellers ran as hard as they could and the leading black dogs howled in glee, loosened now to run down their prey.

Tris took a trail that cut across their path, it led over the side and down a wide ledge that jutted out above the depths below; the thunder of galloping hooves followed not very far behind. The way was becoming steeper and they ran harder, almost flying down the Shortway, with the howling of marauders echoing about them. There was a corner that they could not see beyond, Tris was running quickly and gave a loud cry that was not words; a moment later she was jumping for her life with the others close behind.

The chasm was wide, and fell away to a great depth; Flindas launched himself into space with a cry that was echoed by the others. The landing was a smooth rock surface that sloped downward in the direction that they jumped. Brook and Flindas landed together, they fell and slid down the rock, becoming entangled with Tris. Gram and Wuff both yelped with surprise and scrambled loose; then Simo and Teaker crashed into all of them from behind. They tumbled into each other against a rock face, and then they were quickly on their feet and turned to watch, knowing what must happen now. Tris held Gram who did not want to look away.

Behind them the dogs and horsemen had continued their chase, unaware of the danger ahead. The first group of marauders came into the corner at a flat run. With a howl they saw their mistake and had no time to prepare for the leap. They fell screaming to their deaths far below, followed by all of their companions. Then the leading horsemen came around the rock face and in moments they too were screaming and gone, their cries of terror echoing about the cliffs. More horsemen turned the corner and fell. To the travellers it did not seem as if they would ever stop. Those behind could not hear nor see the fate of their fellows, and at a gallop they all turned the corner and were gone into the depths until there were no more. The last horseman, unable to stop his teetering mount, gaped at them in terror, and with a final cry fell to join his ill-fated company. The travellers climbed the smooth rock shelf and looked into the depths.

"Good," said Gram.

The dust began to settle on the great carnage below, then without a word the small group of dusty travellers turned and hastened down the trail.

The path wound down into a cool basin where a small lake was fed by a stream; from there they could see the road across the valley. They camped that night and risked a small fire. All were hungry and the hot meal was welcome. Tris spoke of the Shortway that they had just survived.

"It was shown to me by my father," she told them. "Though I have never attempted the jump before."

She smiled a little, and then bit hungrily into her bread.

"Perhaps I am worth twice my weight in gold now," she said and no one disagreed.

"Yes," said Gram quietly.

They ate on in silence.

"Maradass is on the move," said Flindas when his small meal was finished.

Tris flinched at the mention of that name but said nothing.

"He is confident and does not need Zard to command his armies," Flindas continued. "It looks as though he intends to strike into the Regions, even before his sons are born."

"There is one man who will no longer command his armies now," chuckled Teaker, remembering the longbow shot.

"Did you note the great many grey soldiers, all spearmen, who walked stiffly and did not seem so human?" asked Simo. "I would say that no more than one in thirty of that army was truly human."

"Yes," replied Flindas. "They were very strange, I have not seen there like before."

"Whatever they may be, they travel to the east," said Teaker. "Perhaps they mean to take Viris-Tan-Vara."

"I do not think so," replied Flindas. "It is not the prize that Maradass has in mind, though it would be an easy one. No, there is but one city that would please him to burn and that is the City Amitarl."

"He has not the power to find Zeta," said Brook. "But Tolth is sworn to protect the Regions, if word reaches him of this invasion, the army of Zeta will come, even without Landin and the piece of the Seacrest that he carries."

"If he still carries it," said Simo thoughtfully. "The black army marches and we may be too late. Perhaps Maradass has taken Elfhand and already holds two parts of the prize he seeks."

"You are not too late," said Tris, looking into the fire.

"What do you mean?" said Brook looking at her intently. "What do you know of this?"

She shrugged off his glare. "I know where Elfhand may be, or perhaps was," she added.

"Why did you not speak of this before?" Brook growled.

"We were going in the right direction," she growled back. "And now you all owe me your lives, and so I can lay my cards openly." She paused and grinned at those around the fire. "I do not need to bargain now," she continued. "I am part of this expedition for good or ill, and only I will say when I leave, this is my right. So now I can tell you of Landin, the one you call Elfhand. I have met him. He stayed with our band at times on earlier visits to the Broken Lands. He is secretive, though my father was one he confided in. Somewhere near Shish-Tan-Vara there is a valley that is an outlaw's camp. The leader is called Aster. I have never been to it but I may know some of those who live there. Landin had a base there, a cave or hollow place. He was hunted by the Mad One and now his evil son will have taken up the chase I think. The terror he now brings to the Border Road proves that it is a fit name for him. He hunts for Landin above all else, or perhaps he has already found him and the army marches to the destruction of all, though somehow I think not." She mused for a moment. "He is very clever and elusive is Elfhand," she whispered in admiration.

"And you were going to bargain with that," scoffed Simo suddenly. "Somewhere near Shish-Tan-Vara, in a valley. That could keep us searching for years."

"It is closer than you knew before," she retorted. "I wish to see Elfhand and tell him of my father's death, though he probably knows already. They were friends from a time when Landin came here so many years ago. My father said that they were young men together, and yet Landin is still a young man it seems to me. Is it the power of the talisman he bears?" She turned to Brook.

"Yes, the Seacrest sustains him and gives him life," replied the big man. "He is beyond mere human strength and age. Tell me now, what more do you know of him?"

"That is all," she replied. "Search near Shish-Tan-Vara. That is all."

Yet again Flindas felt that a lie flickered in her voice. She was not telling all the truth but he did not pursue it. The others seemed to accept her words and Flindas wondered about this for a while, before realising that these men were not accustomed to people using deliberate lies. They came from a peaceful trusting land and Flindas thought regretfully that he seemed to have been suspicious of others all of his life. It had saved him at times, and yet had also caused him to withdraw from those that he most wanted to trust. He had become used to being alone and relying only on himself.

That night Tris answered a question that none had dared to ask, she had been speaking about her father and her life as the daughter of a leader amongst thieves.

"Who cut you?" asked Gram suddenly, she had been silent for a long time.

Tris was herself silent for some time, staring into the small fire.

"When I was younger there was a man who said he loved me," she said, looking at the small girl who reminded Tris of her younger self. "He said he would even die for me. When I did not return his love he cut me. He did not want me to die. He just wanted me to be ugly. He did a good job."

"You are not ugly," said Gram knowingly. "Just different."

Tris smiled, looking deeper into the fire.

"He was an important man and yet my father killed him, and made many enemies in doing so," she added.

There was a long silence amongst the group.

"How far are we from Shish-Tan-Vara?" asked Brook looking at Flindas, who thought for a while before replying.

"By road we are perhaps midway between the two cities of Viris and Shish," he replied. "But the Shortways can change much of that it seems." He in turn looked to Tris.

"About the same as you say," she said. "It is a difficult road to measure, another one hundred leagues perhaps, another twelve or fifteen days without mishap."

"We must be more careful than before," said Brook. "Maradass now owns the road and we must expect his troops at any time."

"What of food?" said Teaker. "We are low, and I do not see loaves of bread growing around here."

"I have a suggestion," said Tris. "One day's march from here there lives a band of thieves. My father took me there not so many years ago. With my presence amongst us we should be welcomed and fed there, perhaps even supplied with food and other needs if you still have some of those pretty trinkets about you."

Simo was against the idea but there seemed little danger in the plan and they needed to find food and other supplies soon. After a short discussion it was agreed that they would visit this band, Tris seemed very pleased with the decision.

"What of the girl?" said Brook.

Gram lay bundled up asleep by this time.

"She cannot remain with us for much longer," said Flindas. "The danger is too great."

"This place that we go to, there may be someone there who will take her," said Tris.

The fire burned low and they settled into sleep. During the night they were woken by a rumbling in the earth. Far off they could see torches passing along the distant road. Many of the stone faced men were marching to the east and the torches took a long time to pass. The next day the travellers continued their march. No one went by them on the road and it was late afternoon when Tris led them down a narrow path that made its winding way into a narrow defile that passed amongst tall cliffs. The possible paths were many and any one of them could have been the correct way to the thieves' camp. Tris led them without hesitation through the labyrinth though she had only been there once before.

"We are getting close," she spoke over her shoulder. "These are thieves and do not harm their victims. It is our code, but they will defend themselves and their homes to the death. If you do not wish to be killed in an avalanche you will show no weapon in your hand, and take no cover from above. We come in peace, they have to see that."

They walked on for a time then Flindas heard the distant

call of a desert bird. It was answered even further off.

"We have been seen," said Tris. "Remember, we come in peace."

She took a trail that cut under a steep overhang and then began to climb a narrow path up the cliff; there was a challenge from above.

"I am daughter of Drask," Tris called back. "We come in peace."

She paused. There was silence from above, then a voice called for them to come on. They came to a ledge where a number of men stood, all ragged but well armed. Flindas noted the good quality in their arrows and bows.

"We seek refuge," said Tris to the leader of the men.

"Yes we know you, Tris daughter of Drask,' he said. "But what of these others? They are not thieves, and nor are they from the Broken Lands if I guess correctly. What do they here? Not anyone may come to our hold and go again. You have the forfeit of their lives in your hands Tris. Go beyond here and your companions may not be allowed to leave."

Tris spoke to the man. "Times have become hard if a thief and her friends cannot find sanctuary amongst my father's friends," she said.

"Times have indeed become hard," replied the man. "There is death on the road and there are many more mouths to feed. Our hospitality has become as thin as our people. I cannot let you pass, not yet."

He turned to one of his companions and spoke in hushed words. The man scampered up another pathway and disappeared around a corner.

"We must wait," said Tris turning to her companions. "I did not expect this. Times indeed have changed."

The travellers sat against the rock face at the back of the ledge. They were trained for endurance but day after day of walking through the Broken Lands were beginning to tell on their strengths, only Tris seemed unperturbed by the distances. She stood and spoke with the leader of the guard but he did not tell her much. Food was not as plentiful as it had been. There was no traffic on the roads now. No food and supplies to steal as the wagons rolled by between the two cities. There were only soldiers and dogs. It was a long time before the messenger returned and spoke with his leader, who eventually turned to the group.

"Agarn allows you to advance, but he requires blindfolds on these others," he said to Tris. "If they see the way in then they may have to die because of it."

"I will not be blindfolded," growled Simo. "To be cut down in the dark. No! I will remain here."

His hand strayed to the hilt of his sword.

"Simo!" called Brook. "No one going to die here."

Brook turned to Tris. "This is not what we expected either," he said sternly. "I cannot comply with this demand. We will leave now."

"I am afraid that is not possible either," said the leader and raised his hand. From rock ledges, and behind boulders, at least twenty archers, bows drawn, showed themselves.

"Curse the girl," spat Simo, the sound of his words burnt the air. "A trap and we are in it." He backed away against the rock.

"Enough!" called Brook, his hands held out in a sign of peace. "We have no choice." He turned to the leader. "I will take the first blindfold," he said.

Swiftly their eyes were bound, though their hands remained free and they were allowed to retain their weapons. Anger smouldering in his eyes, Simo allowed himself to be blindfolded, and then with a hand on the shoulder of the man in front they were led on a long walk, often stumbling on the narrow paths. At one point they were led underground, the air cool and dry, then they emerged into the sun again and were assailed by the smell and sounds of habitation.

Voices called out around them, birds squawked at their intrusion. Food and animal smells wafted on the air, while children called to one another as a crowd began to form around the blindfolded warriors. When their eyes were finally uncovered they found themselves in a dusty circular valley facing a large cave in front of which sat a number of men and women. A large man at their centre began to speak.

"Tris, daughter of Drask, you are welcome here," he said in

a quiet and friendly manner. "The memory of your father is strong in our home. We are on hard times and your companions I am not so sure of. They are obviously warriors and therefore are not on the side of Maradass, which is good. But we now live on a knife's edge in these bitter lands. We can no longer feed all who come knocking at our door. How do you say, daughter of Drask? What redeeming qualities have these warriors that we would feel inclined to house and feed them? Speak!"

"Greetings Agarn," replied Tris, her voice authoritative yet in some way humble. "My father's memory of you is of a generous heart. These men are my travelling companions. We go to Viris-Tan-Vara to seek news of the Evil One. Yesterday these men led a troop of marauders and many black horse soldiers to their deaths. So many died that I could not count them."

At this Brook looked at Flindas and raised an eyebrow.

"Not a day's walk from here, there lies in a deep ravine, not less than fifty horsemen and dogs," Tris continued. "These men are great warriors and those in the ravine were not the first of the enemy to die at their hands. Their journey here in the Broken Lands has great bearing on the future of this region, and those of the south. We need food, arrows and bows. With them we will destroy many more of these foul beasts of Maradass in your name. We will avenge all who die by his hand."

She grew silent and Agarn turned and spoke quietly with those about him. Finally he turned back to the group. "Brave words Tris," he said. "Now let the men speak for themselves. Is there one amongst you who speaks for the others?"

Brook stood forward. "I am the leader on this journey," he said. "My name is Brook and we travel here from the Isles of Zeta."

At this a murmur spread through the gathered people.

"We seek one who came from Zeta before us," continued Brook. "He is Landin Elfhand, and if you can help us with any knowledge of him it may be that you help the lands more than you could know. We are warriors and yet we cannot take any glory from the deaths yesterday." Tris turned and scowled at him, but he continued. "We ran from those that hunted us," he said. "We were saved by Tris and they fell to their deaths. It was not our doing. Tris is the one who led us there."

Agarn laughed from the depths of his belly, his great voice bellowed in mirth. "You are a very honest man I think," he said to Brook. "That is good, good. And the others, who are they?"

Brook turned to his companions, he was about to introduce Flindas when Agarn held up his hand for silence. He leaned forward, his deep brown eyes searching the face before him.

"I think we have met," he finally said. "I know you from somewhere? Tell me, you are not from Zeta, I think."

He continued to look intently at Flindas, who after a time spoke into the silence.

"My name is Mardin and I come from the Westlands," he said. "I have not been here before, no. I think you are mistaken, someone who has my features perhaps?"

He became silent, Agarn continued to look at the man before him, and then he shook his head.

"Yes, perhaps one who looks like you," he said.

For a few more moments he gazed into the face of Flindas then he moved on to greet Simo and Teaker, also Gram and Wuff were brought forward. Tris explained their presence in the group and asked sanctuary for them.

"We have too many mouths to feed already," said Agarn. "What can we do with these two? The girl may become a thief in time but what can we do with yet another dog in camp."

"I will take them," came a woman's voice from the crowd and she stepped forward.

"Ah yes," said Agarn thoughtfully. "I was forgetting you Stell. Yes it would be good for you to have someone at your hearth again."

Agarn turned back to Brook.

"Can you pay for this girl's keep? We are not a charity here," he wore a half smile.

Brook dug into his waist pouch and from it produced one of the precious gems that he still carried. He stepped forward and placed it into the large hand of Agarn.

"Oh ho!" the thief leader exclaimed. "Now this is a pretty

thing." He leaned over the blood red stone, and then held it up to the light, peering into its depths. "You have more of these?" his eyes flashed.

"I cannot give you more," replied Brook. "Our travels will be long and we need what we have."

"Do you not realise that I could kill you and take it all," said Agarn scowling at the big man before him.

Now it was Tris who spoke. "The code of thieves," she reminded Agarn. "We do not harm those that we steal from. Since when did you become a mere robber?" She snarled the words at the seated man. For a moment a look of fire came into Agarn's eyes and Flindas thought these could be their last moments, then the man smiled, great bursts of laughter echoed around the cliff walls that surrounded them. Agarn appeared unable to stop and it became infectious. Many in the crowd laughed with him until he was once again able to gain his composure.

"Well said, daughter of Drask," he smiled. "You remind me of that which I should never forget. You are indeed your father's offspring."

"Yes, yes," he juggled the stone in his hand. "You are all welcome to stay. We will feed you and send you on your way with food enough, weapons too. Now Tris I would speak with you alone." He signalled to a man who had remained in the semi-darkness of the cave entrance. "Binda come here," he called. "I want you to show these men where they may sleep. They will join me for the evening meal. Until then gentlemen."

He gave a slight bow from where he sat.

The man Binda was tall and very thin, his arms hanging long and limp at his sides. He came forward, eyeing the travellers suspiciously, then led them to a small overhanging cave with leaves and dry grass scattered on the floor. The travellers lay in the shade, resting and talking amongst themselves. There were many curious folk amongst the band of thieves, especially the children, who would come as close as they dared, give a yell, and bolt out of harm's way, giggling wildly. Gram soon found herself invited to play. Tris finally rejoined them and watched the children's games for a time then turned to Flindas.

"Why did you lie?" she asked him. "Does Agarn really know you from somewhere?"

"Yes, he knows me, though I had forgotten him," he replied. "It has been ten years or more since we met. I was in the Broken Lands for the first time and was travelling with a wagon load of goods going to Viris-Tan-Vara. I earned my living that way for a time. I was passing through a narrow place when a band of thieves leapt onto the wagon from the rocks above. They were well practiced at thievery of this kind. The ropes were cut and they were beginning to empty the wagon of parcels before I could even turn to fight them. When I did they had not expected a warrior to be driving a wagon. They had no weapons except for knives at their belts, while I used a heavy staff that I carried beneath the seat." Flindas smiled a little at the memory.

"There were three or four on the wagon," he said. "Each one I dealt a blow that knocked him to the road. Others came on but they were easy to repel. The horse and wagon kept rolling and I was able to defend the remainder of the load until the thieves ceased to chase me. Agarn was one who was amongst them. He was a much more agile man then. I remember him now, he was very vocal and swore an oath to find and kill me, I have been threatened before and it is not such an unusual thing. I heard later that his brother had been one of those that I had forced from the wagon, and that he had died from the blow. I meant no injury to them. I defended my livelihood. That was all. I lied to him now because I had to. The sooner we are out of here the better. I would not like Agarn to discover who I am."

Tris nodded. "You used a false name, Mardin, why was that?" she asked.

"The name I used ten years ago was Dran," he said. "Agarn would know that name I think. He would also know the name of Flindas Demsharl. The notice of a reward for me has been circulating throughout these lands for years now. So yet again I must take on another identity. Mardin from the Westlands, yes, that will do for now."

That evening they joined Agarn and many others around

a large cooking pot. It was a thick rabbit and lizard stew with crusty bread and it tasted good to the travellers. There was much conversation around the fire, talk of Maradass and Zeta, and many things besides. They spoke of Landin, and Agarn told them that he knew the man they sought.

"He has been here a number of times, but he has gone north I hear," said the thief.

"North!" exclaimed Brook. "Why did he need to go north? It looks to me that the Armies of Maradass are now here and go to the east and south. Can there be more to the north that he needed to know of?"

Brook's words trailed away, he shook his head.

"That is as I hear it," said Agarn. "The source was a good one. If you find a man by the name of Aster, who at times can be found near Shish-Tan-Vara, you may learn more. He is said to have been the bearer of the news that took Landin into the Desolation. Of that news I know nothing."

His mouth was suddenly full of bread and stew. At his elbow sat the thin figure of Binda, who turned to Flindas with an undisguised look of malice.

"And you Mardin of the Westlands," he said. "It was the Westlands? Yes? Your voice is rather cultured for a peasant from the west."

"Not all those from the west are uneducated," replied Flindas. "You may be surprised."

"Yes I expect I may," said Binda, peering from beneath his heavy brows. "You have not been in the Broken Lands before, you say? I too felt that I may know you. Is it not strange?"

"Perhaps you saw the same man as Agarn," replied Flindas.

He was on guard. Binda knew something and was playing a poisonous game.

"Yes, perhaps I did," said Binda knowingly and said no more.

It was much later, when the group around the fire were retiring, that Binda approached Flindas as he stood alone looking into the starlit sky.

"I know who you are," he whispered with an evil chuckle in his voice.

"And who am I?" Flindas turned and faced the man.

In no time at all the man Binda could be dead without a sign. Flindas had no wish to kill him, and the man had not betrayed him yet. There may yet be a reasonable way out of this he thought to himself.

"You are the one called Flindas Demsharl," replied Binda with a mocking smile. "There is a huge price on your head. Your father would dearly love to see you hang." He chuckled. "If I told Agarn he may be inclined to hold you for the reward," he said. "Sanctuary or no. It is much money. It would feed many mouths."

"And why have you not told Agarn of this, if you are so sure?" Flindas eyed the man with distaste.

"Oh I am sure," replied Binda, and took an old tattered piece of paper from his rags and unfolded it carefully.

"There is a good description of a forked scar on your right forearm," he said smiling. "It is there, I saw it when you washed today. Flindas Demsharl, son of the Governor of the City Amitarl, I am honoured to meet you." Binda gave a mocking bow, his eyes never leaving the darkened figure before him, he was no fool.

Flindas held back the blow, his eyes flared bright. "What do you want of me?" he fired at Binda, his anger coming close to the surface.

"I want what all people want," replied Binda. "Money and power. Is it so much to ask?" He waited for an answer that did not come.

"As for you Flindas Demsharl," he continued. "What I want from you is not so much. Agarn has greed too. He would hold you until he could claim the reward and I would receive but a pittance for my trouble. From you I want the stones that your big friend holds. Is that so much to ask?"

He backed away as Flindas drew himself up.

"I will wait here," said Binda. "If you do not bring me the stones by dawn then I will tell Agarn."

Then he moved silently back into the darkness of the rocks.

Flindas returned to the others, they were talking together and when he joined them he told them of Binda and his demand.

"You must have the stones," said Brook and began to take them from his pouch.

"Wait," said Flindas. "He is a treacherous creature. He could still expose me and have the jewels too. There may be another way."

Simo spoke for the first time. "He waits in the rocks for you," said the Elbrand warrior. "Go to him, pretend to have the gems. When you get close, kill him."

"No," said Flindas. "If my past has caught me then I will look for another escape other than killing this man. I could leave now and meet you later."

"You would not find the way," said Tris. "Even if I told you how, you would not get very far. You saw them. There are bowmen everywhere on the pass. No, but there may be another way out of this. Tell me Flindas, when you had your first encounter with Agarn and he swore to kill you, can you remember his words?"

Flindas thought for a time. "I did not hear more than a curse at first," he told her. "It was later, after his brother had died that I heard he had sworn to kill me. Someone told me, I cannot remember. I think it was sworn in the name of someone I did not know. No I cannot remember now."

"Was it sworn on the Grave of Haydra?" asked Tris smiling, knowing that it must be so.

"Yes, I think that was it," said Flindas, wondering at his friend's smile. "He swore on the Grave of Haydra that he would kill me. How can this help?"

"It is not a common curse," she replied. "It is never given lightly and in this there is a way that it can work for you."

Tris leaned forward and told them her plan, and of a deep superstition held by all thieves in the Broken Lands.

Flindas did not deliver the gems, and he hoped that Binda had a sleepless night waiting for them. The morning dawned heavy with cloud. A change was coming from the west. It was during breakfast that Binda stood and told the gathering that he had an announcement to make. All sat expectantly as an evil leer came to the man's face. He looked at Flindas as he spoke the words.

"There is one amongst us who is not what he appears to be," he told the gathering. "We have one in our midst who has committed the vilest of crimes. A man who killed his own flesh and blood, his own brother, this man should be punished."

A cry went up from the ragged people gathered there. They looked about them, wondering who this evil person could be. Binda stretched a long thin arm and pointed at Flindas.

"This man," he said so all could hear. "One who sought sanctuary among us, the one who calls himself Mardin. This is the man who is truly called Flindas Demsharl and is sought by his father, the Governor of the City Amitarl. The reward is great as many of you must know. There is a reward of five thousand gold pieces on his head if he be taken alive."

There was a gasp from the gathered thieves. They had never heard of a reward so large before. The companions of Flindas also looked in surprise at the tall warrior, not knowing before of his true parentage. Agarn stood and raised a hand, and there was silence.

"Is this true?" he spoke to Flindas, who remained seated on the ground, looking at the men who stood across the fire from him.

"No," he said carefully. "It is not the full truth."

Binda began to splutter.

"I have a poster," he cried. "There is a scar, right forearm. Look, look, it is there."

Flindas came to his feet, slowly, deliberately, and then rolled up his sleeve to expose the unusual scar on his forearm.

"You see, you see," crowed Binda excitedly.

Agarn took the poster and read it slowly.

"You are Flindas Demsharl," he said finally. "You have no sanctuary here. We will hold you until we can collect the reward."

"I am not only Flindas Demsharl," was the strange reply. "You, Agarn, know me by another name," Flindas had rehearsed his part carefully.

"What riddle is this?" Binda shrieked. "Mardin is your false name. We know that, you are Flindas Demsharl and no other."

Flindas spoke loudly for all to hear. "I am a man that Agarn has sworn to kill on the Grave of Haydra."

The crowd gasped almost in unison.

"What is this?" bellowed Agarn, a touch of fear in his voice.

"Stop the riddles and tell me plain," he scowled at Flindas.

"I am the one you know as Dranskar," he told Agarn.

The big man stood for a while in heavy thought, until a slow look of comprehension came to his face. Hate came into his eyes and then his voice.

"You killed my brother," he cursed. "Yes, I swore to kill you and I will."

"Seize him!" he called to those around the circle.

"Wait!" came suddenly the commanding voice of Flindas and all stood where they were.

"On the Grave of Haydra," he said clearly, and then the gathered thieves understood. A moment later the truth came to Agarn. "On the Grave of Haydra," Flindas said again quietly. "You have sworn to kill me with your own hands, with help from no other. This is the oath you have made on the Grave of Haydra. Come then, kill me if you can."

Agarn then saw the trap clearly. He was no match for Flindas and he knew it. An oath sworn on that ancient thief's grave was unbreakable. Haydra meant more than any god to the thieves about him, and they too realised that there could be but one outcome of a fight between these two antagonists. None would step forward to help their leader, for they knew that the curse of Haydra would come down upon them. They could not even harm one who was cursed by another in Haydra's name. Agarn stood, not knowing how to retreat from this dangerous situation. Haydra was Haydra and he a mere leader of thieves, those around him of his band, even the most trusted, would not touch Flindas.

Binda leapt forward and began to speak. His words were garbled in his excitement. Flindas coughed soundlessly and Binda suddenly put a hand to his throat, eyes open wide looking at Flindas; then he fell to the ground, thrashing about as if in a fit.

"What now?" bellowed Agarn distractedly.

"I am a healer," called Flindas and was at the man's side

before any could move.

Flindas deftly removed the small dart as he felt for a pulse at Binda's neck. Others rushed to Binda who had slipped into a deep sleep and eventually he was carried to his cave.

"A fit of an excited and troubled mind," said Flindas calmly. "I have seen it before. He will wake in time and his head will hurt a great deal."

Agarn stood shaking his head, bewildered.

"And now," said Flindas. "Do we fight, or do we leave in peace."

Agarn glared at Flindas but could do nothing, without the support of those around him he was helpless and preferred to live.

"Go," he said with a curse. "You are free to go. Go now!"

He turned and walked into his deep cave, he had lost much respect from those who followed him but his life remained his own.

"Let us take his advice," said Brook. "Now."

Returning to the cave for their packs they found Gram and the woman Stell waiting for them.

"I want to go with you," called Gram as she saw Tris.

"We are going on a dangerous journey," she told the girl. "I am sorry Gram but it is not possible for you to come."

Tris held her as she cried.

"I will return," she promised. "I will come back and visit you here one day."

Stell came forward and gently eased Gram into her arms.

"She will be loved," said the woman. "Only a short time ago I lost my husband and two children to the Evil One's dogs. Have no fear for her."

Wuff sat dejectedly, watching his young friend's pain.

The travellers left quickly, each man newly equipped with arrows and bow. Again they were blindfolded and led to the rock shelf where they had first met the thieves. Tris waved goodbye to the guards who watched, and then led the way until they had rejoined the road.

They walked on into the morning, spending much time as far from the road as possible, and always covering their tracks where they left the paved way. Rain began to fall and remained in the air for several days. It pleased them to know that the marauders would now find little trace of their scent. Whenever an opportunity arose they would take the Shortways that Tris suggested. If Landin was sheltering somewhere to the north of Shish-Tan-Vara there was little need to ask at any of the villages that still seemed inhabited.

They travelled in this way for some days, avoiding the riders and dogs that at times passed along the road. Though there were no more large movements of troops, Marauders might pass in the night, or a solitary horseman would gallop by as the travellers watched from afar. As they came closer to Shish-Tan-Vara all such movement ceased, there were only the occasional ragged denizens of the Broken Lands, who would scuttle away at their approach. Occasionally they would stay amongst thieves. Tris would take them to a "safe" camp, though she did not explain why it might be "safe". They were unhappy places. Thievery was no longer a good business with no one travelling. They did not stay for more than a night in these places and could gather no further news of Elfhand. Soon they would reach the old wizard city Shish-Tan-Vara of which many tales of ancient horror had been told. There would be danger for them in this place, but here also lay there best hope of finding Elfhand.

Shish-Tan-Vara

The road to the west remained clear of Maradass's horsemen and marauders. Rain swept over the travellers until one early evening they saw ahead of them the lights of a city.

"Shish-Tan-Vara," said Tris pointing. "We will be there by tomorrow nightfall."

"That long?" queried Brook.

"Yes," she replied. "It stands alone on a small plateau that is sheer on all sides. There is only one way up to it, and the same way down. The road between here and Shish takes a great many turnings with no shortways."

"What sort of place is it?" asked Teaker, who peered into the gloom at the distant, twinkling lights.

Though Flindas had at times ventured into Shish-Tan-Vara he remained silent, letting Tris speak of this grim place.

"The city was built as a fortress, and though the walls are broken in many places it could still be defended against an enemy," replied Tris. "It keeps a strong line of defence against any mad ones who try to make it their home. Tis a strict place where you must prove your sanity before entering, Mayor Hoglim and his pack of villains see to it. No one lives there who does not meet his demands. There is no choice for the inhabitants, they live by the terrible laws and taxes, or they must leave. Some have been forced to go without the use of the road."

She brought one palm of her hand down hard onto the other with a loud slap to demonstrate her meaning.

"We will be asked to pay a tax just to enter the town and another one to leave," she continued. "We will be charged high prices for whatever we may buy. I do not think that we should all enter Shish if you value the contents of your purse. There is something else we must keep in mind now that I see Shish intact and not burning. It has always been rumoured that Hoglim is in the pay of the Maradass family. We must beware of what we say."

They discussed this for some time and it was eventually decided that as they knew the city, only Flindas and Tris would enter. They would very quietly seek for news of Elfhand and the one called Aster, the traveller's food supplies were low again and they would try to buy whatever they needed.

"It may be that we will stay in the town for a number of days," said Flindas. "We will not come out without news."

This was agreed, and the following day Brook, Simo and Teaker left the road not far from the road up to Shish-Tan-Vara and climbed to a vantage point where they could observe both road and city. There was clean water nearby, and after covering their tracks from the road they felt secure from the eyes and noses of their enemies. Rain fell steadily offering more concealment, while a small overhanging cave would give the three Elbrand some shelter. Tris and Flindas, both carrying almost empty packs, followed the road towards the city. It wound down a steep rock face and then, after crossing a broad river, began to climb the opposite cliff to the city high above. Both had been this way within the last years and they knew what to expect.

The bones of those who had died there still remained scattered along their route, many wished to enter Shish-Tan-Vara but few were accepted. The bones were those of people who had been denied entry and had starved, or had been overcome by the crushing heat of high summer, or perhaps by a knife in a desperate hand. Even now there were people living by the side of the road in crude rock shelters, roofed over with the rags of the dead. All looked to be starving, but those who lived here were not the totally insane ones; they were just the utterly poor. A dark hierarchy governed the road that led to the city above, a hierarchy that forever excluded them. At the bottom of the road were the totally destitute, those who would surely succumb to heat and starvation before the year ended, while far above at the gates and in the rubble of the ruined walls there were the stronger ones. Here, just outside the gates, the garbage from the city was dumped each day to be rummaged through and fought over by those outside. No food scrap was too unclean or rotten that it did not go into a cooking pot, often there were fights and deaths over some pitiful morsel. There were those on this road who would at times eat their own kind, the situation was desperate and finally impossible for nearly all who could not enter Shish-Tan-Vara.

As Tris and Flindas climbed they were at first eyed with envy by those too weak to even beg from them, then as they gained the higher levels they were assailed by many who begged, but took care to remain out of sword reach. Nearer the ruined walls there were some who might have attacked them, and yet they held back, something in the eyes of Flindas told them that it would not be a wise thing to do. Finally the closed gates were before them, tall and magnificent they stood, in stark contrast to the ruined walls and piles of garbage that lay in small mountains nearby; Flindas had heard the story of these impregnable gates.

Shish-Tan-Vara had once been the fortress of one who was either a wizard or who had a power much greater than other mortals. With ancient magic he had been able to place a spell on the gates, magic that they would never allow the gates to be taken by force. Never would an enemy enter by those gates, and none ever had. The fortress was taken by an enemy who had brought with them miners from the mountains in the south. For a year or more these men dug and scraped, while their army had laid siege to the walls above. When all was prepared the leader of those who attacked the city had given the order to retreat.

Those on the mighty battlements had laughed and jeered at this apparent abandonment of the attack, then a huge rock that had been set to fall was released by the miners, and its fall caused a series of supports to collapse one by one. Those above felt the city tremble and then a vast section of wall had fallen into the chasm below. The fortress was taken by the much superior army and Shish-Tan-Vara's leader and citizens put to death. The walls had been ruined further but the gates had withstood all attempts to dislodge them, the gates were never again opened and the road turned left and passed through a breach in the once mighty walls. Here it was that stood the insolent guards who challenged the two travellers as they approached.

The captain of the guard, a surly man with sharp, cunning eyes, first ascertained that they had been to the town previously, and had gained entry before. He then tested them and finally called for them to pay the tax, one piece of gold each. Flindas handed over the gold which Brook had given to him, and they were free to enter. It was a large and tumbled down place that they walked through, many shattered ancient ruins stood amongst the much simpler habitations of those who lived there now. There were many small gardens, growing vegetables and grains that were heavily taxed by the mayor. The small army that was kept by Hoglim were amongst the few who were fed well, and there were always more who wanted to join this mob than there were places to fill.

"I wonder that Maradass has not destroyed this place," said Tris to Flindas. "It would be easy. What good can Hoglim be to him?"

"He must have a use for it," replied Flindas. "His spies are surely here amongst the people and the guards. As you have said I would not put it past the great Mayor Hoglim to be in his pay. We must stay alert and be prepared to leave fast. Whoever the spies may be they are surely keeping their eyes open for travelling warriors. We are being watched even now."

They walked towards the centre of the city, the sun dipping behind a far plateau as they entered the central square. A market had been held that day and the last stalls were being dismantled. There were many people still walking the streets and the taverns were full of drunken men and women. Dirty barefoot children played in the roadway.

"There is a man I know," said Tris. "He was a friend of my father. He owns that tavern." Tris pointed to a dimly lit building from which music and raucous singing came. "He knows the town well and may be able to help us," she said.

They crossed the square and entered the large, crowded, smoke-filled rooms. Though not a customary habit in the Southern Regions, here in the Broken Lands there were many who smoked. A variety of plants which grew wild along the banks of the rivers were cultivated for their intoxicating qualities, long stemmed pipes passed from hand to hand. Most of the gathered folk took no notice of the newcomers, yet there were a few who pointed. Tris indicated a small man who wore a dirty apron and was just then carrying a tray of large tankards across to a corner table.

"That is Jontow," she told Flindas. "He is the man I spoke of. Let us sit and take ale. He will be busy for much of the evening. There may even be a room for us here, and we can talk later."

A young woman served them and eventually Jontow caught sight of the two newcomers and bustled over.

"Tris, Tris my dear, it has been such a long time," said Jontow smiling an almost toothless grin. He hugged her with a friendship that was undisguised. He welcomed the man called Mardin and promptly forgot his name. "A room, yes a room," he replied to Tris's query. "Indeed I have one at the back. Here is the key, down the hall, last on the left. Talk, much later, busy, busy."

Then he was gone as a group of new arrivals joined those demanding a drink. Flindas and Tris found their room, which was small with one shuttered window and two simple beds; there was nothing else in the stonewalled cubicle.

"Very elegant," said Tris with a mocking smile.

They lightened their load, and then decided to take a walk. There were others living in the town that they were both acquainted with, and who may have the information they sought. The night was warm and heavy with expectant rain. Men trundled hand carts along the streets selling small loaves of bread filled with meat or goat's cheese, there were drink vendors and stalls of vegetables left over from the day's market.

"There is still no shortage here," said Flindas with some surprise. "Supplies must still come through, even with the marauders and soldiers on the road."

"I think it comes from the west where there have always been large gardens kept," said Tris. "Maradass must indeed wish that Shish-Tan-Vara remain living."

It was two years or more since Flindas had been to the city, and they soon found that a man he sought, who had been his employer and friend, was no longer living. They hunted for others, but after a thorough search for old acquaintances there now seemed to be no one that could help them with information on Landin Elfhand. Quietly they had approached a few strangers but to no avail, even for a proffered piece of silver. Some knew of Aster by name, but he had not been seen for many moons, and none knew of one called Elfhand or the band of warriors who had accompanied him to the Broken Lands. Tris and Flindas were walking down a quiet narrow street when Tris whispered from the corner of her mouth.

"We are being followed," she said.

"Yes," said Flindas. "A small man with a limp, he has been with us for a time, let us see what he wants."

They turned a corner without looking back then slipped into the shadows. The man eventually peered around the stonework, and then tentatively entered the darkened alley. Flindas came quickly from the shadows and grasped him by the back of the neck; the grip was like a vice. The little man squealed, and then his hand darted to his waist. The blade had barely been exposed when Tris took the thin arm and forced it up the man's back. He dropped the knife and whimpered in fear.

"Why do you follow us?" said Flindas, his voice menacing.

"I was not following," squealed the man. "I was on my way here, you attacked me, ah! You hurt me. Let me go."

"Not so quickly," said Flindas. "You lie little man. You have been following us for some time. Now speak."

His fingers dug into the scrawny neck and the man cried out in pain.

"Yes, yes," he squealed. "I was following, I am a thief. I was going to rob you."

"You are no thief," spat Tris, forcing the arm further up his back. "You are neither clever enough nor careful enough to be one. No more lies. Why do you follow us?"

"I was told to," he almost shrieked. "The captain of the guard, he told me to follow."

"Why?" asked Flindas.

"I do not know," said the man and cried out again as fingers pressed into the side of his neck.

"Tell us," said Flindas, his voice coming in a hiss close to the man's ear.

The man was in a panic. "He told me to follow and watch and report who you spoke to," he said whimpering. "That is all, I swear."

Flindas relaxed his grip and Tris let the man's arm fall to his side.

"Go," said Flindas and pushed him hard with his boot. "Do not let me see you again or you will have much to regret."

The man bolted around a corner and was gone.

"The captain of the guard seems very interested in us," said Flindas. "Perhaps we should become interested in him."

"He has much power here," said Tris. "Almost as much as the Mayor. They fear each other, and use each other. It will be difficult to get anything from him."

"We will see," was all Flindas said and they returned to the tavern where the evening's festivities were beginning to ease.

A number of men still sat at various tables, their eyes unfocused and their words incoherent. Jontow was busy with a mop and bucket, the floor was awash in filth.

"I will join you shortly," he called as they made their way down the hall to their room to rest.

Much time passed before there was a tentative knock at the door and Jontow entered the room.

"Market day," he sighed. "'Tis always the busiest time. Now

Tris, how can I be of service to you and your friend?"

"We seek one who is known as Landin Elfhand," said Flindas. "And also one called Aster. Do you know these men and where they are to be found?"

"Aster, yes I know Aster," replied Jontow. "The other, what did you say his name was? No I do not know him. Aster comes to Shish-Tan-Vara quite often, though I have not seen him for three or four moons, perhaps more. He lives somewhere to the north I believe."

He shook his head.

"I am sorry I cannot be of more help."

"Can you tell us what you know of Aster?" Flindas continued and Jontow thought for a while.

"He is not like many who live in the wilds," he told them. "He is soft spoken and quiet, and for that reason he is a very likeable man. There are few in this horror of a place that I would call kindly, but he is one that I do. He has stayed in this very room a number of times and has always paid promptly. Compared to most of the ruffians and drunkards that come to my establishment he is a prince."

Jontow spoke quietly. His mind seemed to wander into realms where princes actually lived, where peace reigned in a beautiful world. He gave a deep sigh and returned to the room. "I do not know where he is," he said finally and stood to go. "There is one here who may help," he said as he was about to open the door. "Her name is Garla and she and Aster are very close if you know what I mean. She lives nearby. I will take you to her in the morning if you wish."

"Thank you," said Flindas. "Yes, until tomorrow then."

Then Jontow was gone.

"Tomorrow then," repeated Tris and stretched out on her bed.

Morning came with much more unrelenting heavy rain. They ate a breakfast of eggs and bread then Jontow led them through the wet, and in some places flooded streets. They reached a weathered and cracked wooden door in a plain stone wall where Jontow knocked quietly. The door was eventually opened by a young woman. She was dressed in a simple one piece garment and her feet were bare. Flindas noted a distant look in her eyes and he knew that he had seen it before. She was a user of an addictive liquid that was extracted from a plant that grew in the far south. He had seen no such plants this far north and knew the drug to be both rare and expensive. Her voice seemed to float on the air as she asked them what they wanted. Jontow told her that they sought after Aster.

"I do not know where he is these days," she said, her voice soft and far away. "He did not come when he said, and now I do not think that he will ever come again."

"Why do you say that?" asked Flindas.

She looked at him closely, her eyes screwed almost closed to see him better. "He said he would come," she said again. "He did not and now will not, and none of it matters any more anyway."

"Do you know where he might be?" asked Flindas gently.

"Oh, he may be dead," she said and laughed softly. "He may have fallen down his ladder and broken his neck, but nothing matters now, nothing." Her voice trailed off in a whisper.

"His ladder," said Flindas. "What ladder, where?"

"He took me there once," she said after a time. "His place to hide himself and his friends he said. He took me so that if I was in trouble I could find him, but now there is never any trouble. The captain makes sure of that."

She giggled and almost fell. Tris was about to speak but Flindas raised his hand for her to be silent.

"Where is Aster's home?" he said quietly, holding her arm as she seemed about to fall.

"What?" she murmured. "Oh, it is beyond the Twins and high up someplace."

"What are the Twins?" asked Flindas and it was Jontow who now spoke.

"They are two matched hills a league or more to the north," he said.

Flindas turned back to Garla.

"Beyond the Twins and high up," said Flindas. "What more can you tell us. It is most important?"

"I know not," she said finally. "That is all, that is what I told the captain. He knows. He went looking. I showed him the way."

"Why?" asked Tris, unable to be silent, and Garla turned to her and studied her closely.

"The captain gave me the magic" she said and pushed her hair back from her pretty face. "The captain said I could have as much magic as I wanted if I would show him where to find Aster and his friends. He brings me more tomorrows tomorrow and then I can go flying again."

They left her smiling and clinging to the door.

"I have never seen her like this," said Jontow. "There is something strange about her."

"I know what it is," said Flindas. "The captain has given her Topa. It is a drug found much in the City Amitarl. Highly addictive and very dangerous."

He stopped briefly in the street as a plan began to formulate in his mind, then moved on and returned to the tavern. Morning found them both in the street early.

"Today we buy food and tomorrow we will call on the captain," he said to Tris and smiled.

They spent the day buying flour, dried fruit, nuts and cured meat, and by the end of the day they had as much food as they would be able to carry from the city. Flindas asked Jontow for some ragged clothes and the tavern owner had no trouble in obliging his guests. That evening the travellers remained indoors and prepared their packs for a quick departure if things did not go according to plan the next day.

Dawn came wet with a heavy mist as Flindas and Tris left the tavern, making their way back to the house of Garla. Flindas had observed a nearby ruined building the previous day and here they set up watch on Garla's door. It was not until noon that the captain of the guard, accompanied by two of his men, turned the corner into the street. They stopped at Garla's door and the captain entered, leaving his two men lounging outside. Flindas did not wait long. He slipped into the rags of clothing and, disguising his walk and posture, made his shuffling way along the street. For all intents and purposes he was an old man making his way to some unknown destination.

The guards took very little notice, and when Flindas came

opposite them they did not even see the double open handed blows that sent them both unconscious to the roadway. Flindas pounded on the door as the captain had and it swung open to reveal the captain himself. He too did not expect the blow that took him on the jaw and laid him cold on the stone floor. Flindas waved for Tris and together they dragged the unconscious men across the threshold and closed the door; the street was deserted and none had seen the happenings there. Flindas walked to the back of the dwelling and stopped suddenly in a doorway, though he had taken little time in following the captain into the house, he saw that it had been too long. Tris joined him and gasped; lying stretched across a bed lay Garla, her eyes were wide and staring as her life's blood dripped to the floor. There was hot anger in the eyes of Flindas as he turned from the room.

"Tie them," he said to Tris indicating the two guards. "Make sure they cannot speak."

He took hold of the captain and dragged him into a room to the side of the door, there he bound the man's hands then threw a pitcher of water into his face. The man began to come around and Flindas slapped him hard several times. The captain finally opened his eyes and looked with fear into those of his captor.

"Why did you kill her?" said Flindas, anger smouldering in his eyes.

The captain did not speak. Flindas drew a knife and pushed it hard against the man's throat. "Talk or die, it is your choice," he said.

"She knew too much," cried the captain.

"What did she know?" snarled Flindas.

"She knew where to find Aster and she talked with you. I could not trust her." The man was telling the truth to save his life.

"Why is Aster so important to you?"

"He knows Elfhand," was the fearful reply. "He knows where the Cripple has gone. Elfhand is a great prize."

"A prize to who?" asked Flindas bitterly. "To Maradass, yes?"

The captain was silent in his fear until Flindas forced the

knife harder against his throat and a trickle of blood began to appear on the blade.

"Maradass, yes," blurted the captain. "And Mayor Hoglim, he too offered a reward for Aster and Elfhand. There is much I do not understand of their intent. All I know is that if they were in my power, these two outlaws would make me rich." Flindas turned to look at Tris. She stood in the doorway, a look of revulsion on her face.

"Where is Aster?" Flindas asked the captain again.

"He is beyond the Twins," was the reply. "There is a high place with a valley beyond those rocks. My men are already preparing to march. Why not share in the spoils? There is such a huge reward that we could all be rich, yes you too."

He was looking at Tris.

"This Landin is a much wanted man," he continued. "We could retire to the South and live like princes. Come, what do you say?"

"I have heard enough of his voice," said Flindas to Tris turning away.

Tris came to the captain and pushed a ball of filthy rags into his protesting mouth, securing another rag to hold it in place.

"What now?" she asked. "We cannot just leave them."

"We must," said Flindas. "To kill this creature, no matter how evil, would make us no better than he is. No, we will ensure that they are well secured then leave this rat hole. We go north to find Aster, and perhaps Landin."

After checking that all their captives were well tied they slipped from the house. As a parting gesture Tris gave the captain a vicious kick and he began to choke on the rags as she followed Flindas from the house. There was no movement in the roadway and they made their way back to the tavern. Jontow would accept no money from the daughter of his friend and they left him standing at the door waving a cheerful goodbye.

When they reached the gates the head guard on duty would not at first accept their gold pieces that allowed them to depart the city. It was most unusual for the captain not to be at the gate at this time of day he told them. Only the captain or the men next in command could receive the tax he said, but Flindas thought he lied. This man had been given instructions to not let them pass.

"The captain is somewhere in the town and his second officer is with a troop of men below in the valley," the guard said.

The man seemed ready to call on the other guards who played a game of chance near the gate. Flindas took another three gold pieces from his pouch and let the man see them.

"We are in a hurry," he said to the guard. "An extra three pieces of gold if you will let us pass."

The guard looked about to make sure none of his fellows could hear what was being said, and then he grasped the money.

"Be gone," he said. "The captain will not like it. Go, before he returns."

They left the gates and began to descend into the deep valley.

"The captain will certainly not like it," Tris chuckled as they walked down the road.

At the foot of the ravine, on a flat area by the river, they saw a troop of thirty or forty foot soldiers waiting for their captain, who would not be joining them for some time.

Slipping past, unnoticed by the second in command, they made their way back to the place where their three companions had left the road. Flindas gave the high whistle of a desert bird, which was the pre-arranged signal for those above, but there was no sound or sign of them. He dropped his pack and ran up the incline to the ledge, what he found put him in great fear for his companions. There were signs on the earth, swordplay had taken place, and blood lay mingled with the dirt and splattered across the rocks. There was no sign of the Elbrand or their packs and weapons, wedged in a tumble of rocks he found the blade of a knife that he recognised as belonging to Teaker. It had been snapped off near the hilt. Flindas could do nothing more and returned to Tris.

"They have gone or been captured or are dead," he said to her. "There has been much blood spilt above. Come, we cannot linger. We must go north in search of Landin."

He looked back up the slope and shook his head slowly, despondently.

After slipping by the gathered troops near the river who still awaited their captain they made their way to the north. Having walked some distance over the rocky terrain they saw against the sky two almost identical flat-topped hills.

"They will be the Twins," said Flindas.

They continued to walk towards them, eventually passing between their towering sides. They were in a deep valley that continued to run north, and the two companions had travelled for perhaps another league when Tris pointed to their left. A small side valley cut away from the one they were in and high above stood a solitary peak.

"That may be the high place," said Tris and Flindas agreed.

"Let us go and see," he said.

They began to scramble across the broken country that separated them from the valley. The sky had been threatening with more rain all day and it now it began to fall, at first a fine mist hung in the air but it was not long before the skies opened. They trudged on completely soaked.

"We cannot go further," said Flindas finally. "I do not see the high place and we may miss something in the gloom."

They paused beneath an overhanging rock; the light was fading as the rainstorm came on heavier still. There was little that they could do and soon Tris began to shiver with cold. Though she protested, Flindas took her in his arms and together shared their body warmth. It was almost dark and the rain had eased when they heard the sound of trudging feet not far off.

"The captain must have escaped or been found," said Flindas. "Quick, let us hide."

They crawled behind a tumble of rocks as the struggling soldiers drew closer. Soon the troops could be seen coming along the valley floor. At their head walked the captain and his second in command. The two travellers watched them pass by then followed.

"They will lead us to where we wish to be," whispered Flindas.

They held back in the soft rain and mist, following the troops by sound rather than sight. Then they heard the captain barking orders and they paused until the troops began to move again. They continued to follow in this way and almost walked into a group of soldiers who had been left below, while the others scaled the heights. The soldiers were huddled against the cliff and did not see the two bedraggled travellers who, without detection, were able to retreat back into the deepening gloom. Flindas and Tris made a wide circle around them and began to climb. It was not hard to follow the trail of loosened stones made by the soldier's feet, and ahead of them they could soon hear the struggling men.

The rain eased and then ceased all together, though a dense mist still hung in the air about them. The climb was not difficult, and soon they had almost caught up to the troops who were having a much harder time, equipment and arms weighing them down. The sun had set and only a soft light from a haloed moon allowed them to see the way ahead. At last Tris and Flindas reached the high point and not far ahead they saw the soldiers beginning to make camp. It was obvious that the captain had no intention of going further that day, the troops made themselves as comfortable as they could while Flindas and Tris found a dry hollow amongst a pile of broken rock and settled for the night. Again they lay close to each other for warmth and eventually they slept.

It was first light when they awoke, not far away the soldiers were stirring and preparing to move. A light drizzle obscured them and gave the travellers the advantage of being able to remain close, as the troops continued their march. The morning slipped by as the soldiers descended a deep and broken valley, then the sounds of movement ceased at the captain's command. Flindas observed them from a broken pile of rocks near a low cliff. The soldiers stood at the edge of a drop that fell away sharply below them, some who had carried ropes now began to prepare the descent into the valley below.

"This must be the place where Asher has his ladder," whispered Flindas, and after circling the soldiers they were able to look down into the valley.

The armed men were not used to ropes and were having difficulties with the descent. Almost all of the soldiers had begun the downward climb when from behind a crumbling outcrop of rock there suddenly descended a rush of ragged men. They carried swords and spears and with a cry they charged the soldiers; including the captain who had waited above. With a clash of metal the two groups came together in battle. The soldiers were better armed but outnumbered and they were forced back to the cliff's edge.

The captain rallied his men but the sheer weight of their attackers became too much for them. One by one they were cut down or fell to their deaths from the cliff. The struggle was ferocious and did not last long. Finally the captain stood alone, sword in hand, teetering on the very brink. One of the ragged men, taller and stronger than his comrades, came forward and began to speak with the captain, his words lost to those who watched from hiding. The captain gave a cry and lunged with his sword, the tall man turned the blow easily and his own blade took the captain across the face. Screaming and blinded, blood streaming from his wound, the captain attempted to avoid another blow and stepped back too far; for a moment he hovered on the edge, and then with a horrible cry he plummeted to the rocks far below. Tris spat quietly on the ground and smiled.

The ragged men then rushed forward and hacked at the ropes on which dangled many of the terrified soldiers. Some were already down on the valley floor and could only watch as their fellows fell about them, there was a cheer from the men above as the final rope was cut, then they turned to go.

"Stay here," said Flindas to Tris.

Leaving the rocks he made himself visible to the victors of the battle, both hands held out before him in a sign of peace. Flindas called to them.

"Wait! I must speak with you."

The men again drew their various weapons and came to surround Flindas.

"Who are you?" said the tall man who had ended the life of the captain.

"My name is Flindas Demsharl," he replied, "I seek one who is known as Aster."

The tall man looked hard at the warrior who stood before him.

"I have heard of you," he said. "You are worth much in reward money. Why do you seek Aster?"

"I came here with companions from the Isles of Zeta," replied Flindas. "We search for Aster as he may know the whereabouts of one named Landin Elfhand."

"And where are these companions of yours now?" continued the tall man.

"I do not know," replied Flindas. "I left them to enter Shish-Tan-Vara and when I returned for them they were gone. There were signs of a struggle but I do not yet know what happened to them."

The tall man did not speak for a time, he stood looking at Flindas with an unwavering gaze, and then at a signal from him the men lowered their weapons.

"You are in luck," said the man. "I am Aster and I believe your story. I can even tell you of those that travelled with you. They were outnumbered. They fought valiantly but were taken, caught in nets by the soldiers of Shish-Tan-Vara, my guess is that if they still live they are now in the old dungeons beneath the city."

"And what of Landin?" asked Flindas after a pause. "Do you know his whereabouts?"

Again Aster looked deeply into the eyes of Flindas as if judging how much he could trust this stranger, finally he made his decision.

"He has gone north and west," he said. "He goes looking for the Stronghold of Maradass."

Puzzled, Flindas spoke again.

"Why would he go there? He cannot assail a fortress alone."

"He said that there was no choice," replied Aster. "His sister is held captive there by Maradass."

"What!?" exclaimed Flindas. "I had heard that Leana is dead, that she fell to the sword of Zard in the south of Dreardim. I travelled with one who saw it happen."

"Yes," said Aster. "That is as Landin told it to me, for he saw it in a dream. It was later that we learned a different story. His sister Leana did not die that day, but was found by marauders and their masters. They closed her wounds and took her to the north, to Maradass. The body of Zard was also returned to the north. The Mad One is now dead as the old oaths held true. He has been replaced by his second son the one they now call the Evil One. This is the truth of it, and now, single handed, Landin has gone to rescue his sister. He has been gone one full moon and I fear that we will not see that great warrior again."

Flindas shook his head in wonder and then waved for Tris to join them, as she came there was reluctance in her step. Aster turned and when he saw her small dark figure he cursed and moved towards her, there was anger in his step, his hand on the hilt of his sword. He had taken only a few paces when Flindas was between them, a look of warning in his eyes.

"Whatever may be your grievance with my companion you will not harm her," he said in a calm but deadly voice. "Swear to it."

"I have made an oath to kill her," Aster bellowed and made to push by Flindas.

The hatred that Asher held for the young woman was also reflected in the snarling faces of his men. There was the glint of flashing steel in the broadening light as Flindas held two knives at the throat of the outlaw leader.

"Swear," said Flindas again. "Or we die here together."

"I cannot swear an oath to break an oath," said Aster. "You must kill me and then my men will kill you."

Flindas stepped back, in one movement the knives disappeared into his clothes and were replaced by his sword.

"My death will mean the lives of not a few of these men," he said. "Whatever Tris has done, she is my friend and I will defend her with my life."

"She murdered one who was like a brother to all those who stand before you," said Aster, venom in his voice.

"I did not kill him!" Tris cried out. "He fell, but you will not believe it!"

Flindas remained between them. There was no sign of

attack by Aster, who spoke again.

"How can we believe this when he was your sworn enemy?" said Aster darkly.

"He was my father's enemy, not mine," Tris replied in anger.

"When your father died, you took on his oath. That is the way of it," said Aster.

"It is not my way," replied Tris. "My father killed Tias when he did this to me," she said bitterly, pointing at her scars. "My father then died in a fall and I may never know how or why. And then the father of Tias dies in a fall and I am on the same road, I am seen, and I am instantly judged guilty."

"And you ran," said Aster with scorn. "Why did you run if you were not guilty?"

"Because I have seen the justice in these lands," she spat back. "I ran to save myself from that justice."

Aster was silent for a time and then he spoke to Flindas.

"I would not have more blood shed here," he said. "Will you put down your weapon in trust?"

The blade slipped back into its scabbard and Aster looked again at Tris.

"I will hold my oath for one day," he told her. "You may go now if you wish."

"I will stay with Flindas," she said defiantly.

Aster looked at her in surprise, and then spoke again to Flindas.

"We must go from here," he said. "There are still soldiers below. Come, I will take you to the safety of our caves."

He turned to his men and they moved off at a slow quiet run. No sound of metal could be heard, though their weapons were numerous. Aster and Flindas began to follow while Tris stood and watched them for several moments, then she too broke into a run.

At one point there was a precipitous downward climb, where rope ladders took them deeper, and then a narrow ravine cut back into the side of a towering cliff. Deep inside the narrow place they arrived at Aster's camp. There were many people there, children played amongst the rocks, and there was a welcoming smell from many cooking fires, no madness could be seen amongst those gathered there.

"Come," Aster spoke to Flindas. "There must be a meeting now. There is much to discuss."

He turned further and gazed at Tris who came behind. There were looks of astonishment on many faces as the people in the camp recognised the young woman. The massed people began to move toward the cliff where there was a large central fire before the dark mouth of a cave. Aster sat with a number of men and women while Flindas and Tris were motioned to sit nearby. People gathered, wanting to hear the news, and Aster spoke telling the people of the events that day.

"Mayor Hoglim will not be pleased," he smiled. "His captain of the guard is dead. His greatest ally and perhaps his greatest enemy are gone. Hoglim will not try to find us again for a time. It is the troops of Maradass who are closing the road now."

Flindas was asked to tell about his journey from Zeta in search of Elfhand, when the gathering heard of the army that had passed they broke out in surprised voices. Aster did not like the news.

"Maradass is on the move, just as Landin feared," he said. "With Leana as a hostage he may think that he holds the winning of the game. He is impatient to use his new powers. The question is, will the forces of Zeta, should they come, be enough to hold him from the south? And will they come in time?"

"We are but outlaws," he began to explain to Flindas. "We are outside of all laws except our own, but the few that we are will join against Maradass. Tell us, what of your own plans? Your search I think is now impossible, Elfhand has gone looking for Maradass and I think you will not find him alive."

"I will return to Shish-Tan-Vara," replied Flindas.

A murmur ran through the gathering.

"If my companions are there I will try to rescue them," Flindas continued. "After that we shall see, but my intent has not changed, alive or dead I seek Elfhand."

"You cannot return to the city," said Aster shaking his head, a warning in his voice. "Your friends are in the dungeons and one man alone could not rescue them. Hoglim will have a hundred men on watch. Your friends are an important link to Landin and Hoglim will have guessed that. The amount of gold that Maradass offers for Landin is an amount of many fortunes. Greed for that gold is driving many men's thoughts, but the prize is not Landin himself, it is that which he carries. You know of what I speak. Were Maradass to win that prize there would be none to stop him. Landin is a most powerful warrior but I fear he is foolhardy and he now endangers the entire land in an impossible quest. He believes in his immortality. He told me that no one who has borne the piece he carries has ever died in battle, yet that does not mean it cannot be so. He understood that, but would not be denied, the thought of Leana, his beloved sister, in the power of Maradass almost drove him mad. He has gone to his death and so have your companions I fear."

"No," said Tris suddenly. "We will rescue them."

"You would go?" asked Aster in surprise. "What are these men to you? You bear allegiance to no one now. You are an outcast, and your life is forfeit."

"The reasons for my choice of company are my own," she said.

Then a voice spoke from those gathered. "And what of justice?" it said.

A murmur ran through the crowd.

"She has until sundown tomorrow," said Aster for all to hear. "She will not be harmed in any way, and if she wishes to leave, none will deny her. If she remains longer there will be a trial. It is her choice, this I have promised."

There was little more to be said and eventually the people dispersed back to their evening meals. Flindas and Tris ate with Aster and his family. Tris spoke little during the meal while Flindas and Aster told each other of the happenings in the lands. Flindas spoke of his three companions and his determination to rescue them.

"There is only one way to escape the dungeon that has ever succeeded," Aster told him. "It may still be possible, though it was never used as a way in, but as a way out. The dungeons are far more ancient than much of the town above and only one man has ever been known to escape from them. There is an old chimney that comes from the deepest part of the dungeons that once served all of the fires on each level. It is sealed up and not used now. The dungeons do not hold many prisoners in these times, for there is not the food for them. A quick trial and death, or confiscation and banishment, this is the law now, and of course eviction for those without the skills to live in the Broken Lands is as good as a death sentence unless they can find their way here.

"This man who escaped," Asher continued. "Tranta was his name. He had been a locksmith by trade. He escaped from his cell with a key he made from a small piece of bone. It was a key that opened all the doors in the lower levels, but not the ones above, for they are much more recently made and are numerous. Tranta had noticed that the guards carried but one key on his level and so his escape was made that much easier. It is over twenty years since he came to our camp, when I was but a youth. After leaving his cell, instead of trying to go above, Tranta went deeper into the dungeons and eventually broke through a stone wall and entered the chimney. How he knew it was there I cannot say, the climb is difficult but not impossible it seems. It exits near the town square amongst the ruins." Aster paused in deep thought, and then smiled at Flindas. "If you are determined to enter the dungeons then you will need this." He took from his pouch a steel key, he smiled again as he passed it to Flindas. "It is hopefully a good copy, and may allow you to pass through the lower doors. The dungeons have many levels and unused cells, tis easy to get lost it seems and the key may not even fit any the locks. No one has ever wanted to go in and find out if it is indeed a good fit, but I wish you well."

Flindas held the key in the palm of his hand for a while then placed it in a small pocket within his jacket.

"You will not know where to break through the wall," continued Aster. "You may come out in the guard's room and that will be that. I suggest going all the way to the bottom of the chimney. It is less likely to be used now, as the upper floors are enough for Hoglim to keep his prisoners and his treasures, or so tis said."

The evening was drawing on to night.

"I will go in the early morning," said Flindas.

"We will go," said Tris quietly.

"That will solve our dilemma also," Aster said looking at Tris.

She only nodded, looking at him briefly, and then turned her gaze back to the fire.

The morning came dark with cold clouds and rumbling rolls of thunder. As Flindas looked to the sky he saw high above the camp the wide spread wings of a white hawk, on the edge of sight Flindas saw Storm circling and turning on the wind. Often during the journey through the Broken Lands he had studied the sky in the hope of seeing the strange and wonderful bird again, but always in vain. He had wondered if the white hawk had been destroyed in some way and was very pleased that it was not so. Flindas and Tris ate with Aster then shouldered their packs, it was a long walk and they wished to enter the chimney by nightfall; Aster stood up as they made ready to depart.

"I will come also," he said.

"Why risk yourself," asked Flindas surprised. "You do not know those we wish to rescue. You have no reason to come."

Aster looked at Flindas with steady eyes.

"I too, in my own way, am a warrior of the land," he said. "I also fight for peace, just as you do. Maradass is our enemy and Hoglim is his pawn."

He smiled a knowing smile.

"To disrupt Hoglim in his pompous self importance and corrupt ways is enough in itself," he continued. "I have seen many die by the orders of the Mayor, friends and innocents. If I had but one chance I would certainly kill the man, perhaps if these important prisoners escape, Maradass will do it for me."

They walked from the camp, and many who watched them go shook their heads in wonder. Aster, the one they looked to for leadership, was leaving on an impossible mission, with an unknown warrior and an enemy he had sworn to kill.

"He and Landin are both rash men," one old man said to his wife as he lay watching them pass in the early dawn.

The Parting of Companions

Rain continued to fall as Aster led Flindas and Tris along the narrow paths that would lead them back to Shish-Tan-Vara, the march taking them most of the day. There were trails Aster used that he knew to be undiscovered by Hoglim, and they eventually came on the old city from the west. Disguised in rags they made their way towards the gates. Aster held the last pieces of gold that remained to Flindas, he hoped to be able to bribe their way past the guards, and they were in luck. Since the demise of the captain and his second in command the men on the gate were lax, and eager to take their own tax from those few who came and went.

The three companions entered the town and Aster led them to the ruins and the exit of the disused chimney. A rusting steel grate covered the hole and it was something that Aster had not expected. It was secured by a strong unusual lock that looked impossible to break or lever open, he and Flindas were standing over the hole when Tris knelt beside the lock with two small piece of wire in her hand. Within moments she had it opened. The wires disappearing back into her pouch as she smiled at the other's expressions.

"My father was a master," was all she said.

It was not yet dusk and so they waited, Aster left them for

a time saying there were those in the town whose aid he could rely on, he returned as darkness began to fall.

"The town is in turmoil and a curfew has been imposed," he told them. "It seems Hoglim is expecting an attack of warriors, the fight yesterday and the death of his captain have totally unnerved him. We will have support, but with the curfew there are going to be many soldiers in the streets."

"Let us go, and disappear from unwelcome eyes," said Flindas, and he lifted the steel grate.

The shaft was narrow, only a little wider than the broad shoulders of Aster. Looking into the darkened space they saw far below a small beam of light that seemed to cross the chimney. Flindas went first, then Aster, and lastly Tris. The sides of the shaft had been hewn from the living rock and then lined with bricks to improve the draught. The old work was good but over the centuries many bricks had become loose in their mortar, while some had broken away and fallen. In the near total darkness of their descent they climbed by touch more than sight, occasionally side shafts giving them an easy resting place for a while. They moved slowly, making as little noise as possible, for they did not know what might lie beyond the brickwork of the old chimney.

Flindas came to the light source they had seen from above, a number of bricks had been removed or fallen, and when he peered through he was startled to find himself looking directly at the legs of a soldier who sat on a chair near the shaft. Other guardsmen moved about or lounged on beds. It was a soldier's barracks and Flindas climbed past quietly. He continued to descend until he felt the chimney begin to widen, in the darkness he could not see what lay below him, then he came to the point where he knew that he would have to jump into the darkness below or abandon the attempt and climb back up. He knew that a man had once climbed up the shaft and he reasoned that he could not be far to the bottom, for to climb out from below would have been most difficult if the shaft continued to widen. He spoke softly to the others just above him.

"The shaft widens even more, do not move, I will have to

jump."

Flindas also guessed that he was near the bottom from the thickness of ancient soot beneath his hands. With fear crawling up the back of his neck he let go. The shock of the fall was surprising and he almost laughed. He fell no more than two or three hand spans and landed with a jolt, suddenly feeling very foolish.

"Come," he said softly, "I am down."

All three could just stand comfortably in the narrow space and when they lit a small candle, they found they were in the old fireplace of what must be the lowest level of the ancient dungeons. They could see where newer stone had been laid and mortared into an opening, they tested the stonework with their strength, wedging themselves in place and pushing with their legs. There was no movement. Flindas took out a heavy knife and began to dig at the mortar and chunks began to fall away.

'It is quite old and soft," he said and they concentrated on one stone, digging in between it and its neighbours.

The next time when they pushed with their feet it moved slightly and the mortar began to crumble between other stones. They dug again and eventually the large stone fell with a noisy tumble into the darkness beyond. They could see nothing through the hole. They waited for a sound of alarm but there was none. The next stone was easily dislodged and soon they had a hole big enough to crawl through. Flindas held the light ahead of him as he passed through the old stonework into the chamber beyond.

The room that met his gaze appeared to have been unused for a very long time. Stagnant water lay in a pool over the entire floor and the smell of the air almost made him retch. Strange slightly luminous fungi hung from the walls and there was a constant dripping of water from the high ceiling, Flindas held the light near the old fireplace and called the others through. Holding the candle above his head Flindas made his way to a short flight of steps that led to a closed doorway. He had the key that Aster had given him and after pushing without success at the door he tried the key in the lock. It went in but would not turn.

"I was afraid of this," said Aster quietly. "The pattern for that key is gone and it may not have been copied well enough."

Tris tried with her wires but to no avail. The lock was old and probably rusted.

"Can we break it down?" she asked.

They studied its ancient steel and wood. It did not look possible to do the work quietly. Flindas tried the key again, this time forcing it and he felt just the slightest movement.

"It will turn," he said with a smile. "The lock is just clogged I think."

He slipped a small knife through the hole in the key's head and turned it further. With a soft squeak it finally slid into the open position. Flindas pushed the protesting door open into another dark space. The small candle was burning low and Tris lit another from the first, this next room held little of interest and the air was damp and smelt of rotten things. The floor was covered with filth and debris, spider webs hung in great sweeps across the ceiling, while the door opposite them lay open to another flight of stairs. The three companions crossed the floor and climbed the stone stairway to another closed door. A hint of light could be seen around its edges. Flindas pushed softly but the door was locked and they stood still for a time, listening. There was no sound from beyond so Flindas tried the key and this time it turned easily. The light in the room they entered came from a torch hung in a bracket on the stone wall. It illuminated a row of ale and wine barrels and a single crate of bottles on the floor. There was the sudden shriek of steel on steel and Flindas leapt back. Holding the door almost closed, he peered through the slit. The crate of bottles tinkled and then was drawn aloft as a counter weight came slowly to the floor. There was the sound of the bottles being carried away, feet scuffling on the stone floor above.

Flindas did not open the door immediately. He waited until there was no longer any sound, and then entered the room. Tris extinguished their light and left it on the dark side of the door. They did not lock it as they had not locked the one below. Another flight of stairs took them to the top of the pulley shaft where a torch hung on the wall. At the end of a short passage there was a partly closed door, and from beyond came the sounds of men talking. Flindas held back in the shadows as a man closed the door with a slam. They moved to it and listened, noting as they did so two side passages that ran from the one they were now in. There was the sound of laughter and men eating and drinking, these were men of the guard, the ones who would stand watch on these lower levels of the dungeons. From the sounds Flindas guessed that ten or twelve men ate and drank beyond the heavy wooden door. A conversation close to the door came through to them. A harsh voice was speaking.

"And then they cut the ropes," the voice said. "It was a cursed mess, captain. Half a troop all gone and the rest of them down in a hole an' still stuck they say. Glad I missed it."

He laughed raucously until a muffled thin voice spoke into his reverie.

"But that be nothin' I hears." He said. "What about these warriors then? What about this army that be comin.' Reckon to knock old Maradass off 'is perch?"

The big voice spoke again.

"I reckon they be nearby even," he muttered. "I reckon they be real close and these prisoners be scouts or some such. Yeah, scouts."

His words slurred and his voice was silenced as he drank, the sound quite audible through the door.

"Them's tough men," said the small voice. "Drang saying old Hogswill hold back nothin' on the big one, proper poundin' and not a word from him. Reckon tomorrow they get a bit heavier. Softened up, that what Drang said."

His chuckle passed through the door clearly.

The three companions retired along the passage to where the two other tunnels were carved through the stone of the hill, both showing no light. Flindas chose one and they entered its darkness. Other doorways stood on either side of this passage, stone and mortar closing them all. Flindas struck a flame to another candle and they began walking down the passage, the light flickered eerily, a slight breeze brushing their faces.

The closed doorways were many and Flindas wondered at them, until he came to one where some of the stonework had crumbled and lay in the passageway. He peered through and saw the cell beyond stacked with the remains of a great many people, their skin like parchment, the ones below turning to dust by the weight of those above. He moved on quickly.

The passage had been sloping up for some time when they came upon another door, it was locked and the key did not fit this time. They studied the woodwork; it was not as strong as the previous ones, the workmanship less skilled. There did not appear to be any light beyond so the two men placed their shoulders against it, they moved in unison and hit the door a strong blow, it sprang inward with a loud echoing crash. The wood around the lock had splintered far easier than they thought it would; distant echoes died away slowly and they paused for some time in silence.

The space beyond the doorway seemed vast in its darkness. They entered and found themselves in a huge natural cave, by the light of their small flame they could see that here lay such mounds of human bones that they could not believe it. Tens of thousands, uncountable, unknowable. The horror of it struck them all. Aster pointed to the wall near the doorway where they had emerged, another door stood there. There seemed no other exits from this subterranean grave and they forced it as easily as the previous one. They were in another long passage lined with more closed doorways.

"Is this place endless?" asked Flindas.

"I had not heard of the dead who lie around us," said Aster. "They must be from an ancient time and I suppose best forgotten, it seems that there has always been evil in this place."

They began to walk up the curving passage, their sense of direction now totally lost. The air was thick and stale as they were forced to take a steep flight of stairs down again to another cave, smaller this time but again crammed with the bones of the dead. There were two doorways and each led to a flight of stairs, Flindas shook his head and chose one. After the stairs there was another passage, at the end of which they could see a faint light, Flindas put out the candle he carried and they moved down the tunnel silently.

There was no door this time, and the light came from a side tunnel. They approached what was now a crossing of two passages. As Flindas looked around the corner he grunted in disbelief. The others looked. To their right there shone a flaming torch and they saw the top of the pulley shaft. To their left was the door leading into the same guard's dining room. It was quiet now, the evening meal long finished. The sound of one person moving about came through the door to them. Someone was sweeping and moving chairs.

"We need to know where the Elbrand are," said Flindas in a whisper. "There is only one man in here I think. I will take him. Come after me quickly and look for others."

Flindas took hold of the door handle and doused his flame. With a leap he was through the door and the small man who held the broom had no time to call out before Flindas had him in a hold he could not escape, his mouth covered; there were no others in the room.

"Silence, or I will do it for you," said Flindas into the man's ear. "I will not kill you unless you call out."

The man relaxed just a little and Flindas slowly removed his hand from his mouth.

"Where do they keep the prisoners, the three warriors?"

The man could hardly speak.

"Cells," was all he said.

"Which cells, tell us how to find them?" growled Flindas.

"Through the dormitory," and the small man pointed at a closed door.

"Then what?" said Flindas.

"Then you are in the cells," the man began to speak a little easier. "Far to the end of the passage to the right. There be guards. You have no chance."

"We will do our best," said Flindas as he moved his hand to the back of the man's neck, the small man suddenly went limp.

They tied the unconscious man and laid him in the passage beyond the door that they had entered by. Dowsing the torches that had lit the room they could see that no light came from the dormitory. The sound of snoring men could be heard and after opening the door Flindas began to pad softly down the length of the room.

There were perhaps eight or ten men sleeping in what was a large room meant for many more. A light shone from beneath a door at the other end. The three companions made their way across the floor silently and there was no disturbance of the sleepers. From beyond the door they could hear a sentry pacing. Flindas measured the timing of the man's walk, and just as the footfalls passed the door he went silently through. The man turned in surprise to meet a fist that knocked him insensible just as Tris closed the door quietly behind them.

Further along the passage they could see the shadows of guards in the light of torches, there was now little time for caution. They came on the guards unexpectedly where the passage ended. The four men were no match for the two warriors. Tris held back, her knife ready if she was needed, but with shattering blows the guards were knocked to the floor insensible. They had been guarding a locked door, a barred opening showed darkness beyond, Flindas reached for the lock and the two bolts slipped open with ease. Aster plucked a torch from its bracket and they entered the cell, from a pile of straw against the back wall Flindas saw a figure rise.

"What now?" said the strained voice of Teaker, and then under the light of the torch he saw his rescuers clearly.

"Well about time," he scorned them jokingly and fell back to the floor.

Simo lifted his bruised face from the straw, one of his eyes was closed and he was cut badly about the mouth.

"Quickly," called Flindas in a whisper. "We must go, now."

He rushed to the unmoving mound that was Brook and shook him but there was no response, Simo crawled across the straw to them.

"They beat him badly," he told Flindas. "He has not been conscious for a long time."

The words coming from the bloodied lips did not sound like the voice of Simo that Flindas knew. There were teeth missing and he spat blood. Tris helped Teaker to his feet. The small man held his chest and winced. Simo rose but it was obvious that he too was in much pain; his torn clothing was splattered with much dried blood. Flindas could not rouse Brook who lay as though dead.

"We will have to carry him," he said to Aster and the two of them took the big man under the arms and they left the cell. There was as yet no sign of movement from the guards who lay by the door. Teaker was having trouble standing and leaned heavily on Tris. Simo came last, after taking a sword from the floor. A thin trail of blood trickled to the floor from some hidden wound.

"I am well," he said as Tris looked back with concern, but in his voice she heard the lie.

They were passing as silently as they could through the darkened dormitory where the men lay asleep, when there was a stirring from one of the beds.

"What goes?" called a sleepy voice.

Simo crossed to him and hit him hard with the hilt of the sword, but it was too late, others were waking and had heard the sudden groan of their companion. Flindas threw back the door as there were cries from the waking guards. The companions rushed through and slammed the door behind them.

"Quickly, the benches!" called Flindas.

Laying Brook down they had enough time to wedge the door shut before there was a pounding on it from the other side.

"They are held for a time," said Flindas.

They again lifted Brook and moved as fast as they could through to the passage beyond, there was a heavy drumming on the barred door behind them, then as they passed down the stairs all sound was cut off from above.

Brook began to come around and Flindas felt the big man take some of his own weight, his feet no longer sliding on the floor.

"I can walk," he said at last, his voice coming from a painful distant place. "It is my head that is not working."

"We must go quickly," said Flindas to him.

Brook began to move unsteadily on his own, and was soon able to follow the others. They passed quickly through to the bottom floor and came to the entrance of the chimney shaft. Aster took the lead and began to climb, followed by Teaker and then Tris, who helped to support the small man. Flindas followed closely behind Brook, while Simo insisted on the last place. Simo's voice was weary and distant. They all heard the alarm bell when it began to ring in the town square above. Aster reached the mouth of the shaft and helped Teaker emerge, the small man was beaten and he did not seem able to rise, Tris came close behind.

The square was filling with torches, troops marshalled haphazardly, though none seemed to know that the ones they sought were emerging nearby. In the absence of their leaders Flindas thought that the soldiers may not know the exact location of the chimney, he hoped it was so. Brook ended the climb and then lay panting beside the hole, Flindas, who had come close behind him called softly down the shaft to Simo but there was no reply. Aster was standing watch when he returned a whistle that came from the dark shadows, soon he was joined by a man and they spoke rapidly. Aster then rejoined Flindas.

"They have prepared an escape," he said. " It will not be expected by Hoglim."

"Simo has not come," said Flindas. "We cannot leave him."

"He did not tell you," said Teaker through his own pain. "He was wounded, badly, perhaps to his death. I think he did not want to fall on anyone, so he came last."

"The soldiers are moving," whispered the man from the darkness.

Flindas called into the hole once more but there was no answer.

"We go," he finally said, sadness in his voice.

Brook could move more easily now while Teaker was limping heavily and continued to hold his chest. Flindas moved to him.

"On my back," he said to the little man and there was no argument.

Teaker climbed on and they began to run.

Brook stumbled often but kept up, as they were taken through dark streets and ruined buildings to the very edge of the city, the broken wall stood dark against the night.

"Through the wall," whispered the man who guided them. "There is a rope. Climb down to the next level. Then another rope takes you on a longer climb to the valley floor. There are men in the rocks."

"Your men," he said to Aster. "Go now and I must go too. Good fortune."

Then he was gone into the shadows. They began the descent, Teaker remaining clinging to Flindas.

"I am heavy for such a long climb," he protested.

"If you get too heavy I will tell you when to let go," said Flindas and heard the familiar chuckle begin, then it choked off in pain.

The descent was steep but not sheer, their feet having purchase on the sloping rock face for much of the time. They had only begun when a cry went up and the sound of running soldiers came from above, firelight began to flicker on the ruined walls.

"Quickly!" called Aster who was the last on the rope. "They are coming!"

Their descent was rapid but flaming torches were soon to be seen near the cliff top, it was Aster who saw much of what happened next. A marauder appeared, and then there were soldiers on the brink, who laughed when they saw those exposed below. There was no escape they thought, and the fugitives would simply die should the rope be cut. The new captain of the guard commanded Aster to stop or die, there was no choice and Aster ceased moving. Then from where the soldiers stood there came the sudden clash of swords, guardsmen began to fall back in terror and men cried out. Aster saw two die with terrible wounds.

"Go!" he called to those below. "Allies fight for us!"

Flindas was almost down to the second level when he heard the cries from above. He clasped the rope tightly as a screaming soldier fell past him. Flindas quickly slid down the rope until his feet came to a darkened ledge. He heard Tris call from the nearby darkness that she and Brook had found the second rope. Aster seemed to fly down the first rope and as he landed the rope was cut and slithered down from above. He looked up as the end fell to the ledge.

"It was Simo," he said and pointed above. "He attacked them and fought without fear for his own death. It was plain that he did not intend to follow us. Another thing was most strange. A large white bird joined him, and the soldiers seemed in more fear of this flying creature that they were of your friend. What sort of magic do you hold that such a creature will come to our aid?"

Flindas looked up the slope for a moment, and when he turned and looked below he could see the lights of many torches moving up the valley.

"Later!" he said to Aster. "Soldiers come."

Tris and Brook had already begun to descend to the valley floor. Brook was weary and almost fell, it was a much longer climb and in places they dangled in the air, before lowering themselves to touch rock again. The lights of the soldiers' torches were much closer now. They were running in ranks, each carrying a flame.

"There are more," Aster called.

Not far up the valley Flindas saw another group of lights approaching. They would be cut off. There seemed little chance of escape.

He was still climbing down, watching the lights, when those further up the valley began to fall and scatter. They were under attack he realised, probably by a volley of arrows. All of the torches soon lay spluttering in the darkness. Flindas heard the sound of battle from below and then they were down from the heights, a confusion of rocks lying between them and the far side of the valley.

Aster now took the lead. He angled away from the troops and took them across the open space and into a narrow side valley. As Flindas looked back he saw the second wave of lights falter, archers in the rocks taking a heavy toll on those who carried the torches. Voices came from the darkness and they were met by a number of men from Aster's camp, and then Flindas heard the welcome sound of horses. Teaker was unable to ride alone; he was spent and almost unconscious.

"Put him with me," said Tris. "Together we are not so heavy."

They all mounted in darkness, and then Aster led the way from Shish-Tan-Vara into the mist enshrouded hills.

Much later they camped, a fire was lit and food eaten. Flindas examined Teaker who had ribs that were tender and probably cracked. His left side wore a huge bruise. Flindas strapped his chest and Teaker began to feel a lot easier, Brook was more of a concern. Though he was functioning, he seemed in a daze, his brain ached he said. Flindas had seen this before in men who had been severely beaten, some recovered quickly and completely while others never did. They moved on at daylight and eventually had to leave the horses, the way becoming too treacherous for the beasts. Climbing a steep path skirting a deep valley it was not long before they arrived back at Aster's camp without having to use ropes again. Brook took no part in the gathering that night. With revelry all around him he lay by a fire and slept as though dead. Hoglim had been foiled once again and much of his force destroyed. All in Aster's camp rejoiced, for now Hoglim must answer to Maradass who would surely know soon that the important captives had escaped. The presence of a marauder on the cliff edge revealed how much in league Hoglim was with Maradass. The question of Tris seemed to be forgotten for a time, though she stayed close to the Elbrand that night.

Flindas sat by the small fire near Brook and Teaker and took no part in the celebrations. Barrels had been broached and music played for the dancers to follow, even the soft rain did not dampen the spirits of the victorious. Tris sat quietly and gazed into the fire for a long time.

"What will you do next?" she finally asked.

"I do not know," Flindas replied. "Heal my friends and then follow Brook is my guess."

"But he is not himself," she said. "His head is not clear."

"I will wait," said Flindas. "Landin is gone and may not return. We are as safe here as we can be anywhere with Maradass on the move. Even to get back to the coast and Zeta now may be impossible. I have heard that there are ways to the west that will bring us to the Desert Pass and into the Regions, it may be that we will have to take a long way home."

For a moment he wondered at his words, home was something he had not thought of for a long time.

"Yes," said Tris to his words. "Beyond the Place of Puzzles, I have heard that there is a way, it would be a long journey."

"I spoke with Aster," continued Flindas. "There is no news yet of Maradass on the road to the west, though that may change by the time Brook and Teaker are fit to travel. To follow Landin to the north and west will be more difficult now. Brook lost all his travelling pack including Tolth's map that may have helped us. I remember it well but not perfectly. We could wander through the Broken Lands for years and still not find Landin or Maradass."

Tris did not speak of her own plans, if she had any.

For almost a full turn of the moon they remained in Aster's camp, the weather becoming warmer as winter turned to spring. Teaker's ribs had nearly healed but to Flindas's great concern Brook was still unwell. He no longer complained of his head pains but his voice had become dull, and for much of the time had lost its life and emotion. He still spoke of following Landin and then, as his memory wandered, he would speak as if it were decided that they would return to Zeta. Flindas was in a quandary. Brook could no longer lead the expedition and Teaker could see this also. The little man spent much of his time with Brook and spoke with him often.

"He is addled," Teaker said to Flindas one day. "It makes me sad to see him like this. He is not just my leader; he is my friend."

Flindas talked it over with Teaker. If they could be given horses the two Elbrand would ride west and search for the way back into Rianodar, then they would try to reach the City Amitarl and find a boat. Without horses they seemed forced to remain where they were and Flindas approached Aster on the question.

"Yes," said the soft spoken warrior. "We can supply you with horses, but to travel west has many difficulties. It is possible I have heard to take horses through but it will not be easy. Then there is the Wizard's Castle, there is an old magic amongst those ruins and people who travel there do not always return as the same person."

"We need to send word to Zeta," said Flindas. "I have not told Teaker or Brook but I intend to follow Landin."

Aster looked at Flindas in surprise.

"I will go alone," he continued. "Teaker must get Brook to Zeta. I do not know the intentions of Tris, nor do I know of your intentions towards her."

"I have spoken with the Council," said Aster. "When you leave, if she does not go, she must stand before our justice, there are some who wish to see that trial. For myself I can no longer hold to the oath which I swore against her, I now believe that she committed no murder. If found innocent she could remain in safety here if she wished."

"That is good," said Flindas to the man, who in a short time had become a close friend. "It releases me from yet another concern."

All were sitting around the fire that night when Flindas spoke to them of his plans. Tris remained silent when told that she would almost certainly have sanctuary in Aster's camp. With Aster on her side there would not be many to gainsay it. Teaker at first wished to join Flindas. The wiry little man did not want to abandon the search, but then he began to see the reasoning behind this solution. Brook could no longer continue, even though at times he was almost his old self. Teaker could not bring himself to leave his friend and Tolth must know that Leana still lived. That evening by the fire Brook was coherent and aware of the situation. He understood that he might endanger those that he travelled with and reluctantly he agreed with Flindas.

"I can no longer trust myself," he told his friends. "Teaker and I will find our way home. Flindas, you are probably crazy to go alone in search of Landin, for I fear that he is lost."

He looked with concern on his face into Flindas's eyes.

"Do not lose yourself as well my friend," he said.

"I will come with you," said Tris, turning to Flindas.

"No," he replied sternly. "I go alone."

"But our bargain!" she exclaimed loudly.

"Our bargain is at an end, just as this company is at an end," he told her. "I go alone."

Flindas would hear no more and Tris sat in stony silence looking into the embers of the fire. They planned to part company the following day. Well supplied with food and weapons Teaker and Brook would ride to the west, while Flindas was to follow the route of Landin as far as he knew it. Aster told him of a trail that led far back into the complexity of cliffs and ravines of the Broken Lands. Those that had at times gone north of the road in search of gems and gold had returned and told stories of wandering lost in a vast maze of towering plateaus, and of attacks by bands of mad ones or worse. Some had returned with a madness of their own lingering behind their eyes, while most had not returned at all.

During the time in Aster's camp Flindas had tried to draw what he could remember of the map, he had studied it often before it was lost and still remembered much. A lacework of lines showing the pattern of the Broken Lands, a clear area, perhaps a wide open valley, at the centre of which was a range of mountains. A road that was marked through them, and it seemed under them in places. Flowing to the east was what appeared to be a river, and Flindas had heard that far to the north on the Withered Coast, a wide river flowed into the ocean from the Northern Desolation. The drawing was reproduced as best he could. He was prepared for travel and intended to begin at first light.

His weapons had been gladly added to by Aster and his men. During his time in the camp he had made a heavy shirt with many small leather sheaths sewn within its folds. Into the sheaths went a number of throwing blades. There were more at his belt, as well as his sword and two long heavy knives hanging on his belt. Attached to his pack was Aster's own longbow, a stout weapon given as a parting gift to a friend. Many arrows were there, as well as a long length of light but very strong rope. His pack was almost full of dried food and a water container, as well as his healing kit and other small necessities for the journey. Eventually he lay down to sleep but could not. So many thoughts and visions were passing through his mind. He had survived many dangers since leaving Zeta but none compared with the journey he intended to begin the next day. The Desolation had been used as a place of horror in so many stories from his childhood that they invaded his dreams, with the name of Maradass conjuring up nightmares from the darkness.

Crossing the Broken Lands

The day dawned clear. If spring could exist in these Broken Lands Flindas felt it that morning. He had grown stale in Aster's camp and looked forward to moving, even if it was directly into danger. Teaker and Brook were also leaving; a guide would take them back to the road far to the west of Shish-Tan-Vara. Friends they had made in the camp came to wish them well, though Tris was nowhere to be seen.

"She is probably on the road ahead of you," said Teaker with a chuckle. "I do not think you are rid of her yet."

Brook looked hard into the eyes of Flindas, a man he thought of as a brother.

"Come back to Zeta," he smiled. "We will drink some ale and reminisce about our travels."

It was a hard parting for them all, Brook and Teaker rode west and Flindas took the northwest trail as it climbed further into the Broken Lands. The sun was warm and he strode at a pace that he could keep up for many days. The trail was well worn for a time then broke up and was gone, though the direction remained clear. A far ridge that spread to the east and west marked a change in the lands and there was no other path possible, though small ravines began to cut across his way. They were not difficult to climb in and out of but took some time, he often looked behind expecting to see a small dark figure duck from sight, but he saw nothing.

Flindas looked into the clear sky and there was still no sign of Storm either. The white hawk, which he had gotten used to in his earlier travels, had not appeared since the day following the rescue of Brook and Teaker. In the early dawn of that day the hawk had dropped from the sky and landed near the bed of dry grass where Flindas had lain in a dream of the Magical Isles. Storm had given a single loud cry that had disturbed many in the camp and then had flown above, mounting on the breeze then turned and winged swiftly to the east. Flindas felt completely alone in these barren lands and looked behind him once again, almost hopeful that he would see Tris walking on his trail.

For the rest of that day and into the next he crossed the widening ravines and rock ledges. The tall cliffs of the ridge now towered above him. From a distance he had decided to head for a cleft that cut back into the cliff face, when he finally came close to it, he saw that a dusty path entered a narrow way with sheer rock walls hanging above.

Flindas came to the entrance and saw there were names and messages scratched and painted on the rock. Some were old and indecipherable and all showed that much time had passed since the last message was added. Flindas noted two of them. *If you enter and come back to this place you will never enter again.* While the other read, *Beware the Mad Ones.*

He was about to enter when he noticed a large stone near the entrance that had a recent mark scratched on it. It looked to be the high letter "L," but it was turned at an angle as if to make it into an arrow. Landin, thought Flindas, wondering as he touched the scratched letter. He looked back along his trail one last time and then walked into the beginning of what soon became a network of many possible paths, cut across by cliffs or yet deeper ravines. He found that some had water flowing at the bottom of them. Always trying to go north and west he took paths and climbs that led him in that direction. Some came to an abrupt end while others travelled in the desired direction

for a time and then would veer east or west and sometimes turn him so that he travelled again to the south. On the second day he noted a high point far off, if he could get there and climb it he thought he may have a better view of the easiest way ahead. A full day passed before he was able to gain the height. At the top most point he saw a small boulder which had obviously been place on top of another. Here again he found the high letter "L," which pointed to the northeast. In that direction lay a confusion of plateaus and deep gullies. There was little he could tell for his climb. His way ahead continued in the same maze to the horizon and nothing moved in the dry, barren country that surrounded him. He ate the last of a stale loaf of bread and chewed thoughtfully on a stringy piece of meat. There were rabbits, snakes and small lizards in the Broken Lands and they were not hard to find.

Flindas camped one night where there were enough dry bushes to supply him with a small cooking fire. He was about to turn the skewered lizards over the flames when a large rock crashed down into the centre of the fire, which exploded in a shower of sparks. More rocks tumbled from the heights above and shattered around him, rolling quickly aside he was able to avoid the continuing rain of stone and crouched huddled into a cleft where he remained until the last stone fell with a thud to the earth. It was dark except for the red sparks that glowed in the sand, and no further sounds disturbed the silent night. Flindas kept close to the cliff face and quietly made his way back to his camp.

In the darkness he groped about for his pack and weapons. Miraculously his bow had survived the bombardment, though several of his arrows had not. Flindas shouldered his pack and left quickly. Those above would be coming down to see if he was dead. He retraced his steps along the way he had come that day and without losing a clear view of his abandoned campsite he hid amongst the rocks. After a time he saw the light of a torch bobbing into view, and soon a group of ragged men and women appeared. Some moved in strange ways, their bodies distorted. Some called out and cheered as they came, and each carried a large stick.

The man with the torch stooped over the embers of the fire, he lifted pieces of arrow then he picked up something else, Flindas recognised his water bottle and cursed beneath his breath. Many of the ragged ones cavorted about as though they were children, but the one with the torch stood still. He then looked directly into the darkness towards where Flindas lay in hiding. Flindas slipped from the rocks and retreated further. The man with the torch made a decision. He called in a loud voice and began to run. Flindas remained well ahead of them in the darkness and after a short climb was able to watch the torchbearer and his followers run by below. He remained on the ledge for the night and then continued his journey as the sun rose.

Flindas carried his bow as he walked, on guard for any attack, but none came. By noon he was thirsty and neither a river nor puddle had he found that morning, until he came upon a deep chasm that barred his way. On the opposite side was a steep cliff with few handholds. Flindas knew that the jump was impossible and that he would have to retrace his steps for a time, but far below he saw water running over the rock, at least he could drink. Pushing his pack into a deep cleft Flindas took the rope he carried, and after securing it to a large stone he threw the other end into the gulf, it reached to the bottom with lengths to spare. Flindas swung himself over the edge and slid quickly down the rope, the water was cold and clear. He drank deeply then sat back for a moment, satisfied.

He was about to drink a final time when he heard a cackling from above, he looked up and saw a dirty tattered man holding the end of his rope. Flindas cursed himself for his stupidity. His pack lay above with his bow and all his other possessions. Another man came to the edge and looked down. He too broke into raucous laughter and danced about. The one with the rope held it delicately in his fingertips then let it fall into the ravine. They both laughed wildly. Their mood suddenly changed and Flindas saw them disappear away from the edge, he remained where he was until he saw them return with rocks, which began to rain down on him. He ran downstream and they could no longer throw so far, again he cursed his foolish mistake.

Flindas drew a knife but knew the distance to be impossible. All was about to be lost because thirst had overtaken his reason for a time. At that moment there was a sudden sharp sound then a cry from above, then another. A man screamed maniacally and suddenly leapt from the edge, falling to his death upon the rocks below, while the other gave a fearful cry and ran from view. It was over quickly and when Flindas looked to the pathway above he saw a familiar dark figure peering down into the chasm.

"Are you looking for me?" he called up to her.

"No!" Tris called back to him. "I was passing and thought that perhaps you may be looking for me."

He laughed and returned to stand beneath the place where she stood, the ragged man's body lay still, alone and forlorn. Tris lowered a rope she was carrying and he had soon joined her above.

"You have been following me," he said.

"No," she replied. "Mostly you have been following me."

"Why do you wish to come on this search?" he asked, puzzled still by this unusual woman. "You will die young if you stay with me."

"I will die sometime," was all she said.

Flindas retrieved his pack and they began to retrace their steps.

"That man jumped," said Tris. "They are crazy these mad ones. I only wanted to hurt them enough so they would leave."

Flindas did not admit it but he was pleased that she was with him once again.

The Broken Lands stretched out before them and they travelled many leagues over the next few days, but the distance they covered was not great. Tris had a small pack of food and a water bottle, which they refilled at every stream or trickle they found; the weather grew warmer. One day Tris found blooms on a small withered tree and she wore them in her hair, until the petals dropped.

"You are a strange one," said Flindas smiling.

"No," she retorted. "Tis you who are the strange one."

He looked at her and raised an eyebrow.

"Yes," she continued. "You do not have to be here. You could be anywhere, but you choose to go on a mission that will most likely see you end with a spear in your gizzard."

"And what of you?" he replied.

"I am not talking about me," she said. "I know my strangeness, but you are still strange to me."

He looked at her, seriousness in his eyes. "I cannot turn aside," he finally said. "I knew that I would not, even before leaving Zeta."

"It is easy to turn aside," she said and made a comical turn to the left.

"No," he said smiling. "For me this is different. I have done little with my life except please myself, and perhaps helped some who were in need. I have fought for no great causes and I have lain hidden from the law of my own home. I have done enough to survive, that is all. Then I proved to myself in the Games on Zeta that I could be a part of this mission. Now I will prove to myself that I will see it through."

"But what can you achieve?" she said. "If you find Elfhand he will not return with you. He will try to save his sister. His power may be great but he cannot beat Maradass and his whole army."

"He may not have to," said Flindas with a sardonic smile. "Perhaps I can fight the other half."

"Be serious," she said. "I am trying to save your life yet again. So you go to your death because you need to prove to yourself that you can do it? Wonderful!"

"It is hard to explain," he said and paused. "I killed my brother, and there is something that I have to do, call it redemption if you will."

He did not know the answer himself and again he turned it back to her.

"Perhaps I do not know why I search, but you have even less reason to be here."

"I go where I wish," she said. "There is little for me now on the Border Road, I choose my own path and for now it is the same path as yours."

They were silent as the sun began to pass into the west and they camped that night amongst a group of tall boulders. Firewood was becoming scarce and as they travelled they picked up any that they saw, down to tiny twigs and thicker grasses. Flindas built a small fire and settled back, occasionally pushing the dead snake and rabbit deeper into the baking ashes. The evening sky glowed with many colours as the first bright star began to shine in the west. Tris joined him and lay by the fire. They had spoken little during the afternoon and Flindas broke the long silence.

"You too are a riddle, Tris," he told her. "You do not fit the picture of a thief as those did back on the Border Road"

"They were not bands such as my father's," she said. "They

are full of bluff there. They talk of the prizes they will steal but can only find enough to feed themselves. Before my father died he led a band that was much like Aster's camp. The goods of Hoglim got highly taxed by my father. He died in a fall and I may never know if he was pushed, then the band was taken over by another. My place there was no longer as it had been. Thieves are men, and the women cook and must remain with the children. I was the exception due to my father, who taught me to be a thief, but he died and suddenly to all in the camp I was no longer a thief, I was just another woman. I would go at times with no word to any of them and this they could not tolerate for long; but I could not be bound to the camp. It was on one of those escapes that I was seen as a murderer. In a way I am pleased, it broke my ties with a place I could no longer call home."

"How long were you on your own?" Flindas asked.

"A year or a bit more," she replied. "It is not hard to live off the land if you know a few things. I survived and ate well most of the time. In Viris-Tan-Vara I would go in disguise and lift what I could from those who had anything to lift. There is much wealth hidden away in the rich folk's homes. In Shish, Hoglim covets all gems that come to the town. I would like to have robbed his house one quiet night."

The fire burned low, while above them the moon shone brightly, casting dark shadows amongst the boulders. Flindas could not sleep which was unusual, leaning against a rock he watched the stars. Occasionally a fiery spark would fall streaking across the sky, burning, gone. The questions that Tris had asked during the previous days ran through his mind. Almost certain death lay at the end of this road. He would not throw his life away but something told him that he would not turn back. A picture of his father came into his mind, Lord Demsharl, Governor of the City Amitarl.

"There is nothing I need to prove to that man," he thought to himself.

A man of great power and great weakness, and yet his father had called him a wastrel and worthless, long before Flindas had killed his father's heir and had become a fugitive. Perhaps it was his father's words that helped to spur him on, but this was not the most important reason for his deadly resolve.

"It must be done," he said to himself, but that too was not enough.

The sun had just risen and Flindas was asleep against the rock when Tris shook him awake.

"Mad ones," she whispered. "Many."

Flindas looked to where she pointed. Dust rose about the large group of ragged men, women and children as they trudged across the flat plateau. There was one at their head who carried a long staff that was hung with cloth strips. The only colour to show amongst the otherwise drab shuffling party. As they passed by Flindas saw that some were in chains, they trudged on accompanied by cries and mad laughter from their crazed minds.

"Miners I think," said Tris. "Grubbing in the earth all day for a crust and water. I have heard horror stories about the miners in the Broken Lands. 'Send you to the mines,' is a mother's threat to a wayward child."

They remained hidden until the ragged group passed and had disappeared from view.

"Let us be gone," said Flindas, and they ate as they continued their journey.

The north-eastern route was becoming more difficult by the day. Canyons, some very deep, cut across their path. Whole days would pass and end in disappointment, much of their wanderings being futile and leading them far from their desired road. Large flies, which drank their blood, were a constant irritation and the heat was beginning to take its toll on them. It was only the fortune of the occasional rainstorm that kept their water bottle full.

One day, after a long and useless march to the west along a sheer cliff top they made camp amongst a pile of boulders, broken and cracked by time and weather. Firewood was so scarce now that they did little more than scorch their meat before eating it and settling down to sleep. The stars above showed Flindas that it was past midnight when Tris woke him, a finger against his lips.

"Marauders," she whispered and sniffed at the air like a small hunted animal.

A horse whinnied not far off and soon they could hear the sound of harnesses rattling in the night. Flindas looked back along the way they had travelled that day. Torches shone to the east and perhaps a league's distance away, the horsemen who had been little more than a bowshot away could be heard spurring their mounts and moving toward the lights.

"There is a trail in that ravine below, clear enough to take horses," said Flindas in surprise.

"They are going," Tris sighed and watched as the group rode to join their distant companions.

"I would like to know what they speak of, but it would not be wise to go to close," said Flindas. "They may be hunting us. We had best be gone from here and lose our trail, but at least we seem to have found a road in these dismal hills."

He stopped speaking and looked intently at the far torches.

"I think they are making camp," he finally said. "If they have our scent they do not realise how close we are. Come, let us get as far away from them and try to lose our scent."

As he made ready to go he looked back one last time at the distant camp, and then smiled into the darkness. "There is a lone rider coming, and no dogs if I am not mistaken," he said. "A messenger I would guess. I would like to know what he has to tell."

Flindas lowered his pack and quickly stripped himself of his jacket and all but two knives. The horseman rode with care, the moon giving barely enough light for his night ride.

"If you can, gather in the horse once I have the rider," he said to Tris. "We may be able to use it."

Flindas moved low and fast into the gully to a point where he could intercept the horseman's route, the horseman moving slowly, watchful of the way ahead. It was not really a road, just a narrow way broken in many places. They waited silently as hooves struck stone close by, and then Flindas moved at the perfect moment. His leap took the man from his mount and they crashed to the earth. There was a groan and that was all. Tris had moved with Flindas and had the horse by the reins before it could bolt.

"Is he alive?" she asked.

"Of course," said Flindas with a soft laugh. "I can get no information from a dead man."

He dragged the rider into deep shadow and Tris followed with the horse. There was another groan from the man and Flindas turned to Tris.

"Stay in the darkness and make no sound," he said. "I do not want him to see us or know more than my voice."

Flindas pulled the small conical helmet from the man's head and pushed back the chain mail then he shook the man who moaned with pain.

"Are you awake my friend?" spoke Flindas, there was silence and Flindas shook the man again.

"Yes, I hears you," said the man quietly with unconcealed fear in his voice.

"Listen to me," said Flindas. "Your life is in my hands. Tell me what I want to know and you go free, be silent and you will die. Where are you going?"

"Back to garrison," was the quick reply.

"Why?"

"Report," said the man. "Lord Maradass must know."

"Report what?"

The man was silent for a moment.

"Report you I reckons," he finally said. "Marauders got your scent. Two on foot, one warrior, one woman."

"What made them think they tracked a warrior?" Flindas asked, though he guessed the answer.

"The scent known by dog," said the messenger. "Same two went into Shish and broke some out of dungeons. That was warrior work. You I reckon. Lord Maradass wants you... alives."

"Do not reckon over much," said Flindas. "There is another you also seek is my guess. What of him?"

"What?" sneered the man. "You mean that cripple? You not him, you got two hands."

The voice of Flindas was deadly. "Yes," he hissed. "And one holds a knife at your throat, so speak only what I want to hear. What of Elfhand?"

"He got across the Flats," he said uneasily now. "They not expect that."

There was a note of dread in the man's voice.

"What are the Flats?" Flindas asked abruptly and there was a pause.

"Open land, 'tween here and Lord Maradass," was the reply.

"How close are we to Maradass?" growled Flindas. After all their hardship he could not disguise his excitement.

"You not even knows where you are," said the man, and he almost laughed through his fear.

"How close?" snarled Flindas.

The knife pricked the bared throat.

"Followings this ravine takes you to the edge," said the man almost whimpering. "Flats go beyond, 'bout three leagues cross. Lord Maradass a long way into mountains beyond. Too much magic there. Tunnels too, guarded. Troops all over. You not get in..." He began to say more but his voice cut off short as if he had spoken too much.

"What do you hold back?" spat Flindas. "Quickly! Tell!"

"Army goes in four days," squealed the man. "You still not get in. Hundreds, the best, guardings Great Lord Maradass. Maradass and the road. One ways in, no way out for you. Cripple not finds it. He get lost somewheres in mountains sure. He fall or starve, eaten, sure."

"What of his sister Leana?" Flindas asked.

"Ah, that be one ups for Lord Maradass I reckons. Bits of bargainings power there," the man gloated.

"She lives?" Flindas asked, though the answer was already there.

"She lives, but only some little I hears. She be sleep but answers all our new Lord Maradass questions. captains reckons that because of what she says Lord Maradass moves sooner." The man was becoming talkative, almost boastful. "Great warrior Lord Zard not be back for five moons yet, but new one Great Lord Maradass not care I reckon. All says be not likes his brother, and soon Lord Zard comes back anyhows. I reckons new Lords Maradass can rule him now proper. Zard still rule us though, I reckons."

"Tell me about the army and the route through these Broken Lands," Flindas said, wanting to learn all he could that might help his quest, yet sickening of the man's slimy voice.

"Army most Krags, this one and ones before," smiled the devious little man, warming now to his greater knowledge over this fool who would challenge his master. "What are Krags?" said Flindas.

"Not seen em yet, eh?" he sneered now. "Krags most human, I guess, but old Lord Maradass mades 'em. Whole battalions, armies of 'em. They be no match for real man, but be lots of 'em, lots and lots. Whole cursed armies of 'em. You see soons."

The man laughed openly now as Flindas remembered the many strange soldiers that they had seen on the Border Road.

"What of the road south?" said Flindas. "How do your armies get from here to the Border Road?"

"Begin ways along river someplace," replied the man. "Never gone me. Got tunnels, hidden ways. Comes out nears Border Road somewheres, maybe Viris some place..."

Silence grew in the darkness, and then Tris heard the man sigh and Flindas stood and turned to her.

"He will not wake for some time," he said to Tris.

"Why not kill him," she replied.

"He told me what we needed to know," he said. "I will not kill him. We will tie him to the horse and take him with us. He may still be useful."

"What is it that makes men like him be followers of such evil, of Maradass?" asked Tris. "He could just ride away and never look back."

"I think it is not so simple for any who follow Maradass," replied Flindas. "Our friend here may seem normal, if not a little dim-witted, but beneath it all I believe that he is in thrall to Maradass, chained forever by unseen bonds. That family has had dark magic for such a long time that all who come within their grasp are unable to ever escape it again. At some time this man may have been free, but no longer. I believe he feels as we do, and fears as we do, but his greatest fear is of his Master. He could not break away from Maradass no matter how hard he might try."

"But why is it this way?" asked Tris, who did not seem to want to let it go; she wanted to understand. "If Maradass is able to capture men's minds, then why does he not take all of the lands just by corrupting all minds. Why bother going to war? What is to stop him from corrupting you?"

Flindas shook his head and smiled. "I do not think I can answer all of those questions," he replied. "My guess is that some men are attracted to his side by greed, and others by hatred of others. First they begin as his willing servants in the hope of getting something, and then by magical bondage they become his slaves. None of the Maradass family is a wizard, but the head of that cursed family holds wizardry in his hands all the same. I do not know if he could control my mind, though I believe there is nothing he could offer me that could break me. I also think that he would not want to corrupt all minds, for in this he is alike to the old wizards. He creates war because he himself desires the dark pleasure that it gives him. He loves slaughter and destruction for its own sake."

They spent that night picking their way through rocky outcrops and shallow ravines until the moon set. At sunrise they were moving again, quickly now that their packs rode on the horse with its bound rider. They had not travelled far when the deep ravine they had been travelling along began to widen. The far cliffs fell away and then the land spread out to form a wide, flat plain. At its centre stood a distant jagged mountain range. The high crags appeared to have been thrust up from below by a great force, peak towering above jagged peak. On the plain a vast army lay in wait, although there were few tents and campfires amongst the horde. Tens of thousands camped there below and yet few were truly men. Vast battalions of Krags stood in perfect files ready to march.

"They look like stone," said Flindas from their hiding place amongst a tumble of rocks. "There is dark magic in them sure enough."

"I like not your chances against all them," said Tris with a grin.

"Four days and then we shall see," he replied. "We must lose our trail."

He pointed to a narrow cleft that appeared to lead into a large canyon beyond. "You take our guest and his mount ahead," said Flindas. "I will follow and cover our tracks."

For much of the morning they made slow progress, Flindas was meticulous, sometimes doubling back to find a less obvious route. He was bent over, replacing a rock dislodged by the horse, when he felt the first drops of rain, looked up and smiled. He had noticed the dark clouds in the morning, but had not expected the wind to move them so fast, more drops fell and far ahead of them a wall of rain advanced up the canyon towards them.

"The Fortunes smile on us," he murmured and joined Tris at the horse's head. "We will be lost now," he said and they moved further into the vast canyon keeping close to the northern wall.

They were soon drenched and could see little beyond their immediate footsteps, until a deeper shadow in the looming cliff face caught Tris's eye.

"Could be a cave," she called through the strengthening storm.

She left the horse and went to investigate, returning quickly. "Tis dry," she called and they led the horse and its rider into the large overhanging cave.

"Someone lives here," said Flindas as he brought the horse into the shelter. The remains of a fire lay to one side of the open space, and scraps of wood were stacked against the rock wall. Flindas untied the blindfolded messenger from his mount and removed the gag from his mouth.

"I do not want to hear from you unless I ask," he said, and the man said not a word as Tris quickly built a small fire.

Their food was running low, dried strips of meat and oats was all that remained. Flindas had earlier rummaged through the horseman's saddlebags and found what was left of a small loaf of bread and a good sized piece of cheese, and they had shared it between them.

"The horseman's belly can grumble," Flindas had said through a mouthful.

Tris cooked the lizards she had killed earlier in the day and they had almost finished their meal when a scream came from the gloom beyond the shelter. A man leapt into the cave and brandished a stout club; Flindas was on his feet sword in hand.

"What doing here?" The man screamed. "My home, my home, go, go now, go!"

"We are not going," Flindas called back, his sword catching the firelight.

The ragged bearded man let out a wail and fell to the stone floor, great sobs and howls came from the broken creature.

"My home, my home," he cried, tears falling to the stone.

"We do not want your home," Flindas said lowering his sword. "Fire and shelter until the rains go, that is all."

He knelt beside the pile of whimpering rags.

"Come friend, we beg your hospitality," he said gently.

The cries eased.

"Got food?" the man asked slyly.

"Oats," said Flindas, and saw the man's eyes light up.

"Like oats," he said and came slowly to his feet, shuffling towards the fire. Tris served him a bowl and he devoured it quickly and with great relish. He asked for more, and followed that with several strips of dried meat. The ragged creature spoke not a word, but lay down beside the fire and was sound asleep within moments.

"A wonderful host," Tris said and lay back. "Tomorrow I will hunt."

The storm raged for three days, and with the extra mouths to feed their food supply was almost halved. Flindas returned horse and rider to the upper cliffs during the rains, and sent them galloping blindly along the ledge. It mattered little what the man could tell, for his commander and Maradass must know already that Flindas and Tris were in hiding nearby.

On the fourth day the sun shone weakly through the dense clouds, with a strong wind pushing them eastward. They said goodbye to the ragged bearded man who had not uttered a word since the first day, and travelling up the canyon they returned to the cliffs above the plain. The army remained there in camp and there were no signs of imminent departure. Fire smoke trailed away into the wind and the few real soldiers lay near the fires or walked about the plain. Horses stood tethered in long lines, and marauders lay in ordered packs. It was easy to tell which companies contained the Krags, there were a great many of them and they did not relax as the common soldiers did. They stood in their perfect ranks, row upon row, neither moving nor talking, as if they waited only for the order to march. They had no camp fires near them and did not appear to eat.

Flindas and Tris lay hidden for the remainder of the day and there was no sign of a hunt. No horsemen or marauders moved on the cliff tops. It was in the early dawn of the following morning that Flindas heard a voice call from far below. It was echoed from different points across the grassless waste, then a harsh horn blast was heard and echoed from the cliffs above. A murmur became a dull roar as those below began to break camp, tents were collapsed and rolled up, horses whinnied and the sounds of their steel harness rattled in the growing light.

The glow of the sun was lighting the eastern sky. From below orders were barked and men scrambled to their mounts. The Krags stood immobile in their perfect ranks, six abreast, waiting. Flindas saw that all of them bore spears, their weapons catching the first rays of sunlight. Far off to the north and east the head of the army began to move, and the sun was well into the sky before the last troops marched from the plain towards the north. The flat land stretched bare and exposed, from the cliffs to the distant mountains of Maradass.

"Tonight I will cross," said Flindas to Tris. "You must not come."

"I will not be left behind," she said, a stubborn note in her voice that Flindas had heard before. "I have come this far and I will go the rest. You cannot stop me."

The eyes of Flindas grew troubled, but he knew it was useless to say more. The sun passed across the grey sky and a brooding gloom seemed to hang on the plains below.

"There is something moving," said Tris suddenly, and pointed toward the mountains.

Far off, perhaps half way across the open land, Flindas could see a large troop of horsemen galloping hard towards the cliffs where they lay hidden. Flindas concentrated his eyes. There on the plain, far out in front of the horsemen, he could see two figures running. Tris pointed.

"They will not reach safety, the horses run too swiftly," she said grimly.

They watched as the chase continued towards them, the figures ran hard but the horsemen gained rapidly. The runners were less than half a league from the cliffs when they were forced to turn and face their pursuers. They were quickly surrounded, then suddenly horses began to rear and several men fell from their mounts. Flindas could not make out what had happened except that the horse troop seemed to fall apart and scatter, and then the two figures ran again, sprinting for the cliffs further to the west.

The horse troop regathered, and with lowered spears charged down upon the two who ran. Flindas could now make out one as a dark figure, a black man of the Western Desert. The other was fair and his blonde hair flew behind him as he ran. The charge of horse soldiers caught them again and Flindas saw the blonde man fly at his attackers once again. The speed and ferocity of the counter attack again caught the horsemen by surprise. Flindas saw a number of them fall from bloody wounds.

"Landin," said Tris excitedly. "No mistake. No one fights like him."

Again the horsemen were in disarray, the mounts shied and fell back from the warrior before them, but the black man had been struck in some way and he sank to the earth. Landin supported his fallen comrade and made a final dash for the walls of rock. An order was barked and a number of riders broke away and rode hard for the cliffs, there intention was clear. they would cut off the escape while the others pressed in from behind their quarry.

Flindas rose from his position and notched his bow. His first arrow took the leading horseman in the chest, piercing his coat of mail, and he fell without a sound. Then another tumbled screaming from his mount, an arrow protruding from his side; two more crashed to the earth before the others turned away

DURAGOR

from the unexpected danger on the cliffs. Landin reached the rock face. He was now carrying his companion who did not appear to be conscious.

"He will not climb there," said Flindas. "The way is too steep."

The remaining horsemen charged one last time but were met by the expert bow of Flindas who picked his marks with care and wasted no arrows. Landin began to climb. The limp body of the black man slumped over his shoulders. Flindas watched in amazement as the man with one good arm somehow managed to find foot holds in what looked like an impossible climb. Some of the horsemen now dismounted and came forward, several with short bows in their hands. Arrows began to fly from below, some aimed at the climbing man, while others flew to the cliff top, rattling harmlessly amongst the rocks.

Flindas spent three more of his remaining arrows, each found a mark and the fight went out of the horsemen. They held back, out of bowshot, until Landin reached the top of the cliff, then they picked up their wounded and turned back toward the distant mountains. Flindas watched them go and then leapt down from his vantage point to join the two men further along the cliff edge. Landin looked up from his unconscious companion as Flindas and Tris joined them.

"Well met," said Tris as a look of astonishment came into Landin's eyes.

"Tris, what in the lands are you doing here?" he said.

He did not wait for an answer but turned to Flindas. The strangest eyes Flindas had ever seen gazed into his own, a golden yellow colour, they seemed to shine with an inner light. They were like Verardian's his brother's, but they glowed brighter with a magical life of their own.

"Well met stranger," said Landin smiling. "You shoot well. We owe you our gratitude. My friend would also thank you but he took a hard blow back there."

Flindas knelt beside the black man and examined his wound, a large darkening lump from which trickled a little blood protruded from the side of his forehead.

"He will survive," said Flindas after feeling the man's strong pulse. "With a painful head when he awakes I think."

Landin came to his feet and held out his hand.

"I am Landin Amitarl, and again I say well met friend"

Flindas took the hand of the powerfully built warrior.

"I am Flindas Demsharl," he said. "As I have heard of you, you may have heard of me."

"Indeed," said Landin with a smile. "A most wanted outlaw. What is it now, five thousand gold pieces? Your father the governor wants you badly. You are not here by chance I think, but stories should wait until later, shelter and healing for my companion is most important now. There will be many of the enemy here soon. They hunt me with a vengeance."

Landin easily lifted the black man to his shoulder and they all left the edge and fell back amongst the twisted cliffs and ravines behind. Several small rivers now flowed with the rain of the last days and their trail was lost quickly. As the sun touched the distant cliffs they found a deep cut in the side of a rock face, a natural shelter from wind and rain. It was in this safe place during the following day that Landin and later Duragor, the black man, told their stories.

Landin had been delayed in his return to Zeta by the appearance on the Border Road of the Maradass armies. Sadly he told of the death of his Elbrand companions, killed when they had been attacked by an overwhelming pack of marauders. Later Landin had heard of Leana's capture and determined to free her, or die in the attempt.

"I got as far as the mountains," he said. "Then I was lost. Even with my powers they are impossible to penetrate, unless one finds the road. There are hungry beasts living in those mountains. Only once did I see the road, and that was from far above. There are horse troops on the road constantly, though now that the last of their armies have gone perhaps there is more of a chance. Somewhere inside those mountains lie Maradass and my sister. I was unable to reach them, try as I might, and then I met Duragor."

The black man lay near the fire, awake and listening, his head in bandages.

"I was in the mountains for two, three moons," said the dark skinned man.

He spoke in a deep but lively voice, his teeth flashing with a mindful knowing smile.

"I was used as tracker by the Mad One's army, but I escaped into the mountains," he continued. "They hunted me as did their beasts, but I sat on a mountain top and watched them stumble about below. I threw rocks on their heads and they did not like it."

He smiled at the memory.

"A lot of accidents happened to them so they left me and went away. I think they expected me to die up there."

"What did you eat?" asked Tris, sceptical of his story.

"There are many things to eat on a mountain top," replied the black man flashing her a smile. "Even in those dark mountains there are mosses and bugs."

Tris screwed up her face and Duragor laughed, the sound filling their shelter with strange warmth.

"Then I found him," said Landin, smiling with his dark friend.

"I was not lost!" retorted Duragor in mock anger. "One day I sat on my mountain top and I see this one-armed man come into the valley below, and I knew him for a warrior and enemy of Maradass. I joined him then, and after much searching for the road our attempts were in vain. Only the road could take us to the fortress and I do not know the way. Trackers rarely pass beyond the first mountains, unless they are called by Maradass. The way to the stronghold is dark in places. Tunnels pass through the mountains, of this I have heard. Trackers and others enslaved to Maradass are never allowed to know the secret ways."

Flindas rummaged in his pack and drew forth his copy of the map. He passed it to Landin who looked at it with surprise.

"I remember this, or at least the original," he said.

"Tolth said it may be the way you seek," said Flindas. "It was done from memory. Totally accurate it is not, but it may help."

Landin and Duragor examined it closely.

"Yes," said Landin after a while. "The road is clear, and I see now why I could not find it, but for that once."

He ran his finger along the marked road as it first went west and then looped far to the east, joining what they took to be the river.

"Here," he pointed. "Both road and river disappear for a time. Perhaps it is the underground water course you spoke of."

He looked at Duragor who nodded.

"It will be difficult to avoid the soldiers once we find the road," he said, his attention returning to the map.

"You are still going to keep trying?" asked Tris in surprise. "I thought you must have given up and were leaving this place."

"No," replied Landin and passed the map back to Flindas. "We were forced from the mountains by the fell beasts of Maradass, and I cannot sit on a mountain top and eat bugs and air as some mortals are able."

Duragor's eyes grew wide with a look of humorous surprise.

"My sister is in the hands of Maradass," Landin continued. "This cannot remain so. We were driven away but I *will* return."

His hand went to his chest and he touched the talisman which hung there beneath his shirt, Landin had already heard the tale of Kerran and the young man's fortuitous meeting with his sister, and knowingly he now looked at Flindas.

"You came all this way to find me, and now you have," he said. "What do you intend now? I will not return with you to Zeta if that is your thought, not without Leana."

"I came to find you tis true," replied Flindas. "I did not come to turn back. If you go looking for Maradass then I will go too."

Landin looked at Flindas with searching eyes.

"We will probably die," he said. "You know that."

"I have come this far," Flindas said quietly across the fire. "I will go on."

"I will go too!" announced Tris with a stubborn determined look at Flindas.

"No," said Landin. "Your father would never forgive my taking you there."

"My father is dead and I go where I will," she replied. "Unless you bind me, I will follow. I will not remain behind."

There was no arguing with her, and Duragor then spoke.

"I am no warrior, but I may also be useful," he smiled, but his dark eyes did not reflect that smile, a look of hatred flickered across his face and was gone.

"Maradass takes my people and uses them for his eyes when hunting," he said. "The slave masters are cruel, and only those who are the best trackers are allowed to live. I have many a silent oath from my dead brothers and sisters to settle amongst the guards of Maradass."

"We must go soon," said Landin. "They will not expect us to return."

"They will expect us," countered Duragor. "They know that you will not turn back."

"I go tomorrow night," said the blonde warrior, and these were his final words for a time.

Duragor rose and looked beyond the entrance into the night, and then he was gone into the darkness and rain.

"Is he a real black man from the deserts?" Tris asked Landin.

"Yes," he replied. "He was captured by the soldiers of Maradass when they raided his homelands. Six years he has been enslaved by Maradass and he seeks revenge before he returns west. Ask him to tell you a story. He has many of them." Duragor did not return until dawn.

"Been looking and singing," he said, and laid a number of rabbits by the fire. He skinned them quickly and they were soon cooking within the embers, the smell filling the enclosed space.

"I have not seen many rabbits since the Border Road," said Tris. "How did you get them?"

Duragor looked at her, and a wide smile danced across his face.

"I sung them," he said mysteriously.

"Sung them!" exclaimed Tris. "How did you sung them?" She was not smiling.

"Tis a secret," said Duragor continuing to beam at her.

"You be in league with the Devils," said Tris, an almost frightened look on her face.

"No," said Duragor. "Maradass has all the Devils on his side.

There are none to spare for me." He paused. "I will teach you how to sing rabbits," he told her. "They are the easiest animal to sing because they do not know the land so well. They came when the wizards came. They are new here."

Tris was only a little mollified. "How do you sing rabbits?" she asked.

Duragor, instead of answering directly, began an unending soft moan deep in his throat. It varied slightly in pitch for a time and then returned to the first note. He kept this up for some time without appearing to take a breath, and then he stopped abruptly and looked at Tris.

"That is how you sings rabbits," he said. "Lie on the ground very still and make that sound. When rabbit come close." He ran a finger across his throat.

"Is all that true?" Tris asked, not quite convinced.

Duragor gave her a look of great sadness. "Now, Tris, would an honourable and wonderful man such as myself lie to you, or to any other such honourable, wondrous being. No, tis the truth I tell. I only speak true."

"Landin said you tell stories," said Tris, beginning to warm to this strange black man.

"Yes I tell stories," he said. "All true, only true. Old, old, old stories, so old they tell of the beginnings before time. Yes I have many stories."

"Will you tell me one?" She asked.

He looked at her across the fire. "Why would you hear stories?" he asked.

"I want to learn things," came her quick reply and Duragor smiled.

"That is a good answer," he said. "Yes, I will tell you a story."

Duragor reached out to the fire and picked up a piece of charred wood. He mixed the black charcoal with some spit in the palm of his hand and then drew with his fingertip a number of symbols on a flat stone near the fire, and then he told his story. It was an old story of his people, and at its core was a deep sense of morality and understanding. That night Tris slept and dreamed of black tribes crossing vast distant deserts, while Flindas sharpened his knives.

The Dying Mountains

The sun was lowering into the west when Flindas and his companions again stood on the cliff's edge. They had seen fresh signs of horse soldiers upon the cliff tops, and Duragor had found the soft tracks of marauders. Fortunately rain had fallen during the last days and their place of hiding had been far from prying eyes, and muzzles. With ropes they climbed to the flat land below, then crossing the distance at a run, the darkness was almost complete when they came to the first jagged outcrops of the mountains. Duragor's eyes proved to have the best night vision and he led the way, keeping close to the foot of the towering, almost vertical rock face. They had crossed the plain to a point west of where the road must enter the mountains, if the map was at all accurate, and they were careful to look for anything that may be a tunnel or a road. The night wore on without success and they stopped for a time as the wind strengthened and rain threatened again. Sheltering against the biting wind Landin spoke with the others.

"The entrance must be hidden in some way, for we should have seen something of it by now," he told them. "We need daylight. Stumbling in the dark is a waste of our strength. I suggest we find somewhere a little more sheltered and wait til dawn."

Duragor searched in the tumbled rocks and soon returned.

"There is good shelter not far, come, this way."

He led them to where a large rock, fallen from the heights above, had formed a deep cave against the mountain side and here they spent the remainder of the night. Tris was restless and Duragor too seemed disinterested in sleep, and so when she asked for a story he thought for a time, pondering, then he began to speak again.

"This is a new story, the story of the white black man," he said.

"How can there be a white black man?" scoffed Tris, thinking he made fun of her.

"Listen for a time and you will understand," Duragor rebuked her softly, and then continued as the storm came on, thrashing and thick with rain.

"In the new age, long after the wizards came, there was a time when there was much prosperity in the lands. Cities grew, and the white people looked after their kind. There was much happiness. Now in that time there lived a scholar, his name was Drargus, and he had a marvellous mind, and he became well known for his great thoughts and ideas. He was revered by those around him, though he preferred the undisturbed quiet of his workrooms to the more social life of his fellows.

"Among his many studies he deciphered and read ancient works of history. He learned of the black people who had not been in the eastern lands for thousands of years. As he learned more, he began to understand some of my people's history, and he became at first intrigued and later he seemed obsessed with knowing about the black man. He decided that he would mount an expedition to come and find us. Of course if my people do not want to be found then they will not be found. They watched the expedition come through the pass, and they watched it for many days as it travelled further into the desert. They saw men leave the group, taking horses and returning to the safety of the east."

"Others left, until there was just one man and a wagon. He travelled further into the desert and my people followed him.

His wagon broke a wheel and he continued on the horse, until it died beneath him. He walked for many nights, sleeping in hollows during the day away from the sun. One evening he did not rise and my people investigated. He was near death, and they took him to a safe place and began to heal him. He stayed with the people for a long time. He learned our language and much of our history and stories, those that were not kept secret. He burnt horribly in the sun and so my people rubbed the juice of dark berries into his skin, they did this often as a protection."

"His skin after a time became darker and darker, until he was as black as I am. He could bear the sun then, and he travelled with the people, continuing to learn their ways. He became a black white man though he was called 'the white black man' by my people. It was a name of affection for he was a good and kindly person. After some years he wished to return to his own lands. My people did not want him to go. There were bad signs they said. He would not listen, for he wished to tell our ancient story to his own people. They would be interested to hear his stories he said. They would accept their black brothers and sisters with open arms.

"It was not for some years that the story came back to my people. He had returned to his city home and all was much as he had left it. People were happy and prosperous and smiled at each other, but they did not smile at the black man who suddenly walked into their midst. They stared, and ran, and jeered, and threw stones. He finally came into the presence of his fellow scholars and earlier compatriots. He felt that they would surely accept him, and wish to hear his story. Not one of them stood by him, and when he returned to claim what was rightfully his, he was laughed at. He went to the courts of the land, and instead of receiving back what he had owned, he was himself cast into prison where he languished and eventually died." Duragor stopped with a thoughtful look on his face. "That is the story of the black white man, who was Drargus the white black man," he said eventually.

Duragor was silent for a few moments more, the darkness of the night complete. "There are few who would understand the great humour in that story," said Duragor finally, and then laughed quietly into the silence.

First light came with a dense misty rain. Under dark clouds the four companions began to retrace their steps of the turbulent, stormy night before. By midday they had again searched the cliffs for several leagues without finding any sign of road or gateway. The rain had eased and it was Flindas who eventually spoke.

"I know that my map is near accurate on the position of the road where it enters the mountains," he said. "It could be no more than a league in error. I think there is something that we have missed, or Tolth may have been mistaken in some way."

He looked for a long time at the map, pondering on their problem. Duragor, who had climbed to a small ridge, gave a low but penetrating whistle, they looked to where he sat crouched above and he pointed to the Flats. On the very edge of sight something moved across the barren rain soaked plain, they were still looking at the slowly moving mass when Duragor joined them.

"Soldiers on foot and marauders, moving slow," he told them. "They hunt. Perhaps when they finish the hunt they may be kind enough to show us the way in."

A broad grin lit his dark face.

"Yes," agreed Landin. "They could be the key that we need."

During the remainder of the day they stalked the squad of soldiers and dogs who remained out on the Flats.

"The rain has spoilt their hunt I think," said Duragor, his eyes penetrating the gloom. "Now they come this way but they do not sense us. The key is turning."

Keeping the soldiers in sight and upwind they crouched amongst the rocks and waited. It was not long before they could make out the individual men through the misty rain, their direct line of march would now bring them close to the watchers who they sought. Time passed slowly, and then the soldiers drew near to the sheer mountain side, no passage or even a narrow crevasse marred the high rock face that they marched towards.

"I see nothing that would allow them entry," said Duragor

quietly. "It may be they will camp here and continue the search tomorrow."

At this place a large shelf of rock jutted out far into the plains, finally disappearing beneath the sands of the flat lands. The soldiers continued to advance, and at their head rode a commander of the Maradass army, Flindas looked more closely. The man's left arm hung loose at his side as if there was no life in it, and he remembered this man, on the Border Road. Brook had said it would be a long shot, but worth the try. The troop marched directly to the rock face, and then the commander raised his right hand as though to halt the men, but they did not stop. The commander and his tall warhorse walked up to the wall of rock and then simply disappeared into it.

Tris let out a gasp, and then gaped as the marching men and dogs followed their commander, passing silently into the solid rock face. Rank after rank seemed to melt into the sheer unbroken cliff. As the last soldier vanished the travellers looked at each other in astonishment.

"That is High Magic," Landin finally said. "Let us look."

He leapt from their hiding place and ran to the cliff. They soon joined him as he searched for the way in. There was no sign of an entry. Only solid rock met their hands. Baffled, they stood back and looked at the wall. Landin held up his right hand and walked toward the rock as he had seen the commander do. It did not work, his toes meeting hard stone.

"The lock demands more than a simple key," he said and stepped back again. During the remainder of the day they lay hidden close by the concealed entrance, hoping to see someone emerge or enter. Darkness fell and all was quiet.

"The powers of Maradass have grown much," said Landin. "He has mastered rock and stone, and even made fighting men of it, or so it seems. His poison travels through the great ocean as you have told me, and he has saved Leana from death and has her under his power. His magic may be high but I will not let him defeat me."

Flindas heard no doubt in the Amitarl warrior's words.

They held a conference late that evening, and it was decided to attempt the climb over the high cliffs above them.

"It cannot be far to the road, but we must be careful, we must arrive unannounced," said Landin looking up the rock face. "Stealth is our only ally. It will be a hard climb."

"I am not staying behind," said Tris defiantly as Landin looked at her.

He smiled then and nodded, remembering her father. They would start at first light he said.

Early dawn saw them begin the ascent. Landin led the way, though he had only one useful arm he seemed able to climb sheer rock faces with less effort than those with four useful limbs. The way was hard all the same. They used their ropes often and it was not until late in the day that they found themselves on a narrow ledge wide enough to rest and sleep. All were exhausted; even Landin hung his head. A steady rain continued to fall during the night and they sheltered as best they could on the exposed ledge, sleep coming fitfully. At first light they were climbing again.

Eventually the way became a little easier, until they found themselves at a high point overlooking both the Flats behind and the terrain ahead. Nowhere did there seem to be space for a road to be made through this formidable country. High wind worn peaks plunged into the depths, broken treacherous slopes where the disturbing of a few rocks could cause a disastrous fall. In many places such a slide would lead to certain death. Tall minarets of stone stood up like fingers pointing to the sky. Even as they watched a small piece of rock fell, causing others to crumble and spill over a precipice, falling to hidden depths below.

For the remainder of the day they continued to clamber about the outer ramparts of the Maradass mountains. It was Duragor who heard the sound first. He signalled for silence and then they all heard the recognisable sound of horses being ridden at a fast walk. The sound seemed to come from a deep and impenetrably dark chasm which lay beyond a low ridge far below them, and eventually they were able to make their way to a point overlooking the gulf.

"Yes," said Landin in triumph. "The road is there."

His face beamed as if they had already stormed the castle and freed Leana.

"If we follow the road without using it we will be moons in the search," Flindas said. "If we take to the road then the danger of discovery is great."

"I have thought much on that," said Landin. "I see no option but to use the road. With care and darkness we shall win through, we *must* win through."

"What of marauders?" asked Tris. "They will sniff us out, and you tell us there are other beasts here far worse than the dogs."

"We must take our chances with them," Landin replied. "The dogs are the greater danger I think, the strange beasts I encountered seem more likely to live in the mountains above, and I doubt if they are true allies of Maradass. I judge from the map that we could reach the stronghold in two nights if we are not discovered, let us rest for the remainder of this night and watch the road tomorrow."

They dared no fire, though small lizards had been plentiful during the day. Duragor ate some raw rather than the dried meat strips which the others carried.

"Would you tell a story Duragor?" Tris pleaded. "A story about somewhere warm and dry."

Duragor mused for a while before beginning.

"A long way to the west, beyond where white men have ever been, there is a place so hot and dry that rain only falls rarely. Years can pass without a drop. It was not always so, that land was once fertile and rich. Lakes stretched across what is now dry desert, and life was green and abundant. Then the rain stopped." Duragor became silent with a thoughtful smile.

"Is that all?" asked Tris, not amused.

"No," said Duragor. "That is not all, but you must discover the rest for yourself. Short stories are often the best."

"You are a strange man," said Tris quietly. "Tell me, why are you here?"

"I am here because I choose to be, that is all," replied the black man. "I could ask the same of you."

"Yes," said Tris. "I have often asked myself that question.

What I see is greed in our world and that is something I cannot understand. Why does someone like Maradass want it all? A full belly and a warm bed, is that not enough for anyone? There is something very sad in these dark times, and I feel I must do what I can to help. I feel within this sadness that I have a purpose in these times, though I cannot see it, not yet"

"Sadness is something we must all feel at times," said Duragor. "It is often a great teacher. When we are happy we are not so open to listening to our heart." Duragor pondered his own words for a time. "I will tell you a sad story which gives an important teaching," he said.

He sat in silence for a time and Tris waited patiently.

"I am a storyteller and a rememberer," Duragor said into the silence. "I have been taught much of the old histories, of the land and its people. In those tales there are some sad times, but since the white man came there have been more tears than the oceans could hold. The white people's history is sad, and yet but a pebble on the mountain of time, even the wizards lasted but a short span of my own people's history. To speak of greed is to speak of selfishness. There is a sad story I know which tells much of the white man's way, not all of them you understand, but some."

"Once, a long time ago, there was an Old One, a black woman who had outlived her children's children. She lived alone in a cave, except for a dog that was her friend. He was a fine and proud beast, a leader of his kind. One day a white man saw the dog, admired it, and wished to own it. Of course the old woman would not part with her friend and eventually the white man rode away. That night he returned, and with meat he managed to steal the dog away. When the old woman discovered her friend was gone she wailed so much that the Wise Ones heard her cry, and she was given a sign. The dog would return, she need but wait. After many days she was about to give up. She started crying, only to hear her friend barking happily and then her friend came running into her cave, dragging a short length of rope that had once kept him tied. They rejoiced in each other's company once again.

Another moon passed and then again the white man was

at the mouth of her cave, this time demanding his dog back. They argued and he struck her, she was frail and very old and died quickly. The dog would not be taken. He stood guard over the old woman's body and snarled at the white man. The man took up his sword and slew the dog. The white man cared for nothing but himself and left the place with nothing but his darkness for company. This is a story that is sad and true. It taught my people, a long time ago, not to trust the white men. Some are good and some are evil. If we were to look on all as being good we would have been a foolish people, and disappeared into our own darkness long ago."

He grinned into the darkness and turned over to sleep. Duragor, though lightly clad, never seemed to feel the cold or rain.

Much later they were all woken by the harsh blast from a trumpet below them on the roadway. They looked down as a number of foot soldiers marched by bearing torches. The troop disappeared around a corner then shortly afterwards a similar troop marched by in the other direction. The companions watched as this group seemed to vanish into the cliff face below them.

"More hidden doors," said Flindas as the last torch flickered and disappeared.

"Yes," said Landin. "A guardroom perhaps. We could have climbed down right on top of it."

For the remainder of the night they stood watch. The horizon to the east had begun to glow when they saw a troop of soldiers and marauders emerge from the rock and make their way along the road and out of sight.

"That will be the troop going in search of us again," spoke Landin. "This will not be the only garrison point I think. The places on the map, which showed the road entering tunnels, these will surely be guarded. If need be we will climb again, but we must take to the road tonight."

They watched until noon without seeing further movement. Keeping well out of sight from the road they eventually found a deep cleft in the ridge, taking them to a place no more than a rope's length from the valley floor. The road wound upward, deeper into the towering and crumbling peaks.

Tris spoke to no one in particular. "I look at this place and I get reminded of something that is rotting," she said. "The mountains seem dead. Can rocks rot?"

"The rocks are indeed dead or dying," said Duragor, and added mysteriously. "They rot from the inside. Maradass has taken the very life from the stone for his own uses."

"How do you know this?" asked Flindas. "Can a stone die?"

Duragor turned to Flindas and smiled grimly. "Yes, stone can die," he said. 'In these mountains the essential energy is gone. I feel this and know it is true. It is said that the wizards had the power to kill stone. Maradass would emulate them it seems. I would guess that the energy is used to create these part human Krags. From what I have seen they are more earthbound than humans." He paused, and then added slowly. "Their life's energy passes into them from the earth itself. I believe they may kill the very earth on which they walk."

He was silent for a time, deep in thought. "As adversaries these stone men may prove easy to fight but hard to kill," he said eventually. "Their great numbers will draw much of the earth's power. Even as they march they will destroy the lands." A fearful look came into his eyes at the realisation. "It would take a great deal of time to drain the mother of her strength, but the Krags and Maradass have much time. This could be. The plans of Maradass are for total ruin, to destroy all lands and all peoples."

"How do you know this?" said Landin, surprised at his friend's outburst.

"I feel it, I know it," replied Duragor with certainty. "Though I have never had to face any of the Maradass family I know how dark their hearts are. I have seen their evil works. The Mad One's dream was to rule over a dead world, and now the Evil One, his son, follows the same path. Does he not march to war even now? If the Maradass household is not destroyed, all humanity will be lost, and the house of Maradass will be free to play their war games with Krags and such into eternity." A cynical laugh escaped from the black man's throat and he said no more.

During the remainder of the day they lay watching the road and doing fine adjustments to their gear and weapons, Landin noted the array of knives that Flindas carried.

"Not only a bowman I see," said Landin and looked around the strange group. "If there are any among you who do not wish to go on I think now is the last time that there will be a chance. Leana is my sister, and my love for her is the reason that I must try to find her. I have powers that may be strong enough to make such a rescue possible. If I cannot do that I will die in the trying, but to go forward is almost certain death for you all."

No one spoke for a time and then Flindas broke the silence. "I will go on," he said quietly.

"I too will go," said Duragor. "A chance to thwart Maradass is all I wish for, then to go home."

"I thought you had no home," said Tris bluntly. "'A homeless people', I heard you say."

"The west is home, the desert is where I find peace," he replied.

"And I thought you could not die," she said as she turned to Landin.

He smiled and looked at the road below them.

"Yes, I can die," he said. "When I wear the Seacrest I am almost immortal. In battle I could be overwhelmed, but it has not happened yet."

The day lengthened and there had been little movement below. A lone horseman had ridden by and a shambling group of chained men, with spades and other tools were herded past. That had been all. At last light they heard the faint echo of the trumpet come from down the valley.

"Changing the guard," said Flindas as he was first to slip over the ledge and down the ropes.

There would be no moon and they were in a welcome darkening gloom, the road but a faint ribbon ahead of them. In silence they turned and began to run, they made little sound as they went, all having learned quiet stealth in their differing lives until it had become part of their very nature. Duragor took the lead, far ahead of the others. His night eyes and acute hearing would give them early warning if the enemy approached from ahead. The road was never straight. It narrowed to a twisting and winding ribbon between high cliffs. Once over a narrow ridge the road made its way downward into another dark and threatening valley, occasionally they heard rock and rubble falling into the depths. They were at a sharp corner with a high cliff on either side when Duragor ran quietly back and joined them.

"There is a fall of rock ahead," he said. "It blocks the road, it could not have been there during the day. No horsemen would have got by. My guess is that rock slides are not rare. We could meet up with workmen at any moment. Come, at least for a time we have no need to worry about being overtaken."

They soon came to the avalanche of rock and stone that had blocked the way, climbing hand over hand they reached the top of the slide and began to clamber down the other side.

"Who goes?" came a call from the dark roadway ahead. The reflection from the harness told them that a lone horseman stood there.

Landin and Flindas both reacted, leaping down the rock slide and quickly covered the ground between them and the horseman. The astonished rider was slow, and too late he turned to spur away. Landin took him from the saddle as Flindas lunged at the mount. He caught the reins and quickly soothed the startled horse. Landin had the man down, one knee on his chest, a knife to his throat.

"Answer me quickly!" said Landin, a dark threat in his words. "What brings you here?"

"We was told of big rock fall. I was sent out to look." A pleading note hovered in the man's voice.

"You know who I am," said Landin. "What new word is there of my whereabouts? Mind you tell the truth. I know when a man lies."

The rider flinched in the darkness and spoke quickly. "They figures you was still outside. No chance they said come inside. They was wrong."

Landin replied with a hint of mirth in his voice. "Yes they were wrong. I am most definitely here, though I would rather you were not. If you do not report, what will they do?"

The man squirmed, he knew he was talking to save his life. "They send a troop to find me," he blurted.

After a short silence Landin spoke, his voice deep and threatening. "That is the one lie that I will allow you," he told the trembling man. "Now the truth, and quickly."

The man shuddered. "I not be expected back," he said. "The slide thought be passable, more must fell down. I be to stay below at gate barracks. Are you still kill me?" he asked pleading, fear in his voice.

"No I will not kill you," spoke Landin. "You may be of use to us."

Tris gave a disgusted snort and turned away.

"Kill him I say," she was heard to mutter as Landin continued to interrogate his captive.

"How far to the first tunnel?"

"Most two leagues," was the reply.

"Guards?"

"Small garrison, two hundred, more," he blurted. "I never go further in other gates and tunnels. Our Lord Great Maradass in centre. You never make it."

"Kill him," said Tris bitterly. "Tis a weakness you have to see an enemy live."

"He knows the road," said Landin. "He can be of use."

"He will not keep pace," she said. "He will slow us unless we take the horse and what then for quiet and stealth?"

"I will not kill an unarmed man," Landin replied, and that seemed to settle it. The horse they left at the rock slide.

"When it is found they may think that their friend was crushed in the slide," he said. "It will take them some time to find out otherwise. I wish for rain, our scent remains to mark our trail."

They began to run again with Duragor far ahead as before. The rider was panting heavily by the time they had reached a high point in the road where a deep chasm fell away to their left. Duragor had paused and there was no sign of lights or soldiers ahead.

"Take off your heavy gear and throw it over," said Landin to their captive and the man did so.

Tris felt that she would like to throw the man down as well but kept her peace. She watched him always, running behind, her knife drawn. The man ran more easily now. The armies of Maradass were not fit and were heavily reliant on mounted troops. This horse soldier surprised them all by keeping up a hard pace.

Deeper into the mountains they ran, the clouds threatening but no rain fell. In the darkness Duragor joined them. He had scouted far ahead to a place where the road vanished into a cliff face.

"The first tunnel I think," he told them. "I was onto it before I knew. No sign of guards, just another mountain of solid rock."

Landin turned to his prisoner. "Tell me of this place," he said. "Where are the guards?"

"They never on outside," came the sullen reply. "Guard room be on other side, I never be through."

"And what of these rocks that you can walk through?" Landin said. "How can we pass?"

"Cannot," the man replied. "Only some got power, not me."

"There must be a watch kept on the road," said Flindas. "A spying eye to see who comes."

The man became silent.

"Quickly, tell!" said Landin, anger erupting in his voice.

"Yes, a watch is kept," the man squealed in fear. "The guard be called out by now. I not understand. Your friend be so dark they miss him maybe, or maybe sleep."

"There is something here I do not like," said Landin to the others. "I think we should take to the mountains before we reach this place. We must get above and spy out the road."

It was almost dawn when they reached a part of the road not far from the tunnel's closed mouth. They prepared for the climb and the prisoner seemed totally exhausted, he knelt and drew in deep breaths, but he was preparing. He stood slowly then he was gone, running hard into the night towards the tunnel, his voice calling out a warning.

Tris was first to react, she had watched carefully, knowing that he would try to escape sometime. The man ran fast, he again called out but did not expect to be heard yet. Only one of his captors followed him closely he realised, there was little doubt that it was the girl. He ran harder and then realised that he could not outrun her, she was close behind. He turned suddenly to face his much smaller adversary, ready to throw her from the cliff top, but Tris surprised him by avoiding his grasp and then her knife sank into his throat. He stumbled and fell to the roadway without another sound, and then Flindas was by Tris's side.

"Quickly over the side with him," he said and they dragged the man to the brink and slid his body over the edge and into the darkness below, then they returned to the others. No alarm had been sounded.

"We must climb now," said Landin.

They climbed as quickly as they could, high into the surrounding cliffs. Landin forged ahead, making their way to the north and east as much as possible, somewhere in that direction lay the continuing road.

"We are in luck," said Duragor as the first heavy drops of rain began to fall from an ominously dark cloud.

Within moments their vision was obscured by driving rain. It was impossible to continue. Even if they could, they would never be able to see into the depths to find the road. The four companions sheltered as best they could and waited out the storm, they did not find the road that day, but something else found them. Duragor gave them a name. He called them Dreedow.

In the dark of the night three of the tall lumbering beasts came upon the travellers scent, high on their precarious mountain the four companions heard them coming.

"They smell our blood," said Duragor looking below towards the sound. "They are old, older even than the Blackman. They have been in the land since before my people's time. They are mountain creatures and are happier on high slopes than flat land. They climb without trouble."

During the early morning the creatures reached the high ledge, in the darkness little could be seen of them except for their huge hair covered bodies. The fight was ferocious and soon over.

"I have met these ones before," said Landin resting on his sword. Two had died to his blade. "They are not difficult to defeat," he continued. "I have ended the lives of others but they will continue to come. I expected them last night, but they live only in the wild it seems, and are not truly allies of Maradass."

"They are no one's ally," said Duragor into the darkness. "They eat flesh, even their own kind. They are the only creature that my people hunt, yet will not eat. They live in the mountains but will enter the desert at times when they are hungry, and they are always hungry. They are evil, and will take children even in daylight though darkened slopes are their true dwelling place."

It was not until the following morning, which dawned bright and warm, that they once again looked down upon the grey ribbon winding through the mountains to the east. They found a place where they could descend, and made their way to a ledge overlooking a stretch of relatively straight road.

"We will go in darkness as before," said Landin. "Sleep and rest, I will watch the road."

The warm sun was welcome to their tired bodies. The companions dried their gear and relaxed for what seemed the first time in days. The road lay empty until just before dark. They were preparing to descend when from the east, the way they would go, a troop of horsemen and marauders appeared.

"Let us hope no more are on the road tonight," said Landin as they waited for the horsemen to ride by.

They did not climb down until the night was dark, slipping quietly to the roadway, and then they ran on through the night, many leagues passing beneath their feet. By dawn they had reached the second gateway, Duragor having spied it from afar.

"The next gate is near," he said as he rejoined them. "I see no guards, but that does not mean there are none, another climb I think."

The sheer walls of crumbling rock made this climb most difficult. Once they were amongst the higher levels of the mountains the way to the east became a little easier, they were crossing a low ridge when they found the road on the other side, shining bare and quiet in the sunlight.

"In darkness we are safest, but time presses," said Landin. "If marauders have been the way we came last night they will surely know we are close. I will press on in daylight."

None would say no to the Amitarl warrior, although fatigue was taking its toll on his three companions. They ran again, their backs warmed at times by the afternoon sun. The road began to turn northward and ascended through a series of spectacular climbs. Higher into the mountains they marched, too tired now to run. Duragor called an urgent halt, raising a finger to his lips he listened to the air, and then knelt on the ground, his ear pressed to the stone.

"Horsemen coming from behind," he said. "They come at speed, we must climb now!"

That did not prove easy, the way up was difficult even for Landin. The others had not climbed far above the road when a small group of horsemen came into view, travelling fast. The climbers just had time to pull the rope up from the road when the first riders turned the last corner then galloped by. The companions rested for a short time then moved on. The sun was lowering to the west when they found themselves in sight of the last tunnel. It had no bare rock face; instead there lay far below them a wide cavernous opening in the mountainside. To this dark entrance came the road like a thin silver snake, while from it flowed a river the colour of dark blood. Rapids boiled, rocks stood like bloody sentinels against the unnatural flow. Flindas then realised that it must reach the oceans perhaps three hundred leagues to the east, the poison of Maradass stretched that far. They made a climb to the rocks above the foul river and studied this last tunnel.

"Whatever happens now you must rest," said Landin as he looked at his exhausted companions. "I wish to see the road ahead, I will return by midnight."

They did not argue, but slumped to the ground and slept. They were roused by Landin much later under a starlit sky. Flindas was shocked to realise that they had all slept into darkness without heed.

"I am going to chance the tunnel," Landin told them. "It was made for the poisoned river to pass through and there is no sign of guards. It may be that it is a trap set for us. It seems too easy. None of you should come any further. The danger is too great. Return to your homelands. This should be my road alone."

They looked at him but none spoke, each of them knowing that they would not turn back.

"Come then," he said to his silent companions. "If we go now we will be through by daylight."

"We must beware the water," said Flindas. "I have seen what even a small amount can do to a person. It is a most unpleasant death."

They reached the cavern without detection, except for the rushing torrent all lay still, expectant. The road led into the darkness and there would be no light inside.

"We have torches but I think it best that we do not use them," called Landin over the sounds of the river. "I will go first. We must keep to the wall and stay close together."

He led the way into the darkness. The river was below them, the road hugging the upper wall of the tunnel which was smooth and worn flat as if by highly skilled workmen, or perhaps by magic. The roadway beneath their feet sloped upward, following the river to its beginning. They had not gone far when Landin stopped and quickly lit a torch.

"This is as far as I came earlier," he told them. "There is something here I wish to see."

He began to look up, and above them there was a change in the rock, huge beams of hardwood had been placed as braces against part of the wall and roof of the tunnel, a gaping hole in the roadway was bridged with wood planking.

"The rock dies," said Duragor looking above. "Maradass will destroy even his own world for his ultimate aims."

"Yes," said Landin. "And if we manage to return this way tis a place where we could slow any pursuit, the roof begs to fall with but a little help."

After looking at the works closely they moved again into the near darkness, the tunnel continued to climb steadily and they were far beneath the mountains when Tris, who had been looking behind, gave an urgent warning.

"There are lights!" she called to the others.

For a short time there was only darkness, then they all saw the distant trail of torches. Coming from behind around a turn in the road were a troop of horsemen riding hard.

"Run! Quickly!" called Landin. "We must find a place to hide."

They ran together, fingertips brushing the wall. The horsemen could be seen to gain on them, coming on in double file, the width of the road allowing no more than two to ride abreast.

It was soon apparent that the tunnel was not about to give them a safe hiding place, as the horsemen came on, gaining at every stride. Light from the torches caught at the companion's heels as they ran, then a shout went up from the leading horsemen.

"We are seen!" cried Landin, who slowed and turned to face the coming onslaught.

The first meeting of sword and spear was short and furious. Flindas sent two arrows into the leading horsemen while Landin took several more with his sword. Flindas watched in the spluttering light of dropped torches as Landin leapt in the air, a lashing boot catching a hapless rider in the chest, the Elbrand warrior's sword taking another from his saddle in the same movement. Horses and riders were in confusion, thrashing about amongst the dead and dying. A man screamed as he was thrown heavily and slid down the steep bank into the river.

"Quickly! While there is chaos!" cried Landin and they were running again, Duragor now carrying a spear taken from a fallen enemy.

It took some time for the horsemen of Maradass to regroup and attack them again, this time they were more cautious but it did them no good. Their need for light made them easy targets for the arrows which Flindas sent hurtling into their midst. He wasted not a shaft and the horsemen held back and did not charge, content for a time to follow and force them up the tunnel. Twice more during the long dark run the four companions were forced to turn and return the fight, each time Landin fell like a wild demon upon the enemy. Sword in hand he leapt through the air, taking men from their saddles with sword and lashing feet. Flindas watched in awe, no one had ever fought this way he thought to himself.

They turned again and ran. The tunnel was beginning to level out, the river becoming sluggish and silent. Then, ahead of them, they could see a point of light. Up a last slow incline they raced and out into the daylight, none barred their way. They were inside the last gate. Ahead, perhaps half a league away, stood the stronghold of Maradass. High on a cliff face of a sheer dark mountain, carved from the very rock itself stood the forbidding brooding castle. The road now ran level beside a stagnant red lake where nothing grew and nothing lived. From behind they heard a blast of a horn, then again another.

"We must have horses," called Landin. "They will hound and trap us if we are afoot. At the next corner we must turn and face them. I will take the riders. Catch a horse if you can."

The corner was not long in coming, a sharp bend where the horsemen would have to slow their mounts, here the four weary travellers stood in readiness. Landin waited, poised at the side of the road close to the rock face. As the leading riders came into view he leapt at them and two riders were unhorsed instantly. The speed of his attack carried Landin into the path of the next riders and they fell with hardly a blade drawn. Those behind were in panic, horses reared as riders lost their courage in the face of the one they called the Cripple.

Elfhand tore at them, his blade flashing swift and sure. He fought them until none would stand before him. The troop had been decimated. Those still living turned and galloped from his reach. They would not attack again. Landin leapt into the saddle of a tall grey warhorse, the others were all mounted now and they turned as one, riding swiftly along the roadway, which snaked around the western shore of the lake. From behind they heard the trumpet again, a distant call, but answered this time from the castle above. They saw, as if in a dream, the mountainside at the foot of the distant fortress shimmer and melt. From the dark tunnel, which suddenly appeared, a great many horsemen emerged from what had been solid rock.

"We are not going to be welcomed at the front gate!" called Duragor, as he crouched low over his horse's pounding neck, unused as he was to riding such a creature.

Flindas looked at the high castle above them as he rode. It did not seem possible to scale the rock face on which it was built, except by the road ahead of them. Much of the high fortress was overhanging, looming above the poisoned lake, while behind the stronghold the mountain continued, sheer and high. The castle itself looked impregnable. Even should they be able to scale the lower slopes, an army of Elbrand could not take such a place.

Ahead of them the black horsemen were in full gallop, plunging down the roadway from the castle towards them, lances glittering in shafts of sunlight that escaped from the clouds to the east. There were many of the horsemen and the thunder of their charge echoed around the valley. The four companions rode hard until they reached the place where the lake left the roadside, its shoreline sweeping further to the east. From here the road took a direct route to the stronghold and the oncoming riders. To the west of the road stood hills of broken rock, one piled onto the other in unnatural heaps that no horse could climb.

"We must leave the horses!" called Landin as he reined in his mount. "There are too many to resist. Up these hills, quickly!"

The high mounds of broken rock were steep and treacherous, boulders moved beneath their feet; some were dislodged and tumbled down the slope. Below they heard, and then saw the arrival of the enemy. Landin and his companions were now beyond bowshot, and with heaving chests and pounding hearts they paused and looked back to the road below.

"No marauders," said Tris, the sound of relief in her voice, a strange note to hear in such a desperate situation.

"The horsemen cannot follow us here," said Landin. "They will come at us on foot. We must make haste, beyond the western buttress of the fortress there is a place that we can climb."

Without further explanation he again broke into a run up the tumbled rock, Flindas wondered how Landin could know of this climb he spoke of but there was no time for questions. He turned up the slope once more and forced his aching legs to follow the powerful Amitarl warrior. The hills were difficult to cross, the broken rock causing them to stumble and often fall. Fine sand and stone slid dangerously beneath their feet. Far to their right they saw the first of the soldiers climbing to a hilltop. The troops moved slowly, their light but cumbersome armour making it difficult for them in the very broken terrain, and still there was no sign of marauders.

The chase across those broken hills, the soldiers almost won. Cutting at an angle toward the western buttress they tried to intercept the four travellers before escape was possible. Landin led the way. He seemed to be searching for a sign in the cliff face. The soldiers were but a longbow shot away when he spied what he sought.

"It is here!" he called to his companions and climbed to a dark cleft in the towering mountainside. They followed him blindly into the dark enclosed space.

"We must go up using both sides and get beyond their bows," said Landin.

They began the difficult ascent, spread across the narrow space, one hand and foot on either wall, they slowly moved upward. The way widened for a time then narrowed to where they almost crawled up the vertical shaft. Below the sound of soldiers could be heard, but they had come too late, unless the soldiers were prepared to attempt the difficult climb they had lost their quarry for now.

The Evil One

The sun was beginning to set as the four travellers lay high above in a small hollow, eating their cold fare, the poisoned lake and the valley stretched below them; all lay quiet and still.

"No dogs," said Duragor, voicing the thoughts of the others.

"No," said Landin. "I do not understand, unless Maradass wished to take us alive. The marauders will not allow that if they are first at their victims."

"It may be that there is only one of us he particularly wishes taken alive," reflected Flindas as he looked at Landin.

"Perhaps," replied the warrior and then they talked of other things.

They were now high up the western face of the mountain ridge from which the Maradass family had carved their fortress centuries before. Across a deep chasm they could see the dark stone turrets and towers caught in the glow of the westerly sun. There was no sign of the enemy, and no soldiers had followed them onto the mountain ridge. They could see now that the low broken hills which they had crossed were not natural, the stone had been left there in high mounds after being wrenched from the mountain side to build the castle.

"How did you know of the narrow climb which brought us here?" Flindas asked of Landin.

"There is a man who came this way before us," Landin began. "I met him at a thief's camp. He escaped the fortress and by a fortunate guess he found the narrow climb. He was taken captive again when he tried to find his way from this place, and then years later he escaped again. Somehow he made it through to Shish-Tan-Vara. All he could remember of that journey was that for much of it he travelled east and south. He told me his secrets for a piece of gold, and I am glad that he told me the truth. I did not tell you of it before because I did not know the truth of it myself."

Sunlight played on the tips of the surrounding mountains, fragments of light vanishing one by one. They could see, far to the west and south, the many jagged peaks descending to the distant plains of the Flats, the walls of the Broken Lands could just be seen on the very edge of sight.

"We have come a long way into the sky to have such a view," said Duragor sweeping his arms wide to the far horizon. "Do you have a way down from this place that does not include growing wings, or being skewered on a Maradass spear?"

He grinned widely but the great danger they had faced that day had taken its toll on the black man. Tris too was exhausted; she hung her head and was unusually withdrawn.

"Tomorrow I will explore," said Landin. "I will try to find a way to climb down upon the castle from above. I think that the soldiers will not come up here to look for us, Maradass knows we are here and need only wait."

At first light Landin left their camp, he took all of their ropes coiled over his broad shoulders.

"I may not be back by dark," he told them. "Keep a watchful eye."

He was soon out of sight, moving upward toward the peak above the castle. The day passed slowly and Flindas sat alone on a high point for much of the time, his eyes scanning the lands about. Tris and Duragor found shelter from the cold southerly wind that had begun to blow. They had eaten just once from their meagre stores. There were no lizards amongst the rocks, and nothing at all seemed to live at the centre of the Maradass domain. No bird flew, nor creature walked, not a single lichen or moss clung to the dark grey stone.

Duragor told stories to Tris who was eager to hear them, when she asked what the black man knew of the marauders he paused and looked at the dark castle of Maradass, a look of hate coming to his usually peaceful eyes.

"This is the history of the black dogs," he said finally. "First there was the earth and then there was the dog, older than man and empowered with much that is called wisdom. A simple wisdom of the hunt and instinct, and the age old lessons taught through time from parent to the litter. They roamed and they survived. When the black men came they found the dog already in the lands, and soon they were allies. Dog would hunt and black man would kill. For many thousand years this arrangement was successful. Then came the white men and with them the wizards. Most of my people escaped the wars but were pushed to the west. The dog came with us and our history continued."

"Then came Maradass the Mad, this is recent history now I talk of. Maradass took the dog, the large dog, the ones that were the masters of all other dogs. In a clever trap that they did not expect, he captured many of them, and then he changed them. Through dark magic he turned them into the foul beasts that they are today. They were taught to think and feel more than all other creatures except man. They have many traits that live in man, they hate and they fear. They are mostly dog still, and yet part of them is not, for they have thoughts of past and future, and they have long memories. When the Mad One first came looking in the west for trackers and slaves he brought with him these black dogs. Those of my people who were young or frail were left to the beasts. I fear them, but I hate them more." Duragor became silent, a look of revulsion darkening his face.

The afternoon light faded and Landin had not returned. As darkness fell Flindas came down from his lookout to join his companions. He had seen nothing of the enemy all day. It was the dead of night when Landin finally returned.

"There is a way," he said as he crouched beside them. "It is dangerous but possible I think. I have set ropes at crucial points. There is one last rock face to cross before we can reach the castle. It is the most difficult and I must set a long rope from high above, then you will swing across." He smiled into the darkness. "As I said, it will not be easy."

"When do we go?" asked Tris. Much rested now, there was fear deep inside her but she did not let it show.

"If we leave at first light tomorrow we will have time to reach the castle by dark," replied Landin. "They burn no lights it seems, and if there are guards on the battlements they lie hidden. I believe that Maradass is inviting us to enter. He desires the Seacrest fragment most of all, yet he can never take it by force. This is something he knows. It can be lost or given away, but never taken by force."

"Is that true?" asked Tris in surprise. "If it cannot be taken then I feel comforted somehow."

"Yes," replied Landin. "If I were to be killed by someone desirous of the Seacrest they could not use this piece of the talisman and live, it must be lost or else passed on before death. Maradass the Philosopher created the magic to fashion such a spell, though he took not into account that it might turn to such horror."

"Is it told how the piece you carry came into the hands of Amitarl?" asked Flindas, he realised that Kerran probably knew more about this than he did.

"Yes," replied Landin and told them the old tale. "In the wars with the Mad One, before Rubon pushed Maradass from the Regions, it was found upon the battlefield. Somehow it had been lost by Zard and that is the one remarkable event that has led to a relatively peaceful time in the Regions during the last few centuries."

Landin seemed in a talkative mood, he spoke during the evening of Amitarl and his family's long history. Eventually he spoke to them of the present time. "Now for the second time the Maradass Family will go to war with Amitarl," he concluded. "By now the black armies will be assembling on the northern plains. Maradass will have some fear of our family and its power, particularly if he cannot gain another piece of the Seacrest. He knows that Amitarl will come from Zeta if they are not already in the Regions by now. I cannot say for sure but I believe Tolth will have led the warriors to Andrian already."

"It may be that the army of Zeta cannot cross the ocean," said Flindas. "If the red poison has reached to the Magical Isles then they may be imprisoned by the ocean itself."

Landin was silent for a time. "I see now," he finally said. "That must have been his plan all along. The armies of Amitarl may not even be in the Regions yet. Maradass could sweep south with little resistance and destroy it all."

"My father will capitulate," said Flindas quietly. "He will hand over the city to buy his own life and freedom. I fear for my sister and her family."

"Amitarl will come," said Landin, an assurance in his voice. "The warriors of Zeta will come, dead sea or no."

A clear day dawned; cool winds blew from the south as they climbed higher into the mountains. The way was long and hard, while around them the wind played, buffeting them, tempting them to fall. The first rope that Landin had tied above led them to the very crown of the tallest mountain. They looked down the vertical face to the dark castle below, where all was still and foreboding.

"Our way is to the north and downward until we are again level with the castle," said Landin and began to lead them again.

As they came to the ropes and ascended precipitous rock faces they took in the light but strong lengths of cord. The castle had not been in view since they had begun the downward climb when Landin dropped to a wide ledge and held up his hand for silence. They followed him without a sound around a corner to a rocky outcrop; here again was the castle, so close that a long bowshot would reach the walls. The travellers showed nothing of themselves against the skyline and observed the way that Landin proposed to take. It did not look possible to any of the three, between them and the castle lay a deep gulf in the mountainside, falling away to the valley floor far below. The rock face could not be climbed; neither a crack nor foothold could be seen. At the point level with the castle the rock was under cut as if a great hand had gouged it from the mountain.

"Maybe a lizard could get across," said Duragor quietly. "Or we could fly," the stillness of the dark castle softening his speech.

"It is not quite flying I propose, but close," replied Landin smiling at his dark friend. "Last night I climbed to a point above where it is undercut." He pointed high up the rock face. "I will do it again tonight with two of our ropes tied end to end, and secured to my waist, and then I will swing you all across."

Tris let out a surprised snort.

"That is a very long way to fly without wings," said Flindas studying the distance. "How will you secure the rope above? We must be silent if we are not to be detected."

"Yes," agreed Landin. "We must be silent. As for the rope, it will remain about my waist for I could find nowhere to tie it. I will gain a strong handhold and then you will swing across."

Again Tris gave a quiet exclamation.

"The distance and height must be judged well, or you will be swinging in space," continued Landin. "The first to cross will tie ropes about their waist with the other end held on this side by one who is to go next. If either of the first two should not reach the castle they can be pulled back and try again, the last one must fly without this guarantee."

"I will go last," said Duragor. His words had a finality about them that could not be denied.

They waited out the last of the day, studying carefully the rock which Landin must climb that night in darkness. The possibility of flying through the air and crashing into the castle walls was only one of the dangers that they saw.

"When you are across, or have fallen to your deaths, or been skewered on some hidden guard's spear, I will climb down the remainder of the way and join you on the walls." said Landin. "I was prepared to go on alone when I stood here last night. You are all in great danger, and I do not wish that you be killed, but then I knew that you would attempt to find me rather than escape."

"You thought truly," said Duragor.

The last shaft of sunlight was striking the mountain face above them and still there was no sign of guards to be seen upon the battlements. They made their way in silence and darkness along a narrow ledge, a thin pale moon lying cradled in the sky. Landin left them in silence and began his ascent. He climbed and found hand holds where others would have fallen, fingers taking hold in the smallest crack as if they sank into the stone itself. It was a long time before Flindas felt a series of tugs on the rope, Landin was now in position and Flindas would swing first.

Tris and Duragor both held to the end of the rope that was tied around the warrior's waist, and Flindas threw the rest of his into the depths as a possible escape route in case of mishap. With his left hand and wrist entwined in the rope he gave one last tug as a signal and then leapt into the darkness, and the distant battlements hidden in the gloom.

The angle was almost perfect, Flindas saw the ramparts of the castle pass by beneath his feet. On the next swing he would have it exact. He swung back across the gulf and thought of Landin, high above, holding his weight. Duragor and Tris pulled him back to the ledge where he moved along the rock shelf, the rope needed to be lengthened just a little, the angle slightly refined.

When he leapt this time he did not entwine his hand in the rope. He flew across the yawning gulf of blackness, and at the moment that he passed above the castle wall he released his grip on the rope, and his pack. His feet hit the cold stone and he fell into a roll, coming to his feet quickly with sword in hand. If his companions heard no swordplay Tris would jump next.

All was quiet; it was an eerie heavy silence. Flindas stood at the stonework and braced himself to catch Tris. He saw the rope before he discerned the small dark figure flying upward towards him. She let go as he took hold and swung her to safety over the battlements. Then they waited in the darkness for Duragor, Tris alert for any sound.

On the other side of the chasm Duragor leapt into the darkness, but as he was nearing his goal the rope caught in a narrow crevice below. Flindas saw the black man for the briefest of moments then the rope jerked tight and Duragor's grip on it was almost broken. The black man slid briefly down the rope and then he was gone into the darkness. Duragor had made no sound and Flindas could see nothing in the blackness below, he feared for his friend as in silence they waited. Landin took a long time reaching them from his precarious position, there was a soft sliding noise where almost sheer cliff met battlements and Landin was with them. He spoke briefly in the softest whisper.

"Duragor did not fall," he told them. "He may have been hurt, but he made his way downward. He signalled on the rope before leaving it. I hope that he makes it from this place alive. We must go on now without him and find the entrance." Whatever knot or loop had caused the rope to catch was now free and Landin hauled it in. "Duragor has courage and much wisdom," he whispered to the others. "He will find his way, as we must ours."

They crept along the battlements until they came to a flight of steps leading down to the inner courtyard. There were high towers to the west crowned by battlements. Lesser towers and fortifications held to the cliff's edge, carved from its dying stone. After some time their search seemed in vain, nothing that looked like a door presented itself. Not a window showed on the walls of the towers, their sides as smooth as glass. They came at last to the central tower with its tall spire looming high above them. There was no challenge and they stood together beneath the wall, vexed by the strangeness of the unguarded impenetrable fortress. Tris saw it first and suddenly pointed to the side of the tower close to where they stood. A doorway could be seen wide and inviting where no door had stood before. Beyond which was a dark chamber and a flight of stairs that led downward.

"It seems we are invited in," said Landin examining the entrance. "This will be your last chance," he said to his companions.

"I will not turn back now," said Flindas and followed Landin to the stairs, Tris paused then took a deep breath and followed.

The stairway was not in total darkness, a dull blue light emanated from the rock, cold and forbidding, like the eyes of the marauders. The steps spiralled downward into the heart of the stronghold. There were no side entrances and the air became warm and stifling as they continued to descend. Eventually they came to a small chamber, a mirror of the one far above. As they stood by the stairs, the blank stone walls opposite them began to shimmer and then dissolve, a light shone into the chamber, firelight that danced across the floor.

They entered slowly and found that they were in a vast chamber dimly lit by a few burning torches against the walls. Tall pillars of stone held the roof aloft and the floor sloped downward to a large central flame burning in a circular pit. At the far side of the fire a stone structure mounted to the ceiling, in the dim light they could not make out the presence of any guards, and watchfully they moved step by slow step toward the centre.

"Welcome to my home," said a high and rasping voice. "I have been expecting you." Beyond the fire, on a tall throne carved from stone lounged Maradass, the Evil One, a dark smile on his thin lips. The ancient wizened creature sat alone, looking down upon them with baleful half closed eyes. "And to what do I owe the pleasure of your most revered company?" he continued ingratiatingly, his long fleshless hands making small circles in the air, encouraging them towards the fire.

"I am Landin Amitarl as you well know," Elfhand spoke up strongly, his clear voice echoing around the cavern. "I have come for my sister who is your captive."

"Yes, I know who you are," said Maradass, his voice becoming low and sinister. "And of course I also know why you are here. But do you think I would give her to you, at your asking?" He laughed now, a terrible mirthless sound.

"You are a fool, and I would squash you like an insect, but you have something I desire, something that you must give to me before I give anything to you."

"Now you are the fool," said Landin in reply. "You know you cannot take it, for your own ancestor's oath binds it to me. And I will not give it, for I know that if you ever held its power you would ruin the lands for ever."

There was silence for a time then Maradass spoke again, slow and thoughtful. "We seem to be at an impasse," he said quietly. "I have what you want, and you have what I would have, but what of your companions? Do you not mind that they will die for your arrogance in coming here? Challenging me. Maradass!"

His voice grew more excited, breaking into a higher pitch, and then a long cackling laugh slowly trailed off into silence. Turning to the others he spoke to them.

"Why have you come here?" he asked with a sneer. "Why do you follow this benighted son of a charlatan? He has led you to your deaths. There is no escape now. I have a thousand men beyond these walls."

"And you!" he said pointing at Flindas. "Wastrel son of the fat governor, you are such a one as I would expect to find amongst the Amitarl rabble. Kin-slayer and outlaw, who are you to come begging at my door?" His aged, ravaged face then turned to Tris. "And here we have the thief," he snorted, the words spat out at her across the fire. Then he looked about with curiosity, as though he expected to see another. "You seem to have lost one of your number," he said turning back to Landin, mocking laughter on his lips. "Where is the black savage who has disdained the honour of being in my employ? Fallen off the mountain has he?"

The wicked barbs in his voice dug at them like knives. Tris cursed suddenly and then leaped up the steps towards the throne.

"No!" called Landin, but she did not heed him.

Maradass let her come almost to the top step before he lazily stretched his bony hand towards her, there was a blue flash and the air crackled throughout the vast chamber. Tris fell without a sound coming from her lips, her knife clattering from her lifeless hand. Landin held Flindas back as he tried to go to her aid.

"She is not dead, not yet," cackled Maradass. "Though I find your sentiments for such a wretched creature somewhat amusing. I could kill you all this very instant, but there is more at stake here than mere mortal lives. The time is set; the time of the new Maradass has finally come. I will take it all, and soon no one will stand in my way!" His voice had reached a high pitch and it took some time for his words to again become clear, and reach to them from across the fire. "Come Landin, be reasonable and join with me," he pleaded with a mocking sign of prayer. "You cannot tell me that you do not lust for power. I give my word that I will spare your family, and your precious Green Isles if that is your wish. I want the Regions, and they are mine by right. Give me the Seacrest and I will grant you all safe passage from these lands, and anything else you may crave. Come, it is all yours for the taking."

Landin spoke, his voice retaining its commanding tone. "Show me Leana, I will agree to nothing until I see her," he said.

Maradass paused in thought, as though he was playing a complex game against a strong opponent. He then raised his hand, and at the foot of the stairs a section of floor dissolved into blue light. A stone slab rose slowly from the depths and on it lay the still and lifeless body of Leana Amitarl. Now it was Landin who moved forward around the fire, and approached his beloved sister. Flindas hung back, watchful, fearful, an arrow strung to his bow. Maradass took no notice of him, as if the weapon could do him no harm.

"She is alive," said the voice of Maradass from the throne. "Let us say that she is just asleep."

"Wake her!" ordered Landin, looking down at the wan and beautiful face of his younger sister.

"I will not wake her," spat Maradass back at him, a dangerous anger in his voice. "You have seen her and know she lives. Now what do you offer?"

"I cannot give you what you most desire," replied Landin. "It is more dear to the land than all our lives are worth. You may crush me now, but you will never gain that prize. With but one piece of the Seacrest you will not win in the south. Though your forces be vast, Amitarl will fight you until you have lost all you have. Stop it now and recall your troops. You will not succeed with your plans. Withdraw and call a truce before you and your armies are no more."

"Strong words from one who has not heard news for such a long time," laughed Maradass. "Amitarl cannot reach the Regions unless I allow it. The seas are closed to your ships, the Regions are mine to do with as I wish. I will isolate the so called Magic Isles until I have finished my plans for the Regions. Then I will let your warriors come, and my armies will slaughter them before they leave the shoreline. Give me the Seacrest now!" he screamed suddenly. "It belongs to the House of Maradass. It will belong to Zard who will soon come to me again, and not even you, the wondrous Cripple, will be able to stand in his way."

His voice, which had risen again, suddenly became quietened to an evil softness, maniacal and full of madness. "There is one other thing that I now wish to show you," he said, wickedness flowed through his voice like liquid fire. "Your father, the one who is so wise, is but a fool like all men, and even now the means of his death lies beneath his own roof."

"What puzzle is this that you use to confuse and distract us?" said Landin, his voice wondering, unsure.

"Here," said Maradass gloating openly at his jest. He raised a hand, and from the stone pillars behind the throne a woman walked. Flindas gazed at her dark beauty. He had never looked upon a woman so desirable. Though she was obviously with child, the heart of Flindas suddenly yearned for her touch.

A gasp escaped Landin lips. "Luista," he said, his voice soft and terrified.

"Yes," called Maradass, laughing at Landin's bewildered expression. "Luista, who is your step-mother, and soon to be mother of Zard and Darss."

Landin looked up into the eyes of the woman who had been Tolth's wife, and was the mother of Mindis his half brother.

"Why?" he asked. "Why did you take my father's heart and then leave him with Mindis the Silent One?"

"It took a lot of arranging," said Luista, her voice quiet and seductive as she came to stand by the throne of Maradass. "I was emptied of all thought so I could reach Zeta without causing suspicion," she said with a charming smile. "The plan worked very well do you not think." She laughed gaily then, her voice echoing like small bells amongst the shadows.

"Tolth fell in love with me, as did most of the men of Zeta," she continued. "Once I became aware of what I must do I did not hesitate, it was all part of the wonderful plan. As you know Tolth and I married, and I bore the child called Mindis. One day, perhaps very soon, Mindis will strike his father a death blow."

She paused, smiling at Landin's confusion. "I know you will not join us, my sweet handsome son," she continued. "You are too proud and honourable to join with the enemy. You once loved me yourself I think. On Zeta I saw your longing glances." Luista took a seductive step forward, and then another. "You could still have me," she said seductively. As she said this she reached out and stroked the ancient face of Maradass; the gown she wore flowed sensuously against her body, swaying, hypnotically.

Landin shook himself. "You are black and evil," he called to her. "I will not be fooled by your sweet words. You are dark beyond depraved."

He reached in his tunic and brought forth his fragment of the Seacrest and held it close to the body of Leana. A warm yellow light glowed from his hand and flowed about his sister's body.

"Stop that!" cried Maradass coming uneasily to his feet.

In his own hand he held the piece that had been his mad brother's, and his father's before that. A blue light flowed outward, and then with a roar the two battling lights merged. The air crackled and danced. Sparks chased each other through the air between the two opponents. Flindas heard a sudden sound and turned from the flames in time to see hundreds of armed soldiers step through the stone walls as if the rock did not exist. They did not advance, but ringed the mighty hall, swords and spears held before them. Flindas drew his bow. He would not die alone.

The melding of the lights ceased abruptly as Landin staggered and fell, his own light fading, diminished. Maradass stood at the top step high above them and he held the blue light aloft. Triumphant and gloating, he spoke again.

"You cannot match my powers," he cried, as Landin struggled to rise. "Could I not take it from you now? Your strength is drained, and you are finished. All time changes and old oaths fall to dust. It belonged to my family, and we will have it back."

Maradass began his slow descent of the wide stone stairway as Elfhand regained his feet when again a shaft of blue light stunned the very air. Landin crumbled to the floor again, crushed by the awful power that Maradass wielded. Flindas too was forced backward, though the might of the blast had not been directed at him. Maradass came slowly down the stairs with Luista following, basking in her master's power.

Flindas saw the unexpected movement first. All of a sudden Tris was up, with her knife held in her hand; but it was not Maradass whom she attacked. Tris leapt, and her weight crushed Luista to the stone stairs behind the Evil One, the small knife held firmly to the woman's throat. Maradass turned as he heard Luista cry out, his face became an evil frothing rage, and he turned the flickering blue light towards his wife's attacker.

"No!" Luista screamed and Maradass was held in her fear.

She was too close to Tris. Both could die in the fiery blast.

"If she dies, then your children will die, and then the Family Maradass will die," cried Tris, for she knew the truth of it.

Flindas moved forward with bow drawn tight.

"And you will not stop both of us," he said.

With his back to the fire he too held a weapon on Luista, the deadly shaft poised for flight. Maradass glared down at him, fear and hatred raging across his aged face. All had seemed within his grasp, and now suddenly his family hovered on the edge of death. How had he not seen it?

"You would kill a woman and her unborn children?" he said with great scorn, yet edged with fear.

"To end the reign of Maradass, yes," replied Flindas, his bow never wavering. The blue light diminished slowly, flickered and then was gone. Landin had gotten slowly to his feet. He was dazed and greatly weakened.

"Release Leana," Flindas called.

Maradass, a look of vile hatred on his face, held his hand

aloft for a moment and then it was done. Leana stirred and Landin helped her sit, though it seemed that he could barely stand himself. Leana did not seem to understand what was happening, her mind remaining in the fog of the Evil One's spell.

"Order your men away," called Flindas and it was reluctantly done, loathing and fear playing across the face of Maradass.

"Luista will come with us, and you will give us a guide," said Flindas. "One who can open the secret gates and take us through your men. We would not have come this far if we were not prepared to die. One mistake and the Maradass family will be at an end, our lives are but a small price to pay."

"So why do you not end it now?" screamed Maradass. "Let us all die here together, for do you not intend it to be so?" He raised his hands as though to end all things.

"Luista will not die," said Landin through his pain and Maradass knew the truth in his words. "We will release her when we have gone from these lands."

Landin struggled to speak and almost fell again to the stone floor of the chamber. Maradass, his face afire with hate, gave a signal, and moments later a commander of the guard entered. Flindas recognised him instantly, the limp arm and the arrogant haughty air, he did not seem so smug now, but watched in bewilderment as his master was seen standing helplessly upon the high dais. The companions came together, Tris keeping Luista held tightly, the knife still at her throat.

"You will guide us from this place," said Flindas coming towards the commander. "We will have horses and you will open the gates for us. Do not try anything foolish. Luista and the Maradass line will fall forever if you try to betray us." The officer looked at Flindas, and then recognition came into his eyes. "It was you," he spat as though a curse. "You took away my arm."

"Speak no words unless I ask," said Flindas coming close, a knife springing into his hand. "You will lose much more than an arm if you do not do as I say."

They moved towards the wall slowly, Landin supporting Leana with difficulty.

"You must see it through," he gasped, turning to Flindas. "My power is almost done. Maradass has drained me. It is in your hands now."

Flindas held the officer with one hand as they passed through the stone wall and into a tunnel beyond, the others following closely. Luista was silent and did not struggle, the children in her womb would one day rule the lands, and she had no wish to lose her life and have them die with her. The officer led them downward along widening passages, there was no sign of other soldiers in any of the side tunnels or larger chambers they passed through, Maradass held them back, fearful for his family. They came finally to a lower cavern carved from the rock. Stores and arms lay in huge stacks; horses, many saddled, were hitched close to the far wall.

"That is the way out," said the commander, and pointed at the apparently solid wall.

"Take a horse," called Flindas to the others. "Tris you must ride double, we will keep her until we have gotten through. She must not escape."

Leana could not ride alone, and Landin chose a strong and solid horse for them both. They mounted with difficulty and the commander then led them through the outer wall of the Maradass stronghold to where the morning shone clear. It felt strange to Flindas to pass through solid rock as though it did not exist. They were all scarcely through the wall when the commander played his hand. Flindas had expected him to try and escape, but instead he lurched sideways and a well aimed blow caught Tris hard in the side of the face, her feet were not securely in the stirrups and she fell unconscious to the ground.

"Fly!" screamed the commander to Luista. "Fly!"

The wife of Maradass pulled hard upon the reins, turned the horse, and quickly disappeared back into the solid rock. Flindas let out a curse and wheeled on the man, who was causing his own horse to rear up amongst the others. The beasts cried out in panic. Flindas saw the man's hand move to the side of his saddle and draw a long wicked dagger, but the hand of Flindas moved more quickly. From behind his shoulder he grasped a four bladed throwing knife and in the same movement cast it with deadly accuracy into the man's throat, a look of surprise came to the officer's face as he slipped from his saddle, and his horse bolted. Flindas had no time to stop the riderless mount. He leapt from his own saddle and scooped the limp body of Tris from the ground.

"Ride!" he cried to the others, but Landin could barely sit his mount, he swayed in the saddle and held Leana as though she were the only thing that kept him alive.

Flindas mounted with difficulty. Tris slumped across the saddle, and with one hand he pulled at the reins of the other horse. Through his pain Landin urged the horse and they began to ride, they broke into a slow gallop and plunged down the steep sloping roadway. There came a shattering horn blast from the castle above and Flindas did not have to look back to know that the hunt had begun.

The road had not yet reached the lake shore when the mounted troops of Maradass joined the chase. There was less than half a league between the hunters and the hunted and Flindas knew that there was little chance of outrunning them. Two horses and four riders was not a good equation. Tris regained consciousness slowly. The blow had left a vicious bruise on her cheekbone and jaw, while a trickle of blood showed above her hairline.

"Are we still alive?" she called to him, her humour fighting down the pain.

"For how long I cannot say," he said back to her over the rush of wind and the pounding of hooves. "We lost our protection back there."

They rounded the last corner and galloped towards the tunnel, no one stood in their way as they plunged into the darkness. The gallop slowed to a canter, the sloping road being too dangerous for anything faster, Flindas called to Landin across the darkness between them.

"I am here," the Amitarl warrior replied with an effort. "We must stop at the bridge. Try to cave in the roof."

Elfhand's voice seemed not his own, the power that had been there before was barely audible; it was as though his words came from a vast distance.

Flindas had also thought about the crumbling roof of the tunnel but had quickly discarded the idea. He did not think it possible. The wooden beams themselves would take a team of plough horses to pull them from under the hanging rock above. His mind was taken over by the sound of the black horsemen entering the tunnel behind them, they were closer than he had hoped and he spurred his mount to greater speed. Ahead he could see a faint light finding its way in by the lower entrance, and then they came upon the bridge.

"It can be done," said Landin, and with an effort he dismounted.

Tris led Leana and her mount further down the tunnel as Flindas stood with Landin on the wooden planks of the bridge. The sound of horse's hooves came closer from the darkness of the tunnel. The horsemen were coming as fast as they dared without the aid of torches. Landin looked at the beams in the dim light and seemed satisfied.

"Yes," he said, his voice pained and weary. "I have enough strength left to do this, but no more. Flindas, you must go down the tunnel, this is for me to do alone." Flindas looked into the golden eyes of his companion as they caught the light from the tunnel's mouth, there was a desolate look in them, and there was also a great longing.

"Go now, I will be with you soon," said Landin.

Flindas left him in the near darkness, braced against a huge wooden pillar which supported yet another beam above. Flindas joined the others and saw that Leana still did not appear to be aware of what was happening around her. The sound of hooves came ever closer, drumming at them from the darkness. Flindas could not make out where Landin was standing, but the Amitarl warrior's voice suddenly rang out strong and clear.

"Flindas!" the warrior of Zeta cried. "You must carry Leana safely back to our father. I am done, my strength is spent. One more effort and then I can rest."

A faint yellow-white glow came from further up the tunnel, and as Flindas and Tris watched the light grew bright. Elfhand's words had not yet been fully understood, they could see him now and the glow flowing through him from his hand. His muscles bulged and strained beneath his tunic.

"It is done!" he cried over the sound of the galloping hooves. "Flindas, I give this to you to give to Leana along with my love."

Flindas watched in horror as Landin threw the Seacrest fragment through the air towards him, still glowing softly. He caught it by reflex as the roof of the tunnel suddenly caved in upon Landin. Huge rocks and shattered stone fell upon the road way and into the river, the roar overwhelmed them, and turning they raced from the tunnel into the sunlight.

The earth shook beneath their feet and the horses cried out in dismay, as still more rock fell into the deep tunnel. A huge section at the entrance sheered away and plunged into the river, clouds of dust gathered against the sunlight, and they watched silently as it drifted away on the breeze. The river had stopped flowing, only the barest trickle now found its way through the mountain.

The danger was still acute, but Flindas could not make himself leave the spot, a look of great regret and sadness held fast to the lines of his face. Tris stood with him as tears fell freely down her damaged face. Finally Flindas shook himself as if out of a dream.

"We must go," he said quietly.

Flindas hung the Seacrest fragment around his neck, Leana would receive it in time but not yet. She was not herself and may not remember its importance. Flindas mounted and Tris rode behind Leana, holding her steady in the saddle.

"We will ride as long as we can," Flindas said to her. "If we can get as far as the next gate without trouble we will be in luck. Word may not have reached there yet."

They cantered down the road, only once did Flindas look back, not for fear of pursuit but with a last look of remembrance of the one they called Elfhand.

It took them longer to reach the next gateway than Flindas had expected; the road had many turnings, deep ravines causing long and involved deviations. They finally came upon the gate but it was closed to them, and they knew that the only possibility of escape was to leave the road, and their mounts.

The climb downward would take them to the beginning of a long valley that stretched towards the west. It was a good place to leave the road and to become lost from the eyes of Maradass. They had managed to bring but a single rope from the stronghold.

It must suffice, thought Flindas to himself as they sent the horses bolting. Then they left the road.

Leana walked now, but her mind still seemed lost in dreams, and it was obvious that she could not climb. Tris tied her carefully to the back of Flindas, Leana held on as would a child, instinctively, and then together they descended to the darkening valley floor below.